The Last Heiress

BOOKS BY MARY ELLIS

CIVIL WAR HEROINES
The Quaker and the Rebel
The Lady and the Officer

⚛

THE NEW BEGINNINGS SERIES
Living in Harmony
Love Comes to Paradise
A Little Bit of Charm

⚛

THE WAYNE COUNTY SERIES
Abigail's New Hope
A Marriage for Meghan

⚛

THE MILLER FAMILY SERIES
A Widow's Hope
Never Far from Home
The Way to a Man's Heart

⚛

STANDALONES
Sarah's Christmas Miracle
An Amish Family Reunion
A Plain Man

The Last Heiress

Mary Ellis

HARVEST HOUSE PUBLISHERS
EUGENE, OREGON

Cover by Garborg Design Works, Savage, Minnesota

Cover photos © Chris Garborg, Bigstock/Voy

THE LAST HEIRESS

Copyright © 2015 by Mary Ellis
Published by Harvest House Publishers
Eugene, Oregon 97402
www.harvesthousepublishers.com

Library of Congress Cataloging-in-Publication Data
Ellis, Mary,
The last heiress / Mary Ellis.
    pages; cm
ISBN 978-0-7369-5052-7 (pbk.)
ISBN 978-0-7369-5053-4 (eBook)

1. Heiresses—Fiction. 2. Abolitionists—Fiction. 3. Man-woman relationships—Fiction.
4. United States—History—Civil War, 1861-1865—Fiction. I Title.
PS3626.E36L37 2015
813'.6—dc23

2014027020

Printed in the United States of America

14 15 16 17 18 19 20 21 22 23 /LB-CD/ 10 9 8 7 6 5 4 3 2 1

This book is dedicated to my friends Carolyne and Alan Way of Gosport, England, who provided background information on the garment industry of western England during the nineteenth and twentieth centuries.

Carolyne's grandfather owned a coal mine in the Lancashire area that supplied the mills. Thanks also for helping with British slang and customs.

How lucky I am to have British friends willing to open their home and hearts to me.

Acknowledgments

Thanks to the countless authors of history I have pored over for years, including Shelby Foote, Bruce Catton, Ed Bearss, James M. McPherson, and Brian Pohanka. My favorite sources for this book were *Walking to Cold Mountain: A Journey Through Civil War America* by Carl Zebrowski, and *Fort Fisher 1865* by Chris E. Fonvielle Jr. This book contains a collection of photographs taken by T.H. O'Sullivan, apprentice to Mathew Brady, who worked in the Washington studio managed by Alexander Gardner, both famous Civil War photographers.

Thanks to Noah Janis and Caitlyn Rifenburg at the Fort Fisher State Historic Site for patiently explaining the minutiae of the fort and historic battle.

Thanks to the wonderful guides at the Bellamy House, the Lattimer House, and the First Presbyterian Church of Wilmington. Special thanks to Janet Davidson, historian at the Cape Fear Museum in Wilmington, for answering an inordinate number of questions and providing archival photos of the area during the Civil War.

Thanks to the Western Reserve Historical Society, Cuyahoga Valley Civil War Roundtable, the Peninsula Valley Foundation of Ohio, and GAR Hall, whose appreciation for Civil War history has kept my passion alive locally.

Thanks to the Wayne County Writer's Guild Novelists, especially Ruth, Bobbie, Christina, Darrell, Cyndi, and Kira, for your great brainstorming help.

Thanks to my agent, Mary Sue Seymour; my lovely proofreader, Joycelyn Sullivan; my editor, Kim Moore; and the wonderful staff at Harvest House Publishers. Where would I be without your hard work?

One

Manchester, England
February 1864

Amanda slumped in the dressing table chair, thwarting her maid's efforts for the third time.

"Please stop fidgeting, Miss Amanda, or I'll never finish your hair. At this rate you may miss breakfast altogether." As she spoke she swiftly fastened the coiled braid to the back of Amanda's head with a half dozen long hairpins.

"I'm sorry, Helene. I don't know why I can't cut it off since it's such a bother, or at least wear it down until noon. After all, it's only my family at table." Amanda stared at her wavy reflection in the mirror. The dreary winter had robbed her cheeks of all color. She was as pale as the ghost the staff insisted roamed the attic of Dunncliff Manor.

"You can't wear it down because you're not a child anymore. Young ladies must have fashionable *coiffures* unless they are abed with the fever and their continued earthly existence appears in doubt." Helene winked at Amanda's reflection in the mirror. "And cutting it off is advisable only if you plan to book passage to India disguised as a man."

Amanda chuckled at the mental picture of herself dressed in flannel and tweed. "I've seen you in the garden of the carriage house with your hair plaited down your back. And you're older than I."

"True enough, but I'm the widowed daughter of your papa's coachman. My appearance ceased to be of much interest the day I married. But you, Miss Amanda, should make a good impression wherever you are, no matter what time day or night." Helene bent to whisper close to her ear. "How else will you catch a fine husband like a viscount or an earl?"

Amanda emitted a rude noise that would have appalled her mother. "Your suggestion sounds dreadfully dull. Instead, maybe I'll become an actress and travel the world, or perhaps a famous opera singer and appear on the finest stages of Rome, Vienna, and Paris." She closed her eyes, imagining the sound of thunderous applause.

Helene freed two tendrils to soften the severe look of Amanda's upswept hair. "To be a famous opera singer, one must first be able to sing." She tugged on a lock playfully. "Go to breakfast before your mama sends her maid after you."

Without an alternative, Amanda dutifully obeyed. On her way downstairs, she heard rain pelting the window with chilling relentlessness. This time of year *any* career someplace warm sounded preferable to winter in Manchester.

"There you are, my dear. I feared you'd taken ill to be this tardy." Agnes Dunn maintained a hawkish perusal of her daughter while sipping her tea.

"Forgive me, Mama. My hair refused to cooperate with Helene." Taking her usual seat at the table, she asked the footman for coffee instead of tea. "Where is Papa?" she asked, noticing that her mother sat alone at the ornate table for twelve.

"His cough is no better. He's not coming downstairs this morning." Agnes signaled for the footman to serve.

Amanda's unease increased threefold. "Papa is still in bed? He doesn't plan to go to the mill? I can't remember that ever happening—"

Her mother narrowed her eyes. "Please don't overdramatize, Amanda. Everyone gets sick, even your hale and hearty father. You're too young to remember a bout of gout that laid him low for days." She nibbled her toast. The barest coating of lemon cheese provided a sunny glow.

Amanda refused to be put off easily. "But he never misses breakfast. It's his favorite meal of the day. I'll take him a bowl of poached eggs and some kippers. And I know he won't refuse porridge with fresh cream."

"If your father is hungry, ring for the maid and she will carry up a tray. I won't have you doing servant work. Everyone needs to earn their wages." Agnes glanced at the footman, who pretended not to be listening. "But you should visit your father when you finish eating. He asked to see you this morning."

Amanda set down her fork, her taste for food gone. "He wishes me to come to his bedroom?" Her father never spoke to his children except at the dinner table, at tea, or occasionally by the parlor fire if they weren't entertaining that evening. And he certainly never requested an audience while wearing his dressing gown. "Do you know what this is about, Mama?"

"I have my suspicions but prefer not to speculate. When did you become so apprehensive?" Agnes's expression softened. "I would have expected as much from your sister, but not from my fearless girl."

A second oddity within ten minutes was almost too much to

bear. Her mother never mentioned Abigail, as though her twin sister hadn't been born. Since Alfred's death several years ago, it felt as though she'd been born an only child. "Will you come upstairs with me?" Amanda asked.

"No, my dear. I'm merely relaying the message. Your father requested only you, not the two of us. He will impart any decisions he's made to me when the time is right." Mama smiled, but the gesture fooled no one.

Amanda knew her parents hadn't taken rooms at opposite ends of the hall because of his snoring or Agnes's restless tossing and turning. She'd hoped they would become friends, if no longer passionate about each other. But her brother's untimely death put an end to that possibility. Amanda finished her toast and coffee, and then she refilled her cup at the sideboard. "I shall go now."

"Allow me to carry that for you, Miss Dunn." Joseph, the head footman reached her side with a saucer.

Reluctant to argue in front of her mother, Amanda allowed him to precede her up the stairs to her father's suite.

"Miss Amanda to see you, sir," announced Joseph, stopping in the doorway.

"Come in, daughter," said George Dunn, his voice hoarse and scratchy. "Why are you standing there like a statue? Come talk to your old papa."

She hurried then to his bedside, the sight of her robust father under heavy quilts giving her a chill. "Mama said you're not feeling well, sir. I hope that's not true." Amanda smiled as she said this, yet she needed little confirmation from him as to how he was with his face drawn and haggard.

"I'm a touch under the weather, but it's nothing for you to be concerned about. The way Ochs fusses over me, I'll either be right as rain or ready for a nanny and perambulator before long."

As though on cue, her father's trusted valet since before Amanda was born entered the room. "I intercepted your breakfast on the stairs, sir. Everything looks quite in order. I'll have more coal sent up for the fire."

"Getting my room to tropical temperatures will not cure a bit of the flu. Leave the tray on the table and my hearth alone for now. I want to speak privately to my daughter."

The valet turned as though just noticing her. "Good morning, Miss Dunn. Shall I have a tray sent up for you too?" He looked down his thin hooked nose at her.

"No, thank you, Ochs. I breakfasted with Mama."

"Very good. Ring if I can be of service, sir." He bowed and departed with great dignity.

"My, my. The man absolutely never smiles." Amanda perched on the edge of her father's massive bed.

"It's in the valet's rulebook not to." Papa's dimples deepened as he said that, and for a moment he resembled his normal self until a hacking cough convulsed his large frame.

"Oh, Papa, that sounds dreadful. Did anyone send for the doctor?" Amanda patted his arm once the coughing subsided.

George reached for the glass of water on his nightstand and took a tentative sip. "What would that old blighter do? Bleed me again? I feel worse after his therapies, not better. Stop fussing. The cough will be gone once this damp weather breaks. Anyway, that's not why I summoned you. I have a favor to ask of you, one that will be no spring stroll in the garden."

Amanda's spirits lifted. Seldom did her father ask anything of his family other than impeccable manners at social events. "Of course, Papa. What can I do?"

"Only the young and foolish say yes without hearing the question." He covered her hand with his larger one. "Pelton visited yesterday afternoon."

Papa received a mill employee at home in his bedchamber? Amanda's stomach tightened.

"The situation at Dunn Mills is growing critical. None of my overpaid managers have been able to line up sufficient cotton from Latin or South America, and certainly nothing that compares to the quality of the cotton we had access to before this nuisance of a war in the States. I can't run textile mills and continue to pay men's wages without raw materials." His vehemence triggered another round of coughing.

Amanda blinked, unsure of a suitable response. Her father seldom discussed important matters and never his business concerns. "What about wool from the northern counties and silk from the Orient?"

"All well and good, but cotton is more than half the industry of the mill. I need to restore reliable sources."

"How can I help? Shall I write to…Jackson?" She murmured the name of their primary American factor—and brother-in-law—reluctantly. He had fallen from favor with her father, to put it mildly.

He sighed heavily. "I've already written to the elder Henthorne several times. Every reply has been the same: His hands are tied. Their new president, Jefferson Davis, has decreed that no cotton is to be exported to the United Kingdom until Queen Victoria takes a stand for the Confederacy. Why would our Queen choose sides in a dispute affecting former colonies? And I can't fathom why southern states would break away and form a new nation."

Amanda waited to see if he expected her opinion on a political topic—one she would be hard pressed to give—but then he waved off the question like a bee from the honey pot.

"None of that concerns you, daughter. I shouldn't sidetrack myself from our dire circumstances."

"How can I help?"

"Hear me out before making up your mind." He coughed again with alarming intensity. When he caught his breath again, he said, "I need you to travel to North Carolina to do whatever is necessary to restore shipping lines to Manchester through Liverpool. Speak with Randolph Henthorne first, but if you must, call on every cotton factor in Wilmington. There has to be *someone* willing to ignore Davis's edict and transact business with us. I'm willing to pay a thirty percent increase over previous contracts, although you certainly shouldn't open negotiations with our most generous offer." He hesitated and dabbed his mouth with his linen handkerchief. Her flummoxed expression had finally given him pause.

"You wish *me* to board a ship and sail to America? The farthest I've traveled is across the channel to the continent."

"I realize I'm asking a lot, Amanda. Such a voyage may be dangerous. Had your brother lived, he would be the one making the journey." Papa's complexion faded to an unhealthy pallor. "I need someone to represent the interests of Dunn Mills on my behalf. I would go myself, but the doctor insists the damp sea air would hasten my demise."

"Of course I'll go," she said without another thought. The possibility of losing her father negated her personal misgivings. As soon as she agreed, a small seed took root and began to grow—a seed that might break the *ennui* that had consumed her all winter.

"You won't be traveling alone. I will send Pelton with you."

Amanda's spine arched at the mention of the pompous man's name. Their few instances of acquaintance had left her with a sour taste in her mouth. Charles Pelton believed a woman's place was in the home, and that they shouldn't speak on subjects other than drapery fabrics or scone choices for tea. "Why him, Papa? You have several capable managers in your mills. Surely you could select one more amenable for a travel companion."

Papa's brow furrowed. "I understand your reservations, but no one knows the textile trade better. He could answer any question you or the Carolina factors may present."

Amanda lifted her chin. "If you hold Mr. Pelton in such high esteem, why do you wish me to go at all? Perhaps he should represent Dunn Mills while I embroider samplers in the parlor with Mama."

Her father's weary face brightened. "That's what I've always admired—your spirit. Those American aristocrats will expect me to negotiate contracts. They might take offense if I send an employee in my stead."

She squeezed the bridge of her nose. "They would prefer someone who knows little about running a mill and even less about grades and qualities of cotton?"

"You're a Dunn, daughter, besides my heir. You will attend the meetings primarily as my emissary—a figurehead, if you will. Pelton will discuss specifics and negotiate the final terms of contract." Papa reached out to pinch her cheek as though she were still nine years old.

"I wish to visit Abigail if I'm traveling to Wilmington. I won't cross the sea without laying eyes on my sister."

His ebullience faded but he nodded agreement. "Your sister's move to the States is one reason I broached the subject. Because she married a wealthy man, your mother and I won't have to worry you'll land among a rough sort. But that's the only positive thing I can say about Jackson Henthorne." He turned his face into the pillow as another convulsive cough robbed him of breath.

Amanda left his bedside and walked to the window. The rain continued to fall, turning the cobblestones below slick underfoot for both man and beast. She stared blindly into the mist while her mind whirred with ideas. After five long years, she would be able to see Abigail? She could visit America—a brand-new land teeming with opportunity—if that's what North Carolina still considered itself part of. But that arrogant Charles Pelton would doubtlessly prevent her from experiencing any adventure.

By the time her father's coughing spell passed, Amanda had made up her mind. "I would be happy to represent Dunn Mills with one condition, Papa. Mr. Pelton remains here in Manchester while I sail solely with my maid."

For a moment her father's lips opened and closed like a trout floundering on the riverbank. "A young woman traveling alone? That is unheard of. Your mother would never permit such recklessness."

"How could it possibly be reckless? I assume you would book first-class passage. If necessary I could remain in my cabin until we reach the Carolina coast. At that point, I would be the guest of Mrs. Jackson Henthorne and under her husband's protection." Amanda offered a wry smile.

"Nevertheless." He dragged out the word for emphasis. "By your own admission, you know nothing about textiles. How can you be useful in convincing the brokers to restore the cotton trade?"

"The fact I've been little help to you since Alfred's death troubles me. I'm of little use…period."

He shifted against the pillows and waved his hand in dismissal. "That doesn't alter the fact—"

"Please, Papa, I've listened patiently to you. I would appreciate it if you would afford me the same courtesy."

His eyes grew round. "Go on."

"Because we wouldn't set sail before March, I plan to study the textile business until then, night and day if need be. I have a month to learn all about cotton so I can represent Dunn Mills adequately."

He laughed, pressing his fingertips to his eyelids. "I've spent thirty years learning the business. You think you can fill my shoes within thirty days? And a woman, no less."

"Certainly not. I'm not interested in producing garments or managing employees. I merely intend to determine what constitutes quality material and what does not. You and Mr. Pelton can run things here while I deal with those American factors."

"Amanda, my darling girl—"

"May I suggest you book my passage along with Helene's for four weeks from now? If you're not satisfied by then that I can represent you, I will accompany Mr. Pelton merely as a figurehead. After all, I am a *woman* as you pointed out. Would that be agreeable to you, Papa?" Stretching out her hand, Amanda held it steady while he laughed again at her.

But when she held her ground, his expression changed from mirth to contemplation. "You won't abandon us and marry some fast-talking trickster?"

His question caught her off guard. "I will not, sir. I love you and Mama."

He slumped deeper into the pillows and closed his eyes, looking older than when she had entered his bedchamber. "You have a bargain, daughter. Report to Mr. Pelton tomorrow and begin your education."

"Oh, thank you, Papa—" She stopped speaking when she realized he was falling asleep. Creeping quietly from his room, she ran smack into her mother.

"Are you going to America?"

"You were listening?" Amanda asked in surprise.

"Of course I was. You're my only child now. What would I do without you?"

Rely on a houseful of servants the way you always do? Amanda squashed the uncharitable thought and selected the logical reply. "You have another daughter, Mama. She resides in North Carolina."

"Do you think I've forgotten?" Her mother wrapped an arm

around Amanda's waist and led her toward the stairs. "That's the reason I'm overjoyed you'll make the trip."

"Not because hundreds of families depend on Dunn Mills to provide bread for their tables?"

"That is all well and good, but you must check on your sister. I may be a grandmama without my knowledge. And you must convince her to return to England."

Amanda laughed without amusement. "Do you think she would abandon her husband and come home after five years?"

"Your father never thought much of the Henthornes. Perhaps Abigail has had enough frontier living and desires civilization again."

"The coastal Carolinas are not the western territories. They live as civilized as we do."

"How would you know that? And if that's the case, Abigail can bring Jackson along. Your father needs someone in the family to run the mill after he's gone."

"I doubt Papa considers the man who eloped with his little girl as part of the family."

"We must put that behind us, considering…."

Halfway down the grand staircase Amanda halted. "Considering what? Is there something you're not telling me? I thought Papa had a mild case of influenza."

"Yes, of course. But neither of us grows any younger. We need to prepare for the future." Her mother patted her back. "Shall we read in the parlor for a while? I believe Joseph built a warm fire in there."

"No, thank you. I intend to have the carriage brought around for a tour of Dunn Mills. There's no time like the present to begin my schooling."

"Splendid! Take the rest of the day if you like."

If Amanda had wanted to speculate on her mother's response

to her plans, enthusiasm would have been last on the list. All of this continued divergence from Mama's typical behavior made her more than a little nervous.

April 1864

"Do you suppose I should hire another lady's maid?" Abigail Henthorne's question drifted toward the twelve-foot ceilings of the dining room without a corresponding answer. "Jackson," she murmured in her modulated tone.

"What's that, my dear?" Her husband lowered his copy of the *Wilmington Star News*. Lately, he'd picked up the habit of reading at the breakfast table, something her father never would have tolerated.

"My sister will be arriving in a few weeks. I was wondering if I should hire another maid." Abigail sipped her coffee, an acquired taste since coming to America.

Jackson folded his newspaper. "Five years in the Carolinas and some customs still escape your notice. If one needs additional help, the lady of the house doesn't run an advertisement in the paper for available domestics. She informs her husband, who then purchases another slave either from a broker or the auction." He picked up his fork and began eating with great gusto.

Abigail glanced nervously at the slaves lined up by the breakfront—maids, footmen, and the butler—all with faces from light cocoa to deepest ebony. It wasn't as though Dunncliff Manor hadn't an equal number of servants, but they had been paid wages along with room and board. "All right then, dear husband. I wish for another maid to assist Amanda during her visit. You know how horrible I am at sharing."

"And why should you share? I will happily accommodate you,

but don't expect to receive someone who has been styling the latest coiffures." Jackson gestured toward her elaborately arranged curls.

"Why not? Estelle is quite handy with a brush and comb."

He smiled indulgently. "She was a wedding gift to you from my mother. She'd been specially trained to assist a lady. I will certainly inquire among the brokers, but house slaves aren't usually as talented as Estelle." Jackson held out his cup, which was promptly refilled by a footman. "But enough about tiresome subjects. Do you really think your twin will step off a clipper ship here in Wilmington?"

"I do. According to her letter, Amanda should arrive by month's end." Abigail could barely contain her excitement. "And she's sailing alone. Can you imagine my parents permitting such liberty? She must have grown adept at maneuvering Papa."

"Apparently you're not identical in all aspects."

"No, I suppose not. I never could stand up to him. He seldom granted me more than a few moments of his precious time." Abigail folded her hands in her lap, her eggs and ham forgotten.

"Don't trouble yourself with that old codger, my dear. That's all behind you." Jackson sipped his coffee without taking his focus from her.

"According to her letter, the name on her travel documents is *Mrs.* Amanda Dunn, as though she had married a cousin or some such. Papa agreed, saying that a matron wouldn't attract much untoward attention during the Atlantic crossing. Truthfully, I would be surprised if Papa didn't have her locked inside her cabin until the ship docks. He always treated Amanda as though she were a rare porcelain vase."

"Your sister lied on the ship's manifest?"

"Those were her plans. I wonder what the village vicar would say about bearing false witness. Of course, it was probably the best course of action. The captain might have refused passage if he knew she was single."

Jackson sniffed. "Indeed. Just don't get too excited too soon. Storms or overly calm winds, not to mention infernal interference by Mr. Lincoln's navy, could delay her arrival considerably. If the ship is forced to seek port in Virginia, Amanda would have to make her way south overland."

"Perhaps, but with my sister's luck she'll be here when expected and without encountering so much as a mild case of seasickness." Abigail pushed away her breakfast plate.

"Time will tell. Now, what are your plans for today?"

Abigail tossed down her napkin. "I intend to oversee the gardeners among the roses. I wish large bouquets without thorns in every room. Then I plan to take luncheon with Carolyn Lowell. As long as there's no hint of rain, she's having eight ladies on the terrace. Then I'll probably read and nap until your return from the office."

"That sounds delightful, but don't overtire yourself. Remember what the doctor said about resting." Jackson reached for her hand and kissed the backs of her fingers. "I must be off." He paused in the doorway and looked over his shoulder. "Nothing stronger at Carolyn's than lemonade."

"Stop worrying, husband. I'm fine."

Jackson accepted his coat and hat from a footman and strode out the door.

From the window, Abigail watched his carriage until it turned the corner. How she loved that man. He was tall and handsome, generous and kind—at least to her. Anything she asked for he graciously provided and asked for nothing in return except an heir, a son to carry on the family business, the prestigious Henthorne and Sons. Thus far she'd been unable to fulfil his one request. Two earlier pregnancies had ended abruptly within a few months.

But this baby she was carrying would be hearty and strong. Abigail just knew it. And Amanda journeying to the Carolinas was a very good omen.

"Miz Henthorne?" A child appeared in the gap in the privet hedge.

"Yes, I'm Mrs. Henthorne. Who might you be?" Abigail smiled kindly at the young boy—a slave, judging by his clothing.

"I'm Daniel from Mr. Phelps. He's the dockmaster."

"The dockmaster?"

"Yes'm. I was sent to say the *Queen Antoinette* has come to port." He shuffled his feet in the dirt.

"Is my sister, Miss Dunn, aboard the ship?"

"Yes'm. I was 'spose to say that too, but I forgot her name." Daniel stole an anxious glance. "Mr. Phelps say you should send your carriage."

Abigail rose to her feet. "I shall at once. Before you run back, Daniel, stop at the kitchen door and ask the woman there to give you a cookie."

When the child had vanished, she moved almost as quickly. Within thirty minutes her carriage pulled into the loading area of the wharf.

"Looks to be fewer ships than usual, Miz Henthorne." The driver shielded his eyes from the sun with his hat.

"Don't dawdle, Thomas. Find Miss Dunn and then tell the porter to bring her luggage to the carriage."

Thomas jumped down and tied the horse to a post. "How will I know which lady is Miss Dunn, ma'am?"

Abigail giggled behind her fan, trying to stem her enthusiasm. "That's easy. She's my twin sister. She looks exactly like me."

Thomas disappeared down the ramp toward the docks and returned with a pale waif of a woman a few minutes later. Amanda wore a somber gray suit that fell in a straight line to the ground, a drab hat with a veil, and sensible lace-up boots. Except for her face, the two women looked nothing alike.

"Amanda! At long last," Abigail called. "I've been so worried."

"My dear Abby! You have no idea how glad I am to be on solid land without all that swaying from side to side."

Abby. No one had called her that in years. Jackson abhorred nicknames. He even cringed when his brother called him Jack. "I assume it wasn't a smooth voyage?" Abigail extended her hand.

Climbing into the carriage, Amanda clasped her fingers as though too weak to walk another yard. "I refuse to begin our overdue reunion by complaining. There will be plenty of time for that later." Amanda threw her arms around her sister's neck and hugged. "I'm overjoyed to see you." Her dimples deepened with her grin.

Her sister's smile hadn't changed one bit. Abigail said, "And I, you, although you were expected a week ago. I've been sitting atop pins and needles." Suddenly, an ominous thought crossed her mind. "Your dark clothes…oh, goodness. Please don't tell me something dreadful has happened to Mama or Papa."

Amanda's gaze rotated between her charcoal wool and Abigail's aqua silk and lace. "I see why you might assume such a thing, but no. Rest easy. Our parents are fine. Papa had a cold when I left, but the doctor insisted he will be better soon."

"What a relief, although I suppose neither gives a whit about me anymore."

"Then you would suppose incorrectly." Amanda leaned back against the upholstery. "They both expressed their regards, and I am to send word upon arrival to let them know how you are."

"Hmm, I'm sure you exaggerated their fond wishes somewhat, but no matter. You came to see what's become of me, and I'm happy to report that Jackson and I are doing splendidly," Abigail said, smoothing her palms down the expensive fabric of her frock.

"Judging by the opulence of your carriage, I would say that's no exaggeration." Amanda fingered the ornate brass trim. "And you look the picture of health, Abby. Marriage suits you."

Abigail spotted the porter wheeling two huge trunks toward the back of the carriage, with a small, dark-haired woman at his heels. "Who is she? Did you bring your maid overseas?"

"Yes. It was the only way I could leave Manchester without Papa sending one of his mill managers for my chaperone. Her name is Helene. I hope she won't pose a problem."

"Not at all." Abigail opened the window and leaned out. "Helene, you may ride topside with my driver. Thomas, I wish to leave the moment the porter loads the trunks. These docks attract an unsavory type of worker as well as shiftless vagabonds." Abigail closed the window and settled back. As soon as they left the docks, she turned toward her sister. "There may be another reason for my healthy glow. I believe I'm expecting a child." She whispered even though they were alone.

"How wonderful! I'm pleased for you. When does the doctor anticipate the child's grand entrance?"

Abigail snapped open her fan. "I haven't consulted him yet. I wish to be certain first as we've suffered several disappointments thus far."

"That sounds like a wise move." Amanda swiveled around to peer out the side window. "Your adopted city appears quite prosperous."

"Wilmington is small but growing by leaps and bounds." Abigail was happy that Thomas had chosen the most flattering route through town. There would be plenty of time for her sister to learn about the unfortunate privations of war.

"Do you live very far from the river?"

"Perhaps another five minutes." Abigail cracked open the window to let a little of the early spring air in. "I'm sure you're eager to rest in a real bed."

"I had no idea how cramped a ship's quarters could be, especially during so long a voyage. Helene and I were the only female passengers, so other than dining at the captain's table, we mainly confined ourselves below deck. Unfortunately, reading and sewing often triggered nausea, so we had little to occupy the hours."

"That sounds dreadful. I'm glad your ship wasn't further delayed." Abigail smiled as the carriage stopped in front of the mansion.

"Is this where you live, Abby?" Amanda swung the door open the moment Thomas lowered the steps. "It's magnificent! A rather enormous house for a young couple, no?"

Abigail followed her onto the stone banquette, letting her gaze travel up to the soaring roofline. "The house belonged to Jackson's grandparents, but they have since passed on."

"Do your husband's parents live here too?"

"No, they have a plantation in the country, although Jackson's father often stays with us when he conducts business in Wilmington." Abigail turned toward Thomas. "Please see that Miss Dunn's trunks are delivered to her room." Turning back to her sister, she said, "Would you like to rest before tea?"

"Actually, I'm eager to stretch my legs after weeks of confinement. Could you show me your garden instead?"

"Of course. Let's take the path to the left through the roses. We'll end up on the front veranda eventually."

The twins set off at a leisurely pace, with Helene keeping a respectable distance behind them. Amanda asked many questions about the flowers of North Carolina, which were quite different from the blooms of Manchester or the western coast of England. Before long, however, it wasn't the magnolia, climbing wisteria, or flowering crepe myrtle piquing her interest.

"Who lives in there?" With a slender finger, she pointed at two cottages along the back property line.

"Our servants." Abigail kept her answer short and to the point.

"All of them? How is that possible?"

"The single women live in that cabin. Our cook is married to our driver, and they live in that one." She indicated the second narrow doorway. "The other men live in the loft of the carriage house."

Amanda frowned, her lower lip protruding. "Why don't they live on the third floor of the house? There would be so much more room."

"Because that's where the ballroom is located. Besides, as living quarters it would be suffocating during the summer months even with cross ventilation. This is the South, dear sister." She fluttered her fan beneath her chin.

"Yes, of course. I didn't consider that, but their quarters seem rather cramped—"

"They have this entire courtyard for socializing." Abigail spread her arms wide. "Our climate is milder than back home. We stay indoors far less often."

At that moment one of the cook's helpers exited the cabin. Wearing a homespun shift in need of replacing, the young woman plopped down on the stoop with a bowl of peas to shell.

Amanda's eyes nearly bugged from her face. "Do you have *only* slaves here?"

"Well…yes. They came with the house. They belonged to Jackson's grandparents." Abigail felt her forehead bead with perspiration.

Amanda stammered as though confused. "I knew you lived in the South, yet for some reason I never considered the possibility Jackson's family would embrace the loathsome practice."

"*Loathsome?* Mama has a fleet of servants paid little beyond room and board. And you travel with your personal maid." She pointed at the small woman cowering behind a trellis.

"True enough, but our parents don't *own* human beings. Their domestics are free to quit their jobs and seek employment elsewhere."

"Abigail?" A voice sounded from behind them. "Why are you and our guest standing in a dusty stable yard while refreshments are waiting on the verandah?" Jackson's arrival had gone unnoticed during the twins' tête-à-tête. "And the rest of the staff is eager to make your sister's acquaintance…as I am." He bowed gallantly to Amanda. "Miss Dunn, it's been too long a time."

"Mr. Henthorne, I'm pleased to see you again and grateful for your kind hospitality." Amanda extended her hand.

While Jackson kissed her hand with great flourish, two slaves stepped forward. "How do, ma'am? Name's Estelle. I'm maid to Miz Abigail. This here's Josie. She's a fast learner and will catch on before you know it." Both women dropped into the curtsies Abigail had painstakingly taught them.

"How do you do, Estelle, Josie," Amanda murmured.

"Estelle is my maid and Josie shall be yours. She's a gift to you from Jackson." Abigail smiled fondly at her husband.

"Thank you, sir, but that won't be necessary. My maid, Helene, traveled with me from home."

"Then you'll have two attendants, Miss Dunn. Buying a slave is much like ordering a *couture* gown—you can't very well send it back." Jackson peered down his nose at his guest, his lip curling. "You ladies can work out the details in a more comfortable spot than this. Shall we?" He pointed at the stone path leading around the house.

"A wonderful idea, I'm dying for something cool to drink." Hooking her arm through her sister's, Abigail led the way. "Will you join us, Jackson?"

"I'm afraid I must return to the office. I'll see you both at dinner. The dockmaster sent word that the *Queen Antoinette* had arrived. I wanted to make sure Miss Dunn had a smooth transition into our household."

"Thank you for your attention to detail." Amanda bobbed her head politely, yet she maintained an expression of seasickness that should have abated the moment her feet touched solid ground.

Two

Amanda couldn't nap that afternoon despite being weary to the bone. How could she rest when so many problems demanded her attention? And how could she fall asleep when not one, but two maids watched her every move? There was no place for Helene in the house, and staying in the slave quarters was out of the question. Abigail was correct about the third floor not being an option. One quick jaunt up the back stairs quashed the idea of partitioning off an area in the big entertainment room. The top floor of the mansion was stiflingly hot and airless, even in April. She would have to screen off her sitting room and have a cot brought in.

The question of Josie presented its own conundrum, but after some thought it was decided that the girl would take care of the washing and ironing, along with cleaning the suite. Helene would feel those tasks beneath her station anyway. America had a different social structure for domestics, not the least of which was *purchasing* servants.

Amanda hurried downstairs the moment she heard the bell to signal dinner. After instructing Helene to eat in the kitchen, she entered the dining room and found Jackson and Abigail at the bank of windows.

"There you are, sister. We thought we would enjoy an aperitif while we waited. Shall we be seated?" Abigail was dressed in yet another elegant gown. "It'll just be the three of us on your first night, although I must say my friends and Jackson's family are eager to meet you. We've had few visitors from Britain since the war began."

Amanda took the chair on Abigail's right. "I appreciate a quiet evening tonight, but I am eager to meet the elder Mr. Henthorne," she said, waving off the butler's offer of champagne.

"My parents will come to town and dine with us later in the week, but I'm curious as to why you're anxious to meet my father," Jackson said as he opened his linen napkin with a sharp snap.

"I was sent by our father to speak with Mr. Henthorne. Papa appointed me his emissary of sorts—a distinction I hope he won't live to regret." Amanda directed her explanation to her sister.

"But I thought you came to visit me, to see how I'm faring in the new world." Abigail's lip protruded in a childlike pout.

"I did come to see you, Abby, but Papa never would have permitted the journey if he didn't have an ulterior motive." Judging by their expressions, the explanation provided little mollification.

"What ulterior motive did he have in sending you?" Jackson downed his glass of bubbly wine and motioned for a refill.

Amanda prayed she would find the correct words. She didn't want to start off her relationship with her brother-in-law on the wrong foot. There had already been a misunderstanding with the maid. "He wishes for me to restore shipping between Wilmington and Manchester. Dunn Mills is desperate for American cotton. There is none better in the world, and Papa's mills cannot make garments solely out of wool, linen, or silk." She gratefully sipped the cup of tea a footman provided.

She had not anticipated Jackson's reaction. He burst into loud guffaws. "Papa Dunn sent you to transact business on his behalf? Preposterous. Just because you wear cotton garments doesn't mean you know anything about the material."

Abigail leaned forward in her chair. "I know what you're up to, you sly imp. This was a ruse to get Papa to agree to the trip. What a clever fox you are."

Amanda couldn't help but laugh. "Papa declared I had spunk, and now you deem me a sly fox. I hope I can live up to both appraisals."

"Whatever device you used to garner permission is fine by me. I'm overjoyed to see you." Abigail smiled warmly at her sister as she motioned for dinner to be served.

Amanda turned to face Jackson. "Please understand that I've done more than wear the fabric for the last two months. I trained ten hours a day with the mill's chief supervisor. Mr. Pelton tutored me on everything having to do with the acquisition of raw materials. He supplied charts on correct pricing in regards to quality and several books on the diseases that affect cotton plants."

Jackson's skepticism didn't wane. "Perhaps you can speak to my father at some point while you're here."

"With your permission, Jackson, I would like to call at the offices of Henthorne and Sons tomorrow. I wouldn't want to muddle the weekend dinner with your parents by discussing business." Amanda fixed a glorious smile on her face in hopes of persuading him.

He mulled this over for a few moments and then said, "Fine, Miss Dunn. I don't see what it would hurt. I have appointments in the morning, but you may have Thomas bring you around at eleven. That should work out well. My father and I will expect you then."

"Thank you. I'm in your debt. Now, if you would be so kind, please call me Amanda. Since we're related by marriage, I feel it's proper."

Jackson studied her for a moment and then laid his hand atop Abigail's. "I wish to grant my wife's sister every courtesy while she's in Wilmington."

"Splendid," said Abigail. "With that settled, let's concentrate on this fine meal. I do believe Salome outdid herself."

Amanda slept so soundly that night that not even a Chinese gong could have wakened her. Josie wanted to remain on a mat in the alcove, but Amanda insisted she sleep in the woman's quarters and report after breakfast. One maid, in this case the bewildered Helene, would be sufficient for her evening needs. At breakfast Amanda dined alone in the grand salon. Jackson had already left the house, and Abigail usually took a tray in her room. Josie explained that Miz Henthorne seldom appeared downstairs before noon.

Amanda wished to discover her new residence for the next couple months and preferred exploring on her own. Her sister lived in a magnificent three-story mansion set on a corner lot, three blocks from the waterfront of the Cape Fear River. Built of some masonry material Amanda had never seen before, the house had tall white columns, second- and third-floor galleries, and a *porte cochere*. Tall privet hedges surrounded the gardens, providing an oasis within the bustling city. Although her parents' home was the largest in their area, only the nobility owned anything this opulent in Manchester. Judging by the number of nearby mansions, she felt America must truly be the land of opportunity for enterprising souls.

The Henthorne servants kept an eye on her as she wandered through the rooms and gardens. She wasn't sure if they wanted to be helpful or to make sure she didn't fill her pockets with the silver.

All things considered, Abigail had married well if the house, number of servants, and quality of meals were any indication. The fact that those servants were slaves irked Amanda no small measure.

"We best be going, Miz Dunn." The coachman materialized behind her on the garden path. "Master said your appointment was at eleven."

Amanda tried not to cringe at his reference to Jackson as "master."

"Thank you, Thomas. I'll get my shawl and bag."

Her bag was a valise filled with records of transactions between Dunn Mills and area cotton factors for the last several years, including recent contracts. She planned to be prepared for her first business meeting, especially as she had reviewed Papa's list of instructions into the early morning hours. In her austere crepe dress and short jacket, Amanda was as ready as she ever would be.

Randolph Henthorne rose to his feet when the clerk showed her into his office. "Ah, you must be Miss Dunn. Come in and have a seat. Jackson mentioned you would be honoring me with a call today." He flourished his hand at his son lounging on the window ledge and then the upholstered chair in front of his desk.

"Goodness, Amanda. You're dressed like the head mistress of my old boarding school—the one who used to rap my knuckles with her ruler." Jackson's quip met with laughter from the elder Henthorne.

"Thank you for making time for me during your busy morning,

sir." Then to Jackson she said, "If I'm to be taken seriously as my father's emissary, I decided to save my frilly gowns for garden parties." Amanda lowered herself onto the edge of the chair.

"And indeed you shall be," said Randolph. "Would you care for coffee or tea?"

"No, thank you, sir." She clutched her valise in front of her as though it were a protective shield.

"Then let me begin by saying I remember your father well. A fine gentleman, George Dunn. He drove a hard bargain, but he was always honest and a man of his word."

"Thank you, sir. That's kind of you to say." Amanda began to relax slightly in the beautifully appointed office.

"But why on earth didn't he come himself instead of sending his daughter? I'm aware of your brother's death and you have my sympathies, but this is a man's domain. I don't care how much studying you've done or that you're dressed like a stern schoolmarm." Leaning back in his chair, Randolph Henthorne chuckled merrily. "But as you've made the trip, I hope you enjoy your visit with my daughter-in-law. And whenever you're ready for the peace and quiet of the countryside, my wife and I wish to invite you to our plantation, Oakdale, for a few weeks."

Amanda's moment of relaxation vanished. "My father isn't well, sir, or he would have traveled himself. He thought it crucial for me to represent Dunn Mills on his behalf."

Jackson pushed away from the windowsill and approached with a scowl. "You said nothing last night about Abigail's father being ill."

"Papa insists it's only a cold he cannot shake. He's probably better by now, but Dunn Mills cannot wait any longer."

Jackson crossed his arms. "Then he should have—"

The elder Henthorne raised his hand, silencing his son. "It's immaterial what Mr. Dunn should or shouldn't have done.

Abigail's sister is here now, and we shall make sure her visit is memorable. But regarding the supply of cotton to Manchester?" Randolph's light blue gaze pinned her much like a butterfly to a display board. "Our hands are tied. The president of the Confederacy has ordered that no shipments shall go to Great Britain, and you'll not find a factor in Wilmington who will go against his decree. Not one who plans to show his face at any social event this season." Then he smiled patiently, like a grandfather forced to dispense disappointing news. "There's a war on in your former colonies, Miss Dunn. Life is nothing like it used to be." With that, Randolph stood, summarily dismissing her. "But I will inquire with my contacts in Richmond. Maybe progress has been made between our emissaries and Queen Victoria."

"Allow me to see you out, Miss Dunn." Jackson bowed and offered his elbow.

Amanda took his arm because her knees had gone weak. What had she been thinking? That she would be able to produce her charts and price lists and come to terms before lunch? The elder Henthorne had treated her like a child.

Jackson walked her to the carriage, bid her a good afternoon, and turned on his heel. For a long minute she stood on the street while the coachman waited, perplexed. "You 'bout ready to go home, Miz Dunn?"

"No, thank you. I've decided to walk back to Third Street."

"But why, miss? I got the carriage right here."

"Because I wish to tour your lovely city, and what better way than on foot? I remember the route from yesterday."

"I don't know, ma'am. Miz Henthorne might not like you walking alone."

"Why not? I'm a grown woman. Please tell my sister I will be home shortly." To curtail further discussion, Amanda set off at a brisk pace down the street. Once she turned the corner, away from the office of Henthorne and Sons and her sister's slave coachman, she breathed a sigh of relief.

Rome wasn't built in a day. I'm not going back to England until I do my job. With her silent promise made, Amanda's spirits lifted. She scoured the area, studying the different kinds of merchandise in shop after shop until hunger pangs demanded her attention. However, she had no desire to return to the mansion. In the coming days she would share plenty of luncheons with her sister.

Spying a sign for Cooper's Greengrocery, Amanda marched down Water Street and entered the store with a spring in her step.

"Hullo, Mr. Cooper?" She sang out a greeting when she found the shop empty.

"Hold your horses. There's only one of me." A deep voice echoed from the back room. When the man appeared, he remained hidden behind the stack of crates he was carrying.

"Excuse me for shouting. I didn't know if someone was here or not."

The shopkeeper placed his crates near the door and turned, his jaw dropping open. "Excuse me, madam. I thought you were one of my regular customers playing sport with me with a phony accent." Mr. Cooper mimicked a British inflection on his last six words. He pulled off his cap, revealing a head of thick, sandy-brown hair.

Amanda took no offence at his pluck, perhaps because the man was rather handsome in a rugged sort of way. "I'm not a regular customer—at least not yet—but I assure you my accent is quite real. Amanda Dunn, sir, new to your fair city from Manchester, England."

"I humbly beg your pardon, Mrs. Dunn. Now you'll believe the rumors true that all Americans are hopeless boors." He bowed, with less polish than Jackson but with more sincerity.

"I shall reserve my opinion in that regard, and it's Miss Dunn.

Pleased to make your acquaintance." With the spunk her father insisted she possessed, Amanda extended her hand.

Mr. Cooper shook hands as though her fingers might crumble into dozens of pieces. "Nathaniel Cooper, but my friends call me Nate." He immediately flushed to a bright shade of scarlet.

Amanda smiled. "I will remember that in case *we* become friends someday."

Nate couldn't control the dull words issuing from his mouth or his schoolboy blush. "Of course, Miss Dunn. How can I be of service today?" He wiped suddenly damp palms down his apron.

"I'm visiting America for the first time. Today I'm finding my way around town." She tugged on the hem of her odd jacket, the likes of which he'd never seen before. Yet despite the fact she was attired in somber gray from neck to ankle, the woman was breathtakingly, heartbreakingly beautiful.

The longer Nate stared, the larger the boulder in his throat grew. "Do you find our country alien to your tastes?" he asked.

"As I only arrived yesterday, it's too soon to tell. I wouldn't use the term 'alien' but instead merely 'different.'" She smiled as she withdrew a small purse from inside her valise.

"How so?" Nate asked, wiping down his spotlessly clean counter with a rag.

"Everything is newer and grander, at least in my sister's neighborhood. You serve a delicious cup of tea here, but most take it without cream. And your names for things—one would think we spoke two different languages: taxes instead of duties, pickles instead of gherkins, cookies instead of biscuits, privy or water closet instead of loo." Miss Dunn's gloved hand flew to her mouth. "Forgive me. That was indiscreet. I don't know why I'm babbling so much."

"This lovely spring day has set both our tongues free." Nate grinned at her embarrassment. "Think no more about it."

She stepped back to peruse the contents of several shelves. "You display a fine selection of goods, sir. I will remember your shop for future necessities. Do you work here for your father?" Her warm brown eyes sought his.

"No. My father has passed on."

"For your mother, then?" She pursed her rosy lips.

"My mother is at rest, awaiting the Second Coming as well." Nate draped the rag over his shoulder. "They are buried side by side under a fir tree. My ma took sick one winter and died before Christmas."

"Forgive my impertinence, Mr. Cooper, but you appear too young to own a market by yourself."

"I was twenty-five on my last birthday, in robust health and usually sound of mind. Don't forget this is America—the land of opportunity for those with ambition. Even a nobody from the Blue Ridge Mountains can move to the seaboard for a fresh start if they're willing to work long hours. I have few requirements other than keeping my customers happy."

Miss Dunn stared at the floor. "Now I'm the one being boorish. I hope you won't judge all English people by my rudeness."

"I haven't met many Brits. Your countrymen usually send their servants to town to shop. And I don't find your curiosity inappropriate. If we don't ask questions, how can we learn? Now let me ask you one. What brought you into my store today? A bolt of fabric, a bottle of tonic, perhaps candy for your sweet tooth?"

For several moments she appeared perplexed. Then her lips pulled into a smile. "I almost forgot why I'm here. I have been walking all morning and I'm famished. Could I purchase a tin of soup or a potted pie for lunch? Chicken, beef, mutton—the type doesn't matter—but I don't wish to return to my sister's until I finish exploring. Who knows when I'll have another opportunity to escape?" As she ended her explanation, she dropped her voice to a whisper.

"Excuse me just for a minute, Miss Dunn." Nate marched into the stockroom without the slightest idea as to how to fulfill her request. He sold linens, powders, sacks of grain, and canned goods, not meals for those out for the day without a lunch hamper. He scanned burlap sacks of barley, flour, and rice; stacks of foolscap for penning letters; and kegs of apple cider and maple syrup. But he had no cookstove even if he found enough ingredients to prepare a simple meal. Nate reentered the store carrying his only solution.

He spotted Miss Dunn by the front door, assessing tins of salt and spices. "You'll find a basin behind the counter should you like to wash." He rolled out a clean linen cloth and poured a cup of cider. "Here you are, miss. I hope my special-of-the-day meets with your approval."

She washed and dried her hands and then climbed onto a tall stool at the counter. "My, this looks delicious." Miss Dunn lifted the top piece of grainy oatmeal bread and peered at a thick slice of farmer's cheese covered with spicy tomato relish. Holding the sandwich in both hands, she took a bite. "It's wonderful! While I eat, why don't you explain how merchandise finds its way onto your shelves?"

Nate perched on the opposite stool. "Vegetables and sacks of grain arrive in wagons from outlying farms, along with pickled meats and canned goods. I carry smoked hams, dressed turkeys and pheasants, and fresh venison whenever available. Fabric, notions, and cooking implements come by train from the west. Lately, those deliveries have been haphazard. Coffee, sugar, vanilla, and spices from abroad are becoming scarce because of the blockade, while pineapples, oranges, and bananas from the tropics are rare as snowstorms. Many residents are drinking more tea since the plantations around Charleston increased production."

"Splendid. Colonists are returning to the favored beverage of their mother country."

"It's been a long time since Carolinians thought of themselves as colonists. That war is past history. We're smack dab in the middle of another conflict now." Nate tried not to stare as she ate, but her creamy complexion and curvy figure beneath the dark dress drew him like a bee to nectar.

"Weren't you compelled to run off and enlist for the Glorious Cause? Our newspapers made it sound as though men were fighting for noble reasons, but taking someone's life is killing, plain and simple." Miss Dunn dabbed her mouth with the napkin.

Nate felt the tiny hairs lift on his neck. "I'm no coward, if that's what you're implying. I thought about signing up, but Wilmington is the center of trade for the Confederacy. If every man took up arms against the Yankees, who would be left to run the port?" He busied himself cleaning up bread crumbs. "Besides, I'm not from around here. No one back home owned slaves—they were too poor. I can't see the point of dying to maintain slavery. That evil practice only helps the rich get richer." Nate locked gazes with her.

"Forgive me, Mr. Cooper. It wasn't my intention to question your bravery or loyalties. In my attempt to understand the Southern culture, I have insulted you for the second time today."

"I've become quite adept at explaining myself." Nate ran a hand through his hair. "And there isn't one Southern culture. Quality of life depends on whether you're rich or poor, black or white. I suppose the same can be said in..."

"Village of Wycleft, outside of Manchester. And indeed that is the case."

"Where does your sister live, if I may inquire?"

"Abigail and Jackson Henthorne live on Third Street at the corner of Orange. Are you acquainted with them?"

"I've walked past homes in that area. Most assuredly I don't belong to the same social circle as your family." Nate tried unsuccessfully to keep scorn from his voice.

"Like you, I am opposed to slavery. Perhaps I will have little in common with their social circle too." Finished with the sandwich, she rose and walked to the window overlooking Water Street and the wharves beyond. "You mentioned you're from the Blue Ridge Mountains. Is there a high point in town where I might catch a glimpse of these peaks?" She smiled prettily over her shoulder.

He chuckled. "I'm afraid they are four hundred miles to the west. It would take a week to reach them by coach, probably the same by train since the armies keep tearing up the tracks."

"Four hundred miles? Yet we would still be in North Carolina?"

"Yes, ma'am. America is huge, not like that little island you call an *empire*." He winked impishly.

"I will allow you that insult and permit one more before we're even. But I'm keeping you from your noon meal. I should have insisted we dine together. Why don't you eat while I entertain you with tales about my home?"

Nate shoved his hands into his trouser pockets. "As delightful as that sounds, I'm afraid it's impossible."

"Why? Since you own this mercantile, you have no one to answer to and can eat a meal when you wish." She cocked her head to one side. "Are you too shy to eat in front of a stranger? I thought we were halfway to becoming friends."

"It's impossible, Miss Dunn, because *you* ate my lunch." He leaned back against the counter.

Her amused expression changed to abject horror. "I did? Why would you permit such a thing?"

Nate shrugged. "Because you were hungry and I wasn't at the moment. I enjoyed your company and didn't wish to cut our conversation short. Besides, if I sent a starving woman down the street to the hotel, what would that say about American hospitality?"

Miss Dunn fumbled in her purse with trembling fingers. "I have gobbled up a man's sole meal until sundown while insulting him at every turn." She placed several coins on the counter. "My sister left these for me on the hall table, but I'm not familiar with American currency. Please take whatever is fair for the meal."

"Absolutely not. The sandwich was a gift."

"My embarrassment will only increase if you refuse my money. I entered your store with the express purpose of buying something to eat." She pushed the coins across the glass top.

"Your embarrassment is baseless. I wouldn't have given you the sandwich if I didn't want you to have it. And gifts don't require payment." Nate shoved the coins back.

"You are a very stubborn man, Mr. Cooper," she said, returning the money to her purse. "Is that a Wilmington trait or something you brought from the impossible-to-see Blue Ridge Mountains?"

"It's a trait which bodes well for our potential friendship because we have it in common. Is yours an English tendency or perhaps a genetic disposition inherited from a Dunn ancestor?" He selected a shiny red apple from a bin and took a bite.

She paused to consider. "It must be the latter because my twin sister isn't the least bit stubborn. Impulsive, yes. Maybe even flighty, but Abigail is as amenable and pliable as they come."

Nate's apple stopped inches from his mouth. "Are you saying you have a twin? That there are two of you?"

"I am. We are identical in size and feature, but Abby is now a Carolina belle with hoops and frills and ostentatious hats. I compare poorly in my taste for clothes."

Nate studied her while eating the apple. "In my opinion, much of ladies' fashion seems better suited to a theater stage. But the notion that an identical copy of you lives mere blocks away has me stymied."

Miss Dunn stopped fiddling with her change purse and met his eye. "Why is that, Mr. Cooper?"

"Because you're the prettiest woman to ever walk into my store."

For several moments she didn't speak. Then she burst out laughing. "I shall accept that as high compliment, even though not one soul has entered your shop since I arrived. Which reminds me, I should leave and finish my explorations of your lovely town before my sister alerts the authorities. She must be worried that I'm either lost or have fallen in with a bad lot." Miss Dunn headed for the door with a sprightly step.

"Wait. When can I see you again?"

She turned around. "Would tomorrow be soon enough? I could bring a hamper around noon if you're willing to share lunch this time. After all, what's fair is fair."

"Little in life would please me more. But as I have no employees, I have no one to watch the store if we go off on a picnic."

She lifted an eyebrow. "Is this counter spoken for tomorrow afternoon, or perhaps your front stoop if it's sunny and mild?"

"No one has reserved them thus far." He felt a frisson of excitement begin to build inside him.

"Then it is settled. Good day, Mr. Cooper."

A good day to you, Miss Dunn. Nate didn't voice his words because the enchanting woman was already quickly walking up the street. But as he watched her he felt a whisper of unease. He was so out of his league. Amanda Dunn may as well be the Queen of England herself.

Three

*A*manda didn't slow her pace until she came to the two-block hike up the hill to her sister's house. After the long period of inactivity on the ship during her crossing, she was breathless by the time she climbed the steps to the lower verandah, where her sister was waiting for her.

"There you are, naughty girl. I was about to send the carriage in search of you." Abigail shook her finger in a brilliant imitation of their mother.

"Forgive me for worrying you, Abby. I was so fascinated with your city that I lost track of the hour. I browsed shop after shop, admiring everything I saw."

"In that case you are forgiven. We hope you'll enjoy Wilmington enough to remain. Shall we have tea?" Abigail settled on a chaise in the cool shadows and rang a small silver bell. A tea service materialized almost immediately.

"But Papa is depending on me to return to England with signed contracts—"

"Pooh. That's what the postal service is for, or you could hire a ship's courier to transport papers home." Abigail poured a cup of black tea and then handed it to her sister.

Amanda decided not to send Josie for a pitcher of cream, although her maid hovered behind her chair. "I may be here longer than I originally supposed. Mr. Henthorne said he must seek permission from Mr. Davis to conduct business with Dunn Mills."

Abby sipped her tea. "He is *President* Davis, not mister, and these things take time. Jackson said that you comported yourself admirably during the meeting. He expected you to stammer and stutter, if not faint dead away, but you acted like a true woman of industry." She giggled as though the idea amused her.

"That was my intention." Amanda peered through the filmy curtains into the house. "Did you say that Jackson was home?"

"Yes, but then he left for his men's club. He often takes business appointments there, but I believe imbibing alcohol and smoking cigars goes on more than anything else. I heard they also play cards for money late at night. What would our Episcopal priest say about that?" Abby dropped her voice in case the preacher lurked in the shrubbery. "At least Jackson doesn't go out often at night."

"Do you suppose he would venture to Richmond to call on President Davis?" Amanda asked between sips of surprisingly delicious tea.

"Goodness, no. Richmond isn't around the corner, dear sister. It's in another state, Virginia, and an arduous train ride away. Considering the fighting between here and there, that is out of the question. Could you imagine landing within range of Yankee artillery? No, no. A courier will take Papa Henthorne's request to the capital. In the meantime, you can catch me up with news from home. And when we're done with that, we can start calling on my friends during the afternoon. Everyone is eager to meet you." When Abby shook the bell a second time, a three-tiered tray of sweets and savories appeared. "Look! A proper English tea to celebrate your arrival."

Amanda leaned forward to admire crustless sandwiches, orange scones, and tiny iced cakes decorated with pink rosettes. "How lovely. Thank you."

For the next two hours she filled her sister in on changes in the village of Wycleft on the outskirts of Manchester: marriages of childhood friends, the death of their former nanny, scandals among the servants, old beaus who still asked after her. Abigail laughed much, cried a little, and in general appeared homesick, especially when the conversation turned to their mother.

"Grandmama sent a gift to you," said Amanda. "But she insisted that I wait until our birthday."

"Oh, please, may I have it now?" Abby dropped her scone onto the plate, her interest in food gone.

Amanda hurried to her room and a few minutes later presented Abigail with a small box covered in pink silk and tied with a black ribbon. Her sister pulled off the wrapping and extracted a hand-carved cameo bracelet—their grandmother's favorite piece of jewelry. "Are you certain she wanted me to have this?" Her words cracked with emotion.

"Yes. She was quite emphatic it was for you."

Abby clenched her eyes shut but couldn't stem the tears. They trickled down her face like a leaky faucet. After a while, she cleared her throat. "Let's talk about your afternoon before my face turns red and puffy. Jackson doesn't like to see me upset."

Amanda described the dressmaker and milliner she found, along with a resident artist who painted portraits in the front window of his cluttered studio. But before long, the conversation landed on Cooper's Greengrocery, and there it remained until Jackson's carriage pulled up to the mounting block.

"This shopkeeper has accomplished what no Englishman has been able to do—impress my extremely particular sister," Abby teased, finishing her discarded scone.

"I couldn't believe how forthright the man was, quite unafraid to say what he thought."

"Dear me, I hope he wasn't rude to you. Some of those stores on Water Street—"

"Not at all. Mr. Cooper behaved like a perfect gentleman. He just didn't waste time talking in circles like the men of Papa's acquaintance."

"I thought the same about Jackson when we met. He spoke his mind and went after what he wanted in life. Looks as if you've made your first friend in Wilmington. Well done." Abby rose to greet her husband, who had paused on the walkway to give instructions to the gardener.

"May I take a lunch hamper to Mr. Cooper tomorrow? After all, I caused him to go without today."

Abby smiled indulgently. "I don't see the harm, but let's not mention this at the dinner table. Jackson can be overprotective at times, which I'm afraid will include you while you're here."

That night when Amanda blew out her bedside candle, she was filled with anticipation. She had made the right decision in coming to America. Seeing her sister confirmed that five years meant nothing to twins. Her reception at the Henthorne and Sons office portended a successful resolution to the woes at Dunn Mills. And the prospect of seeing Nathaniel Cooper tomorrow? A gently raised young woman never should entertain such thoughts about a complete stranger. Yet when she closed her eyes, visions of his sinewy muscles, silky brown hair, and sky-blue eyes danced across her eyelids. Developing crushes wasn't a common habit for Amanda, but if Helene weren't already snoring on her side of the Chinese screen, she may have waltzed around the room with a pillow for a partner.

The following morning, after her solitary breakfast of grits and ham, she sought out the cook in the kitchen. "Good morning, Salome. May I trouble you to pack a luncheon hamper around eleven o'clock?"

The woman barely glanced up from rolling out pie dough. "Yes'm. Miz Henthorne already told me."

"Could I possibly have hearty selections suitable for a man's appetite instead of a woman's?"

That question triggered a furrowed forehead. "How 'bout fried chicken with corn relish and buttermilk biscuits?"

"Perfect!" Amanda clapped her hands, which drew a second raised eyebrow. But three hours later she and the driver were clattering down Orange Street in the Henthorne coach.

"Miz Henthorne told me to park in the shade and wait for you, no matter how long you take," Thomas said as he helped her down to the street.

Amanda had no desire to argue. She was too busy mentally listing suitable topics for discussion. However, when she reached the front door of Cooper's, all her well-laid plans drifted away on the salty sea breeze. Nathaniel, in a fresh white apron, shot her a smile when she entered. He was behind the counter explaining various types of muscle liniment to a white-haired woman.

Amanda busied herself memorizing labels of canned goods on the middle shelf. After what seemed like an eternity, the matron limped out with her purchase. "Will she improve with your miracle potion?" Amanda asked after the door clicked shut behind her.

Nathaniel stepped around the counter. "I recommended a cabbage poultice—one of my granny's home remedies. She'll be right as rain once she wraps the knee and sets it up on a hassock tonight. What use are grandchildren if not to fetch and carry for their elders?"

Amanda tried not to laugh too loudly. "I ask myself that question almost every day."

"Indeed, Miss Dunn? And how are you on this lovely morning?" He leaned so close she caught the scent of his soap, which was fresh and not the harsh lye some men favored.

"I am well and prepared to fulfill my promise." She lifted the hamper onto the counter.

"Rufus, my good man," he called. "Please come out and say hello to Miss Dunn." Turning back to her, he said, "I rent a room from his parents. They are free people of color who live on Castle Street. When Rufus occasionally fills in for me, I pay him a dime."

A small boy stepped from between the draperies. "How do, miss?"

"I'm well, Rufus. It's nice to meet you," Amanda said, smiling at the child.

"Rufus has agreed to watch the store, allowing us to dine under yonder magnolia." Nathaniel pointed across the street at a band of trees along the river. "Shall we be off?" He picked up the hamper and offered his elbow.

For some reason Amanda was too shy to take his arm. She pretended to dig for a handkerchief in her bag instead as they walked out of the store.

Nathaniel didn't seem to notice her hesitation. "We can't go far. If a customer ventures in without correct change, Rufus will whistle. He's an amazing whistler. Then I will run to his rescue." During his explanation he spread a tattered patchwork blanket on a thick patch of grass.

Amanda attempted to lower herself without revealing her

ankles. "I hope the meal meets with your approval." She unwrapped crispy chicken and opened a tin of biscuits. "I'm eager to hear about your home four hundred miles to the west. Is it similar to the landscape here?" She flourished her hand toward the downtown waterfront.

"It's absolutely nothing like Wilmington. I lived outside a small town in a valley between two mountains. A beautiful place three seasons of the year but brutal during winter. Sometimes my parents were snowed in for weeks, unable to reach the nearest road."

"During those weeks what did you eat?" she asked as she took a dainty bite of chicken.

"Rabbit, squirrel, possum—venison if a deer wandered close to the house—and root vegetables from the cellar. If the well froze up, we melted snow for drinking water."

"Did your parents farm the land?"

"If you could call it that. We raised mostly corn, squash, and potatoes for us, sometimes tobacco to sell when Pa could buy seed. We only owned twenty-five acres, and most of that was timber for the woodstove. At least we didn't freeze during cold months." Nathaniel stared at a ship approaching the harbor. "We had some fine apple trees, plum and pear too, and plenty of pecans and hickory nuts to roast and crack."

"That sounds like a lovely place in fair weather. Is the farm still in your family?" Amanda filled two cups with Salome's sweet tea.

Nathaniel finished his chicken leg before answering. "No. After my ma died, my pa took up the bottle until…until he died too. I tried my best for a while, but I left shortly after we lost the farm." He shook his head as though dispelling a nightmare.

"Were you unable to pay the mortgage?"

"There was no mortgage. We were living on land my grandfather had claimed fifty years earlier as a homesteader." He reached for another piece of chicken.

"Then how could someone just *take* your land?" Amanda didn't wish to be intrusive, but the lack of justice had raised her hackles.

"Maybe it's different where you come from, but here folks leave you alone only if no one desires what you have. If a rich man decides he wants to put a railroad through your land, he'll find a legal way to run you off. But I didn't accept your kind invitation to tell my hard-luck story. It's a beautiful day. Why don't we enjoy this fine repast and each other's company?" He lifted his tea in a toast and brought the cup to his lips, but he never took his gaze off her. And those blue eyes seemed older than those faraway mountains...and infinitely as remote.

Over the next two weeks, Nate lived in a state of constant agitation. He jumped each time the bell jingled over the door. He would cock his head to catch a hint of a British accent among female customers. Even the sound of a passing carriage on the street took his mind away from whatever task occupied his hands. Miss Amanda Dunn had invaded his nights as well. He lay in bed for hours trying to remember every word she said, and he saw her face whenever he closed his eyes.

He was smitten, plain and simple. He had arrived at that conclusion after their lunch under the magnolia. Each time she came in his store to purchase a sweet or pound of rice reinforced his conclusion and gave him hope that the affection might be mutual. Yet what did he have to offer a fine lady? Now his store made a fine profit, sufficient to pay his landlady for a room and nightly supper with money left over to save. The shop's attic could be converted into living quarters, but such an addition wasn't part of his dreams for the future. How could he expect Amanda to live like a church mouse after walking past the Henthorne house on Third Street? It was hopeless. Yet the idea of one day making her his bride made him work harder than ever.

A man had to have dreams, even if they never came true.

On Wednesday he was elbow-deep sifting weevils from the rice when the bell above the door rang. "Be right there," he called, cinching the bag of rice shut.

"Take your time, Mr. Cooper. We'd like to browse your merchandise for a while." The sweet, feminine voice was more than recognizable. It jolted his heart into double-time.

Nate ran a comb through his tangled hair, washed his hands, and donned a fresh apron. "Ah, Miss Dunn, what a pleasure to see you today," he said as he strode from the back room into the shop. Focused on her, he almost knocked over a small black woman.

"You Mr. Cooper?" The woman wore a turban head covering, common among slaves.

"I am. How do you do?" he said, nodding respectfully.

"This is Salome, the cook for the Henthornes. She's agreed to compare your prices and quality to Baxter's on Market Street." Miss Dunn rocked on her heels while delivering the clarification.

"Harrumph!" Salome added punctuation to the statement.

"Mr. Baxter is a man of impeccable reputation and runs a fine establishment. I am honored to be considered for your potential patronage." Nate bowed to both ladies.

"Don't hurt none to look, I 'spose," she said tersely, hooking her market basket in the crook of her arm and marching off toward the fresh vegetables.

Amanda lingered at the counter. "Salome is a bit stuck in her ways, but I have every confidence she'll be impressed." She withdrew a folded sheet from her reticule. "This is a letter of credit from the Henthornes' banker. My sister doesn't allow her servants to carry much money."

Nate rubbed a hand along his jaw. "Because she's afraid they'll stow away on the next northbound train or ship?"

Amanda shook her head. "I don't think so. Salome and her husband appear content working for them, but neither can read nor write. My sister fears they would be taken advantage of with substantial cash."

"Illiteracy is common with plenty of folks where I come from, black and white. Many don't recognize the value of book learning."

"Yet I can tell by the way you speak that you were well schooled."

"I went through the eighth grade in the mountains, but the gentleman who owned this shop before me left three shelves of books in the back room—manuals, novels, poetry, Shakespeare. I have been reading each night before bed and intend to finish every one of them. I ask someone about words I don't know. There's no shame in not knowing. It's only shameful to remain ignorant."

"Well said, and I couldn't agree more." Amanda produced her glorious smile. When their mutual admiration finally grew uncomfortable, she turned to check the cook's progress. Salome was busy filling her basket with all kinds of merchandise. "It appears your quality has met her expectations, and your prices must be fair," she whispered.

"I aim to please." Nate tucked the letter from the bank next to the cash box. Credit wasn't something he usually extended—a man could go broke if he made bad choices—but Miss Dunn could have the shoes off his feet if she so wished.

"So do I, which brings me to my second order of business." Amanda smoothed down the skirt of her pale blue dress. Her somber gray tweed from their first encounter was nowhere in sight, but her hoop was substantially smaller than average. "Would you care to dine tonight with the Henthornes and me?"

"Tonight?" His voice faltered and a squeak ensued.

"Yes, unless you have other plans."

"You wish me to come to the Third Street house for dinner?" He was flummoxed for something intelligent to say.

"Dinner is usually at eight, and I believe you're familiar with the location." Her face couldn't appear more earnest.

"I know where your sister lives, but are you certain she wants me at her table?" Nate's collar tightened around his neck, making it difficult to breathe.

"I asked her this morning. Plus, it was her suggestion that Salome do the shopping here. Have no fear, Mr. Cooper. You'll find us a nonthreatening group." Amanda's laughter sounded like the tinkle of wind chimes.

"But I own no formal dinner attire like society people wear. All I have are the clothes of a working man." Unfortunately, the mountain accent he'd struggled to minimize intensified as he became flustered.

"Then I suggest you wear what you have. I'll tell Abigail to reserve her formal attire for when the Queen comes to call."

"*Queen Victoria?*" He spoke so loudly the cook stopped sorting melons and stared at him.

"I'm joking, Mr. Cooper. You usually possess a quick wit. But if you don't wish to be my guest for dinner, just say so." Amanda rested a hand on her hip.

This will be the only chance I get, he thought. He ran a finger under his collar. "Nothing would give me greater pleasure than dining with your family, Miss Dunn." He sounded far more confident than he felt.

Salome issued another *harrumph* and ambled to where they stood. "If that's all settled, young man, you can tally up my order. I best get home and start cooking since this supper's gonna be mighty special."

Somehow Nate managed to add up the purchases and bid

the two ladies a good afternoon without tripping over his feet. Once they climbed into the carriage and drove away, he released a whoosh of breath.

Dinner at the home of Jackson Henthorne? Why on earth had he said yes? He'd made inquiries among his friends, and every one reported the same assessment: Henthorne was rich, powerful, and arrogant. His father's company controlled most of the cotton and tobacco leaving the port, along with much of the goods entering Wilmington. What topics of interest did a shopkeeper have to talk about with such a man? But the invitation had come from Amanda—a woman he couldn't possibly refuse.

Nate wrote the amount of the credit in his ledger, restocked the shelves, swept the floor, and hung the "Closed" sign in the window. He couldn't worry about loss of business by leaving early, not when he had a presentable appearance to create. For a modest sum, he bought a proper bath, shave, and haircut from the barber. Then he paid Ruth Sims, his landlady, to press his Sunday suit of clothes. Her husband, Odem, gave him a new pair of socks that were too big for him, and Rufus picked a magnificent bouquet of irises from their garden. He left his rented room on Castle Street in plenty of time to walk to the Henthornes' at a leisurely pace. Yet his shirt was sticking to his back by the time he applied the brass knocker at half past seven. Within moments, a tall black man in full livery opened the door.

"Mr. Henthorne?" The ridiculous question was out of his mouth before he could stop himself.

"No, sir. I am Amos. Mr. and Mrs. Henthorne and Miss Dunn are in the parlor. I'll show you the way." Amos pivoted without the slightest acknowledgment of Nate's faux pas.

When the butler paused in the doorway, Nate skirted around him without waiting to be announced.

"Mr. Cooper, so nice to see you." Amanda came toward him

on dainty slippers, wearing a gown only slightly fancier than her afternoon ensemble. "May I present my sister and brother-in-law? Mr. and Mrs. Jackson Henthorne."

Nate couldn't help gaping at the uncanny resemblance between women despite prior knowledge that Amanda had an identical twin.

Mrs. Henthorne graciously extended her hand. "We're pleased you were able to join us this evening, Mr. Cooper. Our Salome sings the praises of your fruits and vegetables. I believe you have gained a devoted customer."

Nate shook the gloved fingers before realizing she'd expected her hand to be kissed. "A pleasure, madam. These are for you." He handed her the massive bouquet before facing his host. "Thank you for your hospitality, sir."

"Not at all. Abigail and I have been eager to meet you. Despite my wife introducing Miss Dunn to her entire circle of friends, only the owner of the local mercantile has captured her attention." Henthorne grinned, revealing perfectly straight teeth and a deep cleft in his chin.

"Oh, Jackson," said Mrs. Henthorne. "Don't embarrass the man. Amanda simply loves American mercantiles. They contain such a vastly superior selection of goods than in Manchester. Would you care for an aperitif, Mr. Cooper?"

"No, thank you, ma'am." Nate didn't know much about spirits. His father drank only moonshine whiskey made by a neighbor during his declining years. Viewing firsthand the whiskey's effect ensured a lifetime of sobriety.

"Would you join me in a glass of lemonade?" asked Amanda. "I believe it will complement the cuisine." Taking his arm, she steered him away from the Henthornes into the hall. "Pay them no mind," she murmured. "Remember, you're my guest, not theirs."

Nate winked to acknowledge he'd heard. But once seated in the dining room, any confidence he had abandoned him. Never had he seen a table so grand—faceted crystal glasses, gold-banded plates, gleaming silver candelabras with dozens of tapers. He counted four forks and an equal number of spoons at each place setting. And the assortments of dishes served had no rhyme or reason: oysters, pâtés, an odd-tasting fish, veal in a sauce that left the meat unrecognizable, and a cold plate of cheeses and smoked meats. Nate had no choice but to watch Amanda select a utensil and then mimic her. If she declined a particular dish, so did he.

Throughout the meal, Jackson's thinly veiled attempts to discern his background left his head pounding to match his churning gut. He would have cut the man short and escaped the ostentatious room if not for Amanda. Throughout the meal she deflected Henthorne's more obvious inquires while smiling pleasantly. Nate would do nothing to cause her shame or regret over the invitation.

Miss Dunn may be an angel sent from the gates of heaven, but the interminable dinner made one fact crystal clear: They could have no future together. It would be like a box turtle attempting to run with a spotted fawn. And that realization saddened him more than the slippery poached pear that fell into his lap, or the cadre of slaves standing against the wall, or the fact Henthorne dismissed him after dessert as though a poorly behaved child. Nate thanked his two hostesses and fled from the house, confident nothing in life would ever equal his mortification.

The next morning Amanda went down to breakfast eager to leave her airless suite of rooms. Josie offered to fan her half the night, but Amanda had declined. Helene filled the tub with cool water, but the bath's effects didn't last very long. Perhaps part of her restlessness stemmed from the disastrous dinner party. Why had she thought Jackson would welcome Nathaniel? Her brother-in-law was a man who judged people by the cut of their clothes, their deportment and manners, and ultimately their bank accounts. He cared naught for social issues unless they directly affected Henthorne and Sons' interests. And literature or poetry? He'd actually bragged that he hadn't opened a book since leaving the boys' academy.

But Jackson couldn't be blamed solely for the meal's failure. She'd sat there like a toadstool, utterly helpless to alleviate Nathaniel's discomfort, as though she'd succumbed to the same lethargy infecting her sister. So she had no one to blame but herself.

"I thought I would find you here. You always were an early bird, even when we were children." Abigail walked into the breakfast room in a scented cloud of rosewater perfume.

"Good morning, sister. I hope you slept well." Amanda automatically straightened her slouched posture.

"Like a baby." Abby filled a cup of coffee at the sideboard before taking an adjacent chair. "Only fruit and toast for me, Amos. Thank you." Once the butler had left, her sister reached out to pat her hand. "I hope that experience wasn't too disheartening for you last night."

"What do you mean?" Amanda asked unnecessarily.

"Poor Mr. Cooper was frightfully out of his element. Don't you agree? He looked so befuddled when that pear slid down the front of his shirt." Abby clucked her tongue in pity.

"Accidents can happen to anyone. I recall you spilling punch down your gown at a cotillion."

"Of course accidents happen, but poor Mr. Cooper acted as though he'd never eaten oysters on the half shell or escargot before," Abby said as she added a teaspoon of sugar to her black coffee.

"Perhaps he never had. He's from the mountains of your new state, not the coastline. He has only mentioned trout in terms of seafood." Amanda felt a pressing need to defend her friend.

"It wasn't just the fish that stymied the poor grocer. Mr. Cooper seemed uncomfortable no matter which subject Jackson brought up in conversation."

Amanda cut a piece of her omelet and chewed carefully before responding. She was no longer a teenager at home but her sister's guest. "I cannot disagree with your assessment, but Jackson didn't choose topics of common ground. The latest vote on the town council about raising taxes on foreign spirits?"

"Discussing imported wines is the closest my husband comes to the mercantile business. Jackson can't very well talk about muskmelons and cantaloupes. He's probably never entered a store like that in his life."

Amanda set her fork on the side of her plate. "Your point is well taken, Abby, but I don't regret extending the invitation."

Her sister dropped her voice. "Jackson is concerned about you, Amanda. He doesn't understand your…interest…in this shop-keeper from the hills. Truly, it's laudable that Mr. Cooper owns a business, but what could you possibly have in common with him? Considering your education and background, you're from two different worlds. Jackson fears you feel something stronger than friendship for the man." She paused to nibble her piece of toast. "Of course, I told him not to be silly. You always loved taking in strays and championing the cause of the downtrodden."

"Mr. Cooper is not a stray dog! He's a man, and a fine one at that. He's generous and kindhearted to everyone who comes into his shop. He's well read, familiar with the American poets, and keeps abreast of legislation at the state level. Maybe local taxes on French wine don't concern him, but he follows what the North Carolinian delegates are doing in Richmond. Too often new laws benefit only rich planters and ignore the poor and working classes."

"And which side of this debate are you on?" Abby's clear brown eyes darkened.

"I'm not on either. I'm *English*, the same as you."

"Not quite. As Jackson's wife, I now consider myself an American."

Amanda shouldn't have been surprised by the revelation, but she was nevertheless.

"Do you find this grocer handsome in a rugged, unpolished sort of way?" Abby's stare didn't falter.

"I suppose so, but you may rest easy. I didn't come to Wilmington to court and marry—not Mr. Cooper or any friend of Jackson's. I intend to enjoy my visit with you, fulfill Papa's wishes, and then return home as unencumbered as when I left."

Abby clapped her hands. "Splendid. Jackson will be relieved. I told him last night as we prepared for bed that he was worried for nothing. I'm so glad we had this little chat." She patted Amanda's arm affectionately.

Amanda found little pleasure in placating her sister. Even though she and Nathaniel were merely friends, putting her intentions as to her future into words felt oddly disloyal to him.

"Excuse me, Mrs. Henthorne. I have a telegram for Miss Dunn."

"What?" Both sisters spoke simultaneously.

"The boy from the telegraph office said it's for Miss Dunn, in care of you, Mrs. Henthorne, at this address." Amos waited with the sealed envelope on a silver tray.

"Very well. Give it to her." Abby sounded harsh.

Amanda felt uneasy as she read the envelope. "This came from an office in Baltimore."

"Baltimore? Do you know someone living there?"

"No." Amanda extracted the short message and read it twice, her breath coming in gasps, her throat constricting painfully. "It's Papa." She lifted her gaze. "He died soon after I left Manchester. Mama and Mr. Pelton sent word on the next clipper leaving port, headed to Baltimore. A contact of Mr. Pelton's telegraphed as soon as he received word." The sheet of paper slipped from her fingers.

"Papa—he's dead?" Abby sounded weak and childlike.

"I'm afraid so, dear heart."

"But you told Jackson his illness wasn't serious and that he would soon recover."

"That was the impression I had when I left home."

"But I haven't seen Papa in five years. I had no chance to say goodbye…or to make amends. What if I'm carrying a child?" Her hands settled on her flat belly. "He will never see his first grandchild." Tears ran down her pale cheeks.

"Send word to Mr. Henthorne's office." Amanda said to Amos, who stood silently beside his mistress. "Ask him to come home." Then she rose from her chair and enveloped Abigail in her arms. "I suspect Papa knew you loved him, but the love of a good man took you across the sea."

Helpless to hold back her own tears, Amanda began to sob too. She cried for Abby, estranged forever from her father, and she cried for herself. Now he would never be proud of whatever she accomplished in America. For several minutes, the sisters sat immobile, lost in their grief.

Then another troubling thought came to mind, far more weighty than a woman not pleasing her father. What about Mama and her father's employees? Those families depended on their pay envelopes for their very existence. Her mother had never written a cheque or taken care of even a modicum of responsibility. What would happen to her mother and Dunn Mills now?

After her sister's sobs diminished to soft mewing sounds, Amanda helped her to the master suite of rooms. Once Abigail was reclining on the daybed with a cool cloth on her forehead and Estella fanning her with ostrich feathers, Amanda walked down the gallery steps to the garden. Hidden by saw palmetto blades, she allowed her grief to wash over her anew. When she had no more tears to cry, Amanda dried her face, blew her nose, and lifted her face toward heaven. *I'll make you proud of me, Papa. No matter what I need to do.*

Four

May

"May I ride with you downtown, Jackson?"

His sister-in-law's voice cut through his thoughts of cards and cigars at the club that night. Jackson looked up to see Amanda, fully dressed and leaning over the gallery balustrade.

"It's not even nine o'clock, Miss Dunn, and you're already eager to go shopping?" He tugged on his gloves as Thomas led the horse from the stable to the carriage.

"Not shopping. I thought I would call on your father to see if he's heard from Richmond yet."

"If there was word from Jefferson Davis, don't you think I'm capable of conveying the message during tea or at dinner?"

Amanda winced with a blush. "Goodness, I implied that, didn't I? Forgive me." She came down the gallery steps to the flagstone courtyard. "Certainly you would tell me, but I've grown impatient since the passing of my father."

Her forlorn tone changed his irritation to pity. "It's been only a month since we sent a letter to the president of the Confederacy. I fear he has more urgent matters than the business concerns of Dunn Mills or Henthorne and Sons."

"I understand that, but I received a letter from Mr. Pelton, the mill's chief supervisor. He is anxious for an update on raw materials. He said his workers will be idle by midsummer if the mill doesn't receive a substantial supply of cotton. I feel responsible for the families working for us."

"I will speak to my father today. Rest assured, we wish to resume trade as much as you do." Jackson climbed into the open carriage. "In the meantime, please try to get my wife out of the house. Why not call on one of her friends this afternoon? Pining away in our bedroom for weeks isn't healthy and won't bring your father back."

"You insist we make social calls while in mourning?"

"I'm only suggesting close friends in the neighborhood, not that she don a ball gown for a cotillion. She can wear her unrelenting black if she chooses, even though mourning attire only worsens her melancholia. Abigail is a lighthearted, carefree woman. At least she used to be. She's barely left our bedchamber since we heard the news." The horse pranced and pulled against his harness. "What say you? Do we have a bargain?"

She nodded. "I will get her out of the house today."

Jackson thumped his walking stick and the carriage began to roll. Talking to his father had been on his mind anyway. Their company thrived and grew with the movement of goods. With less cotton and tobacco flowing out of port, their balance sheet must be suffering. He aimed to find out how bad things were before the situation became irreparable.

He found his father at his desk enjoying his favorite morning breakfast—sweet dough rolled in chopped pecans, coiled into a circle, and then baked. Whenever Randolph left the plantation before dawn, he carried several with him to eat at his Wilmington office.

"Good morning, Father. Will we have the pleasure of your company at dinner this evening?" Jackson asked as he slouched into one of the soft upholstered chairs.

"You shall because I'm staying in town." Randolph set down the icing-topped pastry and looked at his son, his bloodshot eyes ringed with dark circles.

"You look terrible, sir. What's wrong?"

"I went over the books last night. Today I plan to meet with our clerks and bookkeeper. There must be some mistake. Perhaps receivables haven't been properly tallied on the ledgers."

Jackson recognized his perfect opportunity. "If you don't mind, I would also like to meet with the bookkeeper and assess the company's financial condition."

"Very well. I would appreciate your input, but I don't think either of us will like what we see. President Davis's edict of no trade with England has hurt us badly. Britain is the chief market for cotton and a substantial amount of tobacco. Your houseguest isn't the only one needing restored trade routes." He rang the bell for more coffee. "I've spoken to your mother about curtailing orders from her favorite *couturiers* and also to the overseer about not purchasing more people. Tomorrow I have an appointment with the banker about an extension of credit. Our family is trying to maintain standards until this conflict is resolved."

"The situation has become that dire?" Jackson jumped to his feet and began to pace. "Why haven't we spoken about this before?"

"I didn't wish to worry you, son. I felt certain President Davis would realize how vital cotton is to the economy of Southern states and rescind his decision. This war has lasted three years with no end in sight."

Jackson took in a calming breath. "I'm not a wet-behind-the-ears youth, Father. When William ran off and enlisted in the cavalry, I told you I would help run the company in his place."

The mention of his brother's name only deepened the creases around Randolph's mouth. "It's been weeks since we've heard a word from William or seen a newspaper report as to the whereabouts of his division."

Jackson shook his head. "Yankee spies read Southern papers, sir. The less Sherman's troops know about William's regiment, the better."

Randolph stood and brushed sugar from his cravat. "You have helped me, Jackson. You've demonstrated shrewdness at the auction by buying quality materials at the best prices, yet whatever cotton arrives in Wilmington sits moldering in our warehouses. There's little you can do about that."

All at once Jackson's vision cleared. While he'd been blustering with his friends over whiskeys in the afternoon, or losing at cards until the wee hours of morning, his father had allowed Henthorne and Sons to falter. Why hadn't he noticed how aged the man had grown? And with age came cautiousness and hesitancy. Restraint was no way to run one of the foremost brokerage houses on the Carolina coastline. "Allow me to review the books this afternoon. Then I'll visit every warehouse in town and assess the inventory of cotton available to be shipped."

"Shipped to where? If word of sales to England gets back to Richmond, I may be ostracized. The president insists Britain's influence is crucial if the Confederacy is to prevail." Randolph reached for a glass of water with a shaky hand.

"I read the papers too, Father. Munitions and supplies for our army are far more crucial than the Queen's approval. Soldiers need guns, powder, cannon shot, food, shoes—the list is as long as my arm. There may be a way to help the Cause and help ourselves at the same time. We can ship cotton, tobacco, and tea to Bermuda. Fleet ships on a straight course to the island can return with munitions from the continent much faster than from South Hampton or Liverpool."

Randolph scratched his chin. "Bermuda is a colony of the British Empire. Wouldn't that still be disobeying Davis's request?"

"Allow me to assume the day-to-day operations. Later, if we suffer censure or reprisals from my decision, I shall plead ignorance as to the nature of Bermuda's politics. Several of my friends will attest that I paid little attention to geography in school. In the meantime, German manufacturers can get their products to us. This could be exactly what the company needs."

"Let me think on this for a few days."

"No, Father. Now is the time for action for Henthorne and Sons and perhaps for the Cause itself. If we hesitate, our opportunity may be lost." Jackson straightened to his full six feet and squared his shoulders. "Give me a chance to prove myself. I won't let you down."

For a fleeting moment, he saw relief replace resignation in the old man's eyes.

"Very well. I'll turn over the reins for a while. Your mother would like me at home more. With few men around, our people continue to disappear. The overseer cannot be everywhere at once. I'll expect reports from you each week, but I won't interfere with your decisions." Randolph offered his hand.

"Thank you, sir. You won't be sorry." Jackson shook, bowed deeply, and walked to his small office—an office that had contained too much daydreaming and not enough work. But those days were behind him. He'd always assumed he would take the helm once his father passed on, but what if there was nothing left to run when that time came? Considering the state of affairs in Wilmington, bold action was needed, not reminiscing about how life used to be.

For the remainder of the day, Jackson pored over recent correspondence from cotton planters, other area factors, and then studied the books and ledgers for hours. Although many notations for expenditures were gibberish, one thing became crystal clear by day's end. The economic health of Henthorne and Sons had been in steady decline for the past two years. If something wasn't done to turn the tide, they would soon need to sell assets to satisfy creditors. His father should have come to him before now, but Jackson had done little to instill faith in his abilities.

When William left to join Braxton Braggs's troops, his father had been so proud. Randolph had begged Jackson not to do the same because Wilmington had become the most important port on the eastern coast. Nevertheless, Jackson had yearned for a way to make his own mark.

This might be the best chance he would ever get.

Amanda crept down the back stairs to the garden as quiet as a mouse. She had no desire to disturb anyone at this hour, but she couldn't stay in her room any longer. Jackson had kept his word. Now that he'd taken over the day-to-day operations at Henthorne and Sons, cotton would soon leave the Wilmington wharves and head to the sprawling textile mills of Manchester and Derby. The elder Henthorne was apparently required at his country home, but Jackson assured her Dunn Mills would receive their fair share under his leadership.

She had kept her word as well. For the past week, she and her sister had gone out five afternoons out of seven. After a shaky start, Abigail appeared to thrive under the attention. Although she still wore unrelenting black, usually reserved for widows, Abigail secretly confided to Amanda her second reason for sorrow—the absence of a pregnancy.

Jackson was grateful his wife had rejoined society on a limited basis. And Amanda was grateful for an afternoon that didn't
involve sipping tea, eating iced *petits fours*, and listening to gossip about people she didn't know. Today's overdue task involved
a tall shopkeeper with strong hands, an easy smile, and a lock of
hair that was often in his eyes despite his efforts. She had waited
long enough to visit Cooper's Greengrocery. She hoped Nathaniel
didn't believe her opinions matched her brother-in-law's, because
nothing was further from the truth.

"Miz Dunn? You ready for your breakfast? Miz Henthorne
gonna take a tray in her room."

Amanda turned to find Salome under the arbor. "Yes, I am.
Just toast and jam will be sufficient."

The cook frowned. "I already got cheesy grits and ham. That
no good?"

"It will be fine." Amanda followed Salome into the subterranean kitchen. "I could just eat down here to save time and steps.
It's cooler than one would suppose." She wandered around the
immense room, ducking under hanging pots and branches of
dried herbs and spices.

"Don't know who's doing the supposin', but you go on up to
the morning room. I'll have Josie fetch your breakfast shortly.
That's how we do things." There was no censure in her tone, only
concern that long established rules of conduct might be broken.

"Very well, but I'll have coffee with cream and sugar instead of
my usual tea." Amanda walked up the stone steps to the courtyard
but then paused in the doorway. "Do you need anything from
the grocery today, Salome? I noticed the honey pot was low, and
I haven't had parsnips in ever so long."

The cook stopped stirring the grits. "Parsnips? Master Henthorne don't like parsnips. That's why I don't fix 'em. And I got
a whole crock of honey on the shelf. 'Sides, I'm going to Baxter's
on Wednesday."

"Why Baxter's? I thought you liked Mr. Cooper's selection and prices."

"Yes'm, but Miz Henthorne told me to go back to Baxter's. Ain't my place to ask questions. These grits are ready to eat. You go on up, Miz Dunn." Pulling the pot from the heat, Salome added in a whisper, "But if you happen to buy parsnips today, I'll fix them for your lunch."

Five minutes later, when Josie carried her breakfast tray into the morning room, she blinked and stared in disbelief. Helene was seated at the table with Amanda.

"Would you bring a second bowl and plate, Josie? I wish to speak to Helene while I eat."

Helene hated eating downstairs in the kitchen or the courtyard. If she was present—the sole white face—all conversation ceased among the slaves. Amanda decided that as long as they were alone, Helene would share the table with her.

"I'm going shopping in town today, Helene. Would you like to join me?"

The maid exhaled with relief when Josie wordlessly complied. "Of course, Miss Amanda. If you purchase black silk or crepe at the dry goods store, I will start on another mourning dress for you."

"We won't be stopping there. I fear the selection hasn't improved much since my last visit." Amanda divided the ample food on the tray between two plates.

"To the dressmaker shop, then? Your kid gloves need to be replaced."

"No, I prefer to make do for now. I thought we would stop at the greengrocers on Water Street." Amanda flashed her a grin.

Helene had nothing to say to that. Instead, she concentrated on her food, keeping whatever opinion she had to herself.

Amanda hated to drag her maid along, but otherwise Abigail

would insist she ride in the carriage with Thomas. Within the hour the two of them entered Cooper's Greengrocery—Helene with curiosity; she with nervous apprehension. They found the proprietor on a ladder stocking shelves.

"Good morning, Mr. Cooper. It's a pleasure to see you again, sir."

"Good morning, Miss Dunn. If it is such a pleasure, why have you stayed away for a month?" Nathaniel continued lining up cans of peas without turning around.

Helene gasped at his rude comment, finally drawing his full attention to the women.

Nathaniel nearly lost his balance on the rung. "Excuse me, Miss Dunn! I assumed incorrectly that you were alone."

"I see. So my being alone is a prerequisite for your insults?"

He climbed down the ladder and brushed his hands across his apron. "My words weren't intended to insult, only to ascertain the reason for your visit. Has Baxter's burned to the ground or been hit by a tornado?" A smile pulled at his lips.

"I don't believe so. Salome plans to shop there on Wednesday. But I prefer establishments that treat customers in unexpected ways."

"I see. Then how may I assist you?" He walked behind the counter and reached for his order pad and pencil.

Amanda addressed Helene, who appeared fascinated with small packages of thread. "Would you mind visiting the dressmaker's shop on Front Street? I have changed my mind about new gloves." She dug in her purse for money.

Helene stepped closer. "Don't you wish to select them yourself, ma'am?"

"I do not. You're familiar with my tastes, and our hands are the same size."

"Very well, Miss Amanda." The maid cast the shopkeeper an anxious glance before turning toward the door.

Amanda waited until Helene was on her way before giving Nathaniel her full attention. The counter separating them seemed an inadequate barrier. "First of all, I came because I wanted to apologize for my brother-in-law's behavior."

Nathaniel squinted and cocked his head as though unsure he'd heard correctly. "That dinner party was more than a month ago. Your apology for someone else's actions is wholly unnecessary and decidedly tardy." He crossed his arms over his chest.

She duplicated his defensive posture. "Why on earth would it be unnecessary? We'll deal with the tardy aspect later."

"Unnecessary because you're not responsible for his behavior. Besides, Mr. Henthorne did us both a favor."

"Is there no limit to your opacity? Please be more specific."

"In our mutual desire for friendship or due to physical attraction, we overlooked factors obvious to everyone else."

"May I conclude then that you find me physically attractive?"

Nathaniel blinked several times. "All those words and *that's* what you heard?"

"I heard everything but chose to respond to my attractiveness. With that out of the way, what factors are we ignoring?" Amanda felt rusty at verbal sparring, which she hadn't engaged in since her brother's death, but she wanted to rise to the occasion quickly.

"That we have nothing in common. You and I live in separate worlds, so different that never the twain shall meet."

"Forgive my slow wit and clarify."

"Your brother-in-law is a rich aristocrat from a long line of planters. They created their vast wealth by using slaves. On the other hand, I am a poor man from the western hills. Not one of my ancestors ever accomplished much in terms of society's expectations. Although a Southerner born and bred, I'm not an advocate for slavery, which puts me at odds with central and coastal North Carolinians." His voice lifted a notch as he shifted his weight to the other hip.

"You assume I share Jackson's ethical code because I'm not poor? I take offense to your misguided notion. Although my parents are as wealthy as the Henthornes, they and I abhor slavery. Don't forget we're British, and England abolished the heinous practice in 1833."

Nathaniel yanked his apron over his head. "You're correct. I'm sorry I judged you falsely, Miss Dunn. But it doesn't change the fact your family loves you and would prefer you didn't take up with a mere shopkeeper." Something sad lay just beneath his words.

"You haven't met the rest of my family, only the sister who eloped at seventeen to marry an American cotton factor. Jackson spirited her away to a magistrate for a hasty wedding and then onto the next ship leaving port. Knowing he would be refused, he didn't approach my father for her hand in marriage. He simply took what he wanted and has never allowed Abigail to visit her home since."

Tension filled the shop until a boat whistle on the river broke the silence. "Is that the moral behavior you feel you could never aspire to match?"

Pulling off his cap, he slapped it against his leg. "Confound it, Miss Dunn. If you wanted to salvage the worst night of my life, why did you wait so long?"

She clasped her hands together, willing herself not to cry. "I waited because the very next day my sister and I learned that our father had...had died. He passed in March, but we didn't receive word until then. Ever since the failure of the transatlantic cable, messages are at the mercy of the high seas." She gestured toward her black dress, shawl, and shoes. "I am in mourning, but I chose to come to town today expressly to see you."

He stared in confusion. "I saw the dark clothing but didn't put two and two together. I thought your dress was English conservativeness." He dipped his head respectfully. "My sympathies for your loss, Miss Dunn, and for Mrs. Henthorne's as well. Did his death come as a shock?"

"To me and Abigail, yes, but probably not to Mama. I didn't recognize my parents' motivation for the trip's urgency."

"They were protecting you."

"While robbing me of a...of a chance to say goodbye." Amanda shook away the moisture stinging her eyes and drew in a deep, sustaining breath. "Let's not dwell on my loss, please. Life is full of events beyond our control, but your discomfort in my sister's home should not be one of them." She reached for his hand. "I apologize and promise it never will be repeated if you will accept my friendship once more."

Nathaniel's Adam's apple bobbed as he swallowed hard. "There is nothing to forgive. If you want a friend who's never heard of escargot, I offer my services with pleasure."

They shook hands a bit longer than necessary. "I'm glad that's settled—a weight has been lifted. Could we share lunch soon, perhaps next week? I promise not to pack snails."

"I would be honored, Miss Dunn."

She reached for a cluster of parsnips as Helene entered the store. "I must hear why one uncomfortable dinner became 'the worst night of your life.'"

"No need to wait until next week. I had wanted you to like me more than anything. And I reckoned I had a better chance of swimming to France to see that new tower everyone is talking about."

"On one of those prospects you have succeeded." Amanda placed coins on the counter and pivoted on her heel. She grabbed Helene by the arm and hurried from the shop. Her confidence had waned, yet she felt confident that in the verbal battle of wills, she had prevailed.

⚜

Abigail stretched languidly like a cat and rose to her elbows. The nap had done her good. Her headache was gone, along with the strange queasiness she'd experienced during breakfast. Lately she hadn't been able to stand the sight of poached eggs. When she could tolerate eggs at all, they needed to be cooked to death the way most Americans preferred. Perhaps by the time she reached old age, she would have developed a slow drawl and a preference for grits over porridge. She picked up her book and went in search of a cool spot to read with Estelle trailing at her heels. Yet under the shade of an ancient live oak, Abigail hadn't read a chapter when Jackson broke her concentration.

"Amos said I would find you here." He brushed a kiss across her forehead. "Are you feeling better?"

"Yes. Splendid, in fact. Better than I have felt in weeks." Lifting her legs to the ottoman, she fluffed her voluminous skirt around her ankles. "What brings you home at midday?"

"I'm on my way to the docks, but I was worried about you. Salome said you haven't been eating much at breakfast or lunch. At dinner you barely touched the fine ham my father sent from the country."

"Salome is a tattletale. There's nothing to be concerned about."

Jackson peered into the shadows of the garden. "Where is your sister? Has she gone to pay afternoon calls without you?"

"No. According to Salome, she went shopping with Helene." Estelle appeared with a tray of lemonade and handed her a glass.

Jackson waved off the lemonade. "What kind of shopping? I thought you instructed Salome to return to Baxter's." He wrinkled his nose as if smelling something foul.

"I believe new gloves were the object of my sister's desire." Abigail took a sip of her cold drink.

"Why on earth would she take Helene as though they were school chums off on holiday? She could have sent her maid on the errand, or if something required her presence, then Helene should have assisted with chores around here." He paced back and forth on the flagstone path.

"Goodness, Jackson. Are you piqued that Amanda took Helene to town? Perhaps she enjoys the woman's company or didn't wish to carry the *heavy* parcel herself." She chuckled despite her husband's agitation.

He came to perch on the edge of her chaise. "It's not solely about today's excursion. Amanda treats Helene far too grandly for a maid. Did you know that when you take breakfast on a tray in your room, she invites Helene to dine with her as though they are equals? Don't tell me that would have gone on back home at Dunncliff Manor."

"No, certainly not. Helene would eat in the servants' hall with the other maids and footmen."

"Yet Amanda comes into my house and upsets the established order."

Abigail sobered instantly, realizing the extent of her husband's displeasure. "Forgive me, Jackson. Have I been lax or neglectful in other ways too?"

"Not in the least." He took both her hands in his. "But how does it look to the slaves when this maid sleeps in a private alcove, comes and goes as she pleases, and doesn't do a lick of work not directly related to your sister? Which, I might add, cannot be very taxing because I purchased Josie for her."

Abigail swung her legs off the chair. "I will speak to Amanda about Helene's preferential treatment. But you know her opinion of slavery. I've given her a wide breadth until now to not ruffle her feathers."

Jackson reflected for a moment. "You forget, wife, that I have been to Dunncliff Manor. Amanda judges us harshly, yet her parents have a dozen on staff who are paid a mere pittance beyond room and board. Their cold rooms contain stark furnishings, with two or three occupants per room. And the meals? Hodgepodge stews and soups from uneaten leftovers from upstairs. Those workers barely own one set of clothes for Sundays in addition to their uniforms. All of that sounds little different than life here in Wilmington, wouldn't you agree?"

"Goodness, Jackson. How long has this been simmering inside you?" She patted his hand affectionately.

"Apparently for longer than I realized. Forgive me for speaking plainly, but I've heard your sister making comments to Salome, Amos, and Josie—things she has no business saying. I don't want her stirring up trouble where none exists."

"I doubt that is what she's trying to do. Amanda has always been opinionated and headstrong. But I will speak to her about Helene and reach some sort of compromise. We can't make her maid sleep with strangers in the slave quarters, but she will eat in the kitchen and at least help with the laundry and ironing."

Jackson scrubbed his face with his hands. "I shouldn't involve myself with what is your domain, but I have held my tongue around your sister too many times to count. Amanda is so… unlike you."

"That is such a paradox. To look at us, one would think we're mirror images, yet the longer people know us, presumed similarities disappear. We've always been different as night from day. You have every right to express your displeasure with the household, Jackson, but please attempt to like my sister. She won't be here forever, and I so enjoy her company."

"I will try. I would do that and more for you—anything in fact." He stood and straightened his coat. "I'm dining in town tonight. I called a meeting of the cotton factors. Ships are leaving port on a regular basis now on a course for Bermuda."

"I'm pleased for you."

Jackson kissed her lips tenderly and took the walkway to the street at a brisk pace. Abigail settled back to wait for Amanda and Helene's return. She had lost her place in the book she'd been reading because her thoughts kept drifting to one perfect possibility: Her monthly was again two weeks late. Considering her nausea during the early morning hours, hope flamed anew for what had eluded them thus far—a baby. But she would say nothing, not to Estelle or Amanda, and certainly not to Jackson. Her patient husband had been disappointed too many times. She would wait until his son or daughter was ready to make a noisy entrance before she admitted the truth. In the meantime she would hope and pray and let nothing vex her.

Rousing from another nap an hour later, Abigail overheard female voices on the porch and hurried to intercept them. "Amanda, may I have a word with you before you go upstairs?"

Her sister was pink cheeked from her jaunt up the hill in the bright sunshine. "Of course, Abby. Are you feeling better?"

"I am, thank you. Let's talk for a moment." She pointed to chairs in the shade.

"I'll see you upstairs, Miss Amanda." After a cursory nod in Abigail's direction, Helene turned to leave.

"Just a moment, Helene. Where are you going?"

"She usually naps in the late afternoon when I do," said Amanda. "I'm afraid your Carolina heat and humidity have wreaked havoc on our stamina."

"But your maid is needed this afternoon in the laundry. I'm afraid there's a frightful amount of bed linens to be pressed."

"Of course, Mrs. Henthorne. I'll see to it at once." Helene curtsied and vanished down the steps into the garden.

Amanda lifted her chin but remained silent. It was a pose Abigail was familiar with.

"I must insist that your maid tend to housework when you

don't need her, and that she dines in the kitchen or courtyard with the other servants. It's unseemly that she takes her meals in the morning room. It doesn't set a good example for the rest of the staff."

Amanda pursed her lips. "Do you mean the slaves? I doubt they see much connection between Helene and themselves."

Abigail plucked a spent bloom from a potted plant. "But that's just it. They *should* see a connection and so should she. Please maintain my household's equilibrium."

Amanda turned pale as watered milk. "This doesn't sound like you, Abby. Helene's activities haven't concerned you a bit since we arrived. Are these your husband's requests, but he sent you to soften the impact of their delivery?"

She pulled a sour face. "Whether they originated with me or not is immaterial. Jackson is my husband and this is his home. All that you see is his, handed down from several generations of Henthornes. Please, dear sister, show him the respect he deserves."

Amanda staggered back a step. "Of course. It was thoughtless of me not to recognize and implement these changes on my own. I beg your pardon." She gazed down at the porch floor.

"I knew you would understand." Abigail brushed Amanda's cheek with a kiss. "Let's not speak another word about it. I'll see you at dinner. We're having a leg of lamb. Isn't that one of your favorites?" She turned and entered the house with a lighter heart. *So good to have that unpleasant business over with.*

Five

*N*ate swept the floor, dusted the shelves, and wiped down the countertop for the third time. He'd sold the last of his rice, millet, and barley to nuns from the nearby convent. Then he divided the last of his smoky venison between two matrons who had eyed the same slab of meat. Yet it wasn't his dwindling inventory of goods that made him unable to stand still.

Today Amanda would bring a reconciliatory hamper to share for lunch, and he felt like a man awaiting his fate at the gallows. Part of him yearned to fasten the shutters and hang a sign that said "Closed Until Further Notice," but the brave half of his personality urged him on, spurred by one undeniable fact: Miss Dunn knew he wasn't a man of means, yet she still wished to restore their friendship. Surely that gave him reason to hope that something permanent might develop.

But with the war only a day's ride away, now wasn't the time to plan a future. And with the blockade curtailing his supply of merchandise and inflation eroding whatever money he set aside, he was in no position to take a wife.

What should a man do when the woman of his dreams walked into his life? Tell her to come back later when the timing was better? So Nate polished his stools with lemon oil and spread a lace cloth across the counter. After all, God wouldn't bring his perfect mate along unless He had a few miracles in mind.

At half past one, Amanda strolled through the door wearing a straw hat with a big green bow and an even bigger smile. "Am I too late? Have you already eaten?" She walked up the aisle carrying a huge basket covered with a checkered cloth. "I couldn't get away until Jackson left for his office and my sister lay down for a nap. Jackson was cloistered all morning with his father in the library discussing business." She set the basket on the counter.

Nate felt a pin burst the bubble of his grandiose plans. "No, I haven't had lunch yet, but I don't like the idea of you sneaking out to meet me, Miss Dunn. I don't wish to cause friction between you and your family."

"Then you have nothing to worry about. I am a twenty-two-year-old woman, practically a spinster by American standards. I evaded them because I didn't want to offer an explanation about my activities, not because I was ashamed of them. Part of my reason for coming to America was to enjoy a bit of adventure. And I daresay discussing remedies for colicky babies or sewing projects for the church guild doesn't qualify." Amanda winked one sparkling brown eye.

"Does visiting my store quality?" He pulled out her chair.

"Yes, it does. Perhaps I'll become even more reckless the longer I'm here, but for now you will have to do." She unloaded slices of ham and bread, sliced tomatoes, pickled eggs, and a jar of cider from the hamper, along with plates and forks.

He chose not to ask how she managed to remove such a bounty

from the house unnoticed. Perhaps the food shortage in North Carolina had little effect on the Henthornes. "Why don't you tell me the reason for the voyage, other than to satisfy your quest for adventure? You've relayed only dribs and drabs thus far."

Amanda folded a piece of bread to make a half-sized sandwich while Nate made a much bigger one. "My father owns several textile mills outside Manchester on the western coast. We've enjoyed a brisk business with the Wilmington factors until a year ago. Then the supply of cotton began to dwindle, along with the ability for Dunn Mills to turn a profit. We have hundreds of employees dependent on the resumption of regular trade. If I'm not able to restore that, I'll be the last heiress in my family."

The notion that Jackson had run off with the village seamstress, rather than with a rich man's daughter, had fit better into his fantasy, as unlikely as that was. "Because your father was ill, he sent you to restore the flow of cotton. Have you no brother? Is Mrs. Henthorne your sole sibling?"

"We had a brother, but he was killed in a horrible accident. Coal was being extracted everywhere in the area. One of our mills had been built atop a mine; its shaft deep into the earth became a handy convenience." She swallowed hard. "Unfortunately the supports could no longer withstand the weight. Without warning the floor caved in, killing dozens of workers including my brother. According to survivors, Alfred could have freed himself, but he was trying to dig out others when a second collapse claimed his life."

"Do you think the owner's son shouldn't have intervened to save lowly workers?"

She blanched. "Not at all, but the constable felt the others had died instantly, making my brother's death senseless."

"Forgive me, Miss Dunn. That was a cruel thing for me to say in light of your loss."

"No, I often question my motives in wishing Alfred hadn't stayed behind. But in the end everyone must behave in keeping with their personal moral code."

"Do you believe in predestination—that at the moment we are born our destiny is determined, including the circumstances of our birth, who we marry, what tribulations we suffer, and ultimately how and when we die?"

Amanda didn't answer immediately. She chewed a bit of her sandwich as though chewing the idea in her mind and then set the food down. "I suppose so, but I also believe God gives us free will. Then we're eventually judged on what we did with the choices given us."

"God gives us enough rope to hang ourselves with?"

"If that's what it takes to learn our lessons, then yes. The more a person examines the circumstances of their life, the more they realize someone other than them is in control. There's too much serendipity, too many coincidences."

Nate yearned to ask about the serendipity of their meeting but didn't dare. "At least your trip to Wilmington allowed for a visit with your sister. She hasn't been home since her marriage?"

Amanda shook her head. "I suspect Jackson wouldn't permit it for fear Abigail wouldn't come back. And knowing that my father despised him for sneaking around behind his back, he refused to accompany her to England."

"'Despise' is a strong word. I'm sure Mr. Dunn regretted any words uttered in haste."

"Perhaps. I hope Papa came to terms with Abigail's newfound happiness in America. But Jackson married her without letting us participate in her wedding. Abby packed a bag of traveling clothes, left a letter for Mama, and boarded the next clipper. It was as though Jackson stole something valuable from my father." Her smile was brief and unconvincing.

"A woman isn't a personal possession."

"True, but Abby was just a girl of seventeen, not a woman. Jackson was far more worldly and sophisticated at twenty-three. Abigail and I had been sheltered and protected, and we were ignorant of willful men. After she left, I continued to remain sheltered, probably more so." Amanda picked up her sandwich with both hands. "Listen to me ramble on. Life has turned out well for my sister. Judging by what I've seen, Jackson is a devoted husband. I'm sure Abby hasn't a single regret other than not saying goodbye to Papa."

"Mrs. Henthorne isn't alone with that particular cross to bear." Nate regretted his admission as soon as the words left his mouth.

"Do you share that particular burden, Mr. Cooper? Did your father pass after you'd left to make your fortune on the seacoast?"

"No, his death was the reason I came. Nothing remained for me in those lonely hills. But I won't let you change the subject to my uneventful life. Continue the saga of your grand adventure. After you booked passage on a ship, were you forced to keep seafarers at bay with a broadsword and hidden pistol?" Nate finished his sandwich in another three bites.

"I didn't travel alone. My maid accompanied me. And the distinguished captain made sure none of his crew came within ten paces of us. We dined at his table along with the first mate. The captain roped off a section of deck for our private use during fair weather, but we remained in our cabin most of the time. It was oppressively dull but truly nonthreatening."

"You have a maid who serves only you?"

"Well, yes. Helene is a widow. She agreed to travel because she yearned to see America."

He brushed crumbs from the counter onto his freshly swept floor. "What exactly does someone like that do? I trust it's not cooking or scrubbing pots."

"Helene helps me dress for the day or evening, fixes my hair, and tends to my wardrobe. She's also a skilled seamstress and sews any clothes not ordered from abroad."

"Randolph Henthorne is the most prestigious factor in North Carolina. So your job is little more than mending family fences with your brother-in-law. To be restored to the family's good graces, Jackson merely has to make sure cotton finds its way to England. You can sip tea on your sister's verandah while Jackson and his father take care of the details."

She blinked. "I beg your pardon?"

Nate wished the pine floor would open and swallow him whole. "Forgive me, Miss Dunn. That's the problem when two classes of people attempt to find common ground. Covetous envy rears its head, exposing me for the shallow, jealous man I am."

"You're not shallow, Mr. Cooper. And unfortunately envy is a natural human emotion whether one is rich or poor. But that's not why I took exception to your conclusion. I intend to stand on my own two feet as my father's emissary. True, my brother-in-law would prefer to take control and do all of the work, but I won't allow it. My father had faith in me or he wouldn't have sent me. I hope to repay his confidence by restoring Dunn Mills to its former productivity, and that entails conducting business with other factors besides Henthorne and Sons. I yearn for a challenging career, as unlikely as that sounds. My mother has spent her entire life a pampered woman. She controls nothing in her future. That responsibility has been left in my hands."

He refilled their glasses from the jar of cider. "Let's drink to good fortune in your endeavors, but I'm curious about something else you said."

Amanda clicked his glass and drank deeply. "What else intrigued you about my life story?"

"You said that everyone falls prey to jealousy and envy. In your case I find that hard to believe. And I say that with full respect and admiration."

Her sunny expression vanished. "You would be surprised what things a rich little girl falls asleep praying for."

"Where to, Master Henthorne? Your office or the club?"

"Neither, Thomas. Take me to the docks. It's high time I learned the state of affairs in Wilmington."

During the short ride downtown, Jackson mulled over how much his father's languor had cost the company. If their financial future was to be salvaged, swift and decisive measures must be taken.

"Anywhere in particular along the waterfront, sir?" Thomas braked hard on the steep decline to river level.

"I'm not sure. Park the rig anywhere on Water Street and I'll walk."

Once Thomas tied up the horse in the shade, he handed Jackson his walking stick. "I'd better come with you, Master Henthorne. A rough sort hangs by the docks, not quality folk like you're used to."

"No, stay with the horse and carriage. I've lived in this town my whole life. I won't hide behind my slave from a pack of hooligans." Nevertheless, Jackson tucked a silver pistol into his belt under his frock coat.

He had heard about the influx of foreigners since the start of the war. Sailors on the blockade runner *Kate* had carried in yellow fever two summers ago with their coffee and spices, and three hundred souls went to an early grave before the disease had run its course. But seeing the strange assortment of people huddled in alleys, loitering in the doorways of seedy taverns, or accompanied by painted women gave Jackson an entirely different perspective.

He had lived as sheltered a life as Abigail, who read sonnets and sipped tea behind garden walls.

But the site catching and holding his attention wasn't the dock dwellers. Several large steam vessels were tied up alongside the regular bevy of clipper ships and fishing boats. Obviously, ships were getting through the Union naval blockade despite his father's erroneous assumptions. Jackson wasted no time making his way up the gangway of a large side-wheeler.

"Say there, my good man, may I have a word with you?" Jackson addressed a motley-looking crewman in the filthiest clothes he had ever seen.

"What can I do fer ya, guv'na?" The sailor spoke with an almost incomprehensible Cockney accent—one so divergent from his wife's or Miss Dunn's that he felt they couldn't possibly share a country of origin.

"May I board and speak with your captain?" Jackson extracted his business card from a silver case. "If you would be so kind to say Jackson Henthorne of Henthorne and Sons—"

"Save your breath, guv'na." The sailor spat over the railing into the Cape Fear River. "You can come aboard all you like, but the captain ain't here." He wiped his nose with his sleeve.

Jackson struggled not to betray his revulsion. "May I know his name and his whereabouts?"

"I could be persuaded to tell ya that." The sailor mimicked his accent with derision.

It took Jackson several moments to deduce the implication before he flipped the man a gold coin.

Catching the money in midair, the cretin slipped it into a pocket within the blink of an eye. "Captain Elias Hornsby. You'll find him at Flannigan's. He ain't no Irishman, but he does like a good stout." He pointed toward a row of buildings that never would have garnered much attention.

Jackson turned on his heel and marched down the gangway, the coin being his only expression of gratitude. When he located the pub called Flannigan's by way of a badly lettered sign, his hand caressed the pistol with a wave of relief. Dimly lit and hazy from whale oil lamps, the establishment reeked of unwashed bodies, cigar smoke, and fish entrails. Entering the tavern, he strode purposely toward the bar lest he appear as out of place as he felt.

The barkeep approached with a dirty apron and a dirtier rag over his shoulder. "What'll it be?" His heavy brogue indicated he most likely was Mr. Flannigan.

"Whiskey—the best you've got—for you, me, and my friends." Jackson nodded to the men on his left and right.

Once drinks were poured, toasts made, and the fiery spirits downed, Jackson queried in a soft voice. "Could either of you gentlemen point out Captain Elias Hornsby of the *Countess Marie*?"

The sailor on his right squinted at him with watery eyes. "Maybe we can, maybe we can't. What's your business? You ain't here for the boiled beef and cabbage."

The barkeep and nearby patrons broke into raucous laughter.

"I'm the most successful factor in these parts, representing resin producers from all over North Carolina. Cotton and tobacco fills my warehouses as well, since the blockade closed the Savanah cotton exchange for all practical purposes. My name is Jackson Henthorne." He offered his hand.

His soliloquy met with a second, more subdued round of guffaws.

The man stared at his hand and then shrugged his shoulders. "Where you been, Mr. Henthorne? Away at college studying up on history or philosophy? If you was the largest factor in these parts, I would've met ya by now."

Jackson felt a flush climb his neck into his face, but considering the smoke and poor light, his embarrassment probably went unnoticed. "I did go away to college for a year but didn't care for it—too much memorizing worthless information." With a gesture, he indicated a refill of everyone's glasses. "I recently took over management of my father's company. Since he's…trapped in the old ways…he hasn't kept abreast of changes in the economic climate of the South. I intend to rectify that." Jackson lifting his chin imperiously, downed the whiskey in one swallow, and fought the impulse to gag. "I want to speak to the captain of that steamer in port. He and I may be able to do business." He glanced around the room in an attempt to narrow his choices among the patrons.

After a moment the sailor on his right flicked his finger, and the nearby loiterers wandered away, including the drunk on Jackson's left. Even the esteemed Mr. Flannigan sauntered down to the other end of the bar. "I'm Elias Hornsby. Charmed to make yer 'quaintance." He offered his none-too-clean hand.

Jackson shook it, hiding his shock that this gap-toothed ruffian would be at the helm of an expensive ship. "The pleasure is mine, sir. May I ask what kind of goods you recently brought into port?" He judiciously lowered his voice to a whisper.

Hornsby eyed him slyly. "Whatever folks want and are willing to pay for. Wine and champagne from France; fancy cheeses and smoked meats; wool uniforms for those Reb boys of your'n, sewed by the hardworking folks of Yorkshire; muskets, cannon shot, and gunpowder from Germany. Don't make no difference to me." He picked up his mug of stout, took a drink, and grimaced. "This haul was mostly sides of salted beef, smoked pork, and coffee. Bobby Lee's troops can't seem to get enough meat and coffee. Don't know if those boys ever get a spud or chunk of bread."

Jackson seethed from Hornsby's cavalier reference to the leader of the Confederate army. "Soldiers need to eat, and farmers can't supply the demand with the Yankees tearing up their fields."

"You not catch the bug to sign up and fight, Henthorne?"

Jackson's spine arched like a startled cat at both the informal address and the inference he may be a coward. But calling out Captain Hornsby wouldn't advance his purposes. "When my brother enlisted, I was needed at home to oversee family interests."

Hornsby nodded and swept his cap from his head. His hair looked surprisingly clean for a man in deplorable clothes. "I never could understand fightin' for noble causes myself, not when makin' money is much more satisfyin'." His grin revealed a gold tooth, giving him a roguish mien.

"I discern from your dialect that you are British, sir. Yet I noticed the Confederate Stars and Bars flying from your halyard."

"That President Lincoln in Washington said British smugglers would be hung if caught by his gunboats. He called us a pack of pirates. That's why we fly the Rebel flag. That way he gotta take us as prisoners of war instead." Hornsby ran his fingers through his grizzled beard. "Not that I would relish that idea none."

"So you are English." Jackson needed confirmation of the obvious.

"I am, from Liverpool."

"I have a warehouse of cotton that needs to go to Manchester. Dunn Mills will accept the entire load, along with as much as I can arrange in the future. Would you be interested in such a consignment? And would you be able to slip through the Yankee blockade?"

Hornsby looked over at the barkeep. "Flannigan, more whiskey, and add it to Henthorne's bill." His gold tooth flashed again in the lamplight. "I'm still here listening to ya, ain't I? This might be your first visit to the docks, but it sure ain't mine. I've run 'tween Bermuda, Nassau, and Liverpool plenty in the last two years. And Admiral Porter's slow boats ain't caught me yet." He lifted his refilled glass in toast. "But whether or not I'll risk my neck for your cotton depends on the price—and what you want me to haul back here. I sure ain't running the Atlantic without cargo for the return trip."

Jackson's mind whirred with possibilities, besides the dull ache from decidedly not-the-best whiskey in the house. "Worry not, Mr. Hornsby. Your holds will be full. You have my word. Allow me a night to speak with my associates. Meet me at this warehouse tomorrow. You can see for yourself the quantity I need to ship. We can negotiate the price and terms then." Jackson jotted the address on the back of his card.

The captain stared for a long moment. "I don't know you, Henthorne, but I suppose it'd be worth my while to have a looksee. But I ain't comin' alone and I intend to be armed."

"I would expect nothing less. I too will be accompanied by trusted employees, but have no fear. Considering your success in reaching Bermuda, I predict a long and lucrative association for both of us." Jackson tipped his hat, left a twenty-dollar gold piece on the bar top, and walked away from the loathsome place. He felt he'd handled himself well. At least he didn't break into a cold sweat until inside his carriage. Considering the sour stench to his own perspiration, the reason Flannigan's pub smelled so foul became clear.

Amanda knew that opportunities like this didn't come knocking every day. When Jackson announced that afternoon he wouldn't be home for dinner, she seized her chance. With teapot in hand she approached the settee where her sister sat reading. "Did I hear Jackson mention he would be dining in town?" she asked, refilling both their porcelain cups.

Abigail wrinkled her nose in a pout. "You heard correctly. Goodness, ever since he took over for Papa Henthorne, he's gone more nights than he's home. Always meeting with this factor or that planter. And he insists on calling on ship captains down by the docks. They can't be a quality sort if they spend most of their lives at sea."

"The captain who brought me to Wilmington was a true gentleman," Amanda said consolingly, taking a small sandwich from the tiered tray.

"An exception to the rule. I'll be relieved when life returns to normal. I miss having Jackson home in the evening." Abby's face screwed into a scowl. "This tea is tepid. Helene, bring us a fresh pot and see that it's steaming."

The maid set aside her sewing and rose to her feet, frowning as she left the room. "Of course, madam."

Amanda bit back her original comment. "Why don't you and I do something exciting? Let's have dinner in town. Perhaps at the Kendall House?"

Abby gaped at her. "Dine at a hotel four blocks away when we're local residents? Salome probably has dinner preparations already underway."

"Whatever she's cooking will keep until tomorrow. With Jackson out tonight, let's not rattle around the huge dining room alone. Don't you remember Mama going to the Ritz with her friends every now and then? They would have a grand old time." Amanda allowed her eagerness to practically bubble from her ears.

Abigail took little time to decide. "I do remember that. Sometimes they would drink champagne in the afternoon, unbeknownst to their husbands." She lifted her fan to hide her face.

"I don't recommend that for us, but dinner would be a lark."

"I agree." Abby rose elegantly to her feet. "I'll send Thomas to make reservations for eight with the concierge."

Amanda jumped up. "Please reserve the table for six o'clock instead."

"Goodness, no. Only the uncultured *bourgeois* dine that early."

"Just this once, sister dear, because I have a surprise for us afterward."

Abby laughed. "Are you finally breaking from your shell? Very well. Six it will be, but I insist we remain in mourning attire." She strolled from the room, her request for fresh tea forgotten.

Two hours later, they walked through the elegant lobby of the Kendall House, resplendent with crystal chandeliers, dark cherry wood paneling, and Persian carpets. The concierge greeted them immediately and showed them to the best table in the restaurant. The other diners paid little attention to young women in black. Almost every day Wilmington gained another widow due to the war. Their meal of sea bass with potatoes au gratin and roasted asparagus was delicious. Amanda noticed that her sister ate more than a few tastes of everything for a change.

"You have kept me in suspense long enough." Abigail ate a bite of cherry pie and set down her fork. "Did you ask a *couturier* to keep her showroom open late tonight? I'm afraid the selection may disappoint you. Little from Paris gets past the Union navy. Northern wives and sweethearts will be well dressed from everything the Yankees confiscate."

Amanda pushed away her dessert. "No, I would like you to accompany me to the town council meeting that starts in thirty minutes."

Abby choked on her mouthful of tea. "A town council meeting—what on earth for? That sounds stultifying and dull."

"I intend to address the council. Because none of them know me, I would like you to provide the introduction."

"You wish me to stand up at a meeting with landlords airing grievances about slovenly tenants or housewives who don't like the neighbor's cat digging up their gardens?"

Amanda smiled. "Sounds as if you've attended one before."

"I have, hence the description of stultifying." Abby dropped her napkin next to her plate. "I tagged along with Jackson once. He required some sort of variance for Henthorne and Sons. He insisted we stay for the entire meeting to not appear rude, but I honestly couldn't keep my eyes open. I dozed off against his shoulder."

"Once you provide the introduction, I'll explain you are required at home and must take your leave."

Abby narrowed her gaze. "Why do you wish to address the council, Amanda? You're not a landlord and our neighbors own no cats."

"I want their support in restoring trade. All the mills need cotton, not just Papa's. And certainly increased business would benefit Wilmington as well. I've heard tales of shortages throughout the area. Something needs to be done."

Abigail settled her shawl across her shoulders and started toward the door. "You've invited the wrong Henthorne. Jackson would be happy to attend with you next month."

Amanda waited until they reached the sidewalk to respond. "Jackson, bless his heart, is a businessman. He's interested solely in contracts with Dunn Mills to help his father's company."

"What is so wrong with that?" With Thomas's assistance, Abby stepped up into the carriage.

Amanda didn't wait for help. "Nothing on the surface, but Papa placed me into a position of responsibility, first as his emissary and now as his heir. I am charged with running Dunn Mills, Abby. Mama depends on me to make wise decisions to save the company from ruin."

"You're being overly dramatic."

"I assure you I'm not. I want the council to recognize me as a valuable asset to commerce."

Abigail placed an arm around her sister's shoulders. "I hate to point this out, my dear, but you're a *woman*. They're not about to take you or any other female seriously."

Tears flooded Amanda's eyes, unbidden and embarrassing. "Can't I at least try? Won't you help me? You were a Dunn before you became a Henthorne."

Abby sighed and then hugged her tightly. "Of course I'll help, but I'll leave after the introductions. I do feel a bout of sleepiness coming on."

Amanda dried her tears and concentrated on her speech—the one she'd rehearsed for days in her head. Yet despite her preparedness and her sister's position in the community, the end result was less than ideal.

The entire council and most citizens in attendance stood when they entered the stuffy, smoky room. "Mrs. Henthorne, to what do we owe this pleasure, madam? I speak for all when I extend sincere condolences on the loss of your father."

Abigail extracted her fan to flutter demurely beneath her chin. "Thank you, Mr. Rose, gentlemen, for your concern. May I present my sister, Miss Amanda Dunn? She's visiting from our home near Manchester."

Amanda lifted her veil, triggering gasps from several men at the startling resemblance. Apparently, some hadn't known Abby had a twin. General murmurs of greeting and sympathy followed.

"My sister would like to address your honorable council on behalf of our late father. Papa sent Amanda as his spokesman when he became too ill to travel."

Most members continued to gape, their eyes rotating between the sisters like a pendulum until the chairman cleared his throat. "By all means, Miss Dunn. How may the city of Wilmington be of service to your family? I once met your father during one of his visits years ago. He was a man of fairness and integrity."

Amanda offered a half curtsey and launched into her perfectly prepared speech. But it wasn't necessary for Abigail to concoct excuses to slip out early. Nor was it necessary for the sisters to take seats among the disgruntled landlords and irate gardeners. The assemblage of middle-aged and elderly gentlemen, all well dressed and polished, listened patiently until she concluded her presentation. Two of the men looked confused, two seemed bored, and one grinned with ill-concealed amusement.

Then the chairman rapped his gavel to quiet the crowd. "Silence in the chamber," said Mr. Rose. "It's fortunate you have family in our fair city to visit because your errand on behalf of Dunn Mills was pointless. President Davis relaxed his original stand against commence with England enacted during the early years of the war. Although there has been no outright statement of reversal, the leader of the Confederacy recognizes the importance of a strong economy. Goods need to flow in both directions if we are to prevail over the North. Cotton and tobacco have been leaving Wilmington on a regular basis despite the fleet of Union ships attempting to stem the flow. If Dunn Mills needs cotton, Mr. Henthorne, either junior or senior, could make those arrangements. You certainly don't require the approval of the town council. What you need is a fast ship, a brave sea captain, and good fortune to reach England."

Amanda didn't dare glance at the rotund member who continued to chuckle at her distress. "Thank you, Mr. Rose and council, for permitting me to address you this evening. I apparently suffer from a case of misinformation." She bobbed her head politely.

"Goodness, gentlemen," said Abigail. "I thought this a matter better handled by Jackson." Her tone turned sugary as she batted her thick eyelashes. "But when a Dunn is sent across the sea on an errand, we aren't ones to take the matter lightly."

"No harm done, Mrs. Henthorne. Please give our regards to Jackson and Randolph." The chairman reached for a stack of papers. "A pleasure meeting you, Miss Dunn. Enjoy your holiday in Wilmington with your sister, and again, our sympathies to you both."

Dismissed like two schoolgirls, Abigail linked arms and pulled Amanda from the chamber. "Whew, I'm glad that is over with. Let's hurry home to put our feet up and enjoy a cool glass of tea."

Amanda didn't reply. She was absolutely speechless with indignation.

Six

bigail stretched in the late afternoon heat. Even in the shade the air was oppressively warm. It was barely June, yet the refreshing breeze from the east had disappeared unless a storm was blowing in off the sea. Straightening in her chaise, she peered down into the courtyard below at her slaves hard at work. Salome's helpers sat shucking corn and snapping beans at the worktable. Miriam took down a set of sheets from the clothesline to be ironed, while Josie washed Amanda's dainties in a tub of sudsy water. She would hang them discreetly inside the washhouse on ropes stretched end to end so as not to cause embarrassment.

Only the sight of Helene sewing in the shade marred the otherwise idyllic courtyard tableau. Amanda's English maid refused to associate with the Henthorne slaves. Though that irritated her, Abigail understood it stemmed not from bigotry but rather from the peculiar and distinctive British caste system among servants. As a lady's maid, Helene considered herself superior to a woman who cooked meals or laundered clothes. Unless expressly ordered to do so, she refused to pitch in around the kitchen. Instead, the young woman stretched out any chore given to fill her day. And Amanda permitted such blatant lack of ambition.

"Tell me, Helene," Abigail called over the railing. "Where is your mistress on such a lovely afternoon?"

The maid startled as though the question roused her from a stupor. "Miss Amanda was reading in her room the last time I checked, ma'am."

"In her room, when the gallery is so much cooler?" She frowned. Just as when they were children, her sister's aloofness irritated her. Amanda always became standoffish when put in her place.

"Yes, ma'am. Perhaps she fell asleep." Helene's interest in the conversation apparently waning, she refocused on her sewing.

"If she's not sound asleep, Helene, ask Miss Amanda to join me. I desire company." Abigail stood stiffly. Perhaps it was her imagination, but she thought she saw anger flash in the maid's eyes.

"Yes, Mrs. Henthorne. I'll check." Helene dropped the garment on the chair and strode inside the house. She could have easily taken the gallery steps but chose not to.

It was only fitting that her temperamental sister would have a maid who shared the same quality. Why Amanda hadn't spoken during the ride home from the council meeting was a mystery. Hadn't Abigail gone to the restaurant and dined at a ridiculously early hour just to please her? Hadn't she provided the necessary introduction to Mr. Rose and the other councilmen? Amanda would have sat in that airless chamber all night if not for her. Whose fault was it that she didn't have her facts straight?

Abigail rang the bell for tea and waited, but her sister arrived before Amos and the afternoon refreshments.

"Helene said you wished to speak with me?" She looked flushed and damp from hiding in the heat of her room.

"I was worried about you. Why do you nap indoors when I have another perfectly fine chaise here on the gallery?" She pointed so there would be no confusion. "This is America. Servants are allowed to see us sleep without thinking us hopelessly indolent and sluggish. And if they ever *do* think unkind thoughts, they have the sense not to speak them." Abigail chuckled.

Amanda sat but didn't recline on the chaise. "Thank you, but I wasn't napping. I was reading over the contracts and other documents I brought from Dunn Mills. Mr. Pelton furnished me with several books about cotton I need to review. I prefer to study in my room where it's quiet."

Amos arrived with the tea. Abigail waited until he poured and served before speaking. "I can't imagine why you bother with this. If no one is taking issue with trade with England, then Jackson can make the necessary arrangements."

"He could have done so already. I called at his father's office the day after I arrived. I don't understand why he chose not to keep me informed." From her tone of voice, her foul mood hadn't abated.

Abigail felt her own temper flare. "I hear his carriage in the lane. Perhaps you could ask him yourself."

"I believe I shall." Staring with a face devoid of emotion, Amanda lifted her cup and sipped her tea.

"Jackson, I'm up here." Abigail called as he crossed the courtyard. "Would you be kind enough to join me on the gallery?"

Jackson took the steps two at a time, took his wife in his arms, and began kissing her passionately until he spotted Amanda in the shade. "I beg your pardon. I thought Abigail was alone." Few would describe his expression as contrite.

"My sister has some questions for you, darling. Amos, instead of eavesdropping in the doorway, please bring Mr. Henthorne his bourbon." The butler vanished without a word.

Amanda set her teacup on the table. "Hello, Jackson."

"Good afternoon, Miss Dunn. I have some questions for you as well." He leaned against the balustrade and crossed his legs at the ankles. "Where did you two go yesterday evening?"

Apprehension ran up Abigail's spine like a spider. "We enjoyed a delicious dinner at the Kendall House. We both had sea bass. It was too hot for Salome to fuss with dinner just for us. And Amanda reminded me of the larks Mama took with her friends in London." Aware she was rambling, Abigail clamped her mouth shut.

"I've had their sea bass—quite delicious to be sure. But I'm more interested on your exploits upon leaving the Kendall House." Jackson turned to face Amanda squarely.

Her inscrutable shell began to crack. "We attended a town council meeting. I had heard nothing from either you or your father, so I thought it was time to take matters into my own hands."

Amos delivered a more ample than usual drink, interrupting the staring contest between the two.

"So I heard from several of my business associates." His contempt was unmistakable.

"What did they say?" Abigail jumped to her feet. "We stayed less than ten minutes and were politely received by Mr. Rose."

Much to her dismay, Jackson redirected his animosity at her. "Of course they were polite as a courtesy to my father and me, but undoubtedly they laughed all the way to the club. Two women in my household don't have the common sense to approach me with this matter? And my household includes you, Miss Dunn, while you are our guest."

Before Abigail could reply, Amanda stepped in front of her. "Please don't blame your wife. This was entirely my doing. She wasn't aware of my intentions when she agreed to have dinner downtown."

Jackson took a deep swallow of his drink and grimaced as the spirits burned his throat. "I don't blame my wife, Miss Dunn. I know Abigail would never shame me in this fashion."

"How could my actions possibly cause you embarrassment? I made it quite clear I was my father's emissary, not yours."

"Emissary." He spat the word. "You are no one's emissary. Your father realized he was dying and sent you to North Carolina to repair the ill will with this other daughter. He gave you an *all-important errand* to keep you busy and out of mischief during the voyage. George Dunn was no fool. He knew no woman without standing or reputation would be taken seriously by the business community."

Amanda's mouth dropped open in a most unbecoming fashion. "I was with Papa at his sickbed, sir, and I beg to differ. Now, would you permit me a question? Why didn't you tell me cotton was leaving Wilmington? It just wasn't headed to Dunn Mills. Your father assured me he would keep me abreast of the situation in Richmond."

"My father sent a letter. If President Davis chose not to respond, that isn't our fault." Jackson glared over the rim of his glass before downing the contents. "I don't owe you any explanation, but out of deference to my wife I will elaborate. My father had been woefully out of touch with current trade conditions during the war. Since he was needed at Oakdale, I have assumed full control of Henthorne and Sons."

"Oh, Jackson, I'm so proud—"

He curtailed her praise with an upraised palm. "I learned that goods have been circumventing the blockade—just not any I consigned. I have since rectified the situation. Tomorrow a thousand bales of cotton will leave my warehouse on its way to Manchester, more if the ship can accommodate it. I secured a captain unafraid of Union gunboats. If you would have approached *me* and not the town council, I could have explained these recent developments."

Typical of her twin sister, Amanda lifted her nose into the air. "I didn't realize Randolph Henthorne hadn't kept—"

"How dare you judge my father in matters you don't understand. He had more important concerns on his mind than *cotton*." He infused the word with derision, even though the commodity had been vital to Henthorne's for years.

"I didn't mean to criticize your papa." Amanda held her arms stiffly by her side.

Jackson shook his head like an angry bull. "That isn't the point, Miss Dunn. You had no reason to address the town council. And I will thank you not to involve my wife in your lies and schemes to do a man's job. If you choose to make a fool of yourself, you will do so alone."

It took a moment, but Amanda's penitent expression faded. "What lies are you referring to?"

"You stated on the ship's manifest that you were *Mrs.* Amanda Dunn—a married woman."

"The captain may have refused passage had he known I was single." Amanda shifted her weight between her hips.

"That is my point. If you're willing to bear false witness, who knows what else you're capable of. I think you're a willful woman used to getting her own way. Your parents have allowed you too much freedom. But in my house I expect you to behave with some semblance of decorum."

"I don't intend to make a habit of lying, if that's what you're afraid of. But in this case I felt the end justified the means." Amanda's hands balled into fists.

Jackson opened his mouth to retaliate, but Abigail stepped in between them. "Let's all take a deep breath and collect our thoughts before tempers get the best of us." She smiled at one and then the other. "I can assure you, Jackson, that Amanda isn't one to tell tall tales. And I know she'll approach you with any Dunn Mills matters in the future. Won't you, sister?" The two women locked eyes.

"Yes. Of course I will." It took Amanda several moments to reply, and when she did her tone of sincerity fooled no one.

Instead of listening to Jackson at dinner that night, Amanda would have vastly preferred a tray in her room or eating with Helene in the courtyard where the slaves were fed. He blustered endlessly about how well he negotiated terms with a captain by the docks. To hear him relay the story, the seaman was a vicious desperado wielding a cutlass with a dagger clenched between his teeth. Their meeting place was a den of corruption that no God-fearing gentleman of his ilk had ever ventured inside, and their subsequent rendezvous at the warehouse had been fraught with danger. Jackson had taken Amos, Thomas, and a footman, all fully armed. Captain Hornsby arrived equally fortified with henchmen standing guard.

Was this how Americans conducted business?

Amanda had trouble believing the accuracy of his account. It all sounded exaggerated to impress his wife and, to a lesser extent, her. Two things were clear by the time the interminable dinner concluded: First, she needed to give her brother-in-law a wide berth while a guest in his home. And second, if all men were like Jackson—who reminded her of her father with his overbearing style—she would go to her grave an unmarried woman.

When the Henthornes finally retired to their suite of rooms, Amanda retreated to the garden for serenity and cooler air. Slaves weren't permitted among the formal boxwood and bougainvillea bushes unless weeding or trimming. Fortuitously, Helene was nowhere to be found. Amanda had no patience with her maid's thinly veiled complaints about life in Wilmington. As fond of her as Amanda was, she was in no mood for more critical verbiage that night.

Settling on a stone bench, she spent a blissful few minutes watching a hummingbird flit from blossom to blossom in the honeysuckle vines. Just as the last of her anxiety ebbed, the sight of a pair of eyes peering from the gloom jarred her to alertness. "Who goes there?" She spoke in a harsh whisper.

"It's me, ma'am, Rufus Sims." The small ebony boy took a step closer. "Sometimes I work for Mr. Cooper in his store on Water Street."

"Yes, I remember you, Rufus. Come sit with me." Amanda patted the bench beside her.

The child approached but halted two feet away. "I best not tarry, ma'am. My ma said to deliver the message and come straight back. She afraid some slave-catcher gonna grab me after dark and sell me upstate, even tho' I be free." Rufus glanced around tentatively and then smiled.

"We won't worry your mother then. Tell me why Mr. Cooper sent you all the way to Third Street."

"Mr. Cooper told me I can keep this dime if I say his words 'xactly." Rufus pulled a coin from his pocket. "He said if you of a mind, he would like to take you for a drive tomorrow. He gonna hire a buggy to go down the beach road. He's paying my ma to fix the lunch 'cause it's his turn." The child rushed through the final sentence before it slipped his memory. "What say you, Miz Dunn?"

Amanda paused for less than a heartbeat. "I will pay you a second dime when I see you if you deliver *my* message exactly."

He nodded, wide-eyed and eager.

"Miss Dunn accepts with pleasure and will meet Mr. Cooper at the corner of Third and Dock at ten o'clock. Say that back to me, Rufus."

The boy tried and with minor adjustments finally mastered her reply. Then he disappeared down the path before she could thank him. Alone once more, Amanda sat in the dark while her heart raced out of control. Jackson and his demands were forgotten. Abigail with her plans for an afternoon of social calls was also soon dismissed. Instead, she was planning how she would leave the house tomorrow morning.

She experienced a wave of shame about her duplicity. Despite Jackson's accusations, she took the Ninth Commandment seriously and prided herself on honest communication. Yet honesty felt out of the question right now. She yearned to see Nathaniel again. Knowing Jackson, he would probably prefer she approach the town council next month rather than accept a date from a shopkeeper.

The next day she had coffee in her room, declined breakfast, and sent word downstairs with Josie that she was suffering a headache. Because any light, noise, or interruption worsened the pain, she was not to be disturbed under any circumstances. She stationed Helene inside her room to thwart interlopers and made sure Josie would be in the laundry for the day. When Helene confirmed that all slaves were either in the kitchen or the courtyard, Amanda slipped down the front steps and out the door. She took only her shawl, a wide-brimmed hat, and a measure of excitement she hadn't felt in years. Despite her intention to walk at a dignified pace, Amanda ran to the corner of Dock Street.

Nathaniel sat waiting in an open surrey in a pressed shirt and straw hat. "Why, Miss Dunn, fancy meeting you on such a lovely summer morn." He spoke with an exaggerated drawl and offered his hand to her.

"By the English calendar the season is still spring for another few days. Perhaps Carolinians have made changes to long-established seasonal standards?" Amanda climbed up and smoothed her skirt to cover her ankles.

Nate shook the reins and the horse took off at a brisk trot. "If the powers that be made changes, no one bothered to tell me. Then again, I've had my mind on other matters lately." He winked.

It was a playful gesture, one that her papa used often. Yet his wink produced a giddy sensation in her gut. "What has you distracted, Mr. Cooper?" Amanda tied her hat ribbons beneath her chin more securely to keep it from blowing away.

"I have been flummoxed whether to replace my order of wheat with cheaper-priced rice, and if the high cost of shellfish will yield greater profits or give me a financial thrashing. What if folks lose their taste for crabmeat and scallops?"

"Nothing ventured, nothing gained," she said. "I, myself, went into debt ten cents hoping we wouldn't miscommunicate today."

He guided the horse around a sharp corner. "So I heard. Young Rufus repeated your message with such exuberance that I feel your money was well spent." Nate relaxed against the seat. "How long may I enjoy the pleasure of your company, Miss Dunn?"

"Most of the day, I suppose, as long as I return by nightfall. I will need to spell my maid so she can enjoy supper beyond the confines of our suite and perhaps stretch her legs a bit." Amanda also tried to relax as the city traffic began to thin.

He locked gazes with her. "What did Mr. and Mrs. Henthorne say about your spending an unchaperoned day with me?"

Several plausible replies crossed her mind, but she didn't like her recent penchant for lying. Instead, she opted for the truth. "Mr. Henthorne is out for the day, and my sister believes I'm cloistered in my room with a headache."

A muscle in his neck tightened into a ropy cord. "Are you

ashamed of me or reluctant to admit you're seeing me socially? Because that's what I consider this outing to be."

She faced him on the seat. "As do I, Mr. Cooper, and if I were ashamed I wouldn't have come. However, I see no point in upsetting my sister unless I feel this outing may have long-term possibilities." Amanda blurted out the words before her courage evaporated.

"Fair enough. What man in his right mind could ask for better terms?"

"None, yet neither of us can feel certain about our mental state at present." She tried not to laugh.

"This is a day we shall both remember." He slapped the reins against the horse's back. "What is your opinion of pork pulled from the bone, fried cornbread, and turnip greens?"

"I have none, because I've never tasted any of them."

"Then you're in for a rare treat. My landlady prepared a delectable feast, and she's a culinary master of Carolina cuisine."

Amanda grabbed the side of the buggy as it bumped over ruts in the road. "You certainly don't talk like most men I've heard in Wilmington. Even Jackson doesn't express himself as well as you."

"No one talks like me back home, either. When I left the hills I decided to become an educated man, even if I never achieve a fancy degree to hang on my wall. Besides, I like words. I read passages aloud to let the sentences roll off my tongue. A well-turned phrase tastes even better than Mrs. Sims's barbecue."

"When do we eat? You're making me hungry."

"Not until we reach the water. A young lady must learn patience."

"Are you taking me to the ocean? I adore the beach." Amanda clapped her hands.

"I could take you to the Greenville Sound, but we wouldn't get back until tomorrow. A string of barrier islands separate the sea from the Carolina coastline. So we'll head south on the beach road to the river road. Not too far out of town the Cape Fear River widens with lovely spots to picnic along the way. That's where I'm buying a plot of land—rich fertile soil for my wife to plant a garden; shallow water along the bank for children to swim in and yet still deep enough water to dock a fishing boat."

"Do you intend to hang up your grocer's apron and become a fisherman?"

"I do, when the time is right." He flicked flies off the horse with his whip.

"And you intend to take a wife?" After posing the question, Amanda held her breath.

"Yes. All sane men eventually marry, along with most insane ones too." A dimple appeared in his right cheek.

"Into which category do you place yourself, Mr. Cooper?"

"Sane and sober as a judge. But I wish you would call me Nate, at least when we're alone."

"Fine, as long as you call me Amanda."

Nate smiled but kept his eyes on the road.

"What has amused you?" she demanded.

"I have practiced saying 'Amanda' every night before bed, and all the way to our meeting today. Your name rolls off my tongue like butter. You had better hang on tight because I want this gelding to pick up his hooves. I'm eager to get where we're going."

Amanda gripped the edge of her seat, concentrating her energy on remaining inside the surrey. For a man who turned words into a hobby, he certainly could use them to disarm a woman.

Jackson settled back in his upholstered chair and released a satisfied sigh. His dinner of rare ribs of beef with a horseradish glaze, along with mushrooms and wild rice, had been superb. He sipped a glass of aged cabernet from the Bordeaux region in France, a gift from Elias Hornsby, and had a Cuban cigar to enjoy later. Captain Hornsby had been pleasantly surprised by his overflowing warehouses. What man wouldn't have been? His father had been languishing under misconceptions for so long, he should dress in breeches and powdered wigs. Running his country estate would be a better fit for him, especially because his wife appreciated having him home. Since Lincoln's outrageous emancipation edict the year before, slaves were running off from every plantation. Most that remained either expected pay or were too old to work a full day anyway. Their once prosperous peanut estate had shrunk to half its former productivity.

But Jackson didn't need to worry about his parents. From Hornsby's projections, his anticipated profits should be enough to remove a significant amount of debt from the company's books. And Hornsby had only emptied one of his warehouses. Upon the return of the *Countess Marie*, Hornsby promised to deliver the next load to Bermuda and be back within a fortnight. It wouldn't take long for him to wipe the slate clean of creditors. Then who knew what he could do next?

Jackson peered out the window of his club on the bustling street scene. Soon his friends would sit down at the gaming tables to try their luck or test their skills at cards, but he had no taste for gambling tonight. He preferred to savor his wine while mulling over yesterday's exceptionally satisfying conversation with this sister-in-law.

Amanda strutted around his house putting on airs as though superior to Abigail—and him—by sheer virtue of being English. She thumbed her nose at the Southern way of life and reliance on slavery. Yet if she had to eat food grown, harvested, and prepared by her own hands, she would have starved to death long ago. Perhaps slavery was an antiquated institution that needed to be replaced, but what planter could afford to pay wages that workers could live on? Amanda's performance at the town meeting proved she was just as ineffectual and out-of-touch with reality as Jackson's father. At least he knew when it was time to tuck his tail between his legs and go home. Yet Abigail remained devoted to her twin and loved having her with them. Otherwise Jackson would have booked passage for Amanda on the next ship and sent her back home long ago.

"Mr. Henthorne, sir?"

Jackson looked up from his contemplation to see the white-haired butler of the club. "What is it, James? Can't a man enjoy a cigar in some peace and quiet?"

The butler blanched, his silver tray tipping precariously to one side. "I'm sorry, sir. Should I tell the gentleman you're occupied? He asked for you by name."

Jackson picked up the engraved card on the salver. It was of a quality not seen in his circles in some time. His curiosity piqued, he read the name aloud. "Mr. Robert Peterson, cotton factor, Savannah, Georgia." The inscribed address was in the best section of the city. "Show him in, James, and be quick about it." While waiting, Jackson drained the contents of his glass.

James wasted no time delivering Mr. Peterson to the library. "Mr. Henthorne? This is Mr. Peterson." The butler bowed and backed away.

Jackson quickly assessed the man's expensive clothes, diamond cravat stud, and silver-topped walking stick. Either he was a fop or far more successful than most men dining at the club that night. He rose to his feet and extended a hand. "Jackson Henthorne. How do you do, sir?"

Peterson's smile filled his entire face. "Thank you for allowing me to interrupt your evening, Mr. Henthorne. I visited your father several days ago—a gracious and distinguished gentlemen to be sure—but he insisted I speak to you. He told me I could find you here, so I haunted your club, losing money at cards while waiting to meet you."

"Have a seat and tell me what I can do for you."

"Was that a cabernet you were drinking?" Peterson waved to James, who lurked near the doorway. "Bring the best bottle of wine in the house." He sat in the adjacent chair. "It's I who can help you, sir. You will note from my card that my office is in Savannah, although I'm more of a nomad since that infernal blockade hobbled the cotton exchange at home and in Charleston."

"I am aware of current events." The man's patronizing tone caused Jackson's back to stiffen.

"Of course you are. I have a proposition that could make us very wealthy men." He lowered his voice.

"You have my attention."

"Barns in Georgia and South Carolina are bulging. Maybe not as much as before the slaves began hightailing it north, but enough to fill every ship we can contract for the next year. Markets in Europe and Britain clamor for American cotton."

"I have a load that just left port—one thousand bales headed for the mills of England."

With a sly grin Peterson waved over the butler bearing a tray and two glasses. "That's why I'm here. I heard that the *Countess Marie* was loaded from bow to stern. You obviously possess qualities I do not, Mr. Henthorne. Elias Hornsby refused to do business with me. His armed guards prevented every one of my attempts to negotiate. Yet you marched into his favorite watering hole and arranged delivery. I'm surprised you weren't shot or bludgeoned on your way out."

His revelation didn't help with the digestion of Jackson's heavy meal. "We were able to come to terms the next day." He watched

James pour the wine, sure that if he were doing it his hands would be visibly shaking.

"I have contracts with two ships that regularly leave the harbor bound for Nassau or Bermuda. My brother is in Bermuda now. He sells cotton and tobacco to the highest bidder and sends it on its way. We also have a trusted associate in Liverpool who fills ships with canned meat, clothing, shoes, and wool uniforms for the return voyage." Peterson lifted the two wine glasses, handed Jackson one, and then took a deep swallow from his. "Ah, it's been too long since I've tasted wine this fine."

Jackson sipped without taking his eyes off Peterson. "It sounds as though you have the situation well in hand. Why do you need me?"

"This war and the naval threat have made life difficult for everyone. I don't have to tell you that, but the situation has also eliminated much of our competition. There's no exchange here, unlike in Savannah or Charleston. I need to remain in the interior of Georgia and South Carolina to buy up the cotton. I can send it by rail, by teamster wagons, or float it up the Sound on flatboats inside the ring of Yankee gunboats if necessary. This is where you come in, Mr. Henthorne. With a partner in Wilmington, I can get product onto ships faster. And I want a man with your savvy." He paused to take another drink. "I'm prepared to write you a cheque tonight—consider it an advance against your share of future profits. And there will be substantial profits."

Forcing himself to breathe, Jackson picked up the bottle and refilled both glasses, his hands now perfectly steady. "You continue to hold my attention, sir. Because Wilmington is the last port open on the eastern coast, we need to divert whatever flowed through Charleston and Savannah here to augment my tobacco trade in resin and spirits of turpentine." He sipped the dry cabernet.

"I've spoken to several club members. Everyone says you're a man of integrity—a man I can trust. But you don't know me, Henthorne. So I hope this will convince you that I'm a man of my word as well." Peterson extracted a cheque from an inside pocket and laid it on the table. It had been inscribed with Jackson's name and an amount so large his breath caught in his throat.

"You possess great confidence in your ability to recruit, Mr. Peterson."

"Indeed, but that cheque could easily be thrown into the fire if you decline my proposition. Why don't you take it to your banker? A telegram to my Savannah bank will confirm my honest intentions. Should you need time to consider my offer, I'm staying at the Kendall House." He placed both hands on the carved wolf's head of his walking stick.

Jackson stared at the amount, blinked, and gazed again. "Mr. Peterson, I don't need the evening to decide. I'm a good judge of people and can usually recognize an excellent opportunity when I see one." Tucking the cheque inside his frock coat, he pulled out his card case. "Come by my office at nine tomorrow morning. We'll discuss expectations and obligations on both our parts. Your advance money implies profits not seen in many years, but I like to enter partnerships with my eyes wide open."

Peterson smiled as he accepted Jackson's card. "I wouldn't have it any other way. The real profits are to be made in the goods our ships bring back. General Lee is desperate for food, clothing, guns, munitions—all we can import. And the Confederate Treasury still has gold to spend to supply the army with what they need. It's our duty as Southern gentlemen to ensure our fighting men prevail over the Yankees. Why can't shrewd businessmen also get rich at the same time?" He pushed up from his chair and offered his hand. "I'm weary from traveling and anxious to return to my hotel. Enjoy the remainder of the cabernet. I'll be at your office tomorrow to answer to any questions you have. Answers you'll like, I assure you."

The two men shook and Peterson left, but Jackson stayed in the comfortable library for another hour. He'd lost interest in the wine and had forgotten the cigar. Instead, his mind whirred with visions of wealth to fatten the lean Henthorne coffers. He would be able to restore Oakdale to its former glory and lavish gifts on Abigail that she'd long done without. The longer he remained in the rarefied air of his club the happier Jackson became—an emotion he'd long done without.

Seven

The sun was just dipping below the buildings to the west when Nate's rented carriage rolled away on Third Street. Amanda didn't want the afternoon to end. She couldn't remember ever enjoying herself so much. Perhaps she couldn't remember because she never had. The spot along the river he'd selected for their picnic had been perfect. They had shucked off their shoes and splashed in the shallows, dined on Ruth's delicious pork and wilted greens, and laughed and talked and laughed some more.

Nate had entertained her with tender vignettes of his mountain childhood, interesting observations about the society women of Wilmington, and amusing tales of his less than successful attempts at cooking in his landlady's kitchen. He'd put her at ease and then charmed her. Amanda had never once worried about being miles from town and alone with a man she barely knew on a remote riverbank—in a foreign land, no less. But she did know Nate. He was as transparent as crystal clear water, unassuming and pragmatic. If she wasn't careful she could easily fall in love with him. And that would be a foolish thing to do. Whether it was a few more weeks or a few months, one day she would return to England and maybe never come back. Yet after each time they were together, she couldn't wait to see him again.

Amanda skipped down the street, feeling lighter than air until she ducked under the wisteria-covered arbor into the garden. Only then did the late hour and the likelihood that her ruse had been discovered sour her mood. Creeping silently along the hedgerow, she spied on the slaves eating, chatting, and finishing evening chores in the back courtyard. Her sole chance for an unseen entry was through the front foyer, unless her sister happened to be sewing in the parlor. The weaknesses in her plan loomed large as Amanda opened the door and stepped inside. Finding no one afoot in the front public rooms, she tiptoed upstairs and down the hall to her suite. Once inside the overly warm room, she let out her pent-up breath with a rush.

"Ah, there you are, at last." Abigail's musical voice drifted from the open gallery doorway. "I practically dozed off waiting for you to return. Shakespeare's sonnets may be more enjoyable in the winter. This heat makes me drowsy." She smiled and stretched like a cat.

"Good evening, Abby. I hope you weren't concerned unnecessarily." Amanda crossed the floor toward the open French doors, tugging off her gloves along the way. She tossed her broad-brimmed hat on the bed.

"*Unnecessarily?* Certainly not. It's perfectly normal to worry when a loved one takes ill and is neither seen nor heard from for hours." Abigail's features were perfectly composed.

Amanda spotted Helene sewing in the corner. The young woman looked anxious. Her other maid fidgeted on a stool by Abigail. "Helene, please go down to supper. I'm sure a few turns around the garden will do you good too."

Abigail tapped the slave's arm with her fan. "Josie, bring a tray of tea and sandwiches here to the gallery, and then you are dismissed for the evening as well."

Amanda pulled a chair close to her sister as soon as the women departed. "I'm sorry I deceived you today. Truly, I am."

Abby waited for additional explanation. When it didn't come, she said, "I can only surmise you had an errand I might disapprove of or were meeting someone in that same category."

Amanda focused briefly on the embellished plaster ceiling above their heads. "The latter is the case. I met Mr. Cooper for lunch. He packed a hamper for a picnic."

Abby's mouth formed the letter O. "The shopkeeper? I assumed after that disastrous dinner party, you would have realized his unsuitability."

"I realized that Mr. Cooper wasn't comfortable at formal gatherings, but he's another man altogether in less formal settings."

"How so?" Abby arched an eyebrow.

"He's charming and witty and a good storyteller. It's been a long time since I've laughed so hard or enjoyed myself more." Amanda shifted uneasily.

"That doesn't reflect well on my company."

"I beg your pardon, sister. I meant in a man's company." Blood rushed to her face.

"And where was this congenial atmosphere conducive to Mr. Cooper putting his best foot forward?"

"Nate hired a carriage. We took the beach road south and then turned onto the river road. It was quite beautiful along the Cape Fear once we left the city. We found a nice spot to picnic and wade into the water up to our—"

Abby curtailed the narrative with a wave of her hand. "You left the city, with a shopkeeper, without telling anyone where you were going?"

The question hung in the humid air as Josie bustled in with the tea tray. The girl set it on the low table, bobbed a curtsey, and hurried to the gallery stairs.

"Which of those three facts upsets you more?" Amanda tried to tamp down her rising irritation.

Abby filled both cups with tea. "The last one, I suppose. If you hadn't turned up, Jackson and I wouldn't have known where to start looking for you. Even if Mr. Cooper is a trustworthy man, the two of you could have been robbed by army deserters." She nibbled on a sandwich from the tray.

"I had less than a dollar in coins in my purse. And Mr. Cooper doesn't strike me as the sort who would carry a fat billfold full of currency." Amanda sipped her tea.

"Vagabond soldiers would take your horse and carriage, you goose. Deserters from Fort Fisher would cut any throat to get away from the seacoast. You keep forgetting there is a war on."

"You're right. Because I'm not American, I do have a tendency to forget that." Amanda reached for a soft cheese sandwich. Lunch seemed like ages ago. "I won't venture beyond the city limits again, at least not without telling you."

Abby peered at her as though attempting to decipher a difficult secret code. "You plan to see this storekeeper again?"

Amanda's nerves began to fray. "Yes, I do. As I explained, I enjoy his company. I've never had a male friend and we get along famously. But why do you insist on referring to him by his vocation? You don't identify Jackson as a tobacco and cotton broker or Papa as a mill owner. You refer to them by name. So kindly call him Mr. Cooper while I refer to him as Nate."

Abby sniffed with indignation. "What would Papa and Mama say about your cavorting with Mr. Cooper?" Suddenly, she covered her mouth with her hand. "Goodness, I forgot that Papa is gone. It's hard to remember when so many miles separate us from home."

Amanda reached over to squeeze her arm. "I know. I often think about what I'll say to him when I return, but he won't be there. Maybe that's why I'm eager to get to know Nate. Papa ruled with a firm hand. He tried to marry me off to the village vicar or one of his widowed friends several times—someone staid and respectable."

"You no longer wrapped Papa around your little finger?" Abby twirled a lock of hair between her fingers.

"That's what you recall? Dear sister, no one manipulated our father, certainly not Mama or me."

"Don't rewrite history. I was there growing up. You were Papa's favorite. Alfred might have been heir because he was male, but *sweet* Amanda was the apple of his eye." Her sister's chin jutted out and her eyes squinted. For a moment Abby resembled the snappish teenager from one of their sisterly arguments. "You could do no wrong, while I seldom escaped his wrath. I was such a disappointment to him."

With the scab torn from an old wound, Amanda's heart swelled with pity. "You're right. I learned to say what he wanted to hear and act in a ladylike fashion. Papa didn't like women or young girls with spirit. But after you left with Jackson, I also fell from favor." Amanda paused to collect her thoughts and tamp down sorrow inching up her throat. "He realized he couldn't control his daughters, not as long as we had the ability to fall in love. He knew I too would eventually marry and escape his domain, leaving only Mama under his thumb."

For several minutes they sat quietly in the growing darkness. On the street the clatter of horse hooves and steel wheels on cobblestones provided the only sound. "That's why you came—not to see me but to escape from his authority?"

"I came to win his favor, to prove I could be as viable an heir as Alfred would have been. It wasn't until I slipped the yoke did

I realize how strangled I'd been. But I truly did yearn to see how my sister fared in the new world." Amanda squeezed her hand.

Abigail reared back as though bit by a snake. "But I wasn't your priority."

"I didn't know how much I'd missed having a sister until I got here, Abby. Mama still hopes I can convince you to come home—with Jackson, of course—so our family can be together again."

Abby drained her teacup. "Don't be ridiculous. My husband will never leave Wilmington. His family, his work, his life are here. And thus my life is here. Jackson loves me exactly how I am. I'm not second-best to anyone. He doesn't make impossible demands on me like Papa. And because I love him, I have no desire to keep secrets." She set down her cup and stood. "I intend to tell him about your escapade today—not to punish you, but because Jackson has a right to know what goes on in his house."

Amanda chose her words carefully. "I respect your decision, but you should understand that now that I'm out from Papa's control I plan to enjoy my freedom. Maybe that's why I'm intrigued by the *shopkeeper*. I wasn't allowed to make friends among those socially beneath us. I don't care about those standings now."

"You'll care about your reputation and those standings once you are back in England."

"Maybe so, but in the meantime I want to go where my heart leads me."

"Very well, but let's have no more deception while you're my guest. Josie came to me rather upset. You placed her in a difficult position by expecting her to keep silent. She knows that one day you'll board a ship and sail away with Helene. She will be left behind working for Jackson and me. Please don't make life harder for her."

❖

Nate hooked his long apron on its peg and blew out the lamp that hung over his worktable. It had been a long day. A steady stream of customers promised decent profits for the week, but it also meant less time replaying in his mind the delightful hours spent with Amanda. Staying busy may be good for a man's hands and mental state, but when the bell jangled to signal more customers, Nate sent them away.

"Sorry, I'm closed for the day," he called. "I'll be open tomorrow by eight." He pulled on his coat with a frown. No second bell chime indicated that his tardy customer had left. Stepping from the back room, Nate saw a man leaning against a stack of grain sacks. "May I help you, sir? Do you need directions or assistance of some sort?"

The man turned, his face partially obscured by a hat brim. "As I live and breathe, it really is you!" he exclaimed.

His voice sounded vaguely familiar, yet Nate couldn't place him. His rough-spun clothes and long duster coat provided little identification. "You have me at a disadvantage, sir. I apologize if we were previously introduced."

"Mason. Mason Hooks from Balsam. Don't ya 'member me, Nate?" He yanked off his dirty felt hat.

Despite the fact he was thirty pounds thinner, bearded, and sallow-faced, Nate indeed recognized his old childhood friend from the mountains. A man he thought most likely would be dead by now. "Mason, of course. How are you?" Nate asked, slapping him on the back.

"I had a rough patch, but things are lookin' up these days." Mason's smile revealed several missing teeth. "Got me a job offloading ships that come in. Make a good daily wage, more money than I seen in a week back home."

"That's not hard to imagine. Back in the hills we had plenty of whitetails, squirrels, and pretty sunsets, but not much that would put a pair of new leather boots on a man's feet." Nate extracted his hand before Mason pumped his arm from the socket.

"Heard there was a mercantile owner named Cooper on this block. And I also heard tell you came to Wilmington dead set on opening a store. I put two and two together and thought I'd have a look-see."

"I'm glad you did. Do you like coffee? I could reheat some on the woodstove." Nate opened the door on the stove to stir the coals.

"They pour a fine pint down at Flannigan's at a fair price. What say we git something stronger if'n you're done for the day here."

"Does that establishment sell anything besides spirits—coffee or tea maybe?" Nate felt himself flush. "I don't imbibe, not since it killed my father."

"I just see men drink whiskey or beer. It ain't no teahouse." He laughed good-naturedly. "But your coffee sounds fine by me. Why don't we pull up a chair?"

"There's a good spot out back where we could catch a breeze. Take those stools out and I'll be right with you." Nate pointed toward the door. A few minutes later he carried the pot of coffee and some of Ruth's homemade molasses cookies outdoors.

Mason sat by the low stone wall behind the row of shops. He'd already removed his coat and hat. In the harbor, tall masts bobbed with the current as ships moved in and out. "Good location to set up shop. You doin' all right?"

"Can't complain. I'm not getting rich, but I pay my bills on time."

Mason scratched at a crusty scab. "Story I heard was your pap hanged himself in the barn not two years after your ma died. That musta been a sorry site to behold." He shook his head.

"Pa tried his best to drink himself to death, but when that didn't work he decided to hurry matters along." Nate sipped the coffee, not meeting his friend's eye. "Even that old still wouldn't produce anymore."

"When you left, did you leave your little brother back on the farm?"

Nate flinched. "Do you think I would leave a fifteen-year-old alone in Balsam in a shack that might blow over in a good wind? I sent him to my aunt and uncle outside Fayetteville. They grow corn and raise pigs. Joshua liked farming, but that spread we had never amounted to much. The soil was too rocky and worn out."

"Didn't he want to move to Wilmington? That boy used to follow you around like a hound dog."

"He did, but I knew I would have nothing here at first. Took me nigh a week before I found work. I slept in folks' stables and ate from their gardens until I got paid. When I got a job here, Mr. Starkey let me sleep on a pallet in the storeroom. I saved every penny I earned, but it was no place to bring a boy to live. My aunt promised that Joshua would go to school. That's what Ma would have wanted."

"Have you heard from your brother lately?"

"I wrote five or six times but never heard a word back. 'Course, Joshua never was one for letter writing. He said that was sissy doings."

"Yeah, that sounds like your lil' brother. But Josh ain't at your uncle's hog farm no more. He left a while ago."

Nate bristled for the second time that afternoon. "How would you know? I'm betting you never been to Fayetteville in your life."

"You would win that bet, my friend. I saw Joshua at the battle of Shiloh. He enlisted in the Confederate army right after North Carolina seceded. He fought bravely too, as I recall."

Every hair on the back of Nate's neck stood on end while his gut tightened. He ticked off the years in his head. "Why…he would only have been seventeen at the time."

"Yep, sounds about right. Old enough for a poor boy to fight and die in a war started by rich old men." Mason's face screwed into a scowl.

"Old enough to die?" Nate's stool toppled as he jumped to his feet.

"Simmer down. That's just a figure of speech. Your brother was alive and well the last time I saw him at Chattanooga." Mason reached down to pick up the stool.

"But why would he enlist? He grew up listening to Ma preach about the evils of slavery, while Pa ranted about a government that helps only rich landowners. Backwoods folks were left to fend for themselves." Nate scrubbed his face with his hands.

"I recollect your pa standing up one Sunday after church telling folks not to pay their taxes. He said the government shouldn't get another dime from the hill folk," Mason said thoughtfully, taking the last cookie from the plate.

His reminiscences did nothing to lift Nate's spirits. "The Reb recruiters couldn't even raise a regiment in our county. They had to go to Asheville to fill ranks. Joshua knew I wouldn't enlist—not because I didn't love North Carolina, but because it was time to end slavery. If Jefferson Davis had his way, slavery would spread into the western territories."

Mason pulled on his shaggy beard. "I try not to think much 'bout politics these days. But I bet your uncle was the reason Joshua signed up. You know folks in the flatlands 'round Charlotte and Fayetteville don't think like we do. Plenty of them own slaves in those parts. Maybe even your uncle does too."

That possibility had never occurred to Nate, even though his uncle owned at least three hundred acres of land. "Did you speak to Joshua? Did he ask about me?"

"The last time I saw him it was early in the morning before the fightin' started. He said to tell you 'hey' and that he was doin' fine."

Swallowing a lump of regret, Nate stretched his neck from side to side. "What about you, Mason? Did you muster out after your enlistment period ended?"

He snorted with contempt. "All the majors and generals forgot terms of enlistment once the Yankees started thinning our numbers. There was no mustering out. Only way to leave was into a shallow trench beside your fallen comrades. They threw just enough soil atop the graves to keep the crows and wild hogs from pickin' your bones clean."

With a shudder Nate refilled their mugs from the coffee pot. "I'm curious, then, about how you came to Wilmington."

"You callin' me a coward, Nate? I'll take on any man who calls me a yellow-belly."

Nate recoiled from his friend's perceived insult. Putting up his hands in front of him, he said, "Easy. I meant no disrespect. Far be it for a man who refused to enlist to judge someone who did. Everyone must make that decision for himself and live with the consequences."

Mason slumped lower on the stool. "I'm not a coward, but I did desert. They could hang me if they catch me, but I figured I'm as safe here as anywhere. And the coastline is where the jobs are."

"You realize that Fort Fisher is but thirty miles downriver. That place is guarded better than the fortifications at Charleston."

"I know that, but with the Yankee navy out to sea, they'll be too busy to look for deserters on the docks."

Nate was content to let the matter drop, but apparently his old friend wanted to talk.

"I fought hard on the line at both Chickamauga and Chattanooga. But I couldn't abide with those planter sons astride their fancy horses along the back, ordering us privates to take that hill or claim that worthless cornfield against terrible odds. We were always outnumbered. Always." Mason drank the last of his cold coffee. "So the next day I acted like I was headed to the latrine trench and just kept walking. I expected somebody to spot me and shoot me in the back, but nobody did. I kept moving east, foraging off the land like an animal."

"Our paths were destined to cross."

"Say, you like this coat?" Mason tugged on the lapels. "Some man left it in his carriage when he went inside his house for the night. Musta been in his cups not to take care of so fine a garment." He ran his hand down the cloth lovingly.

"That will teach him to be careless." Nate stood rather stiffly, the long work hours sapping his strength. "I'd best get to my rented quarters or my landlady may throw my supper to the hogs out back. Do you need a place to sleep for the night? Mr. Sims probably won't mind if you stay in the hayloft. Nothing but bales of fresh hay up there. Might just remind you of your pa's farm in Balsam."

Mason scowled. "No, thanks. I don't care to remember the past. 'Sides, I don't sleep in barns. I rented me a room above Flannigan's. Nice place until the drunks start shooting. One night a bullet tore right through the floorboards and cut off the tip of my ear." He tucked his hair behind his maimed ear, the scar still a fiery red.

Nate couldn't fathom an appropriate response, so he said mildly, "If you change your mind, I live in the attic of the Simses' place on Castle Street."

Mason stood and brushed crumbs from his clothes. "And if *you* change your mind about that pint of beer, I'm at Flannigan's most evenings, including tonight. At least until my old lieutenant recognizes me and puts a bullet in my head."

The two men shook hands, and then Mason hopped the stone wall and walked down the wharf. He didn't look back, but Nate could hear him whistling long after he disappeared from sight.

For a while he sat contemplating everything he'd learned. His old friend deserted the army and lived in Wilmington. His father's suicide was apparently common knowledge, even though the preacher promised not to spread gossip. And his brother no longer tended pigs on the outskirts of Fayetteville. Joshua was fighting Yankees, if he still walked among the living.

Nate locked up the store and trudged home, wearier than he'd been in a long time. At least his supper was waiting on the table, covered by a clean linen cloth. A glass of water with a saucer over it to keep out flies had also been left. After washing his face and hands, he bowed his head to give thanks—an old childhood habit that refused to die. His fork was halfway to his mouth when Odom Sims stepped from the shadows.

"Didn't take you for a praying man, Nathaniel, but I'm mighty glad to see it. Mind if I join you while you eat?"

Nate shoved the piece of ham into his mouth and waved at the seat next to him. "My ma always said if we don't give thanks for what we got, we'll have even less tomorrow. Sit, Odom. I'm not shy about eating in front of people, but I may slap your hand if you reach for my slice of pie."

"Had two pieces with my supper. You're lucky to get that skinny slice a'tal." Odom laughed with a deep, throaty sound. "You know, my granny used to say something similar to what your ma said, so I never wanted to take chances either. Now I've lived long enough to know it's true."

Nate shrugged. "I see plenty of ungrateful people who still have their worldly possessions the next day."

"God isn't finished with them yet or with us. He has all sorts of plans up His sleeve whether we believe in Him or not."

Nate scooped up some potatoes. "Weren't you a preacher down by Charleston? You sure sound like one."

"Yes, sir, I was. But they don't need any Negro preachers in

Wilmington. I'll just bide my time at the livery stable and sow my seeds out back." Odom leaned back in his chair with his fingers interlaced behind his head.

"This must be my night for company—those with a mind to talk." Nate told him about his visitor at the store and his unsettling revelations.

"What do you think about your friend skedaddling from his regiment? It makes life harder for the boys who stayed to fight."

"It's not my place to judge him or anyone else." Nate focused on cutting up his chunk of ham. "Some might call me a coward for not enlisting after our state seceded."

"Is that how you see yourself, Nathaniel? Afraid to pick up a gun?"

"Nope. I won't fight to preserve slavery; it's evil. But I can't bear arms against the Confederates either. I've lived in North Carolina my entire life. I'm stuck somewhere in the middle, keeping my head down and hoping the war will be over soon."

Sims patted his shoulder. "That's pretty much how I figure it too. Negroes are in both armies."

"The Rebs conscripted them and are forcing them to stay. It wasn't their choice."

"True enough, but you don't see me joining the Fifty-Fourth or Fifty-Fifth Massachusetts or the Twenty-Ninth Connecticut volunteers. I reckon if God wanted me to die for the Union, I would have been born in Boston or New York City. He put us all exactly where He wants us to do the job He has in mind."

Nate scoffed, shaking his head. "You think our lives are that orchestrated?"

"I think it's exactly that orchestrated. You'll see, Nathaniel. God has big plans for you yet. That's why you're here in Wilmington, and maybe why you met Miss Dunn. Which reminds me. Ruth wants to know when we'll meet this special gal."

"It's not that easy. She's reluctant to be seen out because her family doesn't approve of me. I'm destined to hope she'll need a pack of needles or crave a bag of peppermints."

"Why not invite her to have supper with us? None of the society folk will notice her here. I'll ask Ruth to cook something not too spicy."

Nate couldn't imagine a proper British girl dining in their rustic kitchen. What on earth would they talk about? Yet he also couldn't imagine hurting Odom's feelings. "That might work," he murmured as he finished up his skinny slice of pie.

"I'll send Rufus to Miss Dunn with your message. How about Tuesday?"

"That will give me almost two full days to fret about seeing her again." Nate could hear Odom's chuckles all the way to the attic bedroom.

Amanda grinned as the Henthorne carriage rolled down the hill toward the river. Her sister's expression had been one she would remember for the rest of her life. Keeping her promise, Amanda informed Abigail that she would dine with the Sims family that night, Nathaniel's landlords. Questions began flying like salvos on a battlefield.

Who are these Simses, and where do their people hail from—the coast or the interior?

Where do they live?

Shall I have Thomas remain with the carriage until you're ready to come home?

When Amanda explained that Mr. and Mrs. Sims were free people of color and that a carriage and coachman would only be in the way on their narrow street, Abigail clutched her throat as though choking on a bone.

"Have Thomas return after he drops you off. I trust Mr. Cooper will see that you get home safely." Abby walked away, doubtlessly regretting her decision to tell Jackson everything that happened in his household.

Thomas stopped in the middle of Castle Street with the barest glance left or right. "Send word if you need me to come back for you, Miss Dunn."

"Thank you, Thomas, but I'm sure I will be fine." Inhaling a deep breath, Amanda accepted his help down.

Whatever trepidation she felt vanished when Nate walked out the front door. Dressed in a dark coat and trousers, his cravat and shirt were pressed and his shoes polished. But it was his expression that dissolved the last of her misgivings. His blue eyes twinkled from his tanned, clean-shaven face as he beckoned her up the pebble walkway. How could she feel like an animal freed from its cage when the Henthornes lived in a mansion?

"Good evening, Miss Dunn. I'm delighted you could join us." Nate stepped forward and offered an elbow.

"I would reply that wild horses couldn't keep me away, but I don't want your head to swell with pride." Amanda fluttered her fan, a silly habit she had picked up from Abby.

"Is it Mrs. Sims's cuisine which intrigues you or my company?" he asked as they strolled up the rosebush-lined path.

"I'm curious about both."

Blessedly the front door opened and their host and hostess appeared, curtailing their banter. "Miss Dunn, welcome to our home. I'm Odom Sims," said a thirtyish man, his thick beard already streaked with gray. "This is my wife, Ruth, and you've already met our son, Rufus."

A small, almond-eyed woman stepped forward, her arm encircling the boy's shoulders. "How do you do, miss?" Ruth nudged her son.

"Good evening, Miss Dunn." Rufus bowed from the waist.

"Good evening, Rufus, Mr. and Mrs. Sims." Amanda bobbed a tiny curtsey. And that was the final formal gesture all evening. "Rufus, I believe I owe you a dime." She held the coin out in her palm.

Nate and the Simses led her on a short tour of the three downstairs rooms, describing how the family came by a particular piece of furniture or painting on the wall. During the tour they heard about Odom's past. His father had earned his freedom by saving the master's son from a raging river, along with the freedom of his wife and children. Growing up free, Odom's life was unlike most Negroes in the South. Amanda was hard pressed not to ask a dozen curious questions—ones that were none of her business. Throughout the delicious dinner of smoked turkey, butter beans, and sweet potatoes, the tale unfolded of Odom wooing Ruth from a distance while saving his money. He finally secured Ruth's liberty after paying an exorbitant sum to her former owner.

"That makes us appreciate what we were born with," Nate whispered close to her ear.

His breath tickled, while the scent of his spicy shaving balm filled her nostrils like an elixir. Because Amanda had fought tears during the telling of the Simses' saga, all she could do was nod in agreement. Despite being rather silent during the dinner conversation, Amanda was acutely aware of Nate's proximity. She caught his eye more than once, his grin never failing to spike her heart rate. Nate, who seemed to be monitoring her food intake, grinned when she speared another slice of turkey from the platter. Amanda relaxed in the tidy dining room. It was the first time she'd eaten in the home of free blacks. The abolitionists' determination to abolish slavery throughout the states took on new meaning for her. Another member was added to their ranks that evening.

When it was time to take her leave, Amanda felt the flutters in her stomach return. "Thank you, Mr. and Mrs. Sims, for the most enjoyable evening I can remember," she said on their front stoop.

After adding his own words of gratitude, Nate peered up at the starry sky. "May I walk you home, Miss Dunn, or shall I pay Rufus a dime to summon the Henthorne carriage?"

"The way you throw your dimes around, one might get the idea you're a spendthrift, sir," she said once they reached the sidewalk. "I prefer to walk since the evening remains mild and exercise aids digestion."

"And my company? Do you find it remotely appealing?" Nate's dimple appeared in his cheek.

"Because you inserted the word 'remotely,' I can answer with an unequivocal yes." Amanda stepped off the curb onto the flagstones. Yellow streetlamps separated the dark into pools of light and shadow. The only sounds were the faraway whistles and horns on the river, yet she felt not an ounce of fear.

"And I covet your company more with each passing day, Amanda."

"I do like the way you switch to my given name the moment we're beyond earshot of others, *Nate*. It makes me feel independent and modern simultaneously."

And so for the four-block stroll, they exchanged friendly banter along with thinly veiled flirting. But on the front porch, the idyllic evening came to a screeching halt. When Amanda timidly applied the knocker, she fully expected to see the aged face of Amos.

Instead, Jackson opened the massive carved door. "Ah, finally you're safely home, Miss Dunn. Good of you, Cooper, not to send her down the deserted streets alone."

"That isn't something I would do, Mr. Henthorne." Nate offered a polite bow.

"Yes, well, I'm glad to see you. Would you like to join us for dinner on Thursday?"

"Dinner...on Thursday?" Nate stammered.

"Yes, that is two days from now."

The gaslight revealed his flush. "It would be my pleasure. Good evening, Miss Dunn, Mr. Henthorne." Nate offered a brief smile before turning on his heel.

Amanda moved inside and up the stairs before she was tempted to deliver a swift kick to Jackson's shin.

Eight

*J*ackson paced from one end of the parlor to the other, consulted his pocket watch, and then strode to the doors leading to the garden. He spotted his wife close to the property line, instructing a slave on which flowers to cut for a bouquet. "Amos," he called.

A few moments later the grizzled butler appeared. "Yes, Master Henthorne?"

"Where is Estelle? If she's not handy, send a kitchen slave into the garden to fetch Mrs. Henthorne." He let the drapery fall back into place. "I would like her to join me in the parlor."

"Yes, sir." He shuffled off toward the back of the house.

Jackson poured a short drink, intending to keep a quick wit for tonight's festivities. He swirled the amber liquid in his glass until his wife arrived and then took a small sip.

"What is it, Jackson? Have you taken ill?" Abigail's pale face was flushed as though she'd been hurrying. "Estelle said I was needed on the double."

"That will be all. See to your other duties." He waved off both Amos and Estelle, who stood at attention in the doorway. Then he wrapped an arm around Abigail's slender waist. "I left my office early today to make sure preparations were well in hand for tonight's dinner party. And I find you dawdling in the garden, not even beginning to get ready."

Offering an amused giggle, she patted his arm. "Goodness, Jackson. It's only supper with our friends, my sister, and her friend, Mr. Cooper. I usually dress for dinner at half past five. All will be well, my dear."

"I sent word to our guests that the occasion warranted tailcoats and white tie, so I'd like you to wear your favorite gown and jewels." Jackson grinned at the cleverness of his plan.

"A formal dinner when Amanda invited the local shopkeeper?" She dropped her voice to a whisper. "I doubt Mr. Cooper even owns a dinner jacket or cummerbund, let alone a tailcoat. A Sunday meeting suit is the best we can hope for considering his... financial circumstances."

"Precisely, my dear." He enfolded both her hands in his. "Miss Dunn feels that a rapier wit and passing knowledge of literature are sufficient to rub shoulders in polite society. Perhaps your sister believes standards and rules have been thrown out because she's far from home. I wish for her to see how inappropriate her relationship with Nathaniel Cooper truly is."

"Won't it embarrass Mr. Cooper to be so underdressed?" Her luminous eyes widened.

"I doubt the man is capable of such shame. Besides, why should we lower our standards to accommodate a guest who has no business here in the first place?"

Abigail leaned forward conspiratorially. "But weren't you the one who invited him?"

Jackson waved off her question. "Please instruct Salome to add oysters to our menu of escargot and soft-shelled crabs. There will be no down-home cuisine for our little country boy." He finished his drink in a single gulp.

"Very well. I'll tell her and begin my toilette." Abigail didn't sound very enthusiastic. "May I inform Amanda of the change in plans?"

"Of course. I have no desire to embarrass your sister." Jackson's smile remained only until Abigail swept from the room. *But it is high time she realizes what a fool she's making of herself.*

At a little before eight, Jackson joined his wife in the parlor to await their guests. Abigail looked splendid in a dark green gown, the diamond-and-emerald jewelry he purchased with Mr. Peterson's generous advance sparkling at her throat and earlobes. "You look beautiful, my dear." He whispered the words next to her ear.

"Thank you. I've never owned anything quite so exquisite." She fingered her necklace appreciatively.

Footsteps behind them curtailed any subsequent comment. Amanda walked into the room in a cheery pink dress with a small hoop and very modest accessories. Her ensemble was better suited for a garden party than a formal dinner. Instead of an elaborate coiffure of curls like Abigail's, Amanda's hair had been plaited and then simply coiled atop her head.

"Good evening, Jackson, Abby. I checked with Salome, and everything is ready for this evening."

"Of course, why wouldn't it be?" he asked irritably. He was about to send his sister-in-law upstairs to change clothes, but they heard the sound of carriages on the oyster shell turnaround. "Why don't we meet our guests on the verandah," he said instead.

The women followed him outside, and in short order he introduced Amanda to the Honorable and Mrs. Thaddeus Wilkes, the

Wilmington representative to the Confederate congress; Judge Miles Stewart and his charming wife; and Mr. and Mrs. Preston Alcott, Esquire, the attorney who had represented Henthorne and Sons for years. Although Mrs. Alcott had met Amanda previously, all three ladies fixated on the identicalness of the twins rather than on Amanda's informal attire.

Conversation remained lively on the terrace as Amos circulated with glasses of French champagne. The judge and attorney launched into a spirited discussion about eminent domain in regards to tidal flats and the coastline, while Representative Wilkes tried to interest them in pending legislation involving the barrier islands. Nathaniel nearly slipped into the group unnoticed. Almost, but not quite. Jackson spotted the tall young man at Amanda's side, whispering something into her ear. Her cheeks turned rosy with a blush as she opened her fan to cool her face.

"Mr. Cooper, I'm glad you were able to join us."

"Thank you, Mr. Henthorne, for extending the invitation." Cooper bowed low and then straightened to perfect posture. He was scrubbed and clean shaven; his shirt was pressed and his shoes were polished. But his dark wool suit looked threadbare, and although still passable for church, it was ridiculously unsuitable for the occasion.

"Mr. Cooper is our Amanda's favorite greengrocer. He owns a small shop on Water Street." Jackson rocked back on his heels, waiting for the gasps or mute stares to commence. But instead the other guests appeared taken by the novelty.

"Ah, an enterprising young man. That's what the new South needs more of!" Representative Wilkes slapped Nathaniel on the back. "Too many people sit around waiting for life to return to how it was. Even after we lick those Yankees, that's not going to happen."

The judge stepped to his side. "You're in a good location to gauge the influx of new immigrants, Mr. Cooper. I'm worried many foreigners arrive on steamers and aren't departing when the ships leave port. We need to keep track of those emigrating and demand they seek citizenship."

Even Jackson's lawyer was eager to chat with the shopkeeper, but the ladies circumvented his attempt. "My cook insists your store has the freshest vegetables and weevil-free rice," said Sarah Wilkes. "It's not easy to find quality food these days with the rail lines torn up so often." She shook her blond curls with dismay, although Jackson would bet his eyeteeth she had never peeled a potato or boiled a pot of rice in her life.

"My Gertrude insists your prices are fairer than Baxter's, and everyone needs to mind their budget these days." Rosalyn Stewart nudged in between Amanda and Nathaniel in the familiar manner of older ladies. "I want to hear how our food differs from what you're used to, Miss Dunn. It's been years since we sailed to London, and I don't remember the cuisine very well."

"Speaking of which," Abigail said, drawing her guests' attention, "shall we move to the dining room? Dinner is ready to be served."

Everyone trailed the butler into the elegantly appointed room with a beautifully set table. Jackson waited at the rear, grinding down on his molars. This wasn't progressing as he'd intended. His friends were treating Nathaniel like a favored lap dog instead of the interloper that he was. He needed to take matters into his own hands. His pliable wife would be of no use. "Would you care for more champagne, Mr. Cooper?"

"No, sir. This is lemonade in my flute. Amos kindly provided my favorite beverage. Thank you."

"May I have more lemonade, Amos?" Amanda lifted her glass.

"Of course, Miss Dunn." The butler lingered in case others wished to change their drinks.

Jackson waited to pose his next question until the arrival of the first course. "I hope the *vichyssoise* is to your liking, Mr. Cooper."

Nathaniel peered into his bowl with a smile. "I never cared much for potato soup until I learned it could be made with leeks, celery, and garlic and served cold. I'm sure Salome's recipe will meet with my approval." He nodded in Jackson's direction.

Throughout the meal, Jackson kept watch on the shopkeeper from the corner of his eye. Nathaniel waited until others began eating the oysters and followed their lead. He made polite conversation with his nearby companions, while Amanda practically hung on his every word. That woman's appetite improved significantly from her normal pickiness. Abigail chatted away with Judge Stewart about nonsense, while he remained enchanted with Abigail as usual.

Jackson almost abandoned hope of relegating Nathaniel to his rightful place when Mrs. Wilkes brought up an interesting topic.

"Has anyone read any of the ramblings from those transcendentalists from Concord?" she asked. "I dismissed them out of hand at first because they were abolitionists, but some of their thinking is rather interesting." With encouragement from around the table, she continued. "They believe in the inherent goodness of both people and nature, and that society and its institutions— particularly organized religion and political parties—ultimately corrupt the purity of the individual. They have faith that people are at their best when truly self-reliant and independent."

Jackson seized his opportunity. "What is your opinion of these northern rabble-rousers, Mr. Cooper?"

Nathaniel cleared his throat. "I possess far less faith in the inherent goodness of mankind without a strong Christian background, but I have read several essays by Ralph Waldo Emerson and Walt Whitman. They are educated and erudite men, to be sure. History will determine the final viability of their positions."

Jackson gripped the edge of the table. He would have to bide his time. Thwarting the efforts of the shopkeeper would be harder than he anticipated. Yet he definitely needed to bring that upstart down a peg or two, at least in the eyes of his sister-in-law.

Amanda spent the next several days at her sister's side. Abby seemed to have either caught a case of flu or one of the rich dishes served at the formal dinner hadn't agreed with her. For two days in a row, Abby spent her mornings bent over a washbasin in her room horribly nauseated. Then she spent afternoons weak from dehydration. When Amanda wasn't swabbing her forehead with a cool cloth, she was assigning tasks to the slaves to keep the house running smoothly. In England servants knew what their employers expected of them and went about their daily routines without someone constantly commanding: "Do this or now do that." Slaves in America took little initiative. Their owners didn't encourage independent thinking or taking responsibility. No wonder slaves often floundered for a period of time when suddenly set free.

After a final check that her sister had drifted off to sleep on her balcony chaise, Amanda wandered down to the garden. Thus far she'd confined her musings about the party to the ostentation of white tie on an ordinary Thursday, or the bizarre selection of dishes served. It seemed as though Abby had purposely chosen foods that would be difficult to eat. Yet the more Amanda pondered the dinner, the more she suspected Jackson had been at the helm.

The man had done everything possible to embarrass Nathaniel. Yet despite his Herculean efforts, Jackson had failed. Nate asked polite questions about unfamiliar dishes as anyone would without displaying the slightest amount of discomfort. He mimicked her use of the claw-cracker and correct oyster etiquette without mishap. And the fact that he wasn't formally attired didn't seem to be an issue with anyone but Jackson. His comments about "needing to find you a reputable haberdasher should your friendship with Miss Dunn continue" had made her blood boil. But the more Jackson tried to drive a wedge between them, the more she yearned to pack Nate Cooper into her steamer trunk and book the next passage home—not that Mama would find him any more acceptable than her brother-in-law did.

Nothing tastes sweeter than the fruit just beyond reach. And if she needed a second adage to embroider on a sampler, she would choose: *Absence makes the heart grow fonder.* By the third day, she was ready to invent any excuse to escape the house and walk to the shops along Water Street.

The next day, after assuring herself that Abigail was resting comfortably in her darkened bedroom, Amanda skipped down to the river oblivious of the fact it was ninety degrees in the sunshine.

Nate glanced up from his ledger when she entered his store. "Good day, Mr. Cooper. I trust you recovered from the hemlock tea and belladonna sweet cakes served at the Henthornes'."

Her jest took him a moment to comprehend; then a slow smile lifted the corners of his mouth. "Fortunately, I slipped an antidote for poison into my coat pocket that I concocted from herbal remedies. One never knows when you'll encounter a sworn enemy at a formal dinner." He slapped his ledger closed. "I'm surprised to see you here, Miss Dunn. Pleasantly, but surprised nonetheless."

Amanda tugged off her sunbonnet as she advanced up the narrow aisle toward the back. "Why is that? You know I prefer you infinitely more than that sour old Mr. Baxter."

Nate took his time to sweep pencils and notepads off the counter, put the teakettle on the stove, and pull off his apron. "Because it's fatiguing to constantly battle on someone's behalf—fatiguing and disheartening. Eventually all champions of the downtrodden grow weary and must pass the torch to another advocate."

Climbing onto a stool, she smoothed her skirt with a gloved hand. "I'm not your champion; I'm your friend. And you're certainly not downtrodden. I thought you handled yourself splendidly despite Jackson's every attempt to see you fail."

Astonishment registered in his blue eyes. "I didn't think you would so readily admit to Henthorne's objective."

"Why wouldn't I?" she asked, shrugging. "His rudeness was apparent to everyone, I daresay. But his guests didn't appear to share his low opinion of you."

Nate set out two cups, a tin of milk, and the sugar bowl. "I found the Wilkeses and Stewarts to be delightful people. Even Preston Alcott struck me as a fair-minded man."

"What of Mrs. Sarah Wilkes's fondness for the writings of Henry David Thoreau? Did that not run counter to everything you believed about wealthy coastal aristocrats?"

"Tell me honestly, Amanda. Did you send your personal copy of *Walden* to Mrs. Wilkes with some tantalizing bribe if she read the volume?"

"I own few books by American writers. I prefer the work of Lord Byron, Jane Austen, or Charles Dickens. So no, I did not bribe Mrs. Wilkes for my own purposes. Not everyone is as narrow minded and snobbish as Jackson."

Nate smiled, yet his face contained little warmth. "His guests were kinder and more gracious than I gave them credit for. Thus my snap conclusion had been unwarranted. Yet Jackson did convince the principal target of his message."

Amanda pursed her lips, confused. "Who would that be?"

"Me. He aimed to illustrate my unsuitability as a candidate to court you. And in that he succeeded."

She gasped, shocked by his straightforwardness. "Goodness, I doubt no one ever accused you of being overly subtle."

His eyes softened. "No, they have not. I'm twenty-five years old and didn't achieve my success—however limited that might be—without taking chances and, in many cases, risking everything. I must take one of those chances now." He sucked in a halting breath. "I like you, Miss Dunn, more than I've ever liked a woman before. But Thursday's dinner brought me face-to-face with an undeniable truth: I will never achieve the success of Jackson Henthorne—or your parents, for that matter. Not with the economic reality in North Carolina these days and my questionable background from the mountains. Family ties and ancestral blood still matter to these old families just as much as it does where you live. My grandparents were illiterate and squatted on ground that no one wanted until investors decided to put a railroad through. No land grant from King Charles with fancy seals guaranteed their claim to the homestead. My birthright will never allow me to be good enough for you." His words floated on the warm air wafting in through the open window and echoed in her ears for several seconds.

"You seem to have given the matter serious thought while I've been nursing my sister. And you have arrived at conclusions which involve *two* people all by yourself."

He opened his mouth to speak, but she cut him off with a wave of her hand. "I listened patiently while you elucidated your deficiencies. Now I insist on the same privilege."

Nate crossed his arms and leaned back against the wall. "Fair enough."

"I thought the dinner went well despite Jackson's boorish behavior. I saw admirable traits in your personality that had nothing to do with your upbringing or heritage. But now you're acting like my brother-in-law, telling me what I should or shouldn't do, what's best for me, and how I should think. Are you just another male eager to boss me around, perhaps because you feel women are incapable of making rational decisions in life?"

"Absolutely not. My mother spoke her mind and stood up to my father when she disagreed with him. I always respected her for that."

"At least your parents passed on a useful ability to you and no doubt, to many others. You're choosing to dismiss them because they were uncultured."

"See here. I loved my parents and I'm not embarrassed by them. I only wanted you to understand that I have limited prospects—"

"Do you believe my interest lies only in your financial prospects for the future? Really, sir. That makes me sound horribly vain and shallow."

Nate closed his eyes and rubbed his forehead. "You're an impossible woman, Amanda."

"It merely seems that way because we're having a disagreement." She smiled at him. "*We* decide our future—you and I, not Jackson and not my mother. I was impressed with your self-assurance on Thursday. Few men could stand up to open hostility without losing their temper or storming off in a fit of wounded pride."

"Punching my host in the nose did cross my mind once or twice."

"As it did mine, but you didn't act on your impulse and that goes a long way with me."

He blushed to the roots of his hair. "Who's lacking in subtlety now?"

Amanda stood and circled around the counter. "The proper way to eat unfamiliar foods, or knowing which fork is correct, can easily be mastered if a person sets their mind to it. Formal attire with the right accessories can be purchased if those garments become useful. Social etiquette can be learned like baking a pie or sailing a boat. But what you have inside here, Mr. Cooper," she placed a hand on his chest, "is far more important. It's everything, in fact, when a woman is seeking friends…or perhaps someone to assume a more permanent role." Without considering the boldness of her action, Amanda leaned forward and kissed him on the mouth.

His eyes registered utter shock as his lips responded. "Goodness, Miss Dunn! I thought you were peeved with me."

She moved back a step. "I still am. So you had better provide a bag of sweets for my walk home and no more pushiness or thinking for me." She slapped his arm with her fan. "If you ply me with peppermints, I'll find a way to forgive you."

Nate headed toward the rows of brass-lidded canisters along the far counter. "You are a hard woman to anticipate, let alone boss around."

"Finally we've arrived at something we can agree on."

Abigail soaked in her tub until her skin started to wrinkle like a prune. This was the best she'd felt in a week. For the first few days Amanda had doted on her. Now she disappeared most afternoons with ambiguous comments about helping make bandages with the sewing guild or volunteering at the church kitchen. Refugees displaced by the fighting continued to pour into Wilmington. Why they expected every Christian denomination to feed them day after day was a mystery to her, if charity work was indeed what occupied her sister lately. All Abigail knew was that Amanda wasn't spending her time with her. Even Jackson stayed out later more nights than not. Abigail had never been one to wallow in self-pity, but it seemed that everyone was avoiding her.

"Estelle," she called. "I'm finished with my bath." When an

interval passed without the sound of approaching footsteps in the hall, she called again, this time just short of a scream. "Estelle! Where are you?"

Another minute elapsed before her maid sauntered into the room. "Here I am, Miz Henthorne."

"Why must I shout? You knew I was bathing and should have been ready with a towel." Standing, Abigail allowed Estelle to enfold her in a thick wrap.

"I checked on you three times, mistress. Then I went to the kitchen for a bit of lunch." Her maid wrapped a second towel around her damp hair.

"So I warrant a certain amount of your attention but am then abandoned to my own devices?"

Estelle's brow furrowed with bewilderment. "Beg your pardon, Miz Henthorne?" She continued to ruffle her hair none too gently.

Abigail pushed her away. "Stop that. I'd rather comb the tangles myself if you're going to be so rough. Go back down to your lunch."

She expected the girl to apologize profusely and pledge to do better, but instead she just shrugged her shoulders. "All right, Miz Henthorne." She strode out the door with far more energy than had carried her in.

Abigail dressed in a loose summer frock, sans corset, hoop, or silk stockings. It was too sultry an afternoon and her stomach churned with just the thought of tight restriction. Why fuss if it would only be her and Amanda at dinner? With her neck already damp with perspiration, she headed downstairs. Estelle could fix her hair out on the terrace, where it should be twenty degrees cooler. Carrying her brush, a pack of pins, and several ribbons, Abigail entered the kitchen, an unusual destination for the lady of the house.

The fact that the mistress seldom entered that room was

reflected on Estelle and Josie's faces. They had been pulling off heads and tails from large shrimp and shoving them into their mouth as though participating in an eating competition. "What is going on in here?" Abigail asked, aghast.

Mutely the two maids stared, their mouths agape.

"Answer me!" she demanded.

Estelle swallowed her mouthful. "We…we was eating some shrimp, Miz Henthorne."

"I can see that. Is a plate of boiled shrimp what the other slaves are having for their noon meal?"

"No'm. They having chitlins and cornbread," Josie said, licking her fingertips.

"This is like pulling a rotten tooth," Abigail snapped. "Then why are you two *here* eating shrimp instead of in the courtyard with the others?" She was about to shake the answer out of Estelle when the girl finally spoke.

"Salome boiled shrimp to make croquettes for supper. Because no guests are comin' tonight, Josie and I thought we'd sample a few."

"*Sample a few?*" Abigail pointed at the heap of heads, tails, and shells atop the refuse bucket. "You were gorging yourselves without a thought to anyone else. If Salome steamed extra, she probably planned to make a nice gumbo for the slaves. It appears that the others will get plain beans." She marched over to the bin of rice. She took a large scoopful and spread it on the stone floor near the wall. "I'll show you what happens to selfish women. Kneel on that while you ponder what happens to greedy people when they die. And don't you dare tuck your skirts beneath your knees." She waited until both women knelt down, their faces wincing in pain. Then she stomped off to her chaise in the shade.

Several hours later Abigail woke. The heat had turned reading into a long nap. Shaking off her drowsiness, she stretched and walked the length of the gallery. Below in the courtyard a curious sight captured her attention. Estelle and Josie sat on the low stone wall with Amanda bent over in front of them. Her sister was applying wet cloths to their knees as though she'd become a nurse to the slaves.

Abigail felt a frisson of shame as she walked down the stairs, her dress clinging uncomfortably to her back. "What is going on?"

Amanda peered up from her ministrations on Josie's leg. "I was just about to ask you the same question. Why were these maids kneeling on rice?"

"I was punishing them for thievery." She pushed back a damp lock of hair from her forehead.

"Thievery?" Amanda's eyes rounded as she looked from one slave to the other for confirmation. "They told me they had been caught eating shrimp for lunch."

Josie and Estelle stared at the ground, not lifting their gazes to either woman.

"The boiled shrimp was for our dinner, not theirs. Salome had food for them outside. They know where to find the noon meal." Abigail crossed her arms.

"Filching a few shrimp is grounds for torture?"

"I didn't intend for my punishment to be torture. Unfortunately, I fell asleep. I didn't plan to cause injury to their knees."

Amanda hesitated long enough to rinse her hands in the bucket of water and dry them on a towel. "I thought Josie was *my* maid—a gift from you and Jackson while I'm a guest in your home. Wouldn't any reprimands for her be left up to me to administer?"

"How would it look to the other slaves if Estelle was punished for stealing food and Josie wasn't? We both know any reprimands left up to you would be worthless in nature." Abigail matched her sister's tone in vehemence. She'd grown weary of Amanda taking the upper hand.

As Amanda shook her head like a stubborn mule, Jackson emerged from the side garden. Judging by his expression, he had heard plenty of their tête-à-tête.

"I'm curious, Miss Dunn," he said. "Do the servants eat whatever is being served to family and guests at Dunncliff Manor?"

"*What?*" Amanda tossed the rag into the water bucket.

"Your kitchen maids and footmen—do they dine on the pâtés, stuffed pheasant, and ribs of beef like the Dunns?"

"No, but Mrs. Andrews fixes hearty and sustaining meals for the staff."

Jackson approached, loosening his cravat with each step. "As we do here, I assure you. A master would be foolish to starve his slaves and yet still expect a decent day's work from them."

"Therein resides the essential difference. We have employees in Manchester—men and women who aren't owned by us or anyone else." Amanda arched her back with indignation.

"And if those employees were caught stealing or indulging in some other distasteful behavior, most likely they would be dismissed on the spot. They would be given whatever wages they had coming at that point, told to pack their meager belongings, and turned out regardless of the season or whether or not they had a place to go. The Dunn housekeeper or butler would have no trouble replacing the staff member from England's teeming underclass. The discharged maid would join the masses begging for food or selling themselves on the streets for tuppence."

Amanda flushed a deep scarlet as her hands bunched into fists. "How dare you imply that slavery is somehow a noble institution that takes better care of the underprivileged!"

"There is nothing noble about slavery, but at least we don't turn people out to fend for themselves. Slaves have a home with us until they die."

"And you keep working them until their death."

"Everyone is expected to work in this life, Miss Dunn. I see nothing wrong with people earning their keep."

"Some planters abuse slaves in unspeakable ways—tearing apart families, assaulting women, giving cruel beatings. And if slaves aren't permitted to learn to read or write, they have no way to improve their lives."

Abigail could keep silent no longer. "I don't abuse my slaves. Your maid was being punished for stealing shrimp. I'm sorry I fell asleep, but—"

"My dear, forgive me for interrupting you, but I believe I will leave you sisters alone to continue your philosophical discussions." Jackson bowed to both of them and then strode away.

In the heat of the moment, both women ignored him.

"They took *food*, Abigail, not silverware or gold coins."

"Shortages abound in the city, but your head is stuck in the sand. Estelle and Josie ate what could have been shared with others."

"Look at their knees! Perhaps it wasn't your intention to be cruel, but that swelling won't go down for days." Amanda's tone turned brittle.

"If you are able, I would like you two to go back to work." Abigail spoke calmly to Estelle and Josie. Looking around her, she said, "And the rest of you as well." The argument had attracted quite a few onlookers.

Once the courtyard had cleared, she turned to Amanda. "You have lived a charmed, insulated life in Wycleft, but I have visited Father's textile mills. I have seen the slums of his workers. They live in grim hovels on streets without proper sanitation. Their children begin work at an early age without much opportunity to attend school. I've been inside homes where people grow sick and die without calling doctors they cannot afford. When was the last time you visited those places?"

Amanda's eyes filled with tears. "I agree that much poverty exists in Manchester, but those workers are free to immigrate to another town or a new country if they choose."

Abigail was bored with a philosophical debate going nowhere. "When you return to England, sister, you may take up a crusade of social reform. In the meantime I expect you to respect the rules of this household. I love you and you are welcome here, but this is *my* home."

Nine

August

Leaning back in his chair, Jackson sipped a heady cup of West Indian tea. The view from his office window revealed exactly what he loved to see: ships entering and exiting the Wilmington harbor with astounding frequency. As soon as dockworkers loaded a steamer with cotton or tobacco, the captain navigated into the current of the Cape Fear River toward the sound and the ocean beyond. The Union navy had done little to stem commerce thanks to the brave men manning the guns at Fort Fisher.

His relationship with the dubious Elias Hornsby had become amiable camaraderie. After all, who could remain aloof when both men were growing rich from the enormous profits to be made? And forming a partnership with Robert Peterson and his brother had been his best decision yet after taking control away from his father. Jackson's social contacts and resources guaranteed that the majority of the goods left port on ships he contracted, while Peterson maintained a steady flow of cotton and tobacco to refill warehouses. Jackson hired managers, dock supervisors, bookkeepers to maintain ledgers, and clerks to handle the daily minutiae. He had cleared the debts of Henthorne and Sons and was amassing money to help his parents. He gave little thought to the future of the Confederacy, and even less to what his sister-in-law was doing with the local grocer. It was simply more entertaining to watch the hubbub along the waterfront while his account books improved day after day.

"Mr. Henthorne, sir?"

Jackson peered up at his new, sour-faced secretary. Miss Todd wasn't much to look at, but she possessed an uncanny ability to weed requests for an audience with him. Some wished to renegotiate existing contracts, others were old friends trying to borrow money, and a few sought employment or political influence. She had a gift for redirecting visitors to the correct underling, assuring that the only appointments Jackson took were ones that fattened his coffers.

"What is it, Miss Todd?"

"Mr. Peterson is here, sir. He begs your indulgence in not announcing his visit before now, but he insists he has a matter of upmost urgency." Her bland face offered the tiniest of smiles.

"Then let's not keep him waiting. Show him in and bring us a fresh pot of tea."

Jackson stood, straightened his cravat, and strode toward the fireplace. He wished to appear exactly what he was—the savviest and most successful factor in town. He greeted his business partner with one elbow resting on the marble mantel.

"Mr. Henthorne, good of you to see me this morning, sir." Peterson spoke from the doorway.

"You and I stand on no ceremony, sir. I always have time for you. Please have a seat." Pointing to the most comfortable upholstered chair, Jackson noticed Peterson's complexion had taken on an unhealthy pallor. The man appeared thinner, almost dissipated since his last visit.

"Thank you. I rode in from Whiteville last night and barely slept. I couldn't wait to discuss a unique opportunity with you."

"Are you feeling well, sir?" Jackson asked. Indeed, the short walk across the room brought a flush and beads of sweat to Peterson's face.

"Fair-to-middlin', but nothing to concern yourself with. There's plenty of fever in the interior this time of year. Most of the slaves that hadn't run off are sick with the chills. I had a bout of ague myself, but I'm on the mend now." He dabbed his brow with his handkerchief.

"Ah, here's Miss Todd with tea. That should go down easily."

Peterson accepted a cup from the secretary with a shaky hand. "Has much news reached the coast? General Sherman wreaks havoc in Georgia. Atlanta is besieged. The Yankees are leaving a path of destruction wherever they go."

"Is Sherman fighting Joe Johnson's army? He's the best general we got other than Marse Robert."

"Yes, sir, but Sherman is waging war on farmers and towns-folk—men, women, and children—burning houses and barns and slaughtering livestock. Whatever he doesn't need to feed his soldiers, he leaves to rot under the summer sun. His soldiers are nothing but a pack of thieves—filling their knapsacks with silver, porcelain, and anything they can resell up north."

Jackson made the appropriate murmurs of disgust, but he failed to deduce how reports about a Yankee tyrant could be described as urgent. "I've been rather busy to keep abreast of news of the war. Besides, not everything that gets printed in newspapers can be trusted."

Peterson downed his tea and refilled the cup. "You have done an exemplary job of moving cotton and tobacco out of Wilmington.

Truly commendable. But the time has come to strike while the iron is hot. I've recently heard of two side-wheelers available for sale. They left Nassau harbor and are headed here as we speak. The ships could be ours for the right price."

Jackson shifted in his chair. "Someone actually built two ships without a commissioned buyer? By all means I wish to hear more."

"Another factor in town ordered the steamers. I prefer not to mention his name so that social obligations won't prevent us from making the purchase." Peterson inched forward to the edge of his chair. "If we buy these ships, and I assure you they're magnificent side-wheelers—the *Lady Adelaine* and the *Roanoke*—we can double our profits. We can hire our own captains and not have to contract passage."

Jackson rubbed his jawline. Double their profits? He could turn the Henthorne plantation around with paid workers and set money aside for the future. "I gather this unnamed factor cannot make good on his monetary pledge?"

"That is correct, sir. He has leveraged everything but the braces holding up his trousers." Peterson released a raspy laugh.

Jackson failed to find humor in another man's misfortune. "Do you and your brother have sufficient capital to purchase two brand-new vessels?"

Peterson's lips thinned. "That's why I'm here, Mr. Henthorne. I have spent the last month securing all the cotton I can in South Carolina and Georgia before those Yankees turn it into smoke and ash. I have teamsters hauling it to railroad depots as quickly as possible, but many roads are torn up. It will take time to get it to port, but a vast quantity of cotton is coming and we must be ready. That's why we desperately need more ships."

Despite the early hour, Jackson longed for a beverage stronger than tea. Peterson was taking a circuitous route in reaching his point. "Go on," he prodded.

"I've had to pay planters for their cotton. My finances are temporarily stretched paper-thin. I'm hoping Henthorne and Sons can produce the necessary capital for the *Lady Adelaine* and the *Roanoke*."

Jackson sniffed. "How much money are we talking about?"

Peterson murmured a figure so exorbitant Jackson's sole response was laughter. "Who has that kind of money sitting in their bank account?"

"Keep in mind that the price is for both ships. I'm certain we could acquire one if that sort of outlay is beyond your means." Peterson's expression turned patronizing.

"Beyond my means?" Jackson recoiled at the veiled insult. "Mr. Peterson, Union warships lurk in the Atlantic itching to aim their guns on any vessel flying Confederate colors."

"Fort Fisher keeps those Yankee gunboats far enough out that new ships can easily outrun them. It's worked that way for more than two years, and we have no reason to believe the situation will change." Peterson wiped his upper lip before stuffing his damp handkerchief into his pocket. "I intend to send the *Lady Adelaine* to Bermuda for a load of guns and munitions. President Davis will empty the treasury to supply sufficient weapons for our brave soldiers to win. As I began our conversation, this is the time to reap enormous profits, but a venture this bold isn't for the faint of heart." Peterson stood clumsily. "Would you like the day to consider this opportunity, sir? My stamina still isn't what it should be, so I must return to my hotel. May I call on you tomorrow for your answer?"

Jackson rose to his feet and stretched out his hand. "Because time is of the essence, I won't need a day to consider. Send word to whoever is brokering the sale that Henthorne and Peterson will purchase the *Lady Adelaine* and the *Roanoke*."

"Bravo, sir. And I'm sure that if we wish to sell when the war ends, we will find a ready market for those steamers. The eventual lifting of the blockade from Richmond and Charleston will only improve commerce along the seacoast."

"I'll consult my banker today and should have a cheque within a day or two."

Peterson nodded energetically. "By the time the ships arrive from Nassau your warehouses should be overflowing. Thanks to this war, we should be able to retire rich men by the time it's over. Shall I join you at your club tonight to celebrate?"

Jackson considered inviting his partner to dinner at the house, but Peterson's tremors and pallor put him off. Better not to expose Abigail should the man still be ill. "Yes, my club tonight. Shall we meet at nine?"

After Peterson bowed and took his leave, Jackson's puffed-up confidence waned. The combined sale price constricted his chest like a lady's corset. He had recently cleared the company's debts but had barely had a chance to save a tenth of the amount. To obtain so large a sum on short notice, he would have to leverage the business assets and perhaps mortgage his home. He needed to talk to Abigail and then visit his father in the country. After all, despite his current leadership role, Randolph still owned Henthorne and Sons. Packing his papers into his leather case, Jackson rehearsed how to approach them in his mind. But it took little time to conclude neither conversation would take place—not today and not in the foreseeable future. Abigail and his father would fail to recognize a once-in-a-lifetime opportunity. He felt a twinge of apprehension. If he felt this uneasy, he certainly couldn't convince anyone else. He must work harder than ever and keep his head down.

With a little luck this would be the last gamble he would ever have to take.

Nate heard the bell over the door as he hooked the last side of deer meat overhead in the back room. Washing his hands in a bucket of water, he strode to the front to convince a local matron that his produce had no peer in all of Wilmington. But the friendly face was decidedly male. "Well, look who the wind blew in on this lovely September day."

Mason Hooks marched up the aisle with more swagger than usual for someone from a tiny place like Balsam. "A man can grow old and die waiting for you to mosey into Flannigan's for a beer."

"No smoky saloons for me. I'm still waiting for a teahouse to open in town." Nate grinned, not the least bit put off by his friend's challenge.

Mason's guffaws carried through the open window to the street. "I'll keep tryin' till I wear you out, but that's not why I'm making an afternoon social call."

"Work slowing down on the docks?" Nate asked as he perched on a tall stool.

"Not hardly. Ships are tied up two deep waiting their turn to unload and secure new cargo. I'm here because you might be interested in tonight's meeting." Mason whispered as though eavesdroppers lurked between the bins of apples.

"What kind of meeting?"

"Just a few men hopin' to see this bloody war come to an end." Mason's words were barely audible. "With victory for the Union army, that is."

Nate pulled his stool closer. "I trust this gathering won't be on the Square or in the mayor's front yard."

"We're meeting out near Greenfield Lake 'round nine o'clock. There's an old peanut barn there."

"Greenfield Lake? That's three or four miles from town. How did you hear about this?"

"Word travels fast on the docks. Most of them boys ain't too fond of Jeff Davis. All his fancy ideas are for the rich planters. They're not willing to fight a war they can't win. The South is done for."

"Who will be at this gathering? Immigrants just off the boat not eager to die for their new country?"

"Sure, but also plenty of farm boys run off their spreads by one army or the other. Others will be farmers tired of scratching a livin' from worn-out dirt."

Nate slicked a hand through his hair. "Is that why you're going, because you think the Confederacy is licked?"

Mason's expression turned malevolent as though remembering something he would rather forget. "I'm going 'cause of how those brass-buttoned majors treated us privates, just like we were their slaves back home. They didn't care how much of our blood got spilt long as it wasn't theirs. If you know anybody that would rather not have Joe Johnson victorious, bring them along."

"What about free blacks? Would they be welcome?"

"'Course they are. I would say Negroes have the best reasons to see Billy Sherman march his troops into North Carolina too."

Nate pulled down the shade and turned his window sign to "Closed." "I'd better lock up and head home. Greenfield Lake is a long ride."

Mason's eyes rounded. "So you'll come? I took you for a lover of flowery words, not a man of action. I won't lie to you. This could get bloody if those Reb provost marshals get wind of it."

"I'm showing up to listen. Any flowery words that come to mind I plan to keep to myself."

Mason pulled a crude map from his breast pocket and set it on the counter. "Take the beach road south. Watch for the big marsh on your right. Then count the farm lanes on your left. Turn down the fifth one." He tapped the map with his finger. "'Bout another mile, watch for a clearing with one lone oak sittin' by its lonesome. Cut a beeline across the field. Once you find that tree you'll see the barn roof." Mason allowed him to study the sketch for another minute. "Wear dark clothes and carry no lantern. They don't want no uninvited visitors, but you and your friend will be welcome."

"Providing I don't fall into the bog, I'll be there."

Nate had heard about these meetings in the hills—Carolinians supportive of the Union who didn't want their state to secede. He never imagined the hotheads would eventually migrate through the vast plantation land to the coast. The local militia, those not already reassigned to Fort Fisher, wouldn't like a pack of traitors in their midst.

That evening he arrived home so early he was able to eat supper with the Simses. Throughout the meal of rabbit stew and biscuits, he half listened to Rufus's adventures in the woods outside of town even as his mind churned with ideas. Once Ruth took the boy to the porch to practice arithmetic, Nate told his landlord about his afternoon visitor.

Odom stared into his tea leaves as though their arrangement offered insight into the future. "Are you certain Negroes would be allowed in?"

"According to my friend, several free men from the docks plan to attend."

"This ain't no group of rabble fixing to do their own mischief, is it? I want no part of thievery or mayhem."

"Nor do I. If you would rather not go, I take no exception. I cannot vouch that everything Mason said is the truth."

"I understand, but this is one meeting I want to see for myself."

Without further discussion, they scrambled to their feet, provided an ambiguous explanation to Ruth, and saddled their horses. To reach the obscure barn by the appointed hour they would have to ride hard. They would also have to keep their heads down and concentrate on staying astride. But the less time they spent pondering what awaited them at Greenfield Lake the better.

The former peanut barn sat in a moonlit clearing surrounded by swamp willows and sycamores. Despite Mason's request for no lanterns, two burly men held blazing torches near the barn's entrance. Several more brandished weapons, everything from squirrel muskets to old muzzleloaders to the new repeating Spencer rifles. More torches burned inside the barn, the yellow light spilling through cracks and missing slats. Nate and Odom tied their reins to a low branch and approached the entrance warily.

"Stop! Who goes there?" A bearded giant of a man stepped from the shadows, his pistol trained on the center of Nate's chest.

"Nathaniel Cooper and Odom Sims, friends of Mason Hooks." Nate offered this bit of information uncertain if it bettered his prospects or sealed his fate.

"Hooks is mighty quick to make friends," said the giant. "Where you from, Cooper?"

"Balsam, in the Blue Ridge Mountains."

Tilting his torch briefly at Sims, the guard nodded toward the doorway. "Go on in. They're just about to start." He didn't, however, lower his sidearm.

Within the cavernous barn, Nate's eyes smarted from tar smoke. On the far side of the room, Mason waved his arm at them, but he and Odom found seats in the back row. Nate scanned the assemblage curiously. A strange assortment of humankind filled the rows of crude benches. Young and old, black and white—all talked with great animation. Judging by their attire, the men represented every variety of vocation and financial circumstance except for the rich planter. They were united by a common desire to see the war end and the Union restored without slavery, as mandated by Lincoln's edict. But as Nate scrutinized more closely, he saw that most wore rough, cast-off clothing. They appeared to live a hand-to-mouth existence on the docks, or perhaps survived by pilferage, robbery, or worse.

These weren't seasoned debaters eager to sway public opinion with logic and reason.

Someone fired a musket into the rafters, curtailing the din of chatter. "Silence!" a voice demanded. "We haven't come here to socialize like women at a county fair." A tall, wild-haired man climbed onto a wooden dais. His suit, though not in the current style, was clean and pressed. "We've come tonight to take action!" He paused for a thunder of applause.

"As we struggle to earn a living in Wilmington, endless bales of cotton and hogsheads of tobacco flow from the interior counties to the coast. The same goods we load onto steamers bound for Europe. Then we unload food and guns for Bobby Lee's army in Virginia or Joe Johnson's out west. We cannot end this war until we cut off the flow of supplies."

A second roar of approval bolstered the white-haired leader's bravado. Nate felt a dull ache in the pit of his stomach as he glanced around the room.

"Who's with me?" shouted the leader. "It's the tracks of the Wilmington and Weldon railroad that need to be dealt with swiftly and decisively. I say we ride out the next full moon." Men began shouting and talking all at once. Several began thumping their chests and stomping on the plank floor. Nate saw more than one whiskey bottle passed around to fuel their courage. One glance at Odom, and Nate knew his landlord shared his apprehension. "Real slow-like move toward the door as though you're looking for somebody." Nate uttered the words through gritted teeth.

Nodding almost imperceptivity, Odom meandered through the crowd as though in no particular hurry. Outside, the guards paid them no mind, having caught the fever of rebellion. Silently, Nate and Odom mounted their horses and picked their way through the woods to open pasture. Once they spotted the lone oak, bathed in moonlight and standing sentinel, both men released a sigh of relief.

"Don't think I'll be attendin' anymore meetings with you, Nate," Odom said, reining his horse to an easy gait. "Those boys will likely end up dead soon enough."

"I'm sorry, Odem. I didn't know what to expect, but it certainly wasn't a mob bent on destruction."

The men kept their own council as they rode home. What had Nate expected? He should have known it wouldn't be gentlemen seeking a peaceful solution. Despite the fact he wouldn't fight to preserve slavery, he couldn't wage war *against* North Carolina either.

So where did that leave him? Alone in a country gone mad.

Late September

"Please, Helene, just fix a simple chignon for the day." Amanda smiled into the mirror at her maid. "It's too warm for curls against my neck and shoulders."

"Do you realize, Miss Amanda, if we were home the days—and especially the nights—would be getting cooler by now?"

"You're right. Lately I've been longing for one of those misty, damp days I used to complain about."

Helene secured the bun with a few well-placed hairpins. "How goes your late papa's business affairs? I noticed several recent letters from Mr. Pelton."

"Our chief foreman is rather shocked by my success as a negotiator. Large amounts of cotton arrive at Dunn Mills from the port on a regular basis. Garment production has not only resumed but surpassed prior quotas for the month. Now Mama won't have to sell family heirlooms to pay tax obligations to the Queen."

Helene blanched slightly, distressed by the American penchant to make light of important matters—a habit Amanda had acquired since her arrival in North Carolina.

"You are to be commended then, Miss Amanda, for proving the naysayers wrong."

"Thank you, but my brother-in-law expedited the shipments on my behalf. I'm not sure why they had lapsed in the first place." Amanda touched a bit of powder to her shiny nose.

"Will we leave for England soon? I hope we can make the voyage before the seas turn rough."

Helene couldn't possibly sound more eager, but Amanda wasn't ready to leave Wilmington, or Nathaniel, yet. Turning on her dressing table stool, she met Helene's eye. "Not quite. I haven't secured long-term contracts with Henthorne and Sons. Jackson doesn't like discussing business at the dinner table, but he makes excuses when I request an appointment. He is always too busy at the docks and warehouses. If I must, I will show up unannounced at his office and stay until he admits me. Eventually, Miss Todd will tire of my face and show me in." She smiled, but Helene didn't appreciate her humor.

"Aren't you anxious to see your mother and pay your respects at your father's grave?"

Amanda frowned at her maid, but Josie's interruption precluded a response.

"Should I put this tray on your gallery, Miz Dunn? Or you gonna eat downstairs? I brung nuff for her too." Josie angled her head in Helene's direction.

"On the balcony, Josie. Thank you."

"Forgive me, Miss Amanda," said Helene softly. "I spoke out of turn."

"I understand why you're not comfortable here, but I must remain until my duties are complete. Who knows when I will come back to America?" She strode through the French doors and plopped into a chair. Just the thought of never again seeing Nate had turned her knees to mush. "Sit and have some toast and jam."

Helene glanced around to make sure the other maid had left. "Are you certain Mrs. Henthorne won't be angry?"

Amanda snorted. "I'm not allowed to eat in the kitchen and you're not permitted in the dining room. No one said anything about my balcony." She sipped the strong, hot coffee.

"The slaves don't like me. They might tell Mrs. Henthorne if they spot me."

"You have nothing to fear because you work for *me*," she said emphatically as she spread peach preserves across her toast.

Helene didn't seem convinced, but the appearance of a small boy on the steps distracted their attention.

"Rufus, how are you, child? Would you like a pear?" Amanda held the fruit in the palm of her hand.

The child nodded. "Thank you, Miz Dunn." Slipping it into his pocket, he stepped closer. "I have a message from Mr. Cooper. My ma said to give it to you straightaway." Rufus peered at Helene dubiously before pulling out a note. It had been folded many times.

Amanda opened the small square and read while her heart thrummed against her ribs.

My dear Miss Dunn,

I have been arrested by local militia and accused of being a Northern sympathizer and draft dodger. I'm being held in the jail, probably awaiting Confederate provost marshals. If you can exert any influence, perhaps with the town council, I implore

you to do so. I dare not involve the Simses for fear
of repercussions for them. Forgive me, but I have
nowhere else to turn.

Your devoted servant,
Nathaniel

She clutched the sheet to her chest, unable to draw breath for several moments.

"Any answer to take back, Miz Dunn?" Rufus produced a stub of a charcoal pencil. "I 'spose you could write on the back side."

"No, Rufus. This is something I must take care of in person. You run home and tell your parents not to worry."

"I'll tell them, Miz Dunn." He extracted the pear and took a large bite before vanishing down the steps into the garden.

"Is something wrong, Miss Amanda?"

"Yes, but every problem contains a solution. You eat while I think." By the time she finished another cup of coffee Amanda had eliminated three possibilities. The town council wouldn't meet for another two weeks. Nate could be taken to Fort Fisher by then and hanged. The state representative she had met at dinner, the Honorable Thaddeus Wilkes, would be in Richmond for the current assemblage, according to Jackson's dinner chatter. As for the Henthornes' attorney, Mr. Alcott, he would undoubtedly consult Jackson before taking action. Her only hope lay with Judge Stewart or his charming wife, Rosalyn.

Throughout the morning, Amanda prayed her sister would decide to stay home that day. During luncheon Amanda had never seen anyone dawdle so long over a chilled chicken breast and cup of consommé. Finally, Abigail stood and signaled for the table to be cleared.

"I believe I'll pay a call on Mrs. Wilkes this afternoon and then perhaps Mrs. Stewart." Amanda sounded as cheery as possible.

"What on earth for?" Abby wrinkled her nose. "Sarah is dreadfully dull. She talks about nothing but the privations in Richmond."

Amanda opened her fan as they stepped into the center hall. "Both ladies insisted that we call on them and we haven't done so."

"You go on then. I haven't seen my friend Carolyn Lowell in ages. If I go out later it will be solely to her house, but I must lie down for a while." Abby clung to the banister as she ascended the stairs.

"I'll send the carriage back for you," Amanda said, following her up. The moment her sister closed her door, she collected her parasol and hurried down to the courtyard. She found the coachman grooming the horses.

"Thomas, do you know where Judge Stewart lives?"

"Yes, ma'am. Over on Ann Street."

"Could you take me there, please?"

"Isn't it too early to pay visits, Miz Duncan?"

"Not if the horse takes his time. I'm eager to start my calls." She tapped her toe on the flagstones.

"I'll bring the carriage 'round front, miss," he said, tipping his hat.

For some reason it took him twenty minutes to harness a horse and wipe down the leather upholstery. Abigail's slaves wanted to maintain proper decorum even if the foreign guest remained oblivious of social etiquette. At last the carriage rolled to a stop in front of an Italianate with a fourth-story cupola even grander than the Henthorne mansion.

"Thank you, Thomas. Please return home with the carriage."

He placed a stepping block over the gutter. "Shouldn't I stay to take you on to Miz Wilkes?"

Amanda chose not to admonish his obvious eavesdropping. "No, I want Mrs. Henthorne to have her carriage. I'll ask the Stewarts' driver to take me." She hurried up the walkway to circumvent more questions.

Fortuitously, Rosalyn Stewart was reading in the parlor when the butler announced her.

"Miss Amanda Dunn, madam."

"Miss Dunn, what a pleasure to see you." Rosalyn rose to her feet and met her in the center of the thick Persian rug. "Isn't Mrs. Henthorne with you?" She slipped an arm around Amanda's waist as though they were old friends instead of new acquaintances.

"Not today, I'm afraid, but she sends her fondest regards. The heat plays havoc with her stamina."

"My, yes. I've grown frightfully sluggish myself." Rosalyn guided her guest back to the divan before launching into a detailed account of her work with the ladies' auxiliary, in addition to hours spent with the Confederate Sanitary Commission. For a quarter hour she explained her endeavors, which sounded anything but slothful. If the maid hadn't interrupted with a tray of sandwiches, iced cakes, and pot of tea, Amanda may have fallen asleep from sympathetic fatigue if not outright boredom.

"Ah, here's our tea. Shall I pour, Miss Dunn?"

"Yes, cream and sugar, please." Amanda took a watercress sandwich from the maid's tray and nibbled politely.

"Forgive me for rattling on endlessly. What news do you hear from home? I trust your mother is well?"

If permitted, Rosalyn would orchestrate a lively comparison between American and British fashion and customs. "Mama is well, but I actually have a rather urgent matter to discuss with you," she said, setting her cup carefully in its saucer.

"What is it, my dear? How can I be of service?" Rosalyn's forehead furrowed with concern.

"I have a serious situation to discuss with the judge. May I call on him at his chambers?" Amanda couldn't stop her hands from trembling.

Rosalyn dropped her half-eaten pastry on a china plate. "I can do better than that. Court isn't in session today. Miles is reading arguments and depositions in his home office. I'm sure he would welcome a break from the tedium." Patting her perfect coiffure of curls, she stood with the bearing of a queen.

"He won't be angry with my unannounced disruption?"

"Of course not. He loves to assist damsels in distress, especially one who's young, pretty, and English." Rosalyn laughed and reached for Amanda's hand as though she were a child. She led her down a portrait-lined hallway to a set of double doors. After the briefest of knocks, Rosalyn entered the paneled library. "Miles?" she said sweetly. "Look who has joined us. Amanda Dunn, Mrs. Henthorne's sister. She has a matter of upmost urgency to discuss with you."

Judge Stewart peered up from his stack of books and papers. His glasses sat askew on his nose, his silvery hair was ruffled and mussed, and his collar was undone. "Miss Dunn, do come in. Please forgive my appearance," he said genially as he reached for his discarded cravat.

"Please don't trouble yourself on my account, sir." With Rosalyn's prodding, Amanda approached his cluttered desk. "I'm so sorry to impose on you, but I knew of no one else who could assist with this conundrum. You're my only hope."

"Goodness, this sounds dire. Speak frankly, Miss Dunn. Allow me to rectify the matter if I can."

Amanda launched into a disjointed plea for Nate's release from jail, augmenting the little she knew from his note with pure fiction to sway the man to her side. "I assure you, sir, Nathaniel Cooper is not a Union sympathizer. He's loyal to North Carolina and has never lived anywhere else. His reluctance to enlist stems from his pacifist convictions passed down from his parents."

How easily the fabrications rolled off her tongue. She knew almost nothing about his parents, least of all whether or not they would take up arms. Is this what love did to a person—allowed them to lie effortlessly? Because at that moment, she knew she loved him and would say or do anything to keep him safe. "Please believe me, Judge Stewart. Nathaniel is no traitor to the Confederacy."

He removed his quill pen from the inkwell. "Our militia has gone too far. They would demand that all men fight for the Cause, yet if so who would be left to keep our society from crumbling into chaos? I remember talking to Mr. Cooper at length about the great philosophers Immanuel Kant and Jean-Jacques Rousseau and Adam Smith and their theories as to how men might be governed in the future. He struck me as a man of learning and conviction, not cowardice." He pulled a sheet of foolscap from his drawer. "I shall personally vouch for his integrity and usefulness in Wilmington and issue a directive that Mr. Cooper be released at once."

While he scribbled and scrawled, Amanda felt her stiff back begin to relax. She unwittingly had tensed every muscle in her body. "I don't know how to thank you, sir. I will be forever in your debt."

"Didn't I tell you the judge would be happy to help?" Rosalyn hugged her around the shoulders. The woman demonstrated more affection than Amanda's own mother.

"Mr. Cooper has become dear to me," she said, as though obligated to offer explanation for her behavior.

Rosalyn chuckled. "That fact was apparent to everyone at the dinner party."

Judge Stewart blotted his signature and sealed the wax with

his family crest. "I had better accompany you downtown, Miss Dunn. The local militia is filled more with rabble than gentlemen these days. Send for the carriage, my dear, and I will join you ladies in the *porte cochere* in a few moments," he said, smiling at his wife as he rolled down his shirtsleeves.

Amanda's eyes filled with tears as Rosalyn led her from the library. "Splendid! I shall ride along too. I don't mean to make light of this, but I welcome any diversion to my frightfully dull afternoons."

Ten

It was all Amanda could do to sit still in the Stewarts' stuffy, enclosed brougham. Once they arrived at their destination, the judge insisted she remain in the carriage because "jails were no place for ladies of a delicate nature." She didn't feel as though her nature was very delicate. If Rosalyn hadn't ridden along too, Amanda may have followed Judge Stewart into the forbidding brick building. What if the local militia refused to recognize civil authority? What if Nate had already been transferred to the brig at the Confederate fort? One troubling possibility after another came to mind while the judge was inside.

Just as the last of her patience ran out, Judge Stewart and a haggard Nate Cooper appeared in the doorway. He wore no hat or frock coat, his shirt was badly wrinkled, and his vest flapped open. Upon closer inspection, Amanda spotted the reason why. "All his buttons are gone," she murmured.

Rosalyn leaned toward the window. "Be thankful he still has

his boots. I've heard the jailers are less reputable than their prisoners—no offense intended to Mr. Cooper." She smiled comfortingly at Amanda before settling back as her husband and Nate entered the carriage.

"You sit there, Mr. Cooper, next to Miss Dunn," said the judge. "She was very brave to speak to me on your behalf."

"I am grateful for your intervention, sir, and to you, Miss Dunn," Nate murmured, locking gazes with her.

"I see they stole your buttons. Did they treat you miserably? Did they refuse to provide food? You look thinner than I recall." Amanda prattled on as though *she* had just been released from confinement.

His pale face brightened measurably with a smile. "Worry not. I spent only two days incarcerated thanks to your swift action and the judge's mercy. No one can lose much weight in so short a time."

"Was it loathsome, Mr. Cooper? Did the air smell foul and were the walls crawling with vermin?" Rosalyn pressed a hand to her throat.

"Where do you hear such things?" asked the judge, aghast.

"At sewing guild, my dear." His wife's focus remained on Nathaniel.

"No, Mrs. Stewart. My window caught the night breeze and my treatment was relatively humane. When I refused moldy bread and rice, the guard said the meal was the equal to those served at the fort."

Judge Stewart cleared his throat. "Enough talk about bad food. Why don't you and Miss Dunn join us for dinner tonight? Our cook works magic with she-crab soup."

Amanda tried to look encouraging, but Nate shook his head. "Thank you, sir, but I'm eager to check on my store. Besides, I have inconvenienced you enough for one day. Perhaps Miss Dunn can be persuaded."

"What say you, my dear? Shall we take you home or back to the Henthornes'?" Rosalyn's gaze rotated between them.

"If you don't mind, I would also like to be dropped off at Cooper's Greengrocery. I won't be able to sleep until I hear every detail about his arrest."

Rosalyn hid her smile even as her husband laughed heartily. "A woman unafraid to speak her mind? I hope that affliction doesn't spread across America. I already have a hard enough time winning arguments at home." Squeezing his wife's hand, the judge barked orders out the window to the footman.

All too soon the brougham rolled to a stop on Water Street. Amanda stepped down to the sidewalk in front of Nate's beloved shop.

He shook hands with his protector. "I will never forget your kindness, sir. Thank you again."

"Nonsense. It's my sworn duty to rectify injustice wherever I find it. In your case, it was also my pleasure. Keep that signed affidavit on your person. There might be other zealous recruiters to contend with in the future. My signature will not be questioned in Wilmington."

Nate bowed low to the couple as their carriage clattered away.

Suddenly alone with him, Amanda was utterly flummoxed as to how to act. "Shall we check the store?" she asked.

"Might as well get it over with." Nate turned his key in the lock. She followed him into the familiar interior, which seemed forlorn without recent attention. Dust motes swirled as they walked up the center aisle. Nate sniffed the stale air. "Thank goodness Odom removed the bucket of fresh fish I had out back. I sent word that the Simses should take home any produce that might spoil. All in all, I see nothing amiss. With food riots in other parts of the Carolinas, I'm a very lucky man." When he turned around, they were face-to-face a foot apart. "And I'm not talking solely about my livelihood." His hand reached for her but then hesitated. "I couldn't think of anything but you when they arrested me. Now I feel ashamed for burdening you in such a way, perhaps even placing you in danger. Forgive me, Amanda."

"Nonsense. You are my friend if you still cannot accept what my kiss implied. And how was I in danger? Sipping tea in the Stewarts' parlor or perhaps riding downtown in their luxurious carriage?" She clucked her tongue.

"How did it look to Judge Stewart that I relied on a woman to rescue me? Literature, at the very least, mandates the male of the species be the chivalrous one." Nate lifted a towel from the hook to dust the counter, a not very subtle avoidance maneuver.

Amanda yanked on his arm like a spoiled child seeking attention. "Do you value Judge Stewart's opinion over personal liberty? What do we care what others in town think about us? Our opinions of each other should take precedence."

Nate filled a cloth sack with food to take to the Simses. "Did Judge Stewart improve your debate skills during the ride to the jail?"

"He did not. This is a gift inherited from my papa, and a natural reaction when someone you care about behaves like a mule."

A ghost of smile flitted across his face. "Please don't think me ungrateful, Miss Dunn, but now I feel even more unworthy of you." He backed away from her. "I will secure the door and then walk you home. Your sister must be worried about you."

She opened her mouth to argue, but he disappeared into the stockroom. Why was he acting this way? She had assumed his request for help and her immediate reaction would cement their bond, not drive them apart.

Five minutes later they were hurrying down Water Street toward Orange Street as though the waterfront were ablaze. "Have we entered a foot race, Mr. Cooper?"

"Excuse me." He stopped short next to a garishly painted bakery. "But we shouldn't rile your brother-in-law more than we already have."

Amanda pulled her arm from his grip. "Nate, I'm not taking another step until you tell me what's gotten into you!" She fixed him with a glare that would have turned a lesser man to stone.

He considered for several moments. "Very well. I feel you acted on my behalf without full knowledge of the circumstances or the truth regarding my political convictions."

"What do you mean?" She moved under an awning to avoid a sudden light drizzle.

"Judge Stewart read a flowery affidavit attesting to my loyalty to the Confederacy and my usefulness in Wilmington as a civilian. They released me based on his word. Yet there was some truth to the militia's charges. I *have* avoided conscription on several occasions, and not because of religious convictions, so draft-dodging is correct. And I won't fight to preserve slavery. I hope to see our nation restored without the abominable institution. I even went so far as to attend a pro-Union rally not long ago. So I have played you and Judge Stewart falsely. Your actions were based on incorrect assumptions." He grimaced as though in pain.

"That's what troubles you? *We* may have played Judge Stewart falsely, and I also abhor slavery. My behavior was based on loyalty to you, not the South. If you recall, I'm British." She linked her arm through his. "Can we proceed at a respectable pace that won't cause me to faint?"

He bobbed his head to hide a blush. "I'm certain you have never fainted in your life."

"And I don't plan to start today. Now tell me about that pro-Union rally. Was it here in Wilmington?"

"It was terrifying, if you must know. It was held in an abandoned barn outside of town. Crazed zealots were bent on destruction. They were no different from Quantrill's raiders in Missouri. I'll have no part of waging war on innocent citizens. There you have it, Amanda. You are a foreigner stranded in an alien country, whereas I am a native son without affiliation to either side."

"Then we shall be a land of two and take comfort in each other."

They crossed the street, dodging puddles that had quickly formed from the sudden shower. Nate remained silent so long she thought he hadn't heard her. Then he circled her waist with his arm and squeezed until she thought her heart, if not her ribs, would break.

If ever he could have used something memorable to say, it was during the twenty-minute walk back to the Henthorne mansion. Yet for some reason Nate wasn't embarrassed by the silence. With Amanda's small hand in his, he neither minded the gentle rain on his cheeks nor the steep hill separating the waterfront from Third Street. It felt good to have her next to his side. All the unpleasantness from the last two days, along with his dragging her into trouble, fell away. An exquisite possibility that their relationship could thrive took root and began to grow.

When they reached the home of her sister, Amanda turned her perfect, oval-shaped face up to his. "Thank you for walking me back, sir. I know I should go inside, but I fear life will be dreadfully dull compared to my last twenty-four hours."

Nate laughed and brought her hand up to his lips. "I would hope so, dear heart. No well-born lady should be expected to save the day more than once or twice during a lifetime." He kissed the back of her fingers.

Amanda withdrew her hand. "If I did save the day, I feel my reward should be greater than that kind of kiss."

Glancing in both directions on the shadowy sidewalk, Nate leaned down and kissed her with all the passion he could muster.

THE LAST HEIRESS 🜊 183

"An insufficient token of my gratitude and esteem to be sure, but it's a start."

Grinning, Amanda opened her eyes. "Ah, much better. Good night, Mr. Cooper, until the next time our paths cross."

"Good night, Miss Dunn. Sleep well with pleasant dreams." He bowed as he'd seen Jackson do on several occasions.

Amanda hurried up the steps and slipped into the house without waiting for the butler to open the door. Nate remained under the canopy of a crepe myrtle tree, hoping to catch one last glimpse of her in the parlor window. But the visage peering into the night behind leaded glass belonged to haughty, aristocratic Jackson Henthorne. If contempt had a scent, Nate would have caught a whiff wafting on the night breeze. This was a man who placed strict boundaries around himself and those he cared about. How far would he go to keep a man like Nate from marrying into his family? Would he speak to Judge Stewart about rescinding the affidavit? Or perhaps truss up Amanda, stuff her in a gunny sack, and lock her in a cabin until the ship was away from the American coast? After a final look at the residence of his beloved, Nate walked back home with a heart already aching without her.

Nate found his landlord at the table when he entered the Simses' kitchen. Despite his overwhelming fatigue, the sight lifted Nate's spirits. "Odom, why are you still up? Did bad dreams get the better of you tonight?"

"Nate." Speaking in an exaggerated whisper, Odom jumped to his feet. "What a relief to see you." He wrapped his arms around his friend and thumped his back as though he were choking on a fish bone. "I couldn't sleep until I heard the news, but I didn't want to keep my missus awake. This is better than any message, even from a nice lady like Miss Dunn."

Nate tried to wriggle away as Odom fired off a rapid succession of questions. "Did Miss Dunn come to the jail? How did she get you released? Will your arrest cause trouble for her with her family?"

Nate slumped into a chair. "I can explain if you let me sit down."

"Yes, sit, sit. I'll pour you a glass of milk."

Nate let the cool liquid run down his parched throat. Then he filled in the details of his saga, beginning at this store and ending with a memorable kiss at the Henthorne hitching post.

"I'm glad Rufus was there during your arrest or we might not have known what happened," Odom said, lowering the guttering lamp wick.

"A fortuitous turn of events." Nate finished the glass of milk, which Odom promptly refilled.

"My son has a knack for locating Miss Dunn when she's not in the company of her sister."

"I'm grateful to Rufus and to you."

"Glad to help, especially since this turned out so well." Odom gave his suspenders a satisfied snap.

Nate stared at him in confusion. "I don't follow you. Are you certain you heard me right? I was arrested by the Rebel militia, accused of treason, thrown into jail, and fed moldy food. I endangered your son and Miss Dunn just to gain freedom that could be brief in duration. Who knows what Judge Stewart will do if he finds out the charges were true? Besides, I don't work for Henthorne and Sons in a *crucial* capacity as the judge's affidavit states."

Odom leaned back in his chair. "I listened to you just fine, but I heard plenty more than that." Holding up a hand, he extended his index finger. "One, I know that Miss Dunn practically levitated from her chair to help you." He extended a second finger. "She wasted no time in getting you released and then insisted on going with you to check your store." Another finger joined the other two. "And three, she demanded a proper kiss for her payment. That means one thing to me—the gal is in love with you. I would say you should be the happiest man on earth, Nate Cooper." Odom folded his hands like an attorney resting his court case.

"That was my conclusion too, for what it's worth. But what future does such an ill-matched couple have? If rumors of my pro-Union sentiments get around, customers will abandon me for Baxter's Market. And a man without a livelihood has poor prospects for marriage." Nate studied his reflection in the windowpane. "Miss Dunn was raised in a big house with a staff of servants. Now I have less to offer her than before."

"I had worse prospects than you, but Ruth still agreed to marry me, making me the happiest man on earth."

Nate smiled at his friend. "I'm open to suggestions if any come to mind. Seeing your and Ruth's contentment is proof enough for me."

Odom refilled his own mug. "You fixate on Miss Dunn's wealth, assuming her life was rosy at home because of it. Maybe it was, true enough, but rich folks can be unhappy, hard as that is for us to believe. Yet she sees something in *you* she likes, so stop trying to fit into the Henthornes' world. Ask her to spend more time in yours."

"Do you mean invite her to dinner again? I know she enjoyed the evening with your family." Nate felt a surge of hope.

Odom leaned back to study the plaster ceiling. "This weekend Ruth wants to visit her aunt in Wrightsville. Why not invite Miss Dunn for supper? The two of you won't have a fancy cook if you get hitched, so why not show her you know how to put supper on the table?"

Nate burst out laughing. "What on earth could I cook for her? All I know are simple recipes from home."

"Ruth and I sampled some of those when you weren't looking.

They weren't half bad. Decide on your favorites and put your best foot forward. Owning a store certainly comes in handy, and if you need it, Ruth can give you cooking advice."

Nate's mind whirled with ideas as Odom pushed up from the table. "Now that our favorite draft dodger is home safe, I'm going to bed. Don't stay up too late. You have a store to open in the morning and only a couple of days to plan this supper." Shuffling from the room, he paused in the doorway, the hard day of labor evident in his stride. "But if you permit me one final piece of advice, don't question life so much. Sometimes God offers gifts we don't deserve, and in the case of His Son, we never will. The best thing to do is say thank you and try to be as worthy as you can. Miss Dunn may be one of those gifts."

"I guess I haven't spent enough time thinking about God since my ma died," Nate said softly, rubbing the back of his neck.

"I know, but He thinks about you all the time." Odom looked over his shoulder. "And God can be very patient."

After his landlord went to bed, Nate closed his eyes and tried to picture his mother. Faye Cooper had worn her dark hair in a single plait down her back. Her roughened, chore-rough hands had felt soft against his face. The woman could holler across the valley, yet she still whispered prayers each night next to his bed. How he had missed her when she died after months of sickness. Nate rubbed his eyes with his fists but couldn't dislodge the memory of his twelfth birthday dinner: Fried chicken, honeyed sweet potatoes, fresh corn on the cob dripping with butter, and apple pie for dessert. He and Joshua had eaten until their stomachs hurt.

Suddenly ravenous, he scrambled to his feet. He devoured three dry biscuits from breakfast and a wedge of cheese before realizing he had the perfect menu for Saturday. He'd never eaten a more enjoyable meal. Finding a scrap of paper, he scribbled a brief note to Ruth, went to bed, and slept better than he had in weeks.

Abigail tiptoed into the bathing chamber for the second time that morning. Crouching over a basin, she voided her stomach of the toast and boiled eggs she had just consumed. She tried to be as quiet as possible so not to disturb Jackson outside on their private gallery, yet her best efforts were for naught.

"Great Scott, Abigail! Are you ill again?" her husband asked anxiously as he hovered behind her.

She shook her head, unable to speak for a moment. "It's nothing to worry yourself about. Go enjoy your breakfast." She rose clumsily to her feet and filled a clean basin from the pitcher.

He pulled out his pocket watch to consult. "Then you should get dressed. If we don't hurry we'll miss church. The service starts in forty minutes."

Abigail rinsed out her mouth, washed her face, and tried to step past him, but he was too quick. He grabbed hold of her wrist. "You're pale as a ghost and look ready to faint. How long have you been ill? If that Robert Peterson carried swamp fever into the city, I'll summon his second."

"You'll do nothing of the sort, my dear. I'm fit as a fiddle." Sidling past him into their bedchamber, she rummaged through her armoire for a fresh dressing gown.

"You've been sick several mornings this week and haven't eaten more than half a meal in days. I insist that you see Dr. Barnes tomorrow. Perhaps he can supply an herb or tonic to quell your discomfort."

"Absolutely not. I'll not quaff any herbal potion without knowing how it might affect the baby."

Jackson had been tying his cravat in the mirror when his fingers froze on the silk fabric. "Baby? What baby?" He spun on one heel, his jaw dropping open. "What are you saying, Abigail?"

She closed the armoire with a thud. "I'm saying that to the best of my knowledge I'm with child. We should have a new Henthorne by spring if not sooner. All the signs are evident."

"Have you spoken to anyone yet?"

"Only Salome." She tied back her thick hair with a ribbon.

"You may be with child, yet you've consulted only our *cook*?" Jackson gently gripped her forearms.

"Amanda, Estelle, Josie, Helene—none of them have given birth. Salome has. I trust her expertise to answer practical, simple questions."

"I insist that you see Dr. Barnes—for verification, if nothing else. How can we trust an uneducated slave?"

"Because she has borne four healthy children." Abigail patted his chest with both hands. "Allow me another month or two and then I shall. I want to be further along before I visit that gossipmonger. Every woman at First Presbyterian will know our news before my carriage returns home. I want no sorrowful faces and no words of consolation if events don't proceed as planned."

Jackson shrugged his shoulders. "Fine, if you insist, but I could accompany you and threaten him with my horsewhip."

"Such an idea on the Sabbath!" Abigail sighed with disapproval. "Go to church, husband. Pray to be saved from your violent urges and for a full-term pregnancy. I don't believe I've seen the last of my basin yet." Abigail strolled toward the French doors for cooler air.

But he remained at her heels. "I am thunderstruck with joy, my love. I intended to give you this at dinner, but I can't wait another minute." He drew a small box from his weskit pocket, fumbling as though his fingers had stiffened without warning.

Abigail expected a cameo or perhaps a silk scarf from a Parisian artist. What she found instead took her breath away. She lifted a gold-and-diamond sunburst broach from its nest of cotton. At least twenty smaller diamonds orbited a center stone the size of a robin's egg. "Is that a diamond?" she gasped.

"Yes. I hope you like it." Jackson's smile stretched across his face. "A factor from Charleston was selling this creation on behalf of his client. Many fine families are losing everything in other parts of the South."

"I hope this didn't belong to a lady I know." She held the broach in a beam of sunlight, the refraction of colors dazzling with brilliance.

"Rest assured that you'll never cross paths with the bauble's former owner. She's an elderly South Carolinian who never travels."

"Thank you, Jackson. I've never seen a lovelier piece of jewelry. But will such extravagance one day cause us hardship like that Charleston matriarch?"

"That woman's husband failed to adjust to current circumstances, a man without vision for opportunities during wartime. I don't sit on my haunches sipping bourbon and lamenting the past each night. My partners and I are poised to reap great profits during the Yankee blockade. By the end of the war, the Henthornes will be richer than any of our friends, perhaps wealthier than anyone in Wilmington."

"But what if the Yankees prevail? I've heard General Sherman is unstoppable. Despite our noble intentions, the Union army never seems to run out of soldiers."

"Win, lose—the final outcome is immaterial. Profits are to be made *now*." He pulled on his frock coat and shot his cuffs. "Our wildest dreams are about to come true for you, me, and our new son or daughter. While the South rebuilds, we will travel to Europe and live like kings. My father can run the business here if I leave a reliable foreman in charge. You shall be my queen."

Abigail threw her arms around his neck. "Oh, Jackson, you're so good to me. What have I done to deserve a husband like you?"

He kissed her forehead tenderly. "You loved and trusted me when I was young and wet behind the ears. You left your home, your parents, and your twin sister and took a chance in a new world. And now my fondest wish is about to come true." His fingers skimmed her belly.

"I never regretted my decision." She stretched up on tiptoes to kiss him. "Please go to church so that the dowagers don't gossip about the Henthornes."

Jackson bowed and went downstairs to the front hall. He would have to sprint to services if Thomas didn't have the carriage already hitched. But a tardy arrival was of no concern.

For the first time in months, Abigail felt blissfully content.

That evening, while Jackson entertained Papa Henthorne in the library and her mother-in-law napped in the best guest suite, Abigail wandered to the front verandah. True to Josie's information, her sister sat reading a thick, leather-bound volume. "Did you find something interesting in the library?"

Amanda glanced up. "An interesting tale about the French and Indian War, but James Fenimore Cooper's style can be tedious. How are you feeling?"

"Perfectly fine, which you probably deduced at dinner as you and Jackson constantly monitor my food consumption."

"Those ribs of beef were delicious. Give my compliments to Salome."

Abigail ignored the culinary praise, choosing instead to broach another thorn in her foot. "Jackson ran into Representative Wilkes at church this morning with his lovely wife. Sarah asked him to convey a rather peculiar message to both of us."

Amanda's grip tightened on the binding. "What message could she have for me?"

Abigail plucked the book from her fingers. "That she's holding us to our promise of an afternoon call. I found that peculiar because I thought you had fulfilled that obligation."

Amanda appeared stricken. "I ended up spending the entire afternoon with Rosalyn Stewart...and her husband."

"What would you have to talk about with Judge Stewart?" Assessing her sister's expression, Abigail added, "And I demand the truth."

"I needed his help, and he graciously obliged."

"What on earth could he do for you that Jackson couldn't? Stop evading the question."

"Judge Stewart had Nathaniel released from jail by attesting to his loyalty to the Confederacy. He'd been arrested as a draft dodger. Had the judge not intervened, Nate would be in the stockade at Fort Fisher."

"Maybe that's where he belongs," Abigail hissed between her teeth, hoping no one could hear their conversation.

"Must I remind you that Jackson never saw the need to enlist?"

"Everyone knows his work is crucial to the Confederate Cause. The beef and pork he imports feeds thousands of soldiers in General Lee's army. Nathaniel's endeavors feed a few dozen ruffians on the docks."

"Those ruffians load and unload the blockade runners, or did you think your husband handled that single-handedly too?"

"A point well taken, I suppose." Abigail shifted uncomfortably, needing to loosen her corset. "Frankly I don't care whether your beau joins the army or not, but I hope Jackson doesn't find out you enlisted *his* friends to bail out Mr. Cooper. You know that Jackson doesn't like him and would prefer your attentions were directed elsewhere."

Amanda tucked an errant curl into her schoolmarm bun. "Do you intend to tell him?"

"I don't, because I remember what it was like when others tried to mandate who we loved. Besides, Jackson has more important matters on his mind. However, considering men gossip worse than women, I wouldn't count on him not finding out."

Jackson stood on the wharf for a long while after the *Roanoke* left the dock, bound for the Atlantic. His ship—his and the Peterson brothers'. What an extraordinary feeling it was to own not one but two fleet steamships capable of outrunning any of the lumbering Yankee gunboats. True to Robert Peterson's promise, the side-wheelers arrived in port within fourteen days of their momentous meeting at his office.

The *Lady Adelaine* had already departed Wilmington loaded with tobacco bound for Bermuda. European markets clamored for American tobacco and would pay dearly. His shortsighted banker had originally balked about the amount of the loan. He felt Henthorne and Sons assets to be worthy of only half the amount. But the mere mention of the banker's gambling debts garnered the man's cooperation. And Jackson hadn't been forced to produce title to the Third Street mansion as collateral. All the better, because risking the roof over his family's head didn't sit well with him, especially considering Abigail's delicate condition. How he longed for a son or daughter, far more than he revealed. Part of their loving union would carry on long after their bleached bones crumbled to dust in the cemetery at Oakdale.

Consulting his watch in the fading light, Jackson realized he must head to the club if he still wished to be served a meal. New seating for dinner stopped at nine. Abigail and Amanda were dining at the Kendall House with Mrs. Stewart while the judge traveled out of town. What an odd friendship to bloom. The Dunn

sisters were young and spirited, whereas Mrs. Stewart was dignified, distinguished, and sixty-five at the very minimum. Perhaps
Abigail was preparing to assume her rightful place in Wilmington society.

Pivoting on his heel, Jackson headed toward Market Street at a
brisk pace. However, he didn't get far before four bushy derelicts
stepped into his path from the alley between warehouses.

"What's the big hurry, guv'na?" One gap-toothed giant spoke
with a strong Irish brogue.

Jackson bristled at the audacious lack of respect. "I hurry
because there is some place I wish to be," he said with feigned
sincerity.

"I'm thinkin' you're gonna be a tad late." This observation came
from a scrawny wastrel who accompanied his comment with a
sharp jab to Jackson's shoulder.

"See here, you drunkard. If you don't crawl back to the gutter,
I'll have you clamped into chains and leg irons. This town doesn't
tolerate—"

Whatever had been his conjecture regarding Wilmington's tol-
erance for rowdy behavior died on his lips. The giant of a man
delivered a punch to Jackson's midsection, robbing him of air
and the ability to speak for several moments. While he gasped for
breath, a familiar face stepped from the shadows. "Do ya remember me, Mr. Henthorne?" asked Elias Hornsby, grinning like a
madman.

Jackson stared into the watery eyes of the sea captain, strug-
gling to enunciate a single word. Hornsby's thugs jostled him
rudely from both sides. Finally he managed a simple sentence.
"Of course I remember you."

"That rather surprises me, considering your loads of cotton and
tobacco left on the *Lady Adelaine* earlier and now on the *Roanoke*."
Hornsby spat on the plank sidewalk, just missing Jackson's boot.

He attempted to move away from the pack, but the giant clamped a viselike grip on his upper arm. *How does a man find enough to eat to maintain three hundred pounds during wartime?* "The sole reason I utilized those particular vessels is because I own them." Lifting his chin, Jackson tried to resurrect his dignity.

Hornsby's fingers clenched into fists. "You think I don't know that? I spend my life on the docks—right here." He stomped his foot. "Not up the hill on Third Street, sipping tea from porcelain cups with fancy ladies in big hoop dresses." Waving his little finger in the air, Hornsby used a foppish voice to describe their afternoon custom.

The blood drained from Jackson's face. "You've been watching my family?"

"Not me personally. I'm a busy man. But I do make a habit of keeping tabs on business associates." Hornsby inched closer, the odor of cheap whiskey emanating from his stained frock coat.

"I take offense to your boorish tactics, sir." Jackson squirmed to rid himself of the meaty hand on his arm to no avail. "I signed no contract of exclusivity with you. I purchased two steamers, and why wouldn't I make use of my investment?"

"Who's captaining them boats?"

"Captain Russell mans the wheel of the *Lady Adelaine*, while Captain Philips commands the crew on the *Roanoke*."

Hornsby spat a second time into the gutter. "Fancy-coats, that's all they are. One good blow comes up at sea and those lily-livers will sink your ships."

An ominous frisson ran up Jackson's spine. "Russell and Philips came highly recommended."

"By who?" demanded Hornsby. "The blokes who sold you those steamers? I didn't take you for a fool, Henthorne."

Jackson considered a right jab to the captain's beer-bloated gut, but his four companions provided a convincing deterrent. "I appreciate your insight, Captain, and I will pray my boats prove stalwart in a hurricane."

Hornsby snorted with contempt. "I don't give a fig whether your ships sink or not, but I need to rectify a lit'l misconception of yours. When the *Countess Marie* arrives in port, you'll load the next consignment onto her at our previous contract price. If you get more goods to export, then you can fill the holds of the *Adelaine* and *Roanoke*. But I got a crew to pay and nobody seems to have cotton to ship but you. Take a look around. Do these boys look like they plan to stand idle while you grow richer than Midas?" The captain thumped on Jackson's chest with a stubby index finger.

"That shouldn't be a problem. With the cotton I have coming from South Carolina, I'll have enough to keep your ship and mine busy."

"You've got plenty to lose, Henthorne, if you don't. And I ain't talkin' about your fancy new side-wheelers."

After a few more hard jabs to his ribs, Hornsby and his band of miscreants left him and disappeared into the dark alley. Jackson stood for a long while until his heart rate slowed and a wave of nausea passed. How could he feel sick without a morsel of food in his belly? On rubbery legs he ambled toward his club, but thoughts of a delicious supper were long gone. He needed either bourbon or maybe his preacher, because he might need a miracle after all.

Jackson entered his club and headed straight for the quiet reading room. He was in no mood for the convivially of the main hall. Instead, he slumped into a wing chair and buried his head in his hands. Hornsby's bullying tactics had left him uneasy. Not due to the fact he hadn't stood up to the assault. Only an insane man would take on five men, all of whom were well experienced with barroom brawling. No, his anxiety stemmed from his own bold assertions. He had no idea how much cotton and tobacco would find its way to Wilmington with the current condition of roads and rail lines. Peterson could have fallen prey to a Union sharpshooter for all he knew.

"May I bring you something to drink, Mr. Henthorne? And have you dined yet this evening, sir?"

He peered up at one of the club's distinguished butlers. "No, I haven't eaten, but I'm not in the mood for company tonight. Could you please bring me some coffee?"

"Of course, sir. May I also bring you a sandwich? It would be breaking club policy, but I believe an exception could be made. They served a fine roast beef this evening in the dining room."

"Thank you, Marcus. That is very kind of you." Jackson discretely passed the freeman a gold coin.

Sliding it into his pocket, Marcus bowed and backed away. But Jackson's solitude proved short lived.

"I wondered if you would have the guts to show your face, Henthorne."

Jackson spotted Michael Frazier, a tobacco factor of dubious repute, in the doorway. His notoriety at the gaming tables far surpassed his reputation for brokering agricultural goods. "Why would I need guts to visit a club I belong to?"

Frazier bumped into several tables as he tried to cross the room. "Because you're nothing but a thief and a coward." The slur accompanying his words confirmed his inebriated state.

Jackson jumped to his feet. "Lower your voice, sir, or I'll have you thrown into the street. Now tell me what this is about."

Frazier braced a fleshy hand on the back of a chair. "You stole my ships out from under me. I commissioned the *Lady Adelaine* and the *Roanoke*. I staked everything I had on those steamers."

It took only moments for the pieces of a puzzle to fit together in his mind, including Peterson's reluctance to name the original buyer for fear of social embarrassment.

"It seems that everything you had wasn't adequate, sir. Your deal had already fallen through when I was approached about the ships' availability."

"That broker may have continued negotiating with me if you and that Charleston swindler hadn't jumped in. Your father never would have stooped so low." Frazier swayed on his feet.

Jackson glanced uneasily around the room. Although no other member sat within earshot, their conversation was attracting attention. "I will ask you again to lower your voice. Sit down, Frazier, and we'll discuss this like gentlemen."

"What is there to talk about? You stole my ships out from under me and now I'm ruined. That broker won't even return my deposit. You should be ashamed if you have no more honor than this." The tobacco factor staggered from the room, leaving chairs askew and one overturned table in his wake.

Jackson was left with a churning gut and accusatory glares from his peers. He slumped into a chair facing the window. When the butler appeared at this side, he barely acknowledged the man.

"Here is your sandwich and coffee, sir."

"Just leave it, Marcus."

"Will there be anything else, sir?"

Jackson gripped the chair's arms as though clinging for his life. "Yes. See that I'm not interrupted for the rest of the night. Can't a man get some peace and quiet even at his club?" A hitch in his voice betrayed the fragile state of his emotions. He needed to gather his wits before returning home or his astute wife would demand an explanation before he took off his hat.

Eleven

The next morning he hummed a lively tune while completing his chores. Then he penned a formal invitation to Miss Amanda Dunn in his best script on a sheet of parchment from the millinery store next door.

Dear Miss Dunn,

Would you honor me with your presence at dinner at the home of Odom Sims on Saturday? Festivities will commence at eight o'clock sharp. For your convenience, a carriage will arrive at the Henthornes' at half past seven. If no previous commitment demands your attention, kindly give verbal acknowledgment to my emissary, Rufus Sims.

Your devoted servant,
Nathaniel Cooper

When the ink had dried, he added a gob of sealing wax and used an odd-shaped bean for an imprint. Next he sent word to the livery stable that he needed to hire a carriage on Saturday night, along with a note to his poultry purveyor for two fresh hens, plucked, disjointed, and ready to fry. For the rest of the day, he could barely keep his mind on his work. When one young matron requested three pounds of flour, he filled her sack with ground cornmeal, much to her dismay.

That afternoon he closed up shop early and walked home. The person he needed was sitting at the kitchen table practicing arithmetic sums. "What'cha doin' here already, Mr. Nate?" asked Rufus. "I was hopin' to help clean the store after I finished this homework." The boy thrummed his fingers on the last row of problems.

"I have too much on my mind to worry about dusting cans of peas," Nate said as he hung his hat on a peg. "If it's all right with your mother, would you deliver a letter for me to Miss Dunn? I'll pay you five cents."

Closing his book, Rufus swiveled in his chair, his last five problems forgotten. "Can I, Ma?"

Ruth nodded. "As long as you don't dillydally. Supper's almost ready."

Grinning, Rufus said, "You don't have to pay me, Mr. Nate. I like running errands for you. And that house is real fine."

"This is an important job, young man, so don't forgo appropriate compensation," Nate said, chuckling at the boy's perplexed expression.

"Okay, I'll take the nickel. Do you want me to hide in the bushes until I can speak to Miss Dunn alone?" He tugged on his cloth cap.

"Absolutely not. You should walk up to the front door and knock, proper-like. When the butler answers, tell him you have a special delivery for Miss Amanda Dunn."

Shaking her head, Ruth placed her hands on Rufus's shoulders. "Here in North Carolina, deliveries go to the back door, including couriers."

Nate frowned. "Always so many rules to learn. Very well, knock on the back door, but stand up straight and don't mumble. Tell whoever answers that you've been instructed to wait for Miss Dunn's response." He handed Rufus the invitation. "And don't drop it in a puddle."

"I won't, Mr. Nate. Can I go now, Ma?" Rufus hopped from foot to foot.

"Since this dinner is in three days, let's not tarry another moment." Ruth pointed her son toward the door, and he took off like a startled rabbit.

With Rufus gone, Nate and his landlady discussed how to make piecrust, the easiest method of coring and peeling apples, and what spices to add to the cornmeal breading for the chicken. She had just ladled up three bowls of thick fish chowder when Rufus bounded into the kitchen, letting the door slam behind him.

"I seen her, Mr. Nate! I seen Miss Amanda." His words came at a breathless staccato.

"*Saw*, Rufus. You saw Miss Dunn." He smiled while Ruth rolled her eyes.

"That's what I said. I knocked on the door, said I had an important letter, and that I would sit on that stoop till Miz Dunn makes up her mind." Rufus pointed at nothing in particular, as though reliving the event. "Then the lady said, 'Who are you, boy?'"

"I said, 'I'm Rufus Sims.'"

Nate bit the inside of his cheek. "What happened next?"

"The lady just shook her head, made a funny sound, and shut the door. I sat on that stoop for the longest time. Then a different gal gave me a cup of water and a molasses cookie."

Nate made an appropriate murmur of appreciation.

Rufus's eyes turned very bright. "Then, before I had a chance to finish my water, Miss Dunn herself comes out the back door!"

Nate and Ruth produced identical expressions of surprise.

"That's right, with the lady in the apron right on her heels. Miss Dunn said it would be a pleasure to accept and that I should wait one more minute. Then that second gal threw my water into the bushes, filled my cup with cider, and handed me another cookie." Rufus's joy was surpassed only by Nate's. "And then Miss Dunn brung your letter outside with her message at the bottom." With great dramatic flair, Rufus extracted the sheet from inside his shirt.

"You had better read it aloud," said Odom, appearing in the doorway. "We're all in suspense."

Nate took the paper with a trembling hand. "Miss Amanda Dunn accepts your dinner invitation with fond anticipation."

Rufus held up a coin. "Then *she* gave me a nickel too—ten cents, two cookies, and a cup of cider—just for running up the hill and back."

Ruth guided the boy to the tub to wash. "All right, son, let's settle down. Your father is ready to say grace."

Nate reread the ten words twice more and then took his seat. When he bowed his head during Odem's prayer, he added his own silent words of thanks. He finally had more to be grateful about than just food.

Amanda had never so *fondly anticipated* an event in her life. But it didn't take Abigail long to learn she'd received a formal invitation and from whom.

"Regarding this dinner you have been invited to," Abigail asked later that day, "where does Mr. Cooper hope to serve? In the storeroom of his market?"

When Amanda explained that they would be dining in the

Simses' kitchen, without the family present, she thought her sister might faint from shock.

"*Unchaperoned,* just you and Mr. Cooper, in the home of Negroes, no less?" Abigail's face scrunched into a scowl.

"As you noted previously, few members of Wilmington society will witness this breach of decorum, so my reputation—or rather yours—is safe for now."

Abby's nostrils flared in an unbecoming fashion. "A letter to Mama detailing your atrocious behavior will be on Jackson's next ship to Liverpool."

"What can she do? Place me in an ice-cold tub of water the way she did when we were children?"

Abby pressed her hand to her mouth as color drained from her cheeks. "I had almost forgotten her favorite method of punishment. To this day I only take hot baths no matter what the weather." She locked gazes with Amanda. "When did Mama finally stop that cruel tactic of persuasion?"

Amanda softened her stance. "She tried it once after you eloped. I refused to climb into the tub and threatened to run away if she forced me."

Abby's pique over Nate's invitation seemed to fade. "Well, see that you're home by a decent hour. I don't want to explain your whereabouts to Jackson. And if you end up with indigestion, don't come crying to me." She glided away with her chin held high.

During the next three days, Amanda selected her outfit not less than a half dozen times. On the momentous afternoon, she soaked in a tub of rosewater, buffed her fingernails until they shone, and had Helene create a cascade of curls trailing down her back. After applying a touch of henna to her lips and gargling with vinegar, she took a final appraisal in the mirror. Suddenly the sound of Jackson barking orders to the slaves broke her pleasant bubble of anticipation. Hurrying downstairs, Amanda intercepted her sister in the parlor doorway. "Jackson is home early. He'll soon be inside the house."

"Yes, I heard his carriage. We're dining at his attorney's home tonight. He probably wishes to leave with enough time to ride across town."

Amanda blocked her path. "Nate's hired carriage will be here any minute. Where should I say I'm going if Jackson asks me?"

"Of course he will ask," Abby said with a sigh. "I'll try to detain him in the garden. Fetch your shawl and wait beyond the privet hedge. As unseemly as standing on a corner may be, I don't wish to upset my husband. I'll say you have already left for the Kendall House." She strode down the center hall with more than her usual amount of energy.

At first Amanda couldn't fathom Abby's change of heart in regard to deceiving Jackson, but then she remembered that Abby had run away from home to be him. Perhaps she could no longer deny her twin the same right to pursue love. Regardless of the reason, Amanda was grateful. When the carriage turned the corner onto Third Street, she was ready to climb aboard before the coachman slowed to a complete stop.

"Good evening, Miss Dunn." He tipped his top hat. "Let me get that door for you."

"No need. I'm in a bit of a hurry." She hiked up her skirt, jumped inside, and pulled the door shut behind her. Amanda held her breath until the mansion faded from view. But as they neared Castle Street, the butterflies in her stomach took flight. At her destination, she waited patiently until the driver opened the door.

"We're here, miss." He positioned a wooden step and helped her down to the sidewalk.

Amanda inhaled a deep breath when the door opened and Nathaniel stepped onto the porch. He wore a white shirt, black weskit and trousers, a dark cravat…and a red calico apron. She giggled like a schoolgirl at the sight.

Pulling off the apron, he donned a dazzling smile. "You're right on time, Miss Dunn. If you were late I would have to start the biscuits over from scratch. They cannot remain warming in the oven another minute." As he reached her, he extended his elbow. "When should the carriage return for you?"

Temporarily befuddled by the questions—and how utterly handsome he looked—Amanda finally stammered out a meek, "Half past nine should be fine."

"Splendid. That gives me nearly two hours to convince you." Nate nodded to the coachman and the conveyance rolled away, the iron wheels clattering in a cloud of dust.

"Convince me of what, sir?"

"That my culinary expertise in the kitchen, rare among male members of the species, makes me the perfect husband for a woman like you."

Amanda stumbled on the uneven flagstones. "I see your bold self-assurance hasn't abandoned you over the last few days. You have high hopes from one home-cooked dinner." She drew up short. "And what do you mean by a 'woman like you'?"

"If a man has a low opinion of himself, so will others. And I refer to your personal lack of cooking skills."

"Why would you assume that—"

Nate abruptly jumped in front of the door, barring entry, thus she ran headlong into his chest. "I must warn you, Miss Dunn, that the Simses aren't here. If you enter a man's abode alone, your reputation may be compromised. Are you prepared to take marriage vows before a preacher and an armed brother-in-law?"

Amanda ducked around him. "Don't be ridiculous. Jackson would simply shoot you and send me back home, besmirched reputation and all."

Amanda followed the delicious mingled scents of rosemary, basil, cinnamon, and honey to the kitchen. "Goodness, I hope you prepared enough. Everything smells wonderful." She sniffed the air like a hound dog on a trail while pivoting to take in every detail. A kettle of corn bubbled on the stove, fried chicken sat cooling on a platter, and a crusty casserole of something orange was in the center of the pine table. The table had been set with pretty but mismatched china. Tall glasses of milk would quench thirsts instead of bubbly champagne or vintage wine. The jelly jar of wildflowers on the windowsill added the feel of a meadow. All in all, the visual effect took her breath away, making her home-sick for a home that was nothing like this.

Nate extracted a tray of golden biscuits from the oven and placed them in a basket. "What do you think, Amanda?" He sounded less confident than he had five minutes ago.

"I think it all looks delightful. Did Mrs. Sims prepare this before she left except for the biscuits?"

Nate arched his spine with indignation. "I beg your pardon, miss. Ruth left yesterday. Everything you see is *my* doing. I practically broke my neck on the steep slope behind the house picking those flowers."

"Very impressive, sir, but I'll reserve judgment until I taste the food. Appearances can be deceptive." She waited until he pulled out a chair for her before taking a place at the table.

"I stand by my endeavors." Nate carried over platters and bowls and then sat down opposite her. "Will you say grace, Miss Dunn? Odom mandates it in this house."

She bowed her head. "Dear Lord, please let this food taste as good as it looks. Thank You and amen."

"Odom wouldn't be happy with your lack of faith." Clucking his tongue, he handed her the basket of biscuits.

Amanda took one, broke off a piece, and ate. Crusty on the

outside, soft within—it needed no butter or honey. "This is deli-cious! Quick, pass me that chicken." She bit into a plump tender breast, the breading crisp and peppery. "Who taught you to cook like this?" she asked, not hiding her surprise.

Nate took two chicken legs and a scoop of yams. "My mother taught the three of us to cook. She said you never know what life will hand you along the way."

"Are those yams? I would love to try some. We never had them at home." Amanda held up her plate. "Your father was willing to learn to cook?"

"Of course. My pa helped my mother with her chores when his were done. After supper they would sit on the porch shuck-ing peas or coring apples before Ma's canning day. And she would help him plant and harvest corn."

"Your mother worked in the fields?"

"She did. Farming is hard work. During certain times of the year, Pa needed everyone from dawn to dark."

"Just the same, I imagine you had a good life."

Nate issued a dismissive snort. "We survived, some years bet-ter than others. But then my mother got sick and lingered before she died. Good thing my father knew how to cook, because he took care of her and us for a long time."

"He must have loved her very much."

Nate reached for another biscuit, avoiding eye contact. "Yes, he did. When she died, he lost interest in living and took up the bottle. The fact that my brother and I still needed him didn't seem to matter. Eventually, he followed her into the grave and left us to fend for ourselves."

Amanda set down her fork. "He couldn't help it if he became sick, dear one."

Nate focused on the whitewashed wall. "My father tried hard to drink himself to death, but it wasn't fast enough. So one cold

January after we had been trapped in the cabin for days, he cut a length of rope. After we went to bed, he fed the horses and then hanged himself in the barn."

An icy chill ran through her veins. "Oh, Nate, I'm so sorry to hear this."

He patted her hand. "Water long over the dam. My brother and I survived the best we could. Eventually I sent Joshua to live with an aunt and uncle so he could go to school. Apparently, he didn't stay long before running off to join the army."

"The Confederate army?"

"Yes. He was living in Fayetteville at the time, but I don't know where he is now."

"I hope that when the war is over you will find each other," she said, but every word from her mouth sounded wholly inadequate.

"That's enough about me. Tell me what it was like growing up a Dunn. Tails and ball gowns for dinner? Three forks, three spoons, two knives, and every size glass known to man at each place setting?" His blue eyes twinkled.

Amanda remembered meals in their dining room after Abby had left and frowned. Mama and Papa sat at opposite ends of the table, both sullen and aloof, while she picked at her food, hoping they wouldn't snipe at each other until she went to bed. Of course, there never had been shouting or vases hurtling through the air like a West End stage comedy. Instead, her mother would whine and cajole:

Why don't we go to London this weekend, George?

Let's take Amanda to the continent for the summer.

Why don't we spend a fortnight in the Lake District with our friends?

And Papa's answers were always the same.

I have no time for your nonsense, Agnes.

Mills do not run themselves.

I don't want to hear another word on the subject.

So her mother would brood and pout in her room, leaving Amanda alone to dream about life anywhere other than Dunncliff Manor.

"For dinner, yes," she replied, shaking off her memories. "But for breakfast and luncheon we were far less civilized."

When Nate smiled, Amanda felt a surge of warmth in her gut—unfamiliar yet not unpleasant. "My father never lifted a finger to help his wife. Of course, she did very little either. She wouldn't pull the stopper from the washbasin for herself or turn down the covers of her bed. Mama would stand waiting and shivering until her maid returned with a warming pan."

"Your parents were raised with servants, creating a form of helplessness. But your father probably showed his love in other ways."

Amanda shook her head, eating her last bite of yams. "Papa did not love her or she him. It was a union arranged by their parents for practical reasons—her family owned coal mines, his owned textile mills. My mother produced three children because it was expected of her. Duty allows little room for love."

Nate reached out and took hold of her chin. "Then you and I will have few expectations and no obligations to each other. We'll just see where our hearts take us." Leaning across the table, he kissed her lips tenderly.

She lifted an eyebrow when she opened her eyes. "Two kisses is my limit for the evening, Mr. Cooper. Why don't we clear the table before you start thinking about your second kiss?"

"I haven't served the pie for dessert yet. Ruth helped with the crust, but I did the rest by myself."

"What kind of pie?" she asked, furrowing her brow.

"Apple, with fruit picked fresh in Pender County."

"You're in luck, Mr. Cooper. Apple is my new favorite since coming to America. I might have to raise my limit to *three* kisses."

"You're the one in luck, Miss Dunn. Wait until you taste my pie."

Twelve

Two weeks later

When Nate walked the five blocks to his shop, he quickly became soaked to the skin despite an overcoat and hat. The October skies had opened with a deluge of rain that refused to stop. By three that afternoon he had yet to wait on his first customer. Perhaps the matrons of Wilmington were overseeing the construction of arks in their backyards. The rain fell so hard that water began to seep under his front door, along with an oily scum of filth. Nate relentlessly swept the sludge back to the street where it could drain into the harbor. His mind, however, stayed focused on his dinner with Amanda.

The evening had turned out better than his fondest dreams. Amanda had reached for his hand three times and kissed him twice. It would be impossible to count how often she smiled or laughed. Yes, his first culinary adventure had been an unqualified triumph. But if he didn't keep the flood out of his shop, his merchandise would be jeopardized. It seemed the faster he swept, the faster it poured in under the door.

"Looks like you're fighting a losing battle, my friend."

Startled, Nate turned to see Mason entering the store from his stockroom. With an uncomfortable twinge he realized he had neglected to lock the back door. And Mason, thinner, bearded, and more wild-eyed than their last meeting, wasn't alone. Another equally unkempt and dissipated ruffian swaggered down the aisle behind him.

"Mason, why didn't you come in the front door like other folks?" Nate tried to keep his voice level.

"Because I ain't your run-of-the-mill customer." Mason stopped in the middle of the store. "I know old friends from home don't have to stand on ceremony with a man like you." His lips formed a smile, but his eyes remained cool and unreadable.

"You took me by surprise." Nate returned to the futile task of sweeping foul-smelling water out to the street.

"You ain't gonna win that battle, Nate. We'd better move the grain sacks up high. The river has risen over the docks. The flood's coming from the wharf, not from uptown." As he spoke, Mason lifted a sack of rice sitting in the aisle directly in the tide's path.

Nate stared for a moment, embarrassed he hadn't grasped the situation. "Good idea. Thank you." Dropping the broom, he began moving boxes of canned goods to higher shelves. Mason and the unnamed man carried sacks of wheat, barley, and rice into the stockroom, stacking them to the ceiling on the work-table. The stranger moved with far less urgency than Mason but pitched in nonetheless.

Thirty minutes later the three men had done all they could.

"Time to head for higher ground and wait out the storm." Mason touched Nate lightly on the shoulder. "It sounds like the wind is starting to die down. If the building doesn't float away, you can come back tomorrow and see what's left."

Nate glanced around and nodded. "Let's brace the door shut

with this." The three men shifted a heavy crate of ruined dry goods against the door frame, the wood already warping from the water. Then they picked their way through floating debris and locked the back door behind them.

Mindlessly numb, Nate followed Mason through streets and alleys away from the Cape Fear River. While he was busily planning a bright future with Amanda, a flash flood had turned his store into a floating stew. When they reached an uptown area of warehouses and mills, Mason headed into a tavern only a bit less seedy than those on the wharf.

Considering the circumstances, Nate didn't object to his choice of dry refuges. Inside, men seeking shelter were huddled elbow to elbow. After they found a rough-hewn bench by the window, Nate offered his hand to the stranger. "Nathaniel Cooper. I'm much obliged for your help today, sir."

The man shook with little enthusiasm. "I ain't 'sir' to nobody. Name's Billy Conroy. I'm expectin' you to show gratitude with a few cold stouts to wet the whistle." Billy revealed the yellowest teeth with his smile Nate had ever seen.

"Of course. It would be my pleasure." Nate dug out a pile of coins from his pocket. "Don't know what beer costs—take what you need." He held out his open palm to Mason.

Mason grabbed the entire pile, plucked two, and slapped them on the bar. "Three stouts," he called to a one-eyed barkeep. "This should keep us dry for a while." Mason slipped the rest of the money into his pocket.

While they waited for their drinks, they wrung as much water from their garments as possible in a public place. Once the dark, foamy draughts arrived, Mason and Billy endeavored to empty their steins as quickly as possible. Issuing a rude burp, Mason motioned for refills before settling back on the bench. Nate had taken only one sip of the bitter drink.

"Haven't seen you at any more meetings, not since that first one in the summer." Mason wiped his mouth on his sleeve. "Maybe you didn't get my messages?"

Taking a second sip, Nate tried not to reveal his revulsion. "I heard about one or two, but I've been too busy to ride into the backwoods. It's only me working in the store." He kept his back very straight against the wall.

Mason picked up his stein the moment it was refilled. "There's a war going on everywhere but here in Wilmington. You folks tend to business just like normal. Mind if I ask what's so all-fired important that you can't spend a few nights helping out like-minded friends?" He kept his voice low, considering the politics of their fellow imbibers.

Nate looked from one of his companions to the other, gauging how much to reveal. "It seems I've gone and fallen in love. Who would guess it could happen to me?" He lifted his glass in cama-raderie to clink theirs. "So if I plan to take a wife, I can't be run-ning off and leaving my store untended." He forced himself to swallow another mouthful.

"I've been curious about you. That little gal in the hat shop next door keeps her eye on you." Mason grinned with maniacal zeal. "She said this real fancy English lady comes by your store often. And she ain't carrying sacks of food when she leaves."

"Miss Amanda Dunn," muttered Billy Conroy. "I knows all about that one."

Nate recoiled as though struck before grabbing hold of the man's coat lapels. "You are mistaken. You couldn't possibly know Miss Dunn. She's only been in Wilmington since April."

Conroy shrugged off his hand. "I know her from back in Wycleft. Her family lives up on the hill like they was kings and queens. Coming and going in their fancy brougham, pulled by horses wearing feathered hats and silver harness." Conroy spat on the sawdust-strewn floor. "My dah worked in Dunn Mills all his life, right up till he fell fifty feet down a black hole." Conroy clutched his stein tight enough to crack the glass. "What did old man Dunn do? He took his sweet time bringin' them up. Then he sez he's sorry and will pay for the funeral—one funeral for twenty-two men. He buried them side-by-side in a field outside town, not in proper plots inside Saint Luke's churchyard."

As Conroy paused to gulp more beer, Mason's expression turned gleeful. The tale appeared to amuse him.

"Then this foreman paid a visit to each family who lost their dah. He said Master Dunn will forget about this month's rent. But next month the rent better be paid on time or the family will be out on the street."

Nate felt heat rise up his neck to his hairline even as his mind struggled to remember everything Amanda told him about home. "Surely you can't hold Miss Dunn—"

"I ain't finished yet, Cooper. I helped save your store from the muck, so you better hear me out." Beer sloshed over the stein's rim onto Conroy's tattered shirt.

"Go on. I'm listening." Nate checked his peripheral vision for possible weapons other than the mug of swill.

"The foreman said Mum could send two sons to take Dah's place at the mill. Two for one, since they weren't trained. But she wouldn't let her boys set foot in that God-forsaken place. Mum went to live with her sister in Bath and sent her older boys to America with the rent money."

As details clicked into place, Nate forced his fingers to uncurl. "I'm sorry your father was killed, but Miss Dunn lost her only brother in that horrible accident. The floor over the coal shaft supplying the mill collapsed. No one was to blame. It was an accident."

Mason blinked several times in the smoky room. "Is that true, Billy?"

"Aye, a Dunn fell through the floor along with the workers, but they got him out right quick. And that don't change the sorry way they run the mill towns. Folks living in shacks with one bathtub for four families, not enough coal to heat the houses, never raising wages no matter how hard a man worked." Conroy's forehead beaded with sweat despite the cool temperatures.

"I imagine Miss Dunn must feel right at home waited on by all those slaves," Mason said, shaking his head in disdain.

Nate said, "Miss Dunn cannot control the lives of the Henthornes anymore than she could control her father. She brought an English maid with her and pays the woman wages. Amanda abhors slavery the same as me."

Mason shrugged his shoulders. "Since you hate slavery so much, why don't you start riding with us?" His whisper was barely audible. "We tear up rail lines north of here as fast as the Rebs lay down new tracks. When work on the docks slacks off this winter, we plan to form scouting parties around Fort Fisher. It's high time the Yankee generals get a better idea of how many troops are inside. Their navy can't get close enough to do much good. What do you say?"

"I could lie to you and say I will think about it, but since I'm in your debt I won't." Nate lowered his voice and continued. "I won't tear up railroad tracks because that cuts off my supplies as a shopkeeper. And I won't take up arms against the South. Wilmington is my home. Whether the Confederacy wins or loses, there must be a peaceful solution to end slavery once and for all. If there's any way to repay you that doesn't involve turning against North Carolina, you let me know." He stood and pulled on his sodden coat.

Conroy jumped to his feet and reached for something inside his coat, but Mason pushed him back down. "I had a feeling that's where you stood. We'll keep the rest of this as payment till I can think of something better." Mason patted his weskit pocket.

"Be my guest, but if either of you ever bother Miss Dunn, you'll face a worthier adversary than some soldiers watching a railhead."

Nate was halfway to the door before Mason called after him. "Know who you remind me of, Cooper? You and your brother will both end up dead in a rich man's war."

Amanda felt like the Bengal tiger she once saw in a traveling road show—relentlessly and hopelessly pacing from one end of its cage to the other. She had stayed with Abigail all morning while she huddled over a basin in the bathing chamber. Did all expectant mothers suffer so much nausea? It was a wonder that women had an ounce of meat left on their bones by the time the baby arrived.

Not that she wasn't happy for her sister. Amanda couldn't wait to see her new niece or nephew. And seeing the baby was something she intended to do. Now she had two reasons to stay in Wilmington: The little Henthorne due by spring…and Nathaniel. *Nate*…how she loved saying his name and picturing his handsome face and holding his hand. Then there had been his three kisses at dinner. She enjoyed herself more than at the party to introduce her to Abigail's friends, or the Stewarts' ball when she had to dance with Jackson's business associates, or even her society debut in England. It had been the most memorable night of her life.

Yet she'd seen Nate only a few times since and never alone. Abby insisted that Salome accompany her on every shopping trip to this store. Even stout-hearted Nate didn't try to steal a kiss in front of her.

"Miss Amanda?" Helene appeared on the balcony, her face pinched and drawn. "May I speak with you a moment?"

"Of course. I seem to be wearing a groove in these beautiful floor tiles. Let's sit in the shade." Amanda pointed at two chaises under the roof's eave.

Helene glanced back into the bedroom. "Where is Josie?"

"She is helping in the laundry. Have no fear of an eighty-pound girl today."

Helene found little humor in the jest as she perched on the chair. "You know I am eager to return home. It's already October. I fear if I wait too much longer, winter squalls will make travel impossible except for the foolhardy. You have been very kind to me, but I want to spend Christmas by my mum's hearth." Helene extracted a cloth pouch from her apron. "I saved my wages. This should be enough for my passage. Please take the money and make the necessary arrangements."

Amanda placed her hand over Helene's. "Knowing your feelings, I have discussed the matter with Mr. Henthorne on several occasions. He won't let either of us leave on one of his steamers. It's far too dangerous. Yankee gunboats have sunk several ships off the coast of Virginia, blessedly none of the ones Jackson contracted. The Union navy fires on any vessel flying the Confederate flag without consideration for civilian passengers. Those ships sank within minutes with all hands lost. I cannot take a chance on losing you."

"Why not? You have Josie to see to your needs, especially as you refuse to wear any hairstyle other than a coiled braid like a farmer's wife."

Amanda recoiled, as much from Helene's tone as her harsh words. "Because I have grown fond of you over the years, Helene, and appreciate all you have done for me, here and in Manchester, if my brother-in-law agreed I would send you home tomorrow. But he refuses and no other ship leaving port permits civilian passengers." Amanda struggled to keep her voice level as her throat clogged with emotion.

"Forgive me, Miss Amanda. That was a cruel thing to say." She burst into tears. With her apron covering her face, she sobbed for several minutes, despite every attempt to console her.

When the maid finally lifted her head, Amanda patted her arm. "As soon as it's safe to sail from Wilmington, I promise to send you home."

"Thank you, ma'am. I will go see why Josie hasn't brought up your tea yet."

Amanda resumed pacing, but she hadn't crossed the gallery once when Helene reappeared with Josie at her side. The girl seemed to be trying to hide behind her.

"I found Josie on the steps, Miss Amanda. She wants to tell you something but is frightened for some reason." Helene nudged the slave forward none too gently.

"What is it, Josie? Tell me what's troubling you."

Josie wrung her hands until Helene cleared her throat. "I was carryin' up your tea on the outside steps because Miz Henthorne gets mad if I slosh tea on her shiny wood floors." Her dark eyes darted left and right.

Amanda began to grow impatient with the girl's reticence. "Speak up and tell me the rest."

Josie crossed her arms over her homespun dress. "I run into that Mr. Cooper who come here once or twice. He the one who brung Miz Henthorne a bunch of flowers even though we got prettier ones in the garden."

"Mr. Cooper is downstairs in the courtyard?"

"Yes'm. I asked what he's doing comin' round back instead of knockin' on the front door. He sez he's hopin' to run into you, Miz Dunn, when you ain't…predispos'd. Then he asks who I be." Josie angled her thumb toward her chest.

Amanda huffed out her breath. "Go on," she prodded.

"I told him I'm your maid, Josie." She focused on the polished tiles. "He asks what happened to Miss Helene. I sez nothin' because you got two maids—one for the fancy work and one for the hard work." Josie peeked at Helene over her shoulder. "Then Master Cooper took the tray away from me and said he'll wait for you in the rose garden. So I'm here to fetch you."

Several moments spun out while the three women looked at each other, one more perplexed than the next. "Thank you, Josie. You never have to be afraid to deliver a message to me. That will be all for now, both of you." Amanda hurried down the gallery stairs and didn't stop running until she reached the ivy-covered arbor among the roses.

"Nate," she said breathlessly. "What a surprise."

He half rose and bowed. Then he began pouring tea. "A pleasant one, I hope."

"Yes, indeed, but perhaps reckless as well. Jackson often comes home early to check on his wife. If he does so today, he may make an unpleasant scene."

"I don't fear a confrontation with your brother-in-law. In fact, I have grown weary of our clandestine rendezvouses behind his back. I yearn for a bit more transparency between us." He lifted the porcelain pitcher. "Would you like cream, Miss Dunn?"

"Yes, please, and a teaspoon of sugar too." Amanda sat on the opposite bench.

"By the way, I ran into your slave a few minutes ago. I believe her name was Josie. I thought we were of the same opinion regarding slavery."

"I feel the institution is wrong, but I couldn't fathom what to do with the girl. Jackson had already made the purchase before I landed in America." Amanda incautiously sipped the tea and burned her tongue. "At least she's better off in my sister's household than in most. If I refused her, she would have been resold at the slave auction. She seems happy here or at least well adjusted."

"Slaves are not *happy*, Amanda. They merely put on performances for their masters to avoid reprisals."

"You are correct; I misspoke. But I didn't want to enrage Jackson until I restored a supply of cotton to Dunn Mills. After months of making inquiries, Henthorne and Sons remains the only factor with a constant supply. Jackson fills every blockade runner arriving in port."

Nate sipped his tea with a frown. "And why do you suppose that is?" His eyes narrowed into a glare.

"I beg your pardon?" With trembling fingers she set the cup in the saucer.

"Did you ever stop to consider how his business partners are able to find cotton when most plantations lie fallow because the slaves have run off?"

"He must pay a better price—"

"Or perhaps he deals with the most despicable breed of planters—those who refuse to provide manumission papers and keep their slaves in bondage under threat of death."

In the humid, vine-entangled garden, Amanda felt the air leave her lungs. "Even if that is the case, Nate, what can I do? I am a guest in my sister's home."

He threw the rest of his tea into the shrubbery. "You could refuse to do business with Jackson Henthorne."

"But our mills desperately need raw materials. Livelihoods in Manchester are at stake."

"Doing business with Georgia and Carolina planters supports those who refuse to let slavery die. Stop helping the Confederacy. You should be seeking cotton from farms in South America or Mexico—anywhere but here."

Amanda thought about her twin sister, eagerly awaiting the birth of her first child. "Abigail would consider it effrontery if I sever ties with her husband, even though I agree with you on principle. Surely you understand that life becomes complicated when families are involved."

"You shouldn't let family stand in the way of your convictions. Each man and woman must decide for themselves who they are." Nate stood and tugged down the hem of his weskit. "Don't get up, Miss Dunn. I can find my way to the street."

Jackson's stroll home from his club that night did nothing to improve his bad mood. Without minding where he walked, he stepped off the curb into a gutter filled with stagnant water. Little progress had been made to clean the streets since the flood two weeks ago. Too few able-bodied men remained in town, whether slave or free. The local militia had their hands full rounding up deserters from Fort Fisher downriver.

According to sailors on the docks, the Yankee gunboats beyond Bald Head Island were thicker than ticks on a hound dog. That didn't bode well for ever seeing Captain Hornsby and the *Countess Marie*, or his share of the substantial profits from the last shipment. He had loaded the *Countess Marie* with so much cotton the crew would have to sleep standing up on the voyage. Hornsby was supposed to transfer the cargo onto vessels bound for Europe and return with a load of artillery from German foundries. That had been almost six weeks ago.

Certainly the crossing could take several weeks in each direction if a storm blew them off course, but Jackson had had a sour taste in his mouth since agreeing to Hornsby's strong-armed terms. He should have taken whatever beating the thugs dished out and not yielded to that pirate's demands. Now Hornsby had stolen three thousand pounds of first-rate cotton, which he could easily sell to a European buyer. He never should have struck a bargain with the devil. Hornsby had no loyalty to the cause and didn't care that the Confederate army was desperate for guns.

But given enough opportunity, Jackson could make up for Hornsby's thievery. The *Roanoke* and the *Lady Adelaine* were proving themselves worthy of their exorbitant price because each could hold five thousand bales of cotton. It was his conversation with Judge Stewart that ruined his evening of relaxation. And this was one time he wouldn't allow Abigail to interfere with his dealing with his sister-in-law.

Jackson found his butler asleep by the door when he entered the house. "Amos," he said, tapping the man's arm.

"Master Henthorne, I was waiting for you, sir, but my eyes closed of their own accord." Amos pushed up from the chair.

"Where is Mrs. Henthorne?" Jackson tossed his hat and gloves on the round hall table.

"She retired for the evening, sir." Amos smoothed down his grizzled hair.

"And Miss Dunn. Where is she?"

Amos cocked his head in confusion. "I suppose she's in bed too, sir."

"Find Josie. Tell her to inform Miss Dunn that she is to dress and join me in the library." Jackson shrugged off his coat, dropping it on the vacated chair.

Amos stepped closer and whispered, "Sir, it's past eleven o'clock. Miss Dunn may be sound asleep."

Tamping down his irritation, Jackson spoke through gritted teeth. "I am aware of the time, but there is a matter of upmost urgency. Mrs. Henthorne is neither to be awakened nor informed of this meeting tomorrow. I suggest you make that crystal clear to Josie as well."

"Yes, sir. I will tell her." Amos shuffled down the corridor and out the door on stiff legs.

One set of steps led to the subterranean kitchen, another led to the courtyard, gardens, and slave quarters. Needless to say, Josie would approach Amanda's suite from the second floor gallery. The girl always avoided Jackson whenever possible, even though he had never lifted a finger against her or any other female slave.

With the butler gone, he had a few minutes to compose his thoughts and sip a glass of bourbon. But the strong spirits did little to calm his nerves. If anything, they fanned a small flame into a blaze of indignation.

"Jackson, did you really send for me at this hour?" A haughty voice spoke behind him. Amanda stood in the doorway in a prim dress, buttoned up to her throat. Her hair hung loose down her back and her feet were bare. *So like the wild child twin not to plait her hair and cover her unsightly feet.*

"Yes, I summoned you." He strode to the sideboard to refill his glass.

"What's wrong? Has something happened to my sister…or the baby?" Her expression changed to pure terror.

"Everything is fine with Abigail. And I intend to keep it that way, despite your continual efforts to upset this household."

"Perhaps you will explain what couldn't wait until the light of day." Though she sounded composed, a nervous tic appeared in her cheek.

"I spoke with your good friend Judge Stewart tonight at the club."

"Judge Stewart is *your* friend, Jackson. He and I are mere acquaintances, although I have grown fond of his lovely wife," she said, settling at one end of the sofa.

"My, aren't you a cool one?" He took a gulp of his drink. "Miles informed me of your mission of mercy in August. You showed up at his home uninvited under the auspices of a social call but with a personal agenda in mind."

"Rosalyn had extended an invitation, which I accepted on behalf of Abigail and myself." Amanda crossed her ankles, tucking her loathsome toes beneath her skirt.

"How long were you there before asking the judge to release your paramour from jail?" He reached her side of the room in a few strides.

"I made polite conversation for about an hour before deciding it was time to rectify an injustice," she murmured, as though discussing the likelihood of rain.

Jackson stared at his sister-in-law, who possessed more bravado than most men. "You considered the arrest of Nathaniel Cooper, your favorite shopkeeper, an *injustice*? Why would you draw such a conclusion?"

"Nate won't bear arms to preserve the evil institution of slavery, but he is no traitor to North Carolina and doesn't deserve to be thrown into the stockade at Fort Fisher for not enlisting. Plenty of *others* haven't responded to the call."

Jackson was taken aback by her quick wit. "You implied to Judge Stewart that Cooper worked for me, which is a total falsehood!" Though he felt like shouting, he hissed the words. The last thing he needed was to awaken his wife.

Color flooded Amanda's face. Perhaps he had finally hit a nerve. "Judge Stewart drew that conclusion on his own because you are my brother-in-law and he knows I'm sweet on Mr. Cooper." Her blush deepened with the admission. "I should, perhaps, have corrected his assumption, but my emotions prevailed over my better judgment." She focused on the carpet as if suddenly beset by humility.

"Did you think your heartfelt confession would garner either pity or indulgence from me? I'm well aware that you have been sneaking out to see him despite my introductions to far more qualified candidates. I also know Abigail gave Salome permission to shop again at Cooper's despite my preference for Baxter's, and that Cooper paid an afternoon call here."

Amanda fixed her gaze on the potted plant by the window.

"My wife doesn't want your reputation ruined should you come to your senses about this infatuation."

"No, Abigail remembered being in love with a man her parents found unacceptable—*you*, Jackson. Papa hated you because you were American, and yet my sister is happy and as much in love as the day you swept her off her feet." Amanda offered him the smallest of smiles.

Jackson dropped into a chair, suddenly too weary to remain upright. "Thank you for your correct assessment. I love your sister more than anything in the world and I will stop at nothing to make her happy. That is why I overlooked your…indiscretions… at Cooper's store, his home, and in my garden. But he is not who you think he is."

"What do you mean?"

"Judge Stewart approached me at the club tonight. He has friends in the militia, men he respects and who respect him." Jackson pulled a folded piece of newspaper from inside his coat. With his index finger he pointed to an article. "Railroad tracks torn up, bridges north of here burned, telegraph wires cut—all in the dead of night. This isn't the work of Union troops but a devious band of anarchists who have been wreaking havoc around Wilmington. They have disrupted the flow of supplies between the port and Richmond, along with dispatches between Fort Fisher and Generals Lee and Johnson. These hooligans are bent on destroying Southern society, the society that by your own admission has made your sister content."

"What does this have to do with Nate?"

"Cooper is a member of that group of anarchists."

Amanda jumped to her feet. "That's ridiculous! He has a shop to run from dawn to dusk. He has no time for midnight raids and no desire to destroy Wilmington commerce. Think about the nature of his business if not his loyalty to the South."

Jackson held the newspaper out to her. "Read the article for yourself. A detachment of cavalry on patrol stumbled upon this band last Saturday night. A gunfight prevailed and several traitors were killed. Two of the dead men were recognized by members of the militia, including one by the name of Mason Hooks." He studied her face carefully. "Do you recognize the name? Because members of the militia remembered Hooks and the other dead man talking to *your Mr. Cooper* in a tavern not long ago."

Amanda pressed the heel of her hand to her forehead. "There must be some logical explanation. I know Nate to be a man of honor. And he doesn't drink. Jackson, this is a mistake—"

He sighed impatiently, cutting her off. "Go to bed, Miss Dunn. In the morning perhaps a clearer head will prevail and you will know what action to pursue. A man like Cooper will not advance your all-important mission of saving Dunn Mills."

Thirteen

manda quickly discovered it wasn't easy to conduct business on a moral high ground, at least not in North Carolina, while America was embroiled in a bloody war. Not one warehouse contained, or one Wilmington factor had access to, cotton picked solely by free hands. Her brother-in-law wasn't the only cotton factor supporting slavery in the Carolinas. Yet each letter from Charles Pelton was always the same: *Dunn Mills needs all the raw materials you can provide.*

And, apparently, her mother's financial requirements hadn't diminished since her father's passing. Mama's complaints about the social obligations for a widow in Manchester had become relentless.

Amanda had fully intended to implement changes before seeing Nate again. But despite her good intentions, she had little choice but to do business with Jackson until Mr. Pelton contacted potential suppliers in South America. Her shopping excursion to

Cooper's last week yielded no poignant reunion with the proprietor. A hand-painted sign indicated that the store was "Closed Until Further Notice." Salome decided that Baxter's, well away from the waterfront, would receive the Henthorne patronage once again. Amanda yearned to pay a visit to the Simses on Castle Street, yet she knew that Abigail wouldn't approve.

But it had been two weeks since Nate's afternoon visit to the rose garden, and following Jackson's ridiculous accusation, she couldn't wait another day to see him. The idea that Nate could be involved with a band of lawless anarchists would be humorous if not so frightening.

Amanda wrapped a heavy shawl around her shoulders and slipped out of the house as soon as she and Abby finished breakfast. Because her sister usually took a long bath and then read for hours in her room, Amanda's absence wouldn't be noticed until luncheon. The brisk walk in the cool air exhilarated her, lifting her spirits and lessening her burdens. When she discovered the door to the store ajar, Amanda practically burst into song.

"How long have you been open for business?" she crowed as she crossed the threshold. Then she caught the whiff of a foul odor and spotted Nate's shocked face at the same moment.

"Wait there, Amanda, and I'll join you. You don't want to get lye soap on your shoes."

She ignored his warning and entered the shop she'd grown so fond of. "Goodness, what happened here? Was this due to that flood two weeks ago? I couldn't fathom why your market was closed. Jackson mentioned that the river had overflowed its banks, but his home only suffered a soggy garden for a few days. Even the stone floor of Salome's kitchen remained dry."

Nate shucked off his heavy gloves on his way up the aisle. "That's the difference between mansions on the hill and businesses along the waterfront. Even the shops on Market suffered only dirty sidewalks and streaky windows." Pulling off his soiled apron, he draped it over a rung of the ladder. "How are you? You're a sight for sore eyes on this less-than-auspicious occasion." The smile filling his face warmed her heart.

"I am well, thank you. I didn't realize you suffered this much damage. What is that smell?" She pulled a handkerchief from her bag.

Nate sniffed the air. "My nose has grown accustomed to it. You're smelling fermented river muck on my pine floorboards. I've scrubbed the walls, shelves, and windows, but I'm afraid the floor will require extra attention. Many boards are warped and will need to be replaced."

Amanda tried to breathe through her scented linen. "What about your merchandise?"

"Much of it was ruined, I'm afraid. Some of the backroom stock is salvageable, along with my canned goods, but I had to have the rest hauled away. The Simses' home was also damaged, so I helped them first before trying to reopen the store." Nate peered around the room, shaking his head. "This isn't a fit place for you. Let me wash up and meet you up the block. Shall we say under the elm tree?" He turned on his heel before she could utter a yea or nay.

Amanda felt oddly offended being sent away instead of invited to pitch in. She cared for Nate and thus what happened inside his market. She waited for him on the iron filigree bench, a spot she recalled from their first acquaintance. "At least we have a fine day for November," she said cheerily when he arrived.

"Indeed, was it the weather which brought you to town? I hope Salome doesn't require a pound of sugar or flour. I would be forced to send you to one of my competitors."

"I came to see you, Nate. Gossip is being spread and I fear reprisals for you. Jackson awoke me in the middle of the night, furious after a conversation with Judge Stewart."

Stretching out his long legs, he tilted his face toward the late autumn sunshine. "I thought the judge would regret his assertion I worked for Henthorne. I hate falsehoods perpetuated on my behalf, no matter how well-intended the motivation."

"No, that's not what I mean." She wrung her hands in her lap. "The judge approached Jackson with details about a story in the newspaper. A group of hooligans—he called them anarchists—wreaked havoc on rail lines outside of town. Rebel cavalry patrolling in the area caught them red-handed and a gunfight ensued. Some of the anarchists escaped but a few were killed."

Nate's relaxed position on the bench stiffened. "Why would Judge Stewart connect those men to me?"

"A false connection to be sure," she said soothingly. "The cavalry brought the bodies back to the garrison. One of the dead men had papers identifying him as Mason Hooks. Then a member of the militia said he saw you drinking with Mr. Hooks in a disreputable place uptown, along with his dead companion. I told Jackson that the man was mistaken because you never imbibe—"

"Mason Hooks is dead?"

Nate's plaintive query chilled her to the bone. "Yes, shot by Confederate cavalry. Do you mean to say you did know the man?"

He scrubbed his face with his hands. "I do—did—and the militiaman was correct. It was me with Mason and his friend in a tavern on Campbell Street."

"I don't understand." Amanda felt queasy, similar to Abigail on more mornings than not.

"I knew Mason from Balsam. We were friends a long time ago. He joined the Reb army but deserted after two years. He brought me news of my brother when he came to Wilmington. Joshua enlisted not long after the war began. The last time Mason saw Joshua, he was alive and well, serving under General Hoke. Mason and his friend, Billy Conroy, showed up the day of the waterfront flood. They helped me move some of the merchandise. I'm indebted to Mason, both for news of my brother and saving my store from even worse damage." Nate dropped his chin to his chest, his face devoid of expression. "We waited in that uptown pub until the storm passed."

"This deserter...Mr. Hooks...do you think he was an anarchist? Someone bent on destroying the fabric of society?"

Nate locked gazes with her. "What meaning does that term have during wartime, Amanda? Mason opposed fighting to preserve slavery, an institution which benefits only the rich planter and denies people of color their inalienable privileges promised in the Bill of Rights and then demanded by Lincoln's emancipation edict."

"Were *you* involved with tearing up tracks and burning depots, Nate? According to Jackson, Confederate guards were ambushed and killed."

"I was not, but you should know the whole truth. I attended one of their rallies and listened to their speeches. If men don't take action against oppression, rich men like George Dunn and Randolph Henthorne will always have the upper hand." His lips thinned to a harsh line. "But my pacifist nature prevailed over my desire for social reform in the South."

Amanda blinked like an owl on midnight watch. "What on earth does my father have to do with American political differences? Slavery was outlawed in my country during the last century."

"Isn't it the same? Rich men like your father essentially enslave those working in the mills, mines, and foundries. Their families live in crude hovels without proper heat, light, or water. Their illiterate children are put to work at an early age and old people die before their time because they can't afford doctors."

Amanda rose to her feet. "We have no laws against educating children, nor do we sell human beings! Men can quit their jobs and move their families elsewhere. How dare you speak critically of a country you have never been to."

"Have *you* walked the alleys of a mill town? Have you stepped inside those houses and seen for yourself how your father's employees live when not toiling fourteen hours a day?"

She gripped the back of the bench. "How do you know this?"

"The man Mason Hooks brought to Wilmington was born in Wycleft. His father died in the same accident that claimed your brother. A month later the family was out on the street. His name was Billy Conroy, although I'm sure your paths never crossed back in England."

"Was he the other dead man?"

"Yes, Amanda. His was a senseless death after a pitiful life." Nate looked away a moment before returning his gaze to her. "I am no traitor to North Carolina and certainly not an anarchist. Nevertheless, the news of Mason and Conroy's deaths brings me little joy."

"You blame *me* for men like them?"

"Of course not. They died by the sword they chose to brandish. But the rich must realize that everything comes with a price. Whether here in America or back in Manchester, great wealth often leaves behind a trail of broken lives."

For a man who fancies himself in love, I have an odd way of show-ing it. This and other recriminations ran through Nate's head during the next two weeks. Arduous days of restoring his store were followed by interminable nights of tossing and turning in his room. Why had he taken Mason's side in an argument with the woman he cared for? How could he blame Amanda for society's ills, both here and across the Atlantic? She was no more responsible for the mill towns of Manchester than he was culpable for slavery two years after the Emancipation Proclamation.

A man without an effective course of action lashed out at those in close proximity. Was he surprised she hadn't returned? Rufus posted handbills announcing the reopening of his market everywhere. The boy personally delivered one to each cook on Third Street to no avail. So when Nate closed up that afternoon, he had only one destination in mind. He changed shirts, wrapped his finest smoked ham in bright paper, and hiked up the hill to beg forgiveness from the kindest person he knew.

Running a hand through his hair, he knocked boldly on the kitchen door, the most likely place to find servants at this hour. With growing unease, he noticed an absence of people in the courtyard and in the row of slave cabins. Nate pounded again on the carved oak panel with little regard for those who might be napping after a full meal.

"Who's there?" A voice demanded from within.

"It's Nathaniel Cooper."

When the door swung wide, Salome stood in the opening, her girth effectively filling the space. Her husband, Thomas, glowered over her shoulder. The man was only half as wide but towered a foot taller. "Whatcha doin' here, Master Cooper?"

"Forgive my intrusion at a late hour, but I must speak to Miss Dunn. I promise to be brief." Nate mustered a smile for the pair.

"Sorry, sir, that not possible." The cook began to close the door.

"Please, Salome, if you would deliver a message to her, I would be ever grateful." He wedged his boot against the wooden frame.

"You can't see her 'cause she ain't here, Master Cooper." At last Thomas offered a reasonable explanation. "Master and Mistress Henthorne are spending December at his papa's plantation. Not enough parties in town this season, so Master celebratin' Christmas in the country with his folks. Miz Henthorne insisted Miz Dunn come too and wouldn't take nay for an answer."

"She will be gone the entire month?" Having rallied enough courage to visit, Nate couldn't fathom Amanda not being there.

"That right, sir," said Thomas. "They be back after Christmas because Judge Stewart is throwin' a New Year party."

Salome issued a final harrumph on the subject.

"Thank you for telling me. I wish you both a joyous holiday." Nate dipped his chin, took a step back, and then remembered the gift. "This is for you." He extended the wrapped package.

"What that?" Salome appeared suspicious.

"A ham I brought for Miss Dunn and the Henthornes, but I want you to have it instead."

Thomas was hesitant. "Don't know, sir, if we should—"

"Thank you and merry Christmas." Salome tucked the package under her arm and closed the door.

Nate walked back to his quarters on Castle Street more depressed than the night of the flood. It would be two weeks before Amanda returned to Wilmington at the earliest. No way could he pay a social call at the Henthorne plantation even if he knew the location. His sole option for Christmas was to help make the holiday special for Rufus...and pray that God would keep Amanda safe and sound.

On Christmas Eve Nate decided to close the store early. Customers had been few and far between all week. Either Mr. Baxter had dropped his prices or the Henthornes weren't the only residents to abandon the city. After he swept his floors and latched the shutters, Nate heard the bell over the door jangle. "Sorry, ma'am, but we're closed," he called, blowing out the lamp.

"It has been a long time, but surely you can tell the difference between a gal and your brother."

The voice, as familiar as the back of his hand, sounded oddly incongruous in the dark. "*Joshua?*" The name issued forth more like a croak than a question. Nate turned to see the hauntingly thin face of his only sibling...younger in years, but looking much older than his own reflection in the mirror.

"Ah, so you do still remember me."

When Joshua opened his arms, Nate stepped clumsily into his embrace. "I'm *mighty* glad to see you." With a tight throat, his declaration took nearly a minute to deliver. "Have you left the army?" He studied his brother at arm's length. Joshua's uniform, tattered and stained, was the usual Confederate shade of butternut.

"General Bragg sent our regiments to reinforce Fort Fisher. I'm in General Hoke's division. We've been at the garrison for two weeks. Because Admiral Porter keeps sending gunboats up the Cape Fear, Colonel Lamb needed a hand to convince those Yankees it was time to go home."

"How on earth did you find me?" Nate released his tight grip before he bruised his brother's arms.

"One of the quartermasters procuring supplies for the fort asked me if I had kinfolk in town. He said there was a shopkeeper named Cooper who talked just like me."

"We don't sound much alike anymore, but I'm glad he made the connection. Apparently, my attempt to lose the mountain twang is an abysmal failure." Nate laughed. "You're a lieutenant now. Pa would be right proud."

Joshua swept off his hat to finger the braiding. "If enough men in the regiment die, the commanders will make anyone still breathing an officer."

"I'm sure you distinguished yourself on the battlefield." Inexplicably, Nate felt a wave of shame or perhaps regret. He felt confused by his reaction.

"I can shoot straight and try to keep my head down. That's about all we can do at this point. The Yanks got us outnumbered and outgunned at every battle. But we're well entrenched now. If the admiral tries to land troops again, we'll be ready. We built a new breastwork and planted torpedoes in the river." His young face glowed with a soldier's pride of accomplishment—rare for a member of the Confederate army lately.

"How long is your furlough? Are you hungry? When was the last time you had a home-cooked meal?"

"The major ordered our company back to the fort by midnight tomorrow—Christmas Day. Those Yanks wouldn't dare attack on Jesus's birthday."

Again Joshua reminded Nate of a very young man, still filled with optimism, instead of a seasoned veteran who had doubtlessly taken many lives. "It's been a long time since we spent a holiday together."

"Do you live upstairs?" His gaze traveled up to the ceiling. "'Spose you got plenty of vittles to cook since you own a store."

"Nothing's upstairs but dust and spiderwebs. I rent a room from the Sims family a few blocks away. Come home with me. Ruth always has enough for an extra mouth, especially as this is Christmas Eve. Tomorrow morning I plan to show my face in church even if it causes a minor ruckus in heaven."

Joshua grinned. "I'll go with you in case Ma is looking down. But tonight I'd better spread my bedroll here." He gestured toward the whitewashed floor. "My company is uptown at some watering hole. The sergeant won't know where I went if he needs me."

"I have a better idea." Nate tore off a sheet of some brown paper and grabbed his charcoal pencil. "What's your sergeant's name?"

"Baker. Gavin Baker."

Nate drew a crude map from his market to the Simses' house, printed Sergeant Gavin Baker at the top, and let Joshua sign the bottom in his childish scrawl. Once he nailed the notice to his front door, he grabbed a parcel for Ruth and headed toward the door. "No brother of mine sleeps on the floor on Christmas. Let's go home."

Home...with the only family Nate had left in the world, other than Amanda, because that's how he felt about her. Even though he'd had a strange way of showing it, she felt like a cherished member of his family. He hoped this would be the last Christmas they would spend apart.

If Joshua was surprised he lived with people of color, he hid it well. During dinner everyone swapped tales of favorite Christmases gone by—a cherished new toy, a rare gift of oranges in the dead of winter, a boy's first muzzleloader for hunting squirrels and rabbits. Ruth served the smoked ham Nate had given her, along with baked apples, yams, and plum pudding for dessert. After the meal his brother struck up a tune on Odom's fiddle. Joshua had acquired the talent after joining the army. Nate settled back to listen and savor the pleasure of having a brother again.

There were no heartbreaking stories of fallen comrades or grievous battle wounds, no description of loathsome rations or foul water, and blessedly none of the melancholy that defines a soldier's life in wartime. For one magical night he and Joshua were boys again in the beautiful Blue Ridge Mountains. Their pa was sober; their ma healthy and robust. When their eyelids finally began to droop, Nate insisted that Joshua take his small metal bed while he curled up in a blanket against the wall. Nate watched his brother sleep for hours. His face, peaceful in repose, still looked innocent despite all he'd seen and done. While Joshua snored, Nate tried to fathom a way to keep him safe from the maelstrom surely headed to Wilmington.

Odom had asked Joshua during dinner why he was fighting. His brother had shrugged and replied, "If I'm a Carolinian, it just seemed like something I should do." His simple response festered in Nate's mind until he finally drifted to sleep.

Yet his slumber was brief in duration due to the Union army proving to be unpredictable once more. Simultaneously, Odom, Nate, and Joshua bolted toward the incessant pounding on the door. Sergeant Baker, shivering in the damp predawn air, snapped a hasty salute. "Lieutenant Cooper, sir."

Joshua returned the formality. "What is it, Sergeant? It's Christmas Day."

"Yes, sir, but somebody forget to tell the Yankees. They opened fire on Fort Fisher in the middle of the night. We are to return to the fort at once. I've already sent the rest of the company on their way."

Within minutes, Joshua retrieved his bedroll and rucksack, thanked his hosts for supper, and delivered the fiercest hug Nate ever received.

"I must go back. God bless you, brother. Goodbye." Joshua disappeared into the night before Nate could utter a reply. Yet before he reached the top of the stairs, Nate already knew what course of action he would take.

December 28, 1864

Amanda couldn't wait to return to Wilmington. Even though they were slave owners, at least Jackson and Abigail treated their slaves far better than the elder Henthornes. She had seen Randolph's field hands in threadbare rags, while most of the children had no shoes despite cool winter temperatures. Although sufficiently attired in livery or maids' uniforms, household servants appeared nervous and mistrustful, as though the master or mistress's wrath could be easily provoked.

Even her sister expressed concern about the deplorable condition of the slave quarters—leaky roofs, dirt floors, and missing mortar between the rough-hewn split logs. Isabelle Henthorne dismissed Abigail's concerns with a wave of her hand and a disdainful shrug. "We have no cotton left for them to make new clothes," she said. "And our peanut harvest this year was barely enough to provide a new gown for me for the season. Thanks to that infernal blockade, horrible shortages have taken their toll on everyone, my dear."

Yet you appear very well fed, Mrs. Henthorne, Amanda thought uncharitably. Always a reason, always an excuse for their lack of compassion in an atmosphere of injustice.

Amanda already had a bellyful when both ham and leg of lamb were served for Christmas dinner, while the slaves ate thin soup and coarse brown bread. When she'd commented during dessert, she received a glare from Jackson and a patronizing, "I wouldn't expect a *foreigner* to understand our ways" from the elder Mrs. Henthorne.

Was this how Wycleft appeared to American visitors? If the description provided by Billy Conroy was accurate, then she knew the answer. Billy had no reason to lie to Nate. She had buried her head in the sand and never questioned the customs of her parents. *Just like Isabelle Henthorne.* Why hadn't she walked the alleys where her father's employees lived? Her mother always ordered the coachman to take certain lanes to and from the mansion. Amanda had no contact with the village children while growing up. Nannies, governesses, and boarding schools provided an insular world of wealth and privilege for the Dunn offspring. No wonder her sister found nothing distasteful in Jackson's world.

After her last visit to Nate's store, Amanda yearned for him to visit Wycleft. Then he could see for himself that Dunn Mills provided decent employment with freedom and opportunities for advancement. Now she no longer thought that a good idea. She'd been sitting on a pile of self-righteousness. Like Nate, maybe she no longer belonged *anywhere*. And what did that bode for the coming New Year?

With Jackson eager to assess the situation at his warehouses and the wharf, and Abigail needing rest after weeks with a critical mother-in-law, Amanda devised a plan. On her first day back in Wilmington, she headed to Water Street immediately after breakfast. But her hope for a tender reunion with Nate dissolved on his front stoop.

A flurry of workmen carried sacks of grains, sides of smoked meat, and boxes of canned goods to drays parked along the street. Teamsters shouted at passing carriages as they fought to control their skittish horses. Filled with apprehension, Amanda walked into the store as a keg of molasses rolled down the aisle.

"Watch your step, miss!" hollered a burly man.

"Amanda! What timing. I just finished penning you a letter," said Nate. He held up a sheet of foolscap, the ink still glistening.

She sidestepped the runaway cask and closed the distance between them. All around her the shelves were rapidly being emptied. "I hope you wrote me an invitation to—" Her jest froze in her throat like a winter icicle with the realization Nate wore the uniform of Confederate soldier. Amanda's vision clouded, her knees buckled, and the floor rose up to meet her.

"Steady, dear heart." In one smooth motion, Nate caught her, lifted her into his arms, and carried her out the back door.

Away from the chaos, the cold breeze restored her senses better than smelling salts. "I'm fine, Nate. Put me down," she demanded. Once her feet reached solid ground, Amanda straightened her skirt over her ankles. "Tell me you haven't done something desperately reckless!" A piqued tone masked the terror churning in her gut.

"I haven't yet, but I intend to enlist once I reach the fort." He tugged down the hem of his jacket, the many repairs attesting to hard service by its previous owner. "A militiaman supplied this so I won't be shot as a Yankee spy along the way."

Amanda pressed a fist to her forehead, where a dull ache throbbed beneath the skin. "Fight for the Confederacy? But why,

Nate? You abhor the institution of slavery and the rich planters who manipulate laws to benefit themselves."

Guiding her to the stone wall, Nate pulled her down next to him. "Yes, but most Carolinians fight for our state's rights, not to preserve slavery. We want to be able to govern ourselves. As for me, I plan to fight for less philosophic reasons—my brother." He gazed toward the river, obscured today by a blanket of fog.

The word hung in the air as though she could almost touch it. "Your brother is here in Wilmington?"

He nodded without meeting her eye. "Joshua found me on Christmas Eve. His regiment has been reassigned to Fort Fisher. Some army quartermaster remembered my store and told him where to find me."

"Unbelievable! I'm sure you were overjoyed to see him."

"I wish you two could have met. To spend Christmas with the two people I love would have been a dream come true."

With the two people I love? Amanda latched on his declaration like a rope thrown to a drowning man. "Nothing would have pleased me more than to be here with you instead of with the Henthornes, surrounded by dying peanut plants."

"While we slept, Yankees fired on the fort, cutting short our reunion. Joshua's commander called him back and canceled his furlough." Nate wrapped his hand around hers. "Amanda, I-I can't bear the thought of losing him after finding him again."

"Joshua is the reason you enlisted?"

"He is the only family I have, other than you. The army bre- vetted him to a lieutenant. That particular rank leads men into battle instead of giving orders from the rear like generals." Nate tightened his grip. "I plan to fight at his side and, if it be God's will, keep him safe. I can shoot even straighter than he can." His lips pulled into a wry grin.

"Please, Nate, don't go. You will both be killed, and it will be all for naught." Panic changed the sound of her voice. "I came to say I don't belong in the Henthorne world any more than you do. But I don't want to live under Mama's thumb either. Why don't we return to Manchester only long enough to sell Dunn Mills? As Papa's heir I have every right. We could set my mother up on a monthly income in London and use the rest to travel the continent, or begin anew in the western territories. Your brother could join us and start fresh." As her enthusiasm escalated, his expression changed to one of sorrow.

Nate lifted her chin with one finger. "Nothing would please me more than a future with you, my love, but Joshua won't desert the army, and so my fate is sealed as well. Life becomes complicated when family is involved. You said so yourself. I was wrong that afternoon in your sister's garden. I judged you for things beyond your control. Everyone is trapped by the circumstances of their birth. I'm a North Carolinian, even though we were too poor for a tombstone on my mother's grave. I cannot abandon either Joshua or Wilmington in its final hour." He offered her a smile filled with sorrow. "Forgive me, but I must finish packing."

Helplessly, she burst into tears as she followed him back inside. "What will happen to your store?"

As Nate packed ledgers and documents into a leather pouch, workmen carried out everything that wasn't nailed to the floor or walls.

"I sent word to Mr. Baxter about my intention to enlist. I offered him my merchandise at no charge as long as he donated whatever he didn't want to charity. No sense letting good food molder." Nate peered around the room dispassionately as though it was no longer part of his life.

"Do these men work for Mr. Baxter?" she asked as two carried out a pickle barrel.

"They do, but Mr. Baxter wouldn't hear of a gift. He insisted on paying a fair price for everything—shelves, worktables, even my empty burlap bags. He intends to expand his market into the space next door." Nate donned his cap and slung two bags over his shoulder as though their reunion was over. "I want to reach the fort before dark." He pushed the leather pouch across the counter.

"What is that?" she asked with her face awash in tears.

"It contains the money Mr. Baxter paid me, along with a bill of sale for land I purchased on the Cape Fear River."

She stared at it suspiciously. "Land?"

"Remember the spot of our first picnic on the peninsula? You waded up to your knees, hoping no one would catch you showing your lacy petticoats."

"I remember." She delicately pressed a handkerchief to her nose.

"I took money I'd saved and made an offer to the owner. He signed over twenty acres free and clear. I planned to build us a cabin with a dock, and then buy a fishing trawler. If you get a hankering to be a fisherman's wife, you could still travel to Wilmington to order cotton for Dunn Mills."

"I love fresh fish," she murmured.

"Then what better reason would you need to marry me?"

"Let's build your cabin on the river. That's a better idea than sailing back to England."

Nate draped the pouch's strap over her shoulder. "We will, someday. In the meantime, take this back to Manchester with you. I need to know you're safe during the upcoming battle. You could take a train north into Virginia. If you show English documents, you will be allowed to cross into the city of Washington. There will be no blockade to prevent your passage."

"But this is my home now!" She flailed her arms to encompass the room.

"I understand, but with you gone I'll have only Joshua to worry about." In front of several shocked Baxter employees, Nate leaned over and kissed her lingeringly on the lips. "When this American nightmare is over, I will find you in Wycleft. I love you, Amanda Dunn."

She opened her mouth to argue, to demand he listen to reason, but she managed only choking sobs.

Nate strode toward the door with her trailing like a pet. Suddenly, he pivoted on his heel. "I nearly forgot. Tell your brother-in-law not to send his steamers downriver. Water mines have been planted to waylay the Yankee navy. Henthorne will lose his ships along with the cargo they carry."

"Why would you warn Jackson?" Amanda crossed her arms and clutched her elbows.

Nate tucked a lock of hair behind her ear. "For no other reason than he is your twin sister's husband. Family does have a way of complicating a person's life." He ran his fingertips down her face and then he was gone, leaving her in an empty market with a heart about to break.

Fourteen

When Nate thought he could conclude his business at the store and arrive at Fort Fisher by nightfall, he hadn't taken into account the Sims family. He found them all waiting for him at home. Although he had explained his decision to Ruth and Odom after the Christmas church services, he still had to field an inordinate number of questions during dinner—all variations of the same conundrum.

"Why would someone feeling as you do about slavery fight for the Confederacy?" Odom asked.

"I hadn't planned to take a stand on either side, but I would die to save my brother or Amanda. And now that she will soon be on her way back to England, I only have Joshua to worry about."

"But the artillery shelling has stopped, and the Union troops that landed on shore have retreated back to their ships. Maybe both sides have had enough," Odom said, waving his hands through the air.

Nate shook his head. "Ulysses S. Grant is chief commander of the Union army. He's a bulldog of a fighter. He won't give up until the Union is restored, no matter how many attempts it takes or how many men die as a result. Wilmington is too important to ignore. It's the last open port on the East Coast. Grant knows *exactly* how Lee and Johnson receive munitions and supplies for their armies. It's only a matter of time before he directs all of his energies here."

Odom launched his best salvo in the argument. "If the situation is as hopeless as it sounds, then you need to think about Miss Dunn. Both you and your brother may end up dead."

Nate laid his hand on the older man's shoulder. "You're always telling me to do the right thing and leave the outcome to God, my friend. I'm about to take your advice."

"Well, you picked a fine day to start listening to me!" Odom walked to the mantel where he kept his well-worn Bible.

There would be no more war talk between them that day or for many to come. Ruth had cooked and baked more than Nate could carry on horseback. Odom presented him with a small, leather-bound testament, and Rufus loaned him his compass.

"It's what I bought with the message-carrying money from you and Miss Dunn," the little boy said, peering up through wet eyelashes.

When Nate tried to refuse the compass, Rufus started to cry in earnest. "How else will you find the fort or your way back to us?" he wailed. "Especially if we move to my aunt's house in the country?"

In the end Nate took the compass. Later that day, miles from the fort on a rutted road in the pitch-dark, he was mighty glad he had. If he kept the horse headed due south, eventually they would either find the fort or land in the Atlantic Ocean—that is, if Rebel pickets didn't shoot him before he could state his intentions.

Just as the first pink of dawn appeared in the east, Nate caught a whiff of salty air. The breeze had shifted direction and increased in intensity with each furlong he advanced. He dismounted from his gelding before the two of them fell into a bog. When he lifted the feedbag from his saddle horn, he heard the unmistakable click of a revolver.

"Raise your hands, boy, real slow-like. Then state your business or prepare to meet your Maker."

Despite having attended church for the first time in years, Nate wasn't ready for the alternate offer. He dropped the grain sack onto the ground and lifted his palms skyward, grateful that a militiaman had provided the badly used uniform. "My name is Nathaniel Cooper. I've come to enlist in the Confederate army."

A round of sneers and guffaws erupted from the trees.

The speaker stepped forward into the thin light of dawn. The gaunt and sallow-faced officer wasn't smiling. "Is that right? Seems to me if a man wanted to do his duty, he wouldn't wait around almost four years."

"I say he's a Yankee spy. Let me run him through, Sergeant. That way we won't make any noise and tell the Yanks where we're at." Another soldier stepped forward with a bayonet protruding from the barrel of his gun.

"I'm no spy," said Nate. "I'm from Wilmington. The reason I didn't sign up sooner was because my services were essential on the waterfront. The rations you enjoy came off a blockade runner tied up in front of my store. You can verify with Judge Miles Stewart in town." Nate knew the judge's name would mean nothing to these men, but he hoped it would preserve his life until they could reach the fort.

"The rations I ate last night weren't fit for a hog." The officer's mood soured another notch.

The skinny private poked Nate's coat with the bayonet. "You

pull that coat off a dead man? Look at them bullet holes." He poked the tip of his bayonet far enough through the hole to tear his shirt.

Nate mustered an imperious tone he hoped would drown out the sound of his knocking knees. "I insist you take me to Lt. Joshua Cooper of General Hoke's Division. My brother will verify I'm telling the truth."

After a moment's pause, the sergeant stuck the pistol that had been aimed at Nate's chest into his belt. "That's what we'll do. There will be plenty of time for bayonet and target practice if you're not telling the truth, Nathaniel Cooper."

Within twenty minutes, Nate got his first look at Fort Fisher. It was not at all what he'd expected. He'd heard his father talk of seeing Fort Sumter once, sitting tall and impressive in the Charleston harbor. Instead of sturdy brick and stone, Fort Fisher was a long series of earthen mounds, like a native burial ground in the desert. At least an imposing palisade of sharpened timbers surrounded the land and sea faces on the narrow peninsula of land. This was the fortress that had effectively guarded the entrance of the Cape Fear River, the only water approach to Wilmington? It was hard to imagine it provided any protection for the blockade runners headed for Nassau, Bermuda, or England.

When the gate of the palisade swung wide, the skinny private prodded Nate inside. At least he used the butt end of his gun instead of the razor-sharp blade. As they crossed the open parade ground, few soldiers gave him more than a cursory glance. Most likely they assumed he was just another deserter, caught and dragged back to be either locked in the brig or shot. Not many men would wait this long to answer the call to serve the Glorious Cause—which didn't seem very glorious, judging by the atmosphere inside the fort.

Once they reached a low-slung building against the western wall, the pistol-packing sergeant barked orders over his shoulder. "You wait here, Cooper, while I ask 'bout your brother among General Hoke's officers. Don't know all them boys yet." To his emaciated companion, he said, "Don't let him out of your sight. No telling what he's got in mind. Shoot him in the back if he tries to run."

"It would be my pleasure." The private flashed Nate a malicious grin.

For several hours Nate remained crouched on his haunches, cramped, hungry, and utterly exhausted. His plea for a drink of water had been ignored. He'd been stripped of his canteen, bag of food from Ruth, and his knapsack. Thank goodness he had given Amanda his money, the deed to his land and store, and every memento he possessed from home. Even his Bible had been confiscated. He would probably never lay eyes on his horse again. Replacement mounts had become rarer than blooming roses in January. Finally, the clatter of hooves awakened him from an uncomfortable doze.

"Nathaniel!" Joshua reined in his horse and swung down only a few feet away.

"This man insists he's your brother, sir," the sergeant sneered.

"That's because he is." Joshua shot the officer a murderous glare while pulling Nate to his feet. "What have you done here, Sergeant?"

"I ain't sure if—"

"This man is my responsibility. You are dismissed."

A shiver ran up Nate's spine, as much from relief as from the cold settling in his bones. "Right happy to see you, little brother," Nate spoke in a whisper.

"Let's warm you up in my quarters. When was the last time you ate?"

"Can't recall. If you put a thick venison steak in front of me, I won't turn it down."

Joshua laughed from the belly. "These aren't the mountains…

no deer here. But I'll get you something edible." He guided his brother into a low-ceilinged room with two cots, two chairs, a table fashioned from wood slats, and a coal stove. While Joshua went to the common room, Nate dropped onto one of the beds, his back against the wall.

Before long Joshua carried in a bowl of stew, a plate of corn mush, a canteen of water, and a homespun blanket. "Eat, and then tell me what in tarnation you're doing here." He wrapped the blanket snuggly around his older brother.

Nate peered at the bowl of carrots, potatoes, turnips, parsley root, and some unidentifiable meat. Seasoned with onions, peppers, and salt, the thick stew was surprisingly delicious. Or perhaps he'd just never been this hungry before.

Joshua sat on a ladderback chair and patiently watched him eat.

Nate devoured the crumbly cornbread with a spoon, drew in a deep breath, and set the crockery on the floor. "I can't remember anything tasting so fine. Thank you."

Joshua bobbed his head. "Now, why have you come?"

"Isn't it obvious? I'm here to enlist. Better late than never as Ma used to say."

"Feeling the way you do about—"

Nate cut him off with an upraised finger, figuring more than a few eavesdroppers lurked nearby. "Hold up there. Everyone should be allowed to change his mind. The Yankees are breathing down the neck of my new hometown. It's now or never, judging by the number of gunboats I saw out there."

After a long appraisal, Joshua shrugged. "Good enough reason for me. We can use every man we can get. We don't even shoot deserters so long as they promise to give it another go."

"Tell me the news. Have the Yanks stopped shelling and withdrawn?"

Joshua consulted his pocket watch. "I need to return to my troops. We're on patrol until dark. In the meantime, get some rest. Tomorrow the major will swear you into my company. Then you'll learn soon enough our situation at the end of the earth."

His brother's face looked breathtakingly young, yet Nate was the one who slept that night in naive ignorance of what was to come.

Amanda would have preferred to spend the entire day in bed after the fateful parting in Nate's abandoned store. Or perhaps until the spring when the Atlantic calmed sufficiently to sail home. But despite his insistence she leave Wilmington, she knew that was out of the question. And it had nothing to do with winter storms or rough seas. How could she leave the man she loved? His profession of affection came as a bittersweet balm after weeks of self-doubt. He loved her, yet he loved his brother as well. And his sense of duty to family might cost him his life.

Thus, when she heard the clatter of shoes across her bedroom floor, she buried her head deeper under the covers. "Please go away, Helene. I intend to remain in bed today."

Without warning the soft, downy quilt was stripped away. Incensed, Amanda bolted upright and reached for the covers in the chilly room. "Oh, bother!"

"I am your sister, not one of the maids. Of course, you have only *one* maid left after last night." Abigail stood at the foot of the bed with her arms crossed over her rounded belly.

"What on earth are you talking about?" Swinging her legs over the side, Amanda picked up her robe from the chair.

"I'll ask the questions. Where did you go yesterday?" Abigail's eyes narrowed into slits.

"I walked to town to see Nate. After all, we spent Christmas apart from each other." Amanda stood and knotted the belt around her waist.

"Did you go there alone, without your maid?"

"I have no need of a maid during a social call. What is this about?"

"Did you and your precious Mr. Cooper conspire to steal my property?"

She rubbed her eyes, desperate for a cup of coffee to clear the fog. "He would never steal from you or anyone else. Despite his modest upbringing, he is an honest man with more integrity than any of Jackson's wealthy friends."

Abigail rolled her eyes and began to pace. "Then none of this makes a bit of sense."

Amanda rang her bedside bell vigorously. "Can't this wait until after I've had my coffee?"

Her question prompted a sly smile from Abigail. "Ring all you want, but I doubt either of your maids will hear it."

Amanda grabbed her sister's arm to stop her pacing. "Instead of talking in riddles, Abby, tell me what happened."

"Josie is gone, vanished during the night. She took all of her things, so it doesn't look as though she's coming back. And, apparently, your sweet Helene has disappeared as well."

Amanda dropped into a chair. "That can't be. Where would she go if the steamers aren't accepting civilian passengers? She knows no one in America except for me."

"But as you keep saying, Helene is free to quit her job and go wherever she likes. So let's focus on who helped Josie escape. Jackson paid fifteen hundred dollars for the girl. Will you or Mr. Cooper reimburse him for his loss?"

"I told you, neither Nate nor I helped Josie…on her road to freedom." Amanda refused to use the word "escape" because slaves ran off regularly these days. "As your guest I would not betray your trust, and Nate has no use for a slave where he's going."

"No one in this household would dare to help—"

"Stop badgering her, Mrs. Henthorne. It wasn't Miss Amanda; it was I." To the utter shock of both women, Helene stepped from behind the draperies where she had hidden since Abigail's arrival.

"What in tarnation?"

"Why are you hiding back there?"

The two questions simultaneously echoed off the ceiling.

Helene looked from one twin to the other and then looked contemptuously at Abigail. "I gave Josie the money so she could escape. Miss Amanda knew nothing about this."

"That's tantamount to thievery in this country and no different than taking an expensive watch or gold from a bank's vault. I could have the sheriff lock you in jail."

Helene paled considerably.

"But you won't because I shall reimburse you for whatever price you set." Amanda stepped in between them. "But why would you do such a thing, Helene? You didn't even like Josie."

The maid lowered her gaze to the floor. "I didn't, not really, but I pitied her. Without family here, she was almost as much an outcast among the other slaves as I. And Josie was terrified that Yankees would come to town and take her north to work. Apparently she had been betrothed to a man in Valdosta, wherever that is. I gave her half my passage money.."

Abigail clucked her tongue. "Yankees overrunning Wilmington? I've never heard anything so ridiculous."

Amanda faced her sister. "Jackson purchased a woman about to be married in Georgia. He tore her from her family and fiancé?"

"Brokers don't provide personal details about slaves, only what skills they might possess." Abby flushed a bright pink. "I must sit down. This is all too much."

"May I bring you something to drink, ma'am?" asked Helene.

Her laughter turned shrill. "Do you mean you still work for my sister? Or have you begun a one-woman slave relocation program? Perhaps you have become a spy for the Yankees from behind boudoir draperies?"

Helene either didn't recognize the sarcasm or chose to ignore it. "No, ma'am, I'm still a lady's maid for Miss Amanda unless she wishes to fire me."

"I would appreciate help until I can arrange your passage home, Helene," said Amanda.

"Thank you, ma'am. I will expect no wages until I've repaid you for Josie's...value."

Amanda shook her head. "No, I'd already planned to purchase the girl's freedom before leaving. Now it's taken care of. But if you're still my maid, could you *please* bring Mrs. Henthorne some water and a pot of coffee for me?" She opened her fan to cool Abby's face. Her sister indeed looked peaked.

"It would be my pleasure." Helene strode toward the door, but Abigail stopped her in her tracks.

"If you intend to remain, Helene, I'll expect no further mischief in the future."

Helene bobbed a perfunctory curtsey. "You have my word, madam."

Amanda wrung out a damp cloth from the basin for Abby's forehead. "I am sorry, sister. It wasn't my intention to create havoc for you, especially with your delicate condition."

Abby laid her head back and closed her eyes. "What did you mean by 'Nate has no use for a slave where he's going'? Has your paramour decided to move north?"

Amanda blinked back the moisture clouding her vision. "Quite the contrary. He joined the army—the Confederate army. He's on his way to Fort Fisher as we speak."

"Now? Why would he remain neutral for so long and then all of a sudden change his mind?"

"His brother is at the fort. Joshua is a lieutenant who will lead men into battle. Apparently, Josie's prediction wasn't too far from the truth. More Union gunboats have arrived at the mouth of the Cape Fear. Their artillery fired on the fort—on Christmas Eve, no less."

"Colonel Lamb will keep Wilmington safe, as he has done so far." Abby didn't sound as confident as she had earlier.

"I hope that's true. Nathaniel enlisted because he fears for his brother in the coming battle. We must pray it is much ado about nothing."

In a rustle of silk, Abby rose clumsily to her feet and dropped the wet cloth on the floor. "With the mystery of the missing Josie solved, I think I will retire to my room and lie down. I'll leave you to your coffee and breakfast."

"Another minute of your time, please." Amanda walked to the fireplace to add more wood. The room had grown damp and cold. "Nate sent a warning to Jackson. He cannot send his steamers downriver to the sea. The Cape Fear has been planted with water mines to thwart any invasion by Union troops."

"How preposterous! Jackson would have heard if this was true."

"It has been a recent development. Joshua Cooper brought word from Fort Fisher on Christmas Eve."

Abby's mouth formed the letter *O*. "Why would Mr. Cooper help my husband? Jackson has never treated him kindly."

"Astute of you to recognize that. I asked the very same thing. Nate said it's because you are my sister. He loves me, and I love him."

"Yes, *that* has been apparent for some time." Abby braced one hand on the door frame. "Thank you for telling me, Amanda. I'll pass the information along to Jackson to do with as he chooses. Ah. At long last, here is your coffee tray."

Jackson yearned for a quiet dinner with his wife that night. After the exasperating day at his warehouses, he certainly didn't need any more irritation. According to the consensus on the docks, Captain Hornsby had run off with his load of cotton, depriving him of substantial profits. He had yet to share this news with Robert. None of the sailors had seen hide nor hair of the *Countess Marie*, and Hornsby knew better than to show up in Wilmington seeking another load anytime soon. If he did, Jackson would be ready for the scoundrel. He had purchased a derringer that fit discretely in his breast pocket. It held only two shots, but that would be sufficient to discourage further trickery from the blackguard.

Unfortunately, when he entered his foyer, one glance at Abigail's pinched face dashed his hopes for relaxation. "What has happened? Is it the baby?" he asked with growing unease.

"No, we are both fine. Just a bit of distressing news I'll tell you at dinner." She smiled prettily, a gesture that never ceased to lift his spirits.

"Why haven't you eaten? It's after eight. With your delicate condition, you should never wait this long." Wrapping an arm around her waist, Jackson guided her toward the dining room.

"Aren't you having your usual bourbon first?" She turned her face up to his.

"I want you to sit down and eat. Amos, please bring Mrs. Henthorne a glass of lemonade and a weak drink for me. Then ask Salome to send up dinner at once."

"Very good, sir." The butler picked up Jackson's overcoat and hat and disappeared down the hallway.

Once they were seated with cool drinks, Jackson reached for his wife's hand. "Tell me why you waited."

"I tried to dine earlier with Amanda but had no appetite. Perhaps I can eat now."

Jackson leaned back as the footman served bowls of thick onion soup, the crusty cheese still bubbling. "Let's allow this to cool while you tell me what's troubling you."

"Amanda found out that our army planted water mines near the mouth of the river. She believes your ships will be sunk if they venture out to sea."

Of all the things that could upset a society matron, this had to be last on the list. "What the devil?"

"Do not invoke that name, Jackson. It can only make matters worse." Abigail murmured a quiet prayer under her breath.

He finished his drink and then called to the butler. "Bring me a lemonade too." He modulated his tone for his wife. "Explain how my English sister-in-law could be privy to such revelations when I haven't heard a word on the wharf."

"Perhaps our army fears spies among the dockworkers, so they keep silent. Recent immigrants hold all sorts of allegiances these days."

Jackson blinked at the woman who looked like his wife but certainly didn't sound like her. "Yet, *Amanda* was able to find out."

Abigail smiled, grasping the irony at last. "Ah, yes. Mr. Cooper told her before he left town to enlist at Fort Fisher. I believe his brother is a general at the fort. Anyway, his brother told the shopkeeper, who told my sister." She tried a spoonful of soup. "Oh, my. This is delicious. I'm so glad Salome changed from those heavy fish chowders."

"Cooper's brother is a *general* at Fort Fisher?"

Her spoon halted midway to her mouth. "Maybe she said colonel. I don't recall. But Joshua Cooper is the reason Amanda's Mr. Cooper joined the Confederate army. Apparently he's not an anarchist after all."

"If there's a shred of truth to this." He pushed away his soup.

"I believe there is. He loves Amanda and, therefore, he feels a smidgen of loyalty to me as well."

Jackson pressed his fingertips to his temples, where a dull ache had begun. "What you're saying makes no sense, Abigail. Why would soldiers plant mines in the river? The blockade runners bring in food and guns as well as take cotton and tobacco out."

"Because the Yankees landed on the shore and attacked the fort. Colonel Lamb doesn't want any more midnight surprises." Abigail dabbed her mouth with a napkin. "Is a lieutenant ranked higher than a colonel? Because I believe *that's* what the shopkeeper said his brother was."

"No, it is not higher," Jackson replied absently. He closed his eyes as his mind began to spin with the dreadful possibility her story might be true. He'd been too busy worrying about losses from Hornsby's thievery to listen to news about the war. The *Roanoke* should be in Bermuda, consigning another load to bring back, but the *Lady Adelaine* was scheduled to leave port tomorrow once the captain completed the paperwork. He couldn't take a chance on losing his brand-new ship if Amanda's information was correct.

Jumping to his feet, he dropped his napkin next to his plate. "I'm going to the docks. I must inform Captain Russell that he's not to depart under any circumstances until I get to the bottom of this."

Abigail clamped her slender fingers around his wrist, her grip belying her petite size. "You will do no such thing. Captain Russell is probably ensconced at the Kendall House, enjoying an evening away from that boat. Please finish your dinner, my dear. Dawn will be soon enough to cancel the *Lady Adelaine's* departure."

Jackson remained in place, not because he couldn't break free from her restraint, but because never before in their marriage had Abigail given him orders. "First your sister and now you know my business better than I?"

She looked up with her luminous dark eyes. "Certainly not,

Jackson, but unsavory miscreants prowl the wharves at this hour. You are too important to me…to us…to chance being killed over your pocket watch or even the *Lady Adelaine* filled to the decks with gold." Abigail folded her hands over her stomach. "Please, husband, let's finish dinner and go to bed. Tomorrow you will rise to the challenge refreshed."

He could not refuse a request so sweetly asked. "As you wish, my dear." He sat down again, picked up his spoon, and began to eat.

The next morning after his usual ham and eggs, he rode down to the docks in the carriage. When his foreman, Edward Campbell, arrived a few minutes later, Jackson peppered him with questions. The man had heard nothing about water torpedoes but volunteered to inquire. Apparently, the tavern where Jackson encountered the dubious captain of the *Marie Celeste* entertained sailors from first light until after midnight. Within two hours, Campbell returned with news that the river had indeed been mined.

"Who told you this?" Jackson asked. "Can the informant be trusted?"

"Yes, sir. I spoke to the captain of the militia. They have been called to the fort. The captain was ordered to round up stragglers and report at once. The captain sent his men ahead, but he wasn't in any particular hurry to join them. The port has been closed until further notice. No ships are to approach the fort for any reason. What should we do, Mr. Henthorne? Do you want us to unload the steamer?" As though already weary, Campbell leaned his shoulder against a post.

"Give me a minute to think," Jackson said. He clenched and unclenched his hands as he walked from one end of the cotton warehouse to the other. *If the port is closed, how can I sell the contents of the* Lady Adelaine *to the highest bidder? And how can the*

Roanoke *return with its profits, along with a cargo of war materials? But ships blown to pieces won't do me much good either.*

By the time he walked back to Campbell, a plan had taken shape. "Complete the departure manifest. Then handpick eight or nine of your most reliable workers. Make sure they are sober men whose families can spare them for days at a time. Can *you* be spared at home to accept a new position for me, Mr. Campbell? I'm willing to double your salary."

The foreman nodded eagerly. "Our daughter is married and living in Beaufort. Our son is with Joe Johnston somewhere west of here, and my wife can fend for herself. What do you have in mind, sir?"

"Yankees are getting too close. Even if our army protects Wilmington, I don't trust the unsavory lot hanging by the docks, not after my experience with Captain Hornsby. I plan to instruct Captain Russell to sail the *Lady Adelaine* downriver about twelve miles. There is a hidden inlet that maintains deep enough water even at low tide. I'll have him drop anchor there and wait this out. Everyone seems to think the Yankees are itching for a fight and our Colonel Lamb will give it to them."

Campbell pulled on his ear, deep in thought. "Do you want Captain Russell to stay on the ship indefinitely?"

"Of course not. That's why I need you. I'll send a carriage to bring the captain back to town. You and several others will stand guard for three or four days at the time. Then trade off with the other half of your men. Tell them I'll pay their full wages for half the work as long as they keep their mouths shut regarding the inlet's location."

Campbell smiled. "I don't think too many will argue 'bout that."

"As I said, I'll pay you twice your normal amount and give you Sundays off."

"That's mighty generous, Mr. Henthorne. Your wages have always been more than fair."

"I need a man I can trust, Campbell. My entire fortune is tied up in my vessels. I am ruined if I lose those steamships."

"Nothing will happen to the *Lady Adelaine*, not with me in charge."

"I'm indebted to you, sir." Impetuously, Jackson extended his hand.

Campbell looked at it for a moment in stunned silence before brushing his palm down his shirt and then shaking heartily. "You won't be sorry you put your trust in me."

Fifteen

January 1, 1865

Amanda began the New Year resolved to avoid duplicitous behavior. Tradition called for resolutions—changes—to a person's mind-set along with the avoidance of certain habits that threatened a person's well-being in this life and perhaps hampered their chances of obtaining the hereafter. She started down this fresh path by avoiding the Stewarts' gala on New Year's Eve. The last thing she wanted was to don a voluminous ball gown and cumbersome hoop and then mingle with people who found her oddly unsociable. She *was* oddly unsociable.

Although Jackson promised to stop foisting her on Wilmington bachelors, she had no desire to waltz with aging widowers or young men still learning to dance. And conversations with the overdressed, overly made-up female guests would be no better. Even the kindhearted matrons couldn't resist asking: "How is your storekeeper faring these days?"

Why did people insist on identifying a person by their vocation, as though how someone made his living determined his worth as a man? Yet, back at home in England she had done the same thing. A nobleman, even a desperately poor one, was worthy of her time and attention, whereas the gardener or milk delivery man or lamplighter on the street wouldn't warrant the briefest of hellos.

America was the land of opportunity, and Amanda yearned for a clean slate. So she remained home during the two-day affair hosted by the Stewarts. She spent a quiet evening with Helene, Salome, Amos, and the few slaves who hadn't run off while the Henthornes were in the country.

Word of a possible invasion of Union troops had frightened both slaves and free people of color. Slaves didn't fully understand the Yankees' intentions. And along with the freemen, many feared the army would burn their homes and kill their chickens. Exaggerated tales of General Sherman's exploits in South Carolina and Georgia had spread all the way to Wilmington.

Amanda ate supper at the massive trestle table in the subterranean kitchen with the others. Afterward, on a surprisingly mild evening, Amos played a lively tune on his fiddle for those inclined to dance. Even Helene lifted her skirts with one hand and tried to duplicate Salome's footwork, while Amanda clapped her hands to keep the rhythm. Anything to keep her mind off Nate. Where was he on this breezy, cloudless night? Had he safely reached Fort Fisher, or had he been shot by sharpshooters from the same army he intended to join?

That New Year's morning, as soon as the sun rose over the rooflines, Amanda penned a long overdue letter to her mother and a second to Charles Pelton. Although she frequently sent details regarding cotton headed to Liverpool and Manchester, this letter contained a different type of instructions to the man in charge in her absence.

"Ah, you're up bright and early this holiday morn." Helene bustled into the room with a tray containing Amanda's carafe of coffee and a plate of sweet rolls. After opening the drapes and making the bed, she headed for the door.

"Stay, Helene. Have a pastry with me so we can talk." Amanda gestured toward the small table by the window.

Helene glanced at the doorway. "I don't know if that's wise, Miss Amanda…"

"It will be late afternoon at the earliest before the Henthornes return. If Abigail is feeling well, they may drive straight on to Oakdale. We may not see them until the weekend."

"That's good to hear. Tell me what has you so industrious this morning." Helene sat down and took the smallest pastry from the tray.

"I have written a list of changes to be implemented at Dunn Mills."

Helene arched one delicate eyebrow. "Regarding how garments are to be made?"

Amanda snickered. "Goodness, no. I have no knowledge of manufacturing. These are changes within the village of Wycleft." Picking up the letter, she blew lightly on the damp ink. "I want a local school for the mill children so they won't have to travel to the next town. Mr. Pelton is to advertise and then hire a headmaster. We'll use the church hall until a facility can be built. Attending school should be encouraged until age sixteen but mandatory until children are fourteen. A father's wages will be adjusted to prevent hardship from the loss of income if his children are absent from the mill due to obtaining an education." She picked up her coffee cup and sipped daintily.

"A bonnie idea, especially about the new school. 'Tis a tragedy for lads and lasses to be illiterate in this day and age."

"That's not all. Mr. Pelton is to hire a doctor, perhaps a young man fresh from university, who wishes to establish a new practice. The doctor's fees will be paid by Dunn Mills and not borne by the workers. A generous yearly stipend will be agreed upon when the doctor is hired."

"My, these are bold changes, Miss Amanda. Don't you want to wait until you discuss them with your mother?"

"No, I do not." Amanda bit into a cream-filled pastry. "Mama knows nothing about living conditions in Wycleft, and I doubt she would care if she did. According to papers sent me by Papa's solicitor, I am in charge."

"I commend your progressive thinking, ma'am."

"At least it's a start. When I see for myself how much of Nate's assertions are true, I will institute additional improvements."

"I suspected your Mr. Cooper might somehow be involved with this. The citizens of Wycleft will owe their improved lot to a shopkeeper in North Carolina—one they will never meet."

Amanda smiled at the idea of *her* Mr. Cooper. Then the image of him dressed in a faded butternut uniform caused her chest to constrict. "Perhaps Nate will visit my home one day and offer suggestions, but this will get Pelton moving in the meantime." She inserted the letter in an envelope and sealed it with a drop of wax. "I have written to my mother as well. You will deliver both upon your arrival in England."

Helene set down her sweet roll in surprise. "Upon *my* arrival? Where will you be?"

"Right here in Wilmington, waiting for Nate to come home." Amanda swallowed hard, forcing herself not to cry.

"But you told Mrs. Henthorne that he left to fight for the Confederacy. The war could last months or even years more—"

"I can't be in England while he may lie wounded and languishing in some hospital without someone to care for him."

"What could you do, Miss Amanda? You're not a trained nurse, and you cannot search the battlefield for him." Helene shivered visibly before refilling Amanda's cup. "Wait to hear from him in the comfort of your home."

"I have made up my mind to stay, but *you* will not. Thomas will take us to the train station tomorrow. I've made inquiries regarding which rail lines are still functional. We shall travel to Richmond together, where I'll see you safely into territory controlled by the Yankees. I won't leave your side until you're safely on a train to Washington."

"Washington? What will I do there by myself?"

"You will book passage on the next steamer to England. No gunboats will prevent ships from leaving the nation's capital. With proper English documents, no one will deny you passage."

"What should I tell your mother? Mrs. Dunn will be incensed if you don't return with me."

"I explained everything in my letter to her, at least as much as I know now. She won't like it, but I'm a grown woman with plans to follow my heart."

"Like Miss Abigail," murmured Helene.

"Yes, I suppose so, but I never thought I would admit it." She placed a third envelope next to Helene's plate. "This contains traveling money along with your next six months' wages."

The maid shook her head. "I can't take money I haven't earned."

"You *have* earned it by accompanying me to a strange land. This will support you until you find another position."

Helene glanced around the lavish suite. "I suppose America has much to recommend it. If only circumstances were different here…"

"It is splendid to hear you say so! Perhaps one day you'll return for a visit, if and when Nate and I marry and make our home here. But rest assured, Helene. Our circumstances will be vastly different than the Henthornes." Just uttering those words gave Amanda a jolt of courage.

Impulsively, Helene hugged her for a brief moment. "I shall miss you." A tear slipped beneath her lashes.

"And I, you. Now go collect your things while I will pack a bag for a few nights. There's no telling how long it will take to get you back to the United States instead of the Confederate States of America. I'm hoping January will be mild this year."

Helene bobbed her head and went into the alcove to pack. Suddenly the prospect of returning to Red Rose County banished her worries over rough water or seasickness.

Amanda wished she could feel so optimistically about the future. She had no doubts regarding Nate's integrity. It was the mind-set of the Union army that kept her pacing until the wee hours of morning. When sleep refused to come, Amanda penned a note, brief and to the point, to her sister.

Abby, I've gone to Washington to see Helene safely past the Union blockade. She will sail for England but I will return to Wilmington. My fate is irrevocably tied to the outcome of this war, the same as yours.

   With fond regards, Amanda

"Frankly, I don't understand you, Abigail," Jackson said as he thumped on the ceiling of the carriage to signal the coachman. When the carriage started to roll, he turned toward her on the seat. "You insisted on remaining another day after the New Year's brunch because you felt better than you had all winter."

"Rosalyn graciously asked us to stay, and it had been ever so long since we visited…"

"Yes, I understand that. But when I suggested we go straight to the plantation to extend the holiday with my parents, your stomach suddenly felt queasy." He tried not to sound as peevish as he felt.

Abigail remained quiet for half a minute before responding. "I believe your mother upsets my constitution." She giggled behind her fan.

Jackson fought the urge to laugh. "I'm not sure I like your new forthright manner of speech. Is this your twin's influence after the last nine months?"

"Perhaps so. We can't help but affect each other, even though we attempt to remain autonomous."

"How do you affect Amanda?"

"I've observed that she's less judgmental of those not sharing her opinions."

"I don't see much improvement in that regard, but I appreciated her news about the river channel. That could have been ruination for me."

"My point exactly. If she stays in Wilmington long enough, I predict you two shall become fast friends." Abigail lifted her fan to cover her face.

"Pigs will fly first." Jackson thumped again on the ceiling as they turned onto Third Street.

The footman stuck his head in the window. "Yes, Master Henthorne?"

"Tell Thomas to stop at the front hitching block. I'm going to town after I see Mrs. Henthorne inside."

When the footman had withdrawn his head, Abigail said, "Must you, Jackson? I so yearned for us to have a quiet evening by the fire."

He kissed the back of her gloved fingers. "I won't be long, my dear. Then we'll have our evening together. I need to talk to Mr. Peterson while he's in town. He should be informed of the situation with the *Lady Adelaine* and the *Roanoke*."

Abigail issued an unladylike snort. "Business, business. I'll be glad when this war is over and life returns to normal. I liked you better the way you were before—mildly slothful."

He looked twice to make sure the right Dunn sister was sitting beside him. Once they were inside the house, Jackson helped Abigail to her favorite settee under the window. After tucking her up in a quilt and summoning a pot of tea, he returned to the carriage for the ride to Wilmington's best hotel. If truth be told, he was as eager for a quiet evening at home as she was.

"Why have you provided a bell if no one intends to respond?" Jackson chastised the Kendall House clerk. It had taken three rings before the man emerged from the back room.

"Begging your pardon, sir. How can I help you tonight?" The clerk sounded appropriately contrite.

"Kindly let Mr. Peterson know Mr. Henthorne is here and wishes to speak with him. I'll wait in the gentlemen's parlor." Jackson hooked his thumb toward a masculine lounge, thick with blue cigar smoke even at this early hour.

"Mr. Peterson, did you say, sir?" The clerk's thin face paled considerably.

"Yes, Mr. Robert Peterson. Step lively. I don't have all night."

"Uh…please allow me to get the manager, sir." Before Jackson could protest, the clerk disappeared into the private office.

Moments later a distinguished white-haired man appeared with a somber expression. "Mr. Henthorne, a pleasure to see you, sir. I regret to be the bearer of bad news. We sent word to your home after finding your name on several papers in Mr. Peterson's possession. Your butler indicated you were gone for the holiday and wouldn't return for several days."

Jackson bit back a caustic retort as a wave of panic burned inside his belly. "I stand before you now. Perhaps you can convey the news without further delay?"

The manager swabbed his forehead with his handkerchief. "Mr. Peterson checked in on the thirty-first to enjoy the festivities at the club. He left instructions not to be disturbed the next morning. We assumed he wished to sleep late. When a maid checked his room that evening, she found him unresponsive in his chair. She informed me, and I summoned the doctor and the mayor. Because the militia has been called to the fort, we have few civil authorities in town." He dropped his voice to a whisper as though pillagers might soon descend on his hotel.

Jackson braced his palms on the counter. "What exactly do you mean by 'unresponsive'?"

"Dead, sir. Mr. Peterson is dead. The doctor believes that bout of swamp fever weakened his heart and it simply gave out."

"He's *dead*?" Jackson's exclamation revealed his inability to comprehend the manager's words. "Swamp fever?"

"Certainly you knew he was very sick last fall while in the backwater counties. The miasma has taken many men to an early grave."

"Those papers you found…are the ledgers and contracts still in his room?" Jackson felt sudden beads of sweat run down his temples.

The manager's demeanor cooled. "They were gathered into a satchel along with Mr. Peterson's personal effects to await the arrival of his family. I understand he had a brother living abroad."

"That's right, Steven Peterson, who is in Bermuda."

"Yes, sir. I believe that's where we sent notification."

"I was in partnership with both brothers. I demand to see those papers to ascertain what provisions were made in case the unthinkable transpired..." Jackson knew he was rambling almost incoherently, but the demise of Mr. Peterson had discombobulated him.

The manager splayed his hands on the counter. "This sounds like a matter for your attorney, Mr. Henthorne, and perhaps a court of law. I will keep the gentleman's possessions secure pending the arrival of his brother or an order from the court."

Jackson grabbed hold of the man's lapels. "You self-important little— My entire fortune is in jeopardy!"

The manager shrugged away, incensed. "That will be the case for everyone if the war doesn't end soon. Good day to you, sir!" He stomped into his office and closed the door, leaving Jackson alone and shaking in the lobby.

Hornsby and the *Marie Celeste* had vanished with his load of cotton, and now Peterson was dead? What did that bode for the future of their partnership? And what about the *Roanoke*? It could be coming to the Carolinas at this moment, unaware of catastrophe awaiting hapless ships that entered the Cape Fear.

At least he had moved his other ship to safe harbor, as long as unscrupulous guards, shallow waters, unpredictable tidal surges, or *rust* didn't bring about the *Lady Adelaine*'s premature demise.

Jackson staggered back to where Thomas sat with the carriage. He paused on the curb to speak to his driver, dapper in his frock coat and top hat. "Has the horse been fed and adequately watered?" he asked.

"Of course, sir. I take good care of the old boy."

"Good, because I want to ride to Oakdale tonight." Jackson lifted his boot heel to the carriage's bottom step.

"This late in the day, sir? Don't you reckon we should wait till morning?"

"No, I do not." Jackson exhaled harshly, trying to rein in his temper. "I have important business to discuss with my father that won't wait. I shouldn't need to explain this to you, Thomas, but we will return to town tomorrow. You can sleep once we get to Oakdale. Mrs. Henthorne and Salome will be fine for one night alone. After all, Amos is there."

"Amos is an old man, sir, if you don't mind my saying so, and—"

"What I *mind* is standing here arguing instead of leaving! The sooner we go, the sooner we'll get back." He ended up shouting on the street.

"Yes, sir." Releasing the brake, Thomas snapped the whip over the horse's back. The carriage began to roll before the prudently silent footman closed the door behind Jackson.

Picking their way along dark, rutted roads provided Jackson with plenty of time for contemplation as to what he would say when he arrived, but how did a man tell his father he had apparently been duped and swindled by a man he shouldn't have trusted in the first place? Or that he'd leveraged their assets on two shiny blockade runners that could be sunk by an artillery shell or confiscated by the navy as spoils of war? His father had entrusted him with Henthorne and Sons, but in his quest for wealth he may have foolishly and needlessly put at risk their entire future.

By the time they reached the front gate to Oakdale, morning had broken over fallow peanut fields, dormant until spring's warm rains. Jackson sent Thomas and the footman around back to eat and sleep while he entered the grand foyer of his ancestral home. Handing his coat to the butler, he paused in the dining room doorway and bowed low. "Good morning, Mother, Father. Forgive my intrusion at this early hour."

His parents looked at him in some surprise but also in welcome. "You need no invitation to come home, son," said Randolph.

"Sit and have something to eat, dear. Did Abigail come with you?" his mother asked.

"She did not. I came rather spur of the moment." Jackson stiffly lowered himself onto a chair and motioned for coffee.

"You must have ridden all night to arrive at this hour. I trust there is something important on your mind." His father studied him curiously.

"There is, but let's enjoy this fine breakfast first." Plates of fruit, grits, tomatoes, sliced ham, fried eggs, and flakey biscuits were arrayed across the table...all for two diners. Jackson forced himself to eat a small amount despite his lack of hunger.

Isabelle finished her food in silence, and then she stood, brushed her son's forehead with a kiss, and left the room. Jackson didn't wait to be prodded as to why he had come. He launched into a tale of bulging warehouses, inflated prices for tobacco and cotton, sleek ships able to outrun gunboats, and repaid debts on the company books. He then completed his account with the saga of Captain Hornsby, the closing of the port and mining of the river by their army, the death of his business partner, and one undeniable reality: the financial future of Henthorne and Sons rested on the continued success of the *Roanoke* and the *Lady Adelaine*.

His father listened without interruption. He neither cursed nor berated nor shook his fist in anger. His behavior throughout Jackson's narrative remained calm and composed. "So you're telling me our backs are against the wall." He signaled to the servants to clear the table.

"To put it mildly, sir. I feel as though I betrayed you by not coming here earlier." He forced himself to meet his father's eye.

"Nonsense. I gave you the reins because I no longer wanted them. You tried what you thought was our best chance for success."

"I may have been reckless—"

Randolph waved away the adjective as though it were a gnat near his food. "There was no safe course, no predictable road to an assured outcome, during this time of extended conflict. All of that's been taken from us." He gazed out the window at sights he had seen all his life.

For the first time, Jackson noticed accumulated dust on the surfaces of the table and bookshelves and the streaky window glass. The neglect of his parents' pride and joy saddened him as much as his money woes. He turned his attention back to his father, a man almost as worn as the room's appointments. "Who could have predicted this war would go so relentlessly against us?"

"Your brother was certain they would lick the Yankees and be home in time for harvest. Everyone thought after giving the North one or two good thrashings that Lincoln would leave us in peace."

"Now Yankee ships ring the mouth of the river, waiting, daring us to escape from our own state."

"Perhaps the *Roanoke* will stay in Bermuda. You were wise to hide the other steamer." Randolph clumsily pushed up from the table. "Don't persecute yourself, son. We shall manage with whatever comes."

When had his father become so defeated or grown so old? Jackson sucked in a deep breath. "I cannot sit in my parlor awaiting my fate like a condemned man. I have to act. The Confederacy *must* prevail. If we are victorious in the coming battle, and if the Yankee navy sails back north, commerce will resume. Given time, our losses can be recouped."

"Don't talk foolishly. I won't sacrifice both my sons." Randolph walked toward the door, but Jackson blocked his exit.

"If we lose the war, the Yankees could confiscate everything I have left. We will be ruined."

"What can one man possibly do? You must think about your wife and the child on the way."

"I can fight to preserve my home, my ships…my dignity. I intend to take a stand."

"You sound exactly like your brother! William hasn't been heard from in *two years*. He's probably lying in an unmarked grave with other brave souls in Maryland or Virginia and we'll never know where." Randolph's face flushed hotly as he staggered against the wall.

Jackson gripped his father's arms to steady him. "If my brother is dead, he died a hero. I want no man calling me a coward when all is said and done."

"You're not making any sense. No one is trying to raise regiments in town anymore."

"No, but I can still volunteer at the fort. They won't turn away a man who comes to fight." Before his courage faltered, Jackson kissed his father's cheek in a rare token of affection. "Best not to tell Mother where I am going. I'll tell her myself when this nasty business is behind us." He strode from the house, the place where he'd been born, and didn't look back.

In the side yard, he sent a small boy to find Thomas. When his coachman appeared with a chicken leg in hand, Jackson issued instructions. "Have someone saddle one of my father's horses and tie on a bag of food and a canteen of water. After you have sufficiently rested, I want you to drive the carriage home. Inform Mrs. Henthorne she is to pack her bags and return here with you. Bring Salome and Amos, Miss Dunn and Helene, and anybody else who's still there. Lock up the house and leave as soon as possible. Do you understand, Thomas?"

"Yes, sir, I do, but where's you goin'?"

"I'm on my way to Fort Fisher, but Mrs. Henthorne isn't to be informed of that until she's safely with my parents. Is that clear?"

"Yes, sir. I surely don't want to be the one to tell her when we've got a long ride ahead of us."

After his coachman headed toward the stable, Jackson sought the cool shade under a live oak tree. He would rest for an hour or two and leave without seeing his parents again.

He wouldn't need much provocation to change his mind.

January 5, 1865

Nate quickly learned the meaning of purposeless drills, useless exercises, and how truly bad food can taste. But he was now a private in the Army of the Confederate States of America, something he never thought he would be. He also learned the meaning of mind-numbing boredom. Few books were to be found in the sand-and-earthen fort, and he hadn't the forethought to bring any with him.

After morning drills and exercises, Nate took it upon himself to learn the layout and weaponry of Fisher. At first his numerous questions were met with suspicion, but eventually the artillerymen deduced he was just another bored soldier, one who didn't enjoy card games or bawdy singing. In the evening, Nate read a few passages of Scripture, said his prayers for Amanda's safety during his absence, and then studied the defenses of the fort as a way to pass the time.

Unlike typical masonry forts, rendered obsolete by improved weaponry, Fort Fisher was a massive sand fortification with a land face and a long sea face. Along the sea wall, connected by a broad sand rampart, were eight- and ten-inch cannons, along with Brooke rifles and a one-hundred-fifty-pound Armstrong gun. An artilleryman explained that the Armstrong was capable of shooting shells for five miles, but before Nate could feel particularly secure, the man bemoaned the fact that they had very little ammunition for the cannon.

Land defenses included Parrott rifles and Coehorn mortars along the inland wall, with twelve-pound Napoleons guarding the entrance. Any Union troops landing on the northern shore wouldn't stand a chance against such weaponry. The woods were cleared for half a mile, and the area in front of a nine-foot palisade of sharpened pine timbers was mined. Beneath the fort's embankment was a series of interconnected bunkers for ordnance and gunpowder, or to serve as bombproof shelters where soldiers could find protection during a bombardment.

As for himself, Nate intended on keeping his head down and pointing his rifle at anyone with Joshua in their crosshairs. Was such an idea even possible? Having never fought in a war before, he didn't know, but it was the only plan he had.

After he practiced loading and reloading his gun until he could do it in his sleep, Nate went in search of Joshua in hopes his patrol duty was finished for the day. However, the familiar face he spotted on the parade ground didn't belong to his brother. Jackson Henthorne approached on a diagonal path with his head bowed as if deep in thought. If Nate hadn't glanced up, the men may have collided.

"Mr. Henthorne! What are you doing here?"

"Mr. Cooper," drawled Jackson, the first to recover his composure. "Ordinarily I might ask you the same question, but Miss Dunn told us of your wish to fight side by side with your brother. This is an odd turn of events for a suspected anarchist and a mercenary planter's son, wouldn't you agree? Not that I believed that particular rumor about you."

Nate bit back a snide remark and instead said, "Yes, rumors of my insurgent leanings were greatly exaggerated. Tell me what inspired *your* change of heart."

Jackson pulled on buckskin gloves with a slow smile. "My partner in the shipping business is dead. The man had the luxury of dying without current knowledge of our precarious financial state." He glanced up to meet Nate's eye. "I am indebted to you, Cooper, for the message passed through Miss Dunn. If not for your warning, I might have lost the *Lady Adelaine*." He bent from the waist.

Nate didn't know how a gentleman should respond to such a compliment. He returned a less dramatic bow. "We have been cut from different bolts of cloth, you and I, but we share the common ground of the Dunn sisters."

"Indeed, we do." Jackson absently plucked at a seam on his coat. "Whose regiment are you in?"

"My brother's, Lt. Joshua Cooper."

"I've been given the dubious distinction of corporal in Sam Thompson's regiment. Of course, when the shelling begins again, it won't matter which detail we line up in during roll call."

Nate took a step closer. "Why are you here, Henthorne? Miss Abigail needs you at home. Who's to say the rest of your slaves won't run off? There are no doctors left in Wilmington who haven't been ordered here. By now Miss Dunn and her maid are long gone."

"Abigail's sister left North Carolina?" His face bleached pale to the color of milk. "I intended for her to remain at my parents' home with my wife, safe from whatever is coming."

"And I demanded that she catch the next steamer home. I feared that if she stayed she would follow me here dressed as a man and enlist. She can be a very stubborn woman."

"In that case, I hope her ocean crossing will be uneventful." Jackson took in a deep breath and let it out slowly. "At least Abigail has Estelle and Salome looking after her, along with my mother. One of the slaves at Oakdale is a midwife too."

"I will pray they don't decide to run off."

"Estelle and Salome are like family to Abigail. Thomas would never leave Salome's side, and Amos is too old to leave. We should have given them their freedom long ago instead of holding them captive. Now we're trapped in a war we can't win. I'm here to do my part or I'll never be able to hold up my head again."

He looked so miserable that Nate regretted telling him about Amanda. "With a merciful God, we'll live long enough to see them again someday." He offered his hand, which Henthorne promptly clasped.

"That's what I intend to focus on when those Yankees start knocking at the door."

Sixteen

Henthorne Mansion, Wilmington
January 5, 1865

Abigail awoke to a cool room in a downright frigid house. The fire had gone out during the night. She peered at the small silver bell on her bedside table. What a useless bauble. Most of their slaves had run off, including Estelle. Initially, Abigail had felt miffed because her maid hadn't left her a note. Estelle had simply told Salome she planned to find her mother in South Carolina. But then Abigail recalled that because of a silly law that required slaves to remain illiterate, Estelle could neither read nor write.

Sighing and feeling abandoned by husband, sister, and maid, Abigail wrapped a quilt around her shoulders and shuffled to the window. In the courtyard below, rain splashed the flagstones and pooled in puddles that would soon turn icy if temperatures fell any lower. It seldom snowed in Wilmington, which was similar to weather conditions at home in England, where warm ocean currents kept the climate mild. *Home.* How she wished she were there instead of in an empty mansion with only Salome and Amos. With a baby due in a few weeks, Mama would summon the best physician in the shire to be on hand. Despite five years' worth of pent-up hostility, even Agnes Dunn wouldn't deny her daughter proper medical care.

After listlessly stirring the fireplace ashes to no avail, Abigail trudged down two flights of stairs. With her quilt trailing behind like the Queen's coronation train, she padded through empty rooms in search of another human being. Dust motes floated on stale air, but in the kitchen a fire blazed on the hearth. The sweet scent of cinnamon and sugar caused her stomach to rumble.

Salome almost dropped the tray she held when Abigail entered. "What are you doing down here, Miz Henthorne? I'm on my way up with your breakfast—eggs, toast, jam, grits, ham, and fresh cream for your tea, just how you like it." Dishes rattled precariously from Salome's trembling fingers. "Go on back to bed. I'll be right behind you."

Abigail slumped onto a bench at the trestle table—a table that could easily seat a dozen servants. "My room is cold."

"I told Amos to fetch a load of wood, but none's been split. He's trying to chop some now." Salome huffed. "The worthless boys who tended the garden ran off last night. Chopping wood was the only thing they were good at."

"I'll eat breakfast right here where it's warm and cozy." Abigail tucked the quilt beneath her legs and feet.

Setting the tray down with a clatter, Salome perched her hands on her hips. "You can't eat down here, mistress. It's not done. What if somebody sees you?"

"No one is here to witness my departure from social etiquette, so let's not worry ourselves. May I have my tea?" She looked up, feeling like a child currying favor from a nanny. When Salome filled the cup to the rim, Abigail sliced the air with her hand. "Stop. You left no room for the cream."

The cook issued an exaggerated sigh. "Sorry, mistress. I'm not used to being a lady's maid." Her face screwed up with anxiety.

"Let me handle this while you check the stove. I smell something burning."

"I plumb forgot about the johnnycake!" The cook opened the oven door, wrapped a towel around the handle on the pan, and pulled the skillet from the heat. "You sure you don't want to eat breakfast in the dining room?" she asked over her shoulder.

"I'm sure. I don't like being alone in a room."

"When is Miz Dunn coming back?"

"I have no idea." Abigail tried a forkful of grits, unknown in England but served every morning in Wilmington. "The date on her note was January second. That was three days ago. How long does it take to reach Richmond and then return by train?"

Salome shrugged her shoulders, bewildered. "Can't say, ma'am. I've never been there."

Abigail studied the woman as though for the first time. The cook's face was pinched and drawn as she kneaded her hands like bread dough. "It's no matter, Salome. We shall be patient. Tell Amos to come inside and eat with you. Please sit down and finish the eggs, ham, and grits. Don't bother with that burnt cornbread."

"What if Miz Dunn gets back?"

"I doubt she will walk in this early."

"When is Master Henthorne coming home? He'll be mighty hungry after being gone."

"He sent a note saying he had business with Mr. Peterson that might keep him away for two nights. If he was planning to stay at the Kendall House, he will have eaten in town." Abigail's composure began to slip as she forced down a bite of eggs. At least they weren't runny the way Jackson preferred.

Salome tried scraping the burned cornbread with a knife. "Master shouldn't stay away so long, Miz Henthorne. Not with the baby coming."

"The baby isn't due for weeks yet. Stop upsetting me and go fetch Amos. He needs to keep up his strength. You two are all I have left," she whispered as tears sprang to her eyes.

"I'll be back in a minute." Salome offered a sympathetic look, wrapped a shawl around her shoulders, and bustled outdoors.

With only the sound of a guttering oil lamp to break the silence, Abigail reflected on just how true her observation was. The sole servants left in the house were a cook and an aged butler. Amos had to be sixty if he was a day. No one remained to wash or iron her pretty dresses, polish the silver, or deadhead the last of the roses. What would she do if the pair of them decided to pack their bags and head for greener pastures?

These Southerners thought owning slaves would preserve the workforce. As things turned out, nothing could be further from the truth. At least, Salome wouldn't leave without Thomas. Abigail made up her mind to start paying them a small salary, even if she had to do so behind Jackson's back. She could live with dusty chandeliers, but going hungry wasn't an option now that she was eating for two.

Just as she finished her last bite of breakfast, Salome stomped into the kitchen. "Thomas just drove the carriage into the barn." She sounded as though the rain had changed to lightning bolts.

"Thank goodness Jackson is home! Make sure Thomas eats breakfast and inform Mr. Henthorne I'll await him in the parlor. I'm sure he'll want to bathe and—"

Uncharacteristically, Salome cut her off. "Master Henthorne ain't with him, mistress. Thomas came back alone. You were right. They were at Oakdale…" Salome's eyes darted left and right, everywhere but at Abigail's face.

"What on earth? Why would Jackson stay with his parents,

leaving me here to fend for myself?" She sounded every bit as annoyed as she felt.

"Thomas said you're 'sposed to pack your bags. Take everything you set store by, along with Granddaddy Henthorne's silverware and candlesticks. Pack everything made for the baby too. And be quick about it." Salome's dark complexion took on a rosy hue. "Those be Master Henthorne's words, not mine, missus."

Abigail rose from the table with as much dignity as she possessed. "Please tell Thomas he's to come inside once he's seen to the horse. While the three of you eat, he will tell me every single word Master Henthorne said."

"I don't think—"

"Please don't argue with me, Salome. I need to speak to Thomas myself."

"Yes, ma'am." The cook bowed her head and returned to the courtyard.

Over the next twenty minutes, Abigail drank two more cups of tea. She feared she might burst from fluids if Thomas didn't arrive soon. Fortunately, the coachman appeared in the doorway before disaster struck.

"You wanted to see me, mistress?"

"Indeed, Thomas. Tell me everything Mr. Henthorne said and leave nothing out."

He cocked his head to one side. "He wants you to pack everything important, ma'am. Then I am to take you to Master Randolph's plantation. No telling how long you'll be in the country, so you should take all of the baby's clothes and things too." Thomas ducked his head with embarrassment.

"Why didn't my husband come home with you?" Abigail threw her hands up in the air. "He could help us pack and offer protection for the ride to Oakdale." Hysteria was beginning to take hold, turning her voice high and squeaky.

"Please don't fret, Miz Henthorne. Master gave me his derringer in case army deserters bother you 'long the way. He showed me how to reload too if need be." Thomas grinned, first at her and then at his wife.

"Don't you go shooting yourself in the foot." Salome cautioned, quite perturbed with this piece of information.

Abigail used the moment to collect her wits. "Thank you, Thomas. I will feel safe under your protection, but there is something you're not telling me."

The coachman focused on the waxed floor tiles. "Master Henthorne thought we should hurry and leave. You can hear the rest from Mistress Isabelle once we get there."

The coachman's mention of her mother-in-law's name became the proverbial last straw for Abigail. She slapped her palm down on the table. "No, Thomas! *You* will tell me where Jackson is this minute!"

He looked close to an apoplectic fit. Then he cleared his throat and met her gaze. "Master Henthorne went and joined the army, mistress. He says the South has its back agin' the wall. He won't let Yankees take Wilmington without a fight."

"Jackson...he's at Fort Fisher?"

"That's where he was headed. Don't know if he got there yet. He wouldn't let me drive him."

Ten seconds of uncomfortable silence spun out before Abigail could speak. Then she said, "Thank you, Thomas. Be sure to eat heartily, because you'll have another long drive today. You too, Amos." She'd spotted the butler peeking around the corner. "When you are finished, why don't you two pack the Henthorne silver while I collect my clothes?"

"I can do that, Miz Henthorne. I'll start packing your clothes and the baby's." Salome shifted her weight from hip to hip. "That worthless Estelle ran off," she added in Thomas's direction.

"No, I want you to pack the kitchen, pantry, and root cellar, Salome. It sounds as if we'll be gone awhile."

Thomas tugged on his ear while considering her suggestion. "Amos and Salome can take the open buggy while I drive the brougham. That way we can carry more and get all of the horses to Oakdale too."

"Won't it be too cold to use the open carriage?" Abigail glanced from one to the other.

Amos, who had been quiet thus far, shook his head. "Don't worry about us, ma'am. We'll wear everything we own. That way we can stay warm and have more room in the coach."

"Very ingenious." Abigail smiled at the old man, thinking: *I will have trouble fitting my clothes into two trunks, let alone wearing all of them.* "If there are no questions, let's get started."

Once she was upstairs, she bundled herself into a warm robe and then began to pack as methodically as she could, but hours passed before her trunks were finally filled. Afterward, the mistress and three slaves ate a supper of chicken stew in the kitchen. This time not one of them commented on the impropriety of her actions. There was little talk at all, which suited her fine. She was too weary to think, let alone make polite conversation.

"Are you 'bout ready to go, Miz Henthorne?" asked Thomas. "We done everything you asked down here. Soon as I hitch the horses we could leave. I don't mind driving to Oakdale at night. I'm getting pretty used to the dark."

"We'll leave at first light after we get a good night's sleep."

"But Master Henthorne said—"

Slapping her hand on the tabletop, she looked at each one in succession. "Since my husband isn't here, I'm in charge. Do you understand?"

All nodded their heads in agreement. "Thank you. From this day forward you will refer to him as *Mr.* Henthorne, not master, because you are now paid workers, not slaves. We'll discuss wages once we're settled at Oakdale."

Three pairs of eyes rounded like saucers, but only Amos replied. "Thank you, Mrs. Henthorne."

"And because I intend to pay you, there is no need to run off in the middle of the n-night." Abigail's voice cracked, betraying her emotions.

Salome's expression turned sympathetic. "If we were gonna leave, ma'am, we would have done so by now. Don't you worry 'bout us abandoning you." She patted the sleeve of her dress. "We ain't going nowhere."

Abigail clasped her hand tightly. "Thank you, Salome. Now I must retire. You need to sleep as well. Tomorrow we have a long trip ahead of us."

For the next three hours she lay awake on her bed, staring at the ceiling and worrying. What would happen when Amanda came home and found them gone? Was she wandering through Yankee territory with only a maid? She could be arrested as a spy and thrown into federal prison. And Jackson—was he a sitting duck with dozens of Yankee cannons aimed at the fort? How could he survive a battle when, by his own admission, he never even shot a rabbit as a boy? Despite kind assurances from the three domestics, Abigail felt adrift without her twin and her husband.

"Please keep them safe, God," she prayed softly. "And grant us an uneventful journey to Randolph's plantation."

But Abigail wasn't going anywhere the next day or the one thereafter. Not long before dawn, around the same time Thomas was feeding the horses and attaching their harnesses, she experienced a searing pain in her abdomen. Without a shadow of a doubt she knew it wasn't indigestion or a case of spoiled food. Her baby was on the way sooner than anyone imagined. And she was alone in a cold mansion with a handful of former slaves, not one of which was a midwife. Her optimism for the future plummeted another notch. Right about now, she would be willing to tolerate the disagreeable personality of her mother-in-law to be in more capable hands.

Evening of January 6

"This is the end of the line, folks." The conductor's ominous announcement roused Amanda from a nightmare. In the dream she had been jostled and pushed by indignant travelers, questioned by surly Union officers, poked in the ribs to make certain she concealed no weapons, and then prodded onto a ship's narrow wooden beam that extended over a raging sea. Except for walking the plank, her dream hadn't been too different from reality, considering the last few days. Even with British documents, crossing into the city of Washington from Alexandria hadn't been easy.

Finding Helene suitable accommodations within walking distance of the harbor had been nearly impossible. Amanda parted with a substantial amount of gold for Helene's room, along with a ticket on the next ship to Liverpool. Her offer of a cheque drawn on an English bank had been met with either laughter or a sniff of indignation. At least Helene only had another five days in the chaotic American capital. The hotel had an adequate dining room that served a decent shepherd's pie and a delicious cup of tea. Amanda knew Helene wouldn't set foot on the crowded city streets until it was time to board, even if she ate shepherd's pie for every one of her meals.

Then Amanda had as much trouble reentering Virginia as she had exiting, perhaps more. Her short stay labeled her a suspected spy in the eyes of military authorities. Battle lines had recently changed, so that what had been Confederate territory no longer was. Her explanation of seeing her maid off to their homeland begged the obvious question: *Why didn't you get on the boat with her?* Why, indeed? Doubtlessly, that's what a wise woman would have done. But not a woman in love.

After changing trains no less than seven times, they approached Rocky Point, the last town of any size before reaching the coast. *End of the line?* The conductor's announcement sent a frisson of dread through her veins. A quick glance out the window revealed they had not arrived in the city of Wilmington.

"Please, sir, why have we stopped?" Amanda adopted the American penchant for shouting in public instead of waiting for a more decorous moment to make an inquiry.

The conductor ambled back to where she sat. "Tracks torn up, missy. No telling who did the mischief this time. But don't you worry. The local boarding house has plenty of rooms for gentle-folk with money to pay. Everyone else can sleep in the stable's hay-loft. Not many horses are left in town anyway." He produced an indulgent smile. "Tomorrow I'll call for you at the inn. Then we'll walk to where the tracks start again. Be ready by noon, let's say." He tucked his watch back into his pocket.

"I must reach Wilmington as soon as possible, sir. My sister will be frightfully worried. I've been gone far longer than intended and—"

"Now, now. You'll be home by nightfall tomorrow, midnight at the latest." With that he tipped his hat to her and took his leave.

"Excuse me, sir. Where is that stable you mentioned?"

He glanced back with a frown. "You can't sleep there, miss. It wouldn't be safe. Speak to Mrs. Hawkins at the inn if you're short—"

"I wish to inquire about another matter. Please, sir."

With a sigh the conductor pointed in the general direction of town. "Follow the tracks to the square. Turn right on Greene

Street and walk three blocks till you come to the end. You can't miss Waite's Livery." He came back to pull down her bag from the overhead rack.

"Thank you kindly." Amanda grabbed the handle of her valise and moved toward the door.

"Don't forget to meet me on the inn's porch at noon."

But she had other things on her mind than a night at the local boarding house, no matter how comfortable the furnishings. She walked to Waite's Livery as fast as possible without running. Amanda had never run in her life, not even as a child. *I'm developing new abilities in America*, she mused, giddy from fatigue.

When she reached the stable, she was too breathless to speak. "Do you have a carriage for hire?" she croaked between gasps for air.

"Nope. It was stolen by some Yankee major." A teenager in enormous overalls replied while chewing on a long tasseled weed.

"Then I would like to hire two horses. Surely you have some. I see one right there." Amanda pointed at a brown rump and swishing black tail.

The lad pondered for a few moments. "What you be wantin' them for?" He eyed her traveling suit, broad-brimmed hat, and high-topped shoes suspiciously. Thankfully, she'd left her hoop at her sister's.

Once her heart stopped pounding, she recovered a bit of dignity. "I need two horses—one for me and one for you. I want to hire you as my guide. It's a matter of the upmost urgency that I reach Wilmington as quickly as possible."

"You know how to ride a horse? Ha! That's a good one, missy."

"Young man, you apparently have no idea what an English-woman's childhood education consists of. I've had years of riding lessons and happen to ride quite well. I will pay you two twenty-dollar gold pieces if you accompany me to Wilmington." She hoped she wouldn't have to beg.

The young man scratched the sparse stubble on his chin. "Trouble is, I only got the one horse—Bluebells. I hid him in the woods when Yankees rode into town. That's his name 'cause he likes to eat them flowers, not because he's a sissy."

"Fine. I'll rent Mr. Bluebells and see that he's returned safe and sound. I am a woman of my word." Amanda lifted her chin and crossed her arms.

The boy mimicked her posture. "Bluebells is *my* horse, miss. I wouldn't loan him out to Jeff Davis himself. I don't want to lose him to thieves or stragglers looking for a way home."

Weary beyond forbearance, she broke into tears. "Forty dollars is all I have, but I'll pay you whatever you demand once I reach home."

"Ain't no call for cryin'. Let me think on this a minute." The young Mr. Waite snaked a hand through his thick hair and lifted one boot heel to a bale of hay to assist the process.

Amanda swabbed her face with a handkerchief much in need of laundering.

"Wilmington ain't exactly 'round the next corner. You would get lost for sure if you took Bluebells alone. More likely he would throw you off, and then Yankee cavalry would find him wandering around. They're always crisscrossing these parts."

"What do you suggest?" Amanda asked, trying to stifle her sniffles.

"The name is Bobby Waite. This was my pa's place." He indicated the surroundings with a wave. "'Spose we could both ride Bluebells, seeing as neither of us weighs much. I can take you where you need to be, collect forty dollars atop the forty you pay me now, and then hightail it back home. That second forty includes the price of shipping."

"Shipping?" she asked, straightening her hat.

"For your satchel." He pointed at her valise. "I'm only taking

you and the little purse on your wrist. Bluebells ain't no pack mule."
Bobby narrowed his eyes, the point obviously nonnegotiable.

"You have a deal, Mr. Waite." Amanda offered her ungloved
hand. She was becoming an American by leaps and bounds.

"Bobby. Mr. Waite was my pa." He shook her hand as though
pumping a handle.

While Bobby hung a "Closed" sign on the door, Amanda prepared herself for an unladylike ride minus a sidesaddle. Soon
Bluebells was tossing his mane down the road, seemingly pleased
to be leaving Rocky Point.

Regardless of whether Amanda was a new American or still an
Englishwoman on holiday, it was dawn before the flower-eating
beast, the stable heir, and textile mill heiress arrived at the Henthorne residence. She paused at the back door to address her companion of the last several hours. "You'll find plenty of hay and
oats in the barn for Bluebells. Once he is situated, join me in the
kitchen for breakfast." She pointed at the entrance. "I'll pay you
what I owe and show you to a guest room. You can rest before
starting your journey home."

Bobby's gaze traveled skyward to the roofline three stories
above them. "If it's just the same to you, Miss Dunn, just set my
plate of vittles on that bench along with the money. I prefer to
bed down next to Bluebells for the night and keep an eye on him."

"All right. I'll also set out a quilt and a pillow for you." Suddenly, a piercing wail distracted Amanda from her guide. "Thank
you for helping a damsel in distress, Bobby." With that she left
him and hurried into the house. Upstairs she found her sister
bathed in sweat. Abigail's wrinkled nightdress was sodden despite
the room's cool temperature.

"Goodness! Is the baby on the way?"

Salome jumped to her feet from where she sat on a bedside stool. "Praise the Lord! You've returned, Miz Dunn."

Abigail opened her eyes. "Mandy, you have come back. I thought surely you were on your way home."

"You haven't called me that since we were little girls," Amanda said as she smoothed her sister's damp hair from her forehead. "I wrote that I would return after sending Helene off, and here I am."

"I'm very glad to see you. Salome doesn't think she can handle one wee babe, even though she's already birthed four children." Her weak voice still managed to convey amusement.

"All I said was that I never seen it done from the other end of things." Salome wrung out a cloth in the basin and placed it on Abigail's brow. To Amanda she said, "Don't know why it's taking Miss Abigail so long. She's had the birthin' pains since early yesterday morning."

With Salome's observation, Abigail's face blanched with terror. "I don't know what to do."

Amanda turned to the Henthorne cook. "Could you fix a plate of food for the young man who brought me home from Rocky Point? He's tending to his horse in the barn. He'll also need a quilt and a pillow. He insists on sleeping in the hayloft."

Salome nodded, relieved to be useful in a familiar way. "Be happy to, Miz Dunn." She practically flew out of the room.

Turning to her sister again, Amanda said soothingly, "Aunt Mandy is here to convince her new niece or nephew it's time to make a grand entrance."

Tears streamed down Abigail's cheeks. "I'm so grateful to you, sister."

Amanda took her hand and squeezed. "We're not just sisters; we're twins. I'm not going anywhere, not now and maybe not ever. Don't you worry. Salome and I will figure this out one step at a time."

When Nate looked back on his brief career as an infantryman in the Confederate army, everything would be a blur of confusion. Had the troops been organized and efficient during the early days of the war? He'd heard reports that both battles of Bull Run, along with the battle of Antietam Creek, had been resounding Confederate victories. Reportedly, generals and other officers in command displayed finesse and military brilliance. Perhaps the thing causing morale to falter so badly was fatigue from lack of good food and insufficient rest. Or perhaps it was the *ennui* and despondency that set in when a war lasted too long. Or, most likely, it was the fact that the Rebels were outnumbered and under-gunned in each confrontation. But no matter the reasons, conditions deteriorated with each passing day of bombardment.

The Union navy began shelling Fort Fisher on January 12. Several ships that had been blockading the mouth of the Cape Fear River aimed their guns at the battery mounds and palisade and opened fire. Nate would learn later that fifty-six Union ships were used during the artillery assault. Had Confederate soldiers inside the fort known that *one* fact, they may have thrown up their hands in surrender, saved hundreds of lives, and prevented hundreds more from becoming prisoners of war. Instead, the artillerymen manning the guns and mortars did their best to repulse the barrage for a full two and a half days. During this inordinate period of time, Nate couldn't form a concise thought, let alone sleep or eat or prove useful as an infantryman. His regiment was ordered to remain underground in a bombproof shelter along the rampart on the inland face. On January 15, at three o'clock under a low winter sun, the Union army attacked from both the inland side and the beach where the sea wall met the land face of the fort. Nate would remember no clear command to load and fire, parry forward and retreat, or any semblance of a plan. He focused only on his task at hand against enormous odds—to fight beside Joshua and die for him if necessary. After several hours of attempting to repulse the uninvited guests, the Yankees entered the fortification at Shepherd's Battery. Wave after wave of bluecoats swarmed through the hole in the palisade like black ants from a threatened colony. After battling for several hours in fierce hand-to-hand combat, Joshua's commanding officer had little alternative but sound the retreat from Fort Fisher—Nate's military home for a scant twenty days.

"Head upriver to Fort Anderson, men! We'll regroup and form ranks to give it another go."

Amid the smoke and appalling carnage, it occurred to Nate that his brother might not know where to find Fort Anderson. Nate knew it was on the western side of the river, visible from the river road back to Wilmington. He knew exactly how to get back to town. After fixing bayonets, Nate and Joshua fought their way out of the fort in a melee that if he lived another hundred years he could never describe adequately. Once they broke free of the hailstorm of artillery smoke, gunfire, and savagery, they received their first accurate assessment of how outnumbered they were.

"Head north into the marshlands, men! We'll reconnoiter upriver." The hoarse cry of their major cut through the din moments before the thrust of a bayonet ended his command forever.

"This way!" yelled Nate. Joshua and half a dozen comrades quickly fell into step behind him. He tried not to focus on the fact their detail had thrice that number when they exited the doomed fortress.

"Keep your heads down and don't fire your gun!" shouted Joshua. "That will only draw bluecoats onto our trail." His brother resumed control of their little group with no idea as to where they were going.

Throughout the night they picked their way across tidal flats thick with cordgrass, stunted pines, and scrub-covered hillocks. They were wet, covered in bloody scratches if not battle wounds, hungry, and exhausted when they finally reached a patch of dry land where a lone swamp willow held its ground against shifting tides. Pulling up their jackets to protect their faces against ravenous insects, the six men huddled beneath the tree without uttering a single word. Confident the Yankees were no longer in pursuit, they fell into an exhausted sleep without posting a guard. None of them could have handled such a task anyway.

If the Yankees end our misery, so be it, thought Nate. *Better a well-aimed bullet than a poisonous copperhead or cottonmouth.* He had never been particularly fond of snakes. Before drifting off, he thought about Jackson Henthorne and his odd change of heart. Of course, it wasn't more peculiar than his. He uttered a silent prayer for Henthorne's life for the sake of Abigail and their coming child. And he prayed for Amanda, that she would remember him fondly if this night turned out to be his last. Nate fell asleep with the mental image of her lovely face framed by an array of blond curls etched on his eyelids.

His sleep, however, would be brief in duration. Just after daybreak an enormous explosion shook the ground they reposed on. Dry leaves, still clinging to winter branches, showered down on the sleeping soldiers.

Joshua drew his sword with his right hand and aimed his pistol with his left into the scrub brush. The sky brightened eerily as though the sun itself had exploded at the southern horizon.

"What was that?" asked Nate, rising to his full height.

"I believe the powder magazines at Fisher just exploded. It was definitely from that direction." Joshua lowered his weapons.

"Why would the Yankees do that? If they control the fort, they could use the munitions for their own artillery."

"I have no idea. There's no figuring bluecoats." Joshua busily plucked chiggers and burrs from his coat and trousers. "Let's get moving. We'll rest once we get to our destination."

"Where would that be, Lieutenant?" asked a bearded private.

"North of here. We'll try to join up with others who escaped. We need to move closer to the river." Joshua looked to Nate for confirmation.

Nate suspected Joshua had no particular plan. How could anyone prepare for a chaotic rout in the dead of night? But he had to give his younger brother credit—he sure seemed as though he had a plan, and his choice to seek the Cape Fear proved beneficial. Within an hour they came upon a detail of pickets patrolling the perimeter of an impromptu encampment. Blessedly, all uniforms were Confederate gray or butternut.

"Captain Tucker," Joshua called once they drew close enough to recognize the man. He snapped their commander at Fisher a salute. Besides having a bandage around his upper arm, the captain also sported a gash above his right brow, the blood already drying into a scab.

"You're a sight for sore eyes, Lieutenant. How many men are with you?" Tucker returned a quick salute.

"Five, sir. My brother and four others."

Nate stepped forward to salute, uncertain if this was proper or not. His abbreviated training didn't cover the finer points of military protocol.

The captain nodded, assessing their party with a cursory glance. "I hoped more from our company had escaped from the fort."

"Plenty more did, sir. We're not licked yet."

"Infantry and artillerymen have found their way here all night. I suppose that will continue throughout the day." Shielding his eyes, Tucker scanned the bank. "At least there has been no sign of Yankees this far upriver."

"We'll be ready for them, sir, when they come."

"Oh, they'll come, Cooper. The Yankees are as relentless as hounds after a fox."

Considering his optimism, it was hard to imagine that Joshua had enlisted four years ago. Nate's respect for his brother grew with each passing day.

"How bad is your wound, sir?"

Tucker smiled. "Not bad enough to kill me, Lieutenant."

"What are your orders?" Joshua stood at attention.

"After you get some food and rest, try to find more from your company." He gestured toward soldiers milling around campfires or sound asleep on bedrolls. "General Whiting and Colonel Lamb were both wounded. General Hoke has positioned three brigades along this eastern ridge, or he will have once we are assembled. Across the river, General Hoke positioned another brigade at Fort Anderson. That fort is the last stronghold between here and Wilmington. We can't allow the last southern port to fall into enemy hands. We must hold our ground here on Sugar Loaf to protect Anderson. I cannot overstate how important our jobs are today."

"My men and I are prepared to do our duty." After a final salute, their company left to seek familiar faces, a hot meal of cornmeal mush, and some sleep. There would be no more fighting for Joshua's bedraggled band of Confederate infantry that day. They would have time to lick their wounds.

Nate had plenty of time to think about Amanda, and how close several Union soldiers had come to ending his earthly existence forever.

Seventeen

The Northeast Bastion of Fort Fisher

*H*ow long do you plan to keep us here like muskrats?"

Cold, wet, and faint from hunger and thirst, Jackson scooped up a mouthful of brackish black water and spit it out.

"Until I know those Yankee sailors went back to their boats. Just keep your head down and your mouth shut." The sergeant spat a stream of brown juice into the murky water.

How the man managed to keep his plug of tobacco during a maelstrom of artillery and swarming Yankees with bloodlust in their eyes remained a mystery. Jackson rubbed his eyes to stop the images of men dying. He would never forget the human cruelty he witnessed. He could handle shooting a man from twenty paces away. The poor soul usually crumpled to the ground to await death or an eventual stretcher bearer. But what Jackson had witnessed on the blood-stained grounds of Fort Fisher left him weak-kneed and nauseated. Nothing in life could have prepared him for so much bloodshed, and nothing would ever replace this as the worst day of his life.

"We've been sitting in this tree for almost two days," he said wearily, stretching out his legs.

"You're just a corporal. I'm the one givin' orders round here, Henthorne."

"Yes, sir. But if we don't find good water to drink soon, we'll drop over dead from dehydration."

"The rest of you boys got something to say 'bout this?" The sergeant swiveled around to two privates in uniforms so covered with mud, their loyalties would be unrecognizable.

"Can't stay here another night, sir." The taller of the two drawled. "Them bloodsuckers just 'bout ate us alive."

"What exactly you got in mind, Corporal?" asked his equally emaciated companion.

Jackson looked to his sergeant, a gap-toothed boor of a man. If this was the typical caliber of Confederate officers, the end could be near for their Glorious Cause. "With your permission, sir."

"By all means, Henthorne. Tell us your humble opinion after three stinkin' weeks as a soldier."

Jackson ignored the barb. "If I were in charge of this outfit, I would head toward higher ground. Once we're away from the sea, we should find water and may locate the rest of our company."

"Maybe they's all dead," said one young private.

"We're not the last ones standing," the sergeant snapped. "Regiments will regroup upriver to give it another go. We'll keep fightin' till they kill every last one of us, but that ain't gonna be today. So I'm of a mind to take your advice, Henthorne. Why don't you lead the way since you're so eager to leave our little hidey-hole?"

Jackson nodded but dispensed with a salute. After watching his superior officer in battle, he had little respect for the man. Sergeant Womack spent more time positioning himself out of harm's way than shooting and reloading. Jackson had shot his share of Yankees and would have continued until a bullet found its way to him. But when an explosion blew open their shelter, the sergeant ordered them through the breech in a hail of gunfire. With men dropping to their knees on both sides of him, Jackson tried not to step on fallen comrades. Blindly he followed his superior officer into a maritime wilderness, running from the inevitable collapse of Fort Fisher.

Sergeant Womack's new order was no particular honor. Leading them up the peninsula made him an easy target for Yankee sharpshooters who loved to pick off Rebel stragglers. But Jackson would rather take his chances than spend another night in that bug-infested tree.

They slogged for hours until finally gaining higher ground as the moon rose over a shimmering Atlantic Ocean. They had encountered no Yankee patrols. Their enemies had either returned to the gunboats anchored around the mouth of the river or were celebrating their victory in the newly acquired fort. But Jackson's joy in avoiding capture and a federal prison camp was soon eclipsed by the view out to sea. Sitting off the coast, surrounded by the Union navy, was a familiar-looking blockade runner. From her sleek lines and exquisite details, Jackson knew for certain it was the *Roanoke*. While he stood frozen on a bluff of land, the *Roanoke* went up in flames and thick, black smoke.

"Looky there." The sergeant pointed one blunt finger. "Who'd ever reckon one of those iron boats could catch fire?"

Jackson stared mutely for a full minute before responding. "Anything will burn after being hit by cannon shot or if it triggers a water mine. What doesn't burn will soon sink to the bottom of the sea." Without visible emotion, he delivered the information like a schoolmarm speaking to her pupils. Same as his companions, Jackson watched the *Roanoke* curiously as half his earthly fortune burned out of control. Why mention that it was his ship providing their entertainment and give the sergeant another reason to despise him? Womack already resented that he entered the service a corporal instead of a private, as though one level of rank made much difference to pay, or whether or not a man lived to see another day.

The contents of my pay envelope will be little consolation, he thought as the crow's nest crashed into the flaming hull. It was an inglorious conclusion to a reckless investment.

"Let's keep moving. Show's over."

The sergeant's bark pulled Jackson from his trance, and then they set out again on a meandering course north that crossed marshland, sandy floodplains, and skirted around treacherous bogs that could suck a man into a gruesome death. They ate what little remained in their knapsacks and foraged for berries and edible roots. One of the untidy privates knew which plants could be eaten and which would wreak havoc from just touching the leaves. The men caught rainwater in their caps until they found fresh water. The rushing stream seemed like a mirage after days of walking through tidal pools.

Without much military experience, several days passed before Jackson realized Sergeant Womack was carefully avoiding contact with all troops, friend or foe. The two brothers from Macon seemed content to wander wherever their commander decreed, but after choosing a dry place to sleep on the third night, Jackson decided it was the time to ask questions.

"I would have thought we'd find the Confederate encampment by now. Surely General Bragg intends to regroup and make another stand against the bluecoats."

Womack pulled an insect from his grizzled beard. "Reckon that's what *General Bragg* plans to do." He imbued the commander's name with blatant contempt. "But as far as I'm concerned, Corporal Henthorne, I don't give a rat's arse what General Bragg intends to do." He imbued Jackson's surname with almost as much disdain.

"What are your plans, sir?"

Womack consulted his compass. "I figure if we keep moving north, sooner or later the river will narrow down and get shallow enough to cross. Then we'll be off this infernal peninsula and back on the mainland. I plan to head west and south, keeping out of sight the best I can. By the time I get home to South Carolina, this war should be just about over. Nobody's gonna count on their fingers what day I left the army. I'll tell them I caught me a fast-moving train."

"You intend to desert?"

"You could call it that, rich planter boy." Cocking his revolver, Womack aimed it at Jackson's chest. "Or we could just say I'm letting *you* finish my enlistment, seeing that you're one of our newer recruits. Can't imagine what business was so important that it took you nigh on four years to do your duty."

The gun barrel didn't waver. He could end Jackson's life with the twitch of an index finger.

Jackson slowly lifted his palms from his knees. "There's no sense getting all riled up over a harmless question." His languid drawl masked his fear. "I'm simply curious about your plans, that's all. I judge no man for their past or future deeds." He forced himself to meet the sergeant's eye.

"I might be willing to let you live if you give your word as a *gentleman* to keep your mouth shut."

"On my honor and on the graves of Henthorne ancestors, I will speak to no one about this."

Womack considered his pledge and then aimed his weapon at the brothers. "What 'bout you two?"

They exchanged a glance. "If it's all the same, we'd like to tag along with you, Sarge, seeing that South Carolina is in the same general direction as Georgia."

Womack grunted before turning back to Jackson. "And you,

Henthorne? Do you intend to head toward the river to find what's left of our army or are you comin' with us?"

"Let me mull this over and give you an answer in the morning. Either way, don't worry about my overzealous loyalty to General Hoke. As you succinctly pointed out, my enlistment has been a scant three weeks."

Once his comrades had bedded down for the night, Jackson stared off into the brush, deeply cloaked in shadows. In his mind's eye he saw his father's plantation. Not faded and overgrown as it was now, Oakdale sat like a polished jewel in the middle of fields of peanut plants. Abigail sat on the verandah stitching some tiny garment for his son or daughter. People there bathed, changed their clothes, and led civilized lives. He came to the conclusion the Georgia brothers had been dirty *before* the battle had even begun. In the morning, after a restless night of weighing honor against practicality, dignity against his overwhelming intuition the Yankees would soon control the Cape Fear River, Jackson made up his mind.

"I'm coming with you boys until we get to Wilmington. My folks have a farm about a day's ride from there. I'll hole up in the city for a while." He didn't mention the word "plantation" or refer to his mansion in the city. No sense giving the sergeant a reason to shoot him in the back.

"Suit yourself, Corporal. Don't make no never-mind to me." Womack spat tobacco juice into the dirt.

All day they followed a rutted wagon track north, close to the river. They kept off the road, lest patrolling militiamen drag them back to the army or shoot them as deserters. That evening, when the sun dipped low in the sky, the other three bade him farewell and waited for their opportune moment to swim to Eagle Island unseen. Jackson continued north until the familiar landmarks of his hometown appeared. Only then did he assess his present physical state. No one would recognize him for the wealthy man he was. Or at least, the wealthy man he used to be. Memories of the *Roanoke* burning in grand spectacle churned his empty gut.

Knowing Abigail would be appalled to see him like this, he chose Third Street as his destination. He would bathe, don clean clothes, and burn his uniform in the fireplace. Then he could leave for Oakdale after a good night's sleep in his own bed. Surely Salome left something behind to eat when she packed up the kitchen. After the past few days, he wouldn't be too particular.

It was a little past dawn when Jackson trudged up the oyster shell driveway of home. Glancing down at his muddy boots, he chose the back door, half a dozen steps below ground level, and entered a warm kitchen. He'd assumed the room would be empty.

"Master Henthorne!" Three voices chimed in unison from the trestle table.

Jackson stared at Amos, Salome, and Thomas in succession. "What are you doing here? Why haven't you gone to the plantation with Mrs. Henthorne?"

"Mistress Henthorne is upstairs sleeping, sir." Amos was first to respond as he helped Jackson off with his wet coat.

"Why on earth didn't you take her to Oakdale as I instructed?" He posed this question to Thomas.

Salome bustled toward him with a cup of water. "We were of a mind to leave come that morning, all packed up and ready. But your baby had other ideas. He made up his mind to be born, but then took almost two full days to get 'round to it."

Relieved of his outerwear, Jackson slumped into a chair to pry off his boots. "Did you say *he*?"

"I did, sir. You got yourself a strong, healthy son with quite a set of lungs on him."

Jackson grasped the table for support. "And Abigail—how is my wife?"

Salome patted his back as if he were a small child. "Miz Henthorne be just fine. We was sure glad to see Miz Dunn that day, sir. 'Tween the two of us, we handled the situation fine."

"Miss Dunn? She's here too?" He shook his head as though waking from a dream. *I have a son my sister-in-law helped deliver?* He was too exhausted to process the information. "I thought she sailed back to England."

"She told Miz Henthorne she was not going anywhere until her new niece or nephew was born."

Jackson struggled to his feet. "I want to see my wife…and the baby."

"No, sir, Master Henthorne," said Salome, shaking her head vigorously. "You'll scare her the way you look. Thomas will fill the giant washtub with hot water, and Amos will find you clean clothes to wear. You need a bath and a shave, if you don't mind my saying so. And I'm gonna cook you up a breakfast that'll stick to your ribs."

Jackson felt a wave of relief that decisions were being made for him. "Thank you, Salome, all of you, for taking care of my family."

She shrugged her shoulders. "Just so you know, Mr. Henthorne, we ain't slaves no more. Miz Henthorne told us we're paid workers. She just don't know how much to pay us yet."

"That should have been done long ago." He scrubbed his face with his hands, overwhelmed by fatigue, hunger, and worry. He had to bite his lip and hold his breath to keep from crying in front of his new domestic employees.

"Well, it's done now." She walked into the pantry as Amos and Thomas left to do their tasks. Jackson was left alone in the kitchen, savoring for the first time the true meaning of home, family, and loyalty.

But his solitude was short lived. He heard the soft patter of feet on the steps, and then his wife stepped into the kitchen.

"My word, Jackson! It *is* you at long last," Abigail said breathlessly.

"I-I was told you were sleeping," he said softly, taking a step toward her.

"I was, dear heart, but I thought I heard your voice coming through the vents in the floor and had to check." Abigail shifted the tiny bundle in her arms. "I told myself it was just my imagination, but here you are." Her voice turned raspy.

"I wanted to come to you right away, my love, but Salome told me to wait until my appearance was more presentable." He grimaced as he slicked a hand through his dirty hair.

His wife stared at him for a long moment, her eyes glistening. "Your appearance, untidy as it may be, erases every worry from my mind, every burden on my heart." Her sudden smile shone like the sun. "Don't just stand there, husband. Come kiss me and then say hello to your son. I named him Jackson, but Mandy and I have been calling him Jacky."

No matter how he bit his lip or held his breath, tears streamed down Jackson's face as he viewed his son for the first time. As unworthy a man as any could be, God had answered each one of his prayers.

Early in the morning of February 21, 1865, a bedraggled Nathaniel Cooper knocked on the door of the Simses' residence on Castle Street. His brow dripped sweat, his muscles ached, and hunger made his gut clench. Because he no longer rented a room there, he waited on the stoop for someone to rouse from their bed.

A wan-looking Odom opened the door as Ruth hovered behind his shoulder. "Nate! Why didn't you just come in? We don't stand on ceremony here, son." Odom almost dragged him across the threshold.

Nate could have hugged his former landlord instead of shaking his hand. "I didn't know if you would entertain a guest wearing this color uniform."

"Shucks. We know your heart. That's what's important."

Ruth didn't bother asking whether he was hungry. Instead, she swiftly mixed batter for flapjacks while her skillet heated up. "Ain't your brother with you, Nathaniel?" she asked softly.

"No, ma'am. I've been sent into Wilmington with a detail to alert the citizens. Joshua and what's left of our regiment are trying to move artillery so it doesn't fall into Union hands." He gratefully accepted a cup of coffee, sweet and thick with cream.

"What's the news?" Odom practically forced him down onto a chair with a gentle hand.

"None of it is good for the South. Fort Anderson fell to the Yankees. We've been routed from the Sugar Loaf as well. Admiral Porter's gunboats have moved up the river within range of Wilmington. When they retreated from Fort Anderson, they burned the bridges over Town Creek and the Brunswick River. Those bridges and our cavalry will slow the Yankees down some, but we can't stop them." He gazed from one of his friends to the other.

Young Rufus crept from the staircase, wide-eyed and frightened without knowing why. "Hullo, Mr. Nate," he said.

Odom folded his hands on the table. "Will there be a battle on the city streets? Have you come to warn us?"

Nate smiled at the boy before answering. "Probably not, but you should pack everything you value and leave at once. Braxton Bragg has ordered Wilmington evacuated."

"What does 'vacuated' mean?" asked Rufus, his eyes soulful.

"It means 'leave the city.' For now staying would be unwise, but you'll be able to come back someday."

"Come along, young man," said Ruth, setting a plate of food in front of Nate. "Let's go upstairs and pack our clothes." With a firm hand she guided the boy from the room.

"There won't be fighting here." Nate continued once he and Odom were alone. "At least, not much. But we have no choice but to surrender the city. There are too many Yankees with too much artillery."

"Why should we leave, Nathaniel? The Union army should have no truck with us."

"Our commanding officer ordered the cotton and tobacco warehouses burned, along with the foundries and any ships tied in the harbor. Bragg doesn't want them falling into enemy hands."

"All of Mr. Henthorne's warehouses?" asked Odom.

"Yes, and everyone else's too. If his ships are in port they will be destroyed."

"All that waste." Odom shook his head sadly.

"I'm surprised you would take pity on a slaver." Nate began eating ravenously.

"I harbor no hatred and wish no ill on any man."

"I would warn Henthorne, but I don't know where he is. There's nothing he can do anyway." Nate dropped his chin to his chest. "The storehouses and mercantiles are to be burned as well."

"Not *your* store?" Odom slapped a palm on the table.

"I'm afraid so, but it's time for me to change careers anyway." Nate gobbled up the last bite of his food. "Let's pack your tools into the wagon and hitch the horses. You need to leave as soon as you can."

Odom stood. "We'll go live with Ruth's sister until this blows over. You're welcome to join us, son."

"Thank you, my friend, but I must remain to make sure people understand what's coming." Nate offered his hand again, but Odom wrapped his arms around him.

"Make sure you're gone before the Yankees arrive. Keep yourself alive for when Miss Amanda comes back."

Nate couldn't speak. His throat burned with emotion. These three kind people had been like family to him since he arrived on the Carolina coast. "I aim to do my best."

Once Odem and his family were packed up and gone, Nate allowed himself a long howl of frustration. Then he returned to the business at hand—pounding on doors and preparing citizens for the inevitable.

By the time he worked his way down to Water Street, further endeavor had become unnecessary. Clouds of black, acrid smoke poured from the rooftops of the warehouses on Walnut. The streets were filled with wagons, horses, and people carrying belongings strapped to their backs. Pandemonium reigned on the waterfront. Yet despite the panic and smoke-filled air, Nate fought his way to his beloved market. He arrived just as the roof— *his roof*—fell with a thunderous clash, sending sparks and flames twenty feet into the air.

"Great Scott, Cooper! What are you doing on the waterfront?"

Nate slowly turned to see Jackson, dapper in civilian clothing, astride his gelding. "It should be obvious, Henthorne. I am bearing witness to the destruction of my business."

"I am aware that your shop is on fire." Jackson struggled to control his horse. The smoke filling the beast's nostrils turned him skittish. "So are my cotton and tobacco warehouses. We'll suffer financially to be sure, but we must move swiftly to protect those who matter most." The horse reared, almost unseating the rider.

It took Nate a moment to pull his gaze from the inferno. "What are you talking about?"

"There is no telling how far this fire will spread. If it reaches Third Street, our womenfolk and my new son will be in danger."

Nate took several steps back from the intense heat. "Then

stop jaw-boning with me and move Miss Abigail and your son to safety." The knowledge that Henthorne now had an heir sent a jealous rage through his blood. Would he ever know the happiness of hearth and home with the woman he loved? "Congratulations on your new son." He forced himself to speak the words.

"Much obliged, but I didn't come here for that. I promised my sister-in-law I would check to see if by some miracle you had come back to the harbor. And here you are. Let's go, Cooper. Climb up behind me." Jackson removed his foot from the stirrup and offered a hand.

Nate grabbed the bridle of the prancing horse. "What are you talking about? Amanda went back to England—"

"You have much to learn about stubborn women if you think that. She saw her maid off in Washington and then returned to Wilmington. She helped deliver our baby."

With his head swimming with confusion, Nate doubled over in a coughing jag. *Amanda is here in this melee with the Yankees breathing down our necks?* When he was finally able to speak again, Nate looked at Jackson, all pride and anger gone. "She's truly here?"

"I have no reason to lie to you. Apparently, she feels the same about you that you do for her." Henthorne extended his hand a second time. "Please, let's get away from the waterfront. I would welcome your help in moving the ladies to safety."

Nate jammed his boot into the stirrup and swung up smoothly. The horse reared again, annoyed by the additional weight. As Jackson tightened his grip on the reins, Nate hung on for dear life. Once the horse's hooves met the cobblestones, they took off through smoky lanes and alleys, away from the spreading inferno. In the courtyard behind the Henthorne mansion, Nate slid off the horse.

Jackson dismounted and threw the reins to Thomas. "Give him a good rub, and when he cools down, give him water and a bucket of oats, and then harness him to the coach."

Nate followed Henthorne in through the kitchen. Unbelievably, inconceivably, Amanda was packing food into a hamper at the table. Abigail sat on a bench, discretely nursing an infant under a coverlet.

"Amanda," he croaked.

"Nate!" she cried, dropping a jar with a clatter.

Abigail rose to her feet with the baby in the crook of her elbow. "Oh, I'm glad you found him, Jackson! Will you help me finish upstairs while these two get reacquainted?"

"Very well, but you both need to be brief."

Nate shook off his astonishment as his mission came roaring back to him. "Braxton Bragg has surrendered the city. We must leave at once."

"We'll be down in fifteen minutes. Everything else is ready to go." Jackson set his arm around his wife and guided her toward the steps.

Suddenly Nate was alone with his beloved. Facing the Union infantry swarming the fort had been less intimidating. "No one should impede our flight until tomorrow..." he stammered.

"'Tis a blessing, then." Amanda took hold of the hamper handles.

"I assume Henthorne wishes to take you and Miss Abigail to Oakdale."

"Not anymore. He sent Salome and Amos ahead with the Henthorne heirlooms and planned for us to follow in the coach. Although he's certain they got through, a neighbor reported that Union troops have closed the road."

Nate nodded. "Will he head down the peninsula? My plot of land is there. I started a cabin, but I haven't progressed very far."

She smiled as though pleased. "Jackson intends to find the *Lady Adelaine* if he can reach her. His ship is anchored in a hidden inlet downriver."

Nate nodded a second time as a plan knit together in his mind.

"I know of an old farm trace we can take. I'm not sure where his ship is, but there's a good chance I can get us close to it without being detected by Yankee soldiers."

Silence spun out as they both digested what they learned. Then Nate lifted his gaze and prayed for her to do the same.

First their eyes met and then their hearts. They ran into each other's arms, hugging and kissing and hugging some more. Each whispered sweet endearments they wouldn't want anyone else to overhear. Amanda chastised him for joining a dangerous war, while he scolded her for not leaving during the darkest days of America's illustrious history. All the while they continued to hug and kiss, making up for lost time, until someone cleared their throat behind them.

Dressed in traveling cloaks, the Henthornes stood in the doorway. "Are you two ready to go?" asked Abigail with mischief in her voice.

Nate withdrew from Amanda, but only to arm's length. "Yes, ma'am, I believe we are. By the way, congratulations on your new son." He bowed in Abigail's general direction.

"Thank you," she said as Jackson herded them outside. "We'll have plenty of time to catch up once we reach the *Lady Adelaine*."

"Then let's get started," Nate and Amanda replied simultaneously.

Nate left the mansion with his hand wrapped around Amanda's. Although he was still a private in the Confederate army, getting the woman he loved safely out of a burning city was more important than anything else.

Amanda paused to pick up her valise on their way out the door. In a fortuitous turn of events, it had arrived by teamster wagon that morning. Mr. Bobby Waite had been true to his word.

"Let me carry that," Nate said as he pulled the handle from her fingers.

"Much obliged," she murmured, her stomach tightening from his touch. Considering the events of the last few weeks, Amanda feared the gentle shopkeeper with a knack for turning a phrase would never be the same. Nor would she.

Out in the courtyard, Jackson took charge. "The women will ride inside the compartment with Jacky and the food we're taking. You and I will ride topside with Thomas," he said to Nate.

"*Jacky?*" asked Nate, strapping Amanda's valise to the back.

Abigail paused on the coach's step and smiled over her shoulder. "Jackson Jr., but Jacky seems appropriate for now. You look exhausted, Mr. Cooper. We could make room for you inside."

Nate shook his head. "Your husband needs me to guide us to the river trace, assuming that the roads I remember are still open. Are you sure we can't reach Oakdale?" he asked Henthorne.

"I am. The Yankees will confiscate the horses, carriage, and food, leaving us along the road to fend for ourselves. You, they will shoot with that uniform. Why not change into civilian clothes?"

The two men locked eyes. "I will not," said Nate.

"Suit yourself. We'll head in the direction the Yankees came from, hopefully *not* on the same roads. Do you agree, Cooper?"

"I do. Let's get going." Nate climbed up beside the coachman.

Jackson latched the door closed behind Amanda. "You ladies keep the windows shut and the curtains closed. I don't know how rough the road will be or what sights we'll pass along the way."

"As you wish." Although Amanda was happy to help Abby with little Jack, she yearned to be near Nate—to hold his hand and assure him that one day this madness would be over.

They rattled over bumpy roads for hours. When the sun set and they could no longer see ten feet in front of them, they stopped for the night. Amanda jumped down the moment the wheels stopped spinning. "What can I do to help?"

"Can you bring water from that stream for the horses?" Nate handed her a wooden bucket. "I'll hobble them so they can graze without wandering too far."

"Of course I can." Amanda sprinted away as though her chore held great importance. To feel useful in any fashion pleased her. Once both horses had drunk deeply, she went in search of Nate.

He was exiting the woods with an armful of branches. "This is all fairly dry. It should get us through the night without creating much smoke." He dumped the pile near the small fire Jackson had started with newspaper and twigs.

Abigail pulled food from the hamper, and soon they were gathered around the blaze, munching sandwiches. Amanda passed around jars of cistern water from home. With everyone tired and sore from the rough ride, there was little conversation during the meal. Longing to get a few things off her chest, Amanda tried to catch Nate's attention.

The moment they finished eating, Jackson ordered the women back to the coach for the night. "Cooper, Thomas, and I will sleep by the fire," he said.

Abigail rose with the baby to comply, but Amanda held up a hand in protest. "No, brother-in-law. I believe I'll spend the first half the night out here while you rest." She pointed at a rock close to Nate. "Midway through the night, I'll go to the coach while you keep watch. Nate can sleep then. In the meantime, he and I have catching up to do that won't wait." Her tone of voice brooked no argument.

"A splendid idea." Abigail hoisted the baby higher in her arms and reached for her husband's hand. "If you recall, my dear, we were once young and in love."

Jackson helped her across the uneven ground. "You and Miss Dunn are *exactly* the same age, and I love you just as much as—" The closing coach door obscured the remainder of his protest.

Thomas looked at the two of them, and he then turned and discreetly walked off.

Amanda prayed her courage wouldn't abandon her. "I hope you don't mind staying awake a tad longer, but I wanted to explain why I'm still in America." Settling primly on the rock, she smoothed her skirt over her ankles.

Nate plopped onto a log and moved his boots toward the heat. "I can remain upright long enough to listen to a few things I already know." A grin tugged at his lips.

"And what would those be, Mr. Cooper?"

He stuck out his left thumb. "You were worried about your sister and refused to leave until her baby arrived."

"Go on," she encouraged.

Nate extended his index finger. "You were also worried about *me* and wouldn't leave while the fighting continued."

"Absolutely the truth on both counts. Have you a third conjecture to add? Perhaps you wish to venture a guess regarding my heart?" Amanda held her breath as she waited for his response.

His grin faded, replaced by a somber expression. "I hope you love me so much you will wait on the *Lady Adelaine* until I return, Amanda. That's what I yearn to hear more than anything."

"*What?* Surely you're not going back to the army...that would be suicide! Everyone whispers that the Confederacy will soon be defeated. What difference can one man make now?" Tears collected in her eyes. "But *your* life makes all the difference in the world to m-me." Amanda choked on the final word.

He knelt next to her and folded her hands in his. "If God is merciful, the war will end soon. It can't last much longer. Then we can be together for the rest of our lives—"

She pushed him away, along with his condescension and willingness to gamble with their future. "Jackson burned his Rebel uniform in the fireplace. Burn yours here, Nate, before some

Yankee shoots you." She pointed imperiously toward the dying fire.

"I don't judge Henthorne or any man, but I must make my own choices. Before God I gave an oath to remain loyal until the end." Nate tossed a handful of sticks into the fire, the flickering light reflected in his eyes.

"*Oooooh*! You are an obstinate man!" Amanda jumped to her feet. "I had planned to beg forgiveness for *my* narrow-mindedness. I intended to tell you about changes I implemented at Dunn Mills and the village of Wycleft. But there is no talking to you, Mr. Cooper!" Overcome with hurt and anger, she stomped to the carriage and yanked open the door. A moment later, Jackson stumbled out, hastily buttoning his frock coat. Her brother-in-law would simply have to adjust to the change in plans because if she spent one more minute in Nate's company, she would forget she was a well-bred, genteel Englishwoman.

The next day they found the *Lady Adelaine* anchored in an idyllic little cove. Because the ground was soft and muddy, they carefully concealed the coach behind briars and walked to the ship. Abigail refused to mount the horse, so Amanda rode carrying little Jack. Nate led the way, clutching the gelding's reins tightly, followed by Jackson and Abby. Thomas brought up the rear with his double-barreled shotgun.

Several armed guards patrolling the deck looked rather surprised when they emerged from the cover of foliage. "Mr. Henthorne, I didn't think you would arrive on foot," called a pink-faced man with red hair. "Come aboard, sir. All's well here. The *Lady* lists to the side in low tide, but she floats nicely in high."

When Nate lifted Amanda off the horse, she murmured an embarrassed, "Thank you," and approached the gangplank without hesitation. He followed at her heels after handing the reins to Thomas.

"Mr. Campbell, you're a sight for sore eyes," said Jackson. "May I present my wife, Mrs. Henthorne, and her sister, Miss Dunn?"

"How do, ma'am, miss?" Campbell doffed his cap and bobbed his head. "I trust you will find the *Lady Adelaine* comfortable."

"My husband expresses everyone's sentiments, sir. We are all glad to finally arrive from Wilmington." Abigail extended her hand.

Campbell kissed the back of her gloved fingers lightly. "If I can be of any service, ma'am, do not hesitate to ask." He dropped his gaze politely.

Amanda smiled at Campbell as Nate stepped past the introductions and onto the ship. "Shall we explore *my* new home for the foreseeable future?" she asked him. Sarcasm dripped from the question, but she couldn't help herself. Now that they had found each other again, why did he insist on returning to the battlefield?

Although not as large as the steamer that brought her to North Carolina, the *Lady Adelaine* was beautifully trimmed with brass, well stocked with food, and had several cisterns of fresh water for baths and washing clothes. Jackson's guards took turns on watch and seemed to be a responsible lot. That night the weary travelers dined on fresh trout, sweet potatoes, buttermilk biscuits, and canned peas. She and Nate made polite conversation during the meal and passed the night counting stars on deck. She slept in a feather bed with a down pillow, lulled to sleep by the night sounds.

But on the morning of the third day, he crept into her stateroom, kissed her softly on the lips, and whispered goodbye. Amanda didn't speak or return the kiss. She was too terrified for their future to do anything but pretend she was asleep.

Eighteen

March 1865

Abigail stood on the deck of the *Lady Adelaine*, her attention focused on a blue heron fishing for lunch in the shallows. She'd grown accustomed to the boat canting to the side during low tide. She'd adjusted to the confining size of even the largest of the staterooms. She'd learned to tolerate the mosquitoes feasting on any exposed skin now that spring had arrived. But what she couldn't stand was Jackson sneaking off while she and little Jack slept.

Sometimes he rode to Wilmington alone. On other occasions he took Thomas when they needed food for his family and crew. How could he be so certain Yankees wouldn't shoot him just for sport? The boat's inhabitants could manage without supplies from town. With the fish caught by Mr. Campbell and the game snared by Thomas, they had enough to eat. She knew Jackson worried about their house. Blessedly, the fire had not spread past the waterfront. And thus far, Jackson's clever plan to keep Yankees from inhabiting had worked. Few men were brave enough to enter a home marked: *Plague patients. Enter at your own peril.*

Abigail could live without the Henthorne mansion on Third Street. She could survive splendidly without ever crossing the threshold of Oakdale again. But she couldn't live without her beloved husband. He had grown even more doting and tender since Jacky's birth.

"Shall I hold Jack Jr. for a while?" asked Amanda.

Abigail startled. "I was so lost in thought I didn't hear you approach. Here you are, Aunt Mandy. But I won't go far in case he becomes fussy."

Amanda took the infant from her. "I have good news for you, sister."

"Did Thomas snare a hapless rabbit last night? You and I are becoming adept at cooking rabbit stew. Your Mr. Cooper will be quite pleased with your new skills. Although I won't have much call for the recipe once we leave our backwater home."

Amanda grinned over the baby's tiny head. "No, the news has nothing to do with supper tonight. Guess again."

"Stop teasing and tell me this instant. You're still as contrary as you were when we were children." Abigail leaned over the rail to gauge the tide's progress.

"One of Mr. Campbell's guards spotted Jackson riding along the river from the crow's nest. He should be reaching the gangplank any minute now." Amanda gently chucked the baby under his chin. Jacky gurgled and grinned as though having great fun.

Abigail huffed with annoyance. "I'm going to pull your hair when you least expect it!" Her chastisement held little conviction. *Jackson is home, safe and sound, once more.* Hurrying to the lower deck, she tucked a few loose curls behind her ears. Her days of elaborate coiffures festooned with ribbons and feathers were gone. Now she plaited her hair into a long braid that she coiled at the nape of her neck. At night she unwound the braid for Jackson with great showmanship.

She ran back up the stairs and arrived topside just in time to say, "Why, Mr. Henthorne, what an inconvenient time to come calling." She feigned a tone of disapproval. "You're too late for luncheon and too early for tea. I ask you, sir, were your born in a barn?"

Jackson knocked his boot heels against a post before stepping on deck. Then he picked her up and swung her in a full circle. "I'll be sure to mention to Mother that you questioned her standards in the nursery."

"Heavens! Put me down!" she shrieked, giggling. "What will the neighbors say if someone sees such foolishness in broad daylight?"

"I don't care about the opinions of nosy squirrels and muskrats. You keep watch for any tattletelling possums." He kissed her firmly on the mouth the moment her feet landed on deck.

"You will tell your mother nothing about my questions. Married couples should keep their own confidences." Strolling the length of the *Lady Adelaine*, she hugged him around the waist.

"In that case, my love, I have a confidence to share. Soon everyone will know, but today I choose to impart this information solely to you." Jackson kissed the tip of her nose.

"Tell me at once or I'll make you walk the plank."

"This water is too shallow to drown in, but as you wish. General Schofield has organized his men in preparation to leave the city. According to my informant, the Yankees will soon march west toward Fayettesville to join that troublesome Billy Sherman." Jackson's grin filled his face.

"That's wonderful news! I cannot fathom why the soldiers were still in Wilmington. All the Confederate troops moved out in February to join General Johnston."

"They needed to rebuild the railroad tracks leading to and from the city, along with several bridges."

"Then you can start shipping again, my dear?"

He laughed with surprising good cheer. "Not hardly. Whatever wasn't burned by General Bragg became Yankee property. If steamers start arriving in port from Nassau or abroad, the food and munitions with be confiscated for the Union army, not ours. They still control the fort and the entire Eastern Seaboard, for that matter."

"Then I'm confused why this news has lifted your spirits." Abigail looked up at him, bewildered.

"Because it means we can go home soon. We can leave our floating refuge in the woods and return to civilization." Jackson brushed a kiss across her forehead. "The Yankees left only a few details of men and provost marshals to maintain the peace. They will ensure civilians don't interfere with Union supplies being offloaded and ferried to the railroad depot. But no one will bother an upstanding family going about their business uptown."

"Does this mean Nate will be coming home?" Amanda stepped from the shadows where she had been lurking, the baby sleeping soundly in her arms.

"Were you eavesdropping, sister?" Abigail chastised, reaching for her son. "Some things never change."

"Yes, I was. Twins shouldn't keep secrets from each other. Please, Jackson, what did you hear about our troops?" Amanda's eyes were glassy with unshed tears.

"Very little good news, I'm afraid. The fighting continues west of here. Cooper's regiment was under General Bragg's command. When Bragg retreated from Wilmington, he headed toward Goldsboro to join up with General Johnston. They need more men for a final stand against the Yankees."

"You make it sound hopeless," whispered Amanda.

"It is hopeless and has been for some time. There's talk of General Grant offering terms of surrender to General Lee. Apparently, those terms haven't been to Bobby Lee's liking thus far."

In a rare burst of temper, Amanda knocked a jelly jar of water lilies off the railing. The jar landed in the murky water below with a loud splash. "You Americans are so blasted stubborn! The South will keep fighting until not one man remains to plant a seed, or harvest a crop, or sire a child." She punctuated the tantrum with a stamp of her foot.

Abigail hoisted the baby to her shoulder so she could slip an arm around her sister. "Aren't you glad we were born in a rational, *civilized* nation?" She angled a wry smile at Jackson.

"If not for our stubborn streak, ladies, we Americans would still be under Queen Victoria's thumb. Opportunities for citizens to rebuild the city or start fresh elsewhere would be sharply curtailed." Leaning back against the rail, he crossed his legs at the ankles. "Try not to worry, sister. Cooper's desire to forge a life with you exceeds the sovereignty of states' rights. I believe he'll dodge any bullet shot in his direction."

Amanda looked from one to the other, miserable. "When do we leave for the city?"

"Tomorrow at first light. I'll send Thomas to the coach this afternoon with a bucket and scrub brush to give it a thorough cleaning. That man will truly be glad to see his wife again. Amos and Salome returned from Oakdale days ago, apparently with my mother's blessing. Why don't we start packing up our things here?"

"What about the *Lady Adelaine*?" Abigail asked. "I've grown fond of the old girl. Can't we sail her upriver when the tide lifts her from the sand?" She ran a finger along a brass filigree molding.

"Not if we wish to keep her. The Yankees may not be looking to confiscate Confederate ships any longer, but if we dangle this plum under their noses, they won't be able to resist."

"Will the boat be safe here?"

"For now, yes. I'll keep Mr. Campbell and his guards on my payroll. Let's pray this war ends and the Yankees go home before I go bankrupt. When they leave us in peace, Henthorne and Sons will start over with one ship—a decidedly smaller fleet, but far less risky."

"When we can use the *Lady Adelaine* without fear of confiscation, I want to travel to England to see my mother. And I wish you to come with me."

He considered her request for only a moment. Then, smiling at her, he said, "I delight in granting your every wish, my dear. Of course I will accompany you. My father can run things until we return, and then he wants no part of the business. He wishes to become a real peanut farmer, not a gentleman planter."

She giggled at the idea. "I can't wait to see your mother in the fields come harvest time. It will be a sight worth the long drive to Oakdale."

"Physical labor does a body good. Perhaps she will invite *you* to join her among the rows." Jackson pulled opened the door to their stateroom. "Come draw me a bath, dear wife. I want to hear all about Jacky's exploits in my absence. What new mischief did he discover?"

And so Abigail and Jackson left Amanda alone with her fears and concerns. Until the war ended, there wasn't anything she or anyone else could do.

Despite the fact Robert E. Lee had signed terms of surrender with Ulysses S. Grant at Appomattox, Virginia, on April 9, hostilities continued in North Carolina for seventeen more days. How very sad for the unfortunate souls who died *after* the War Between the States officially ended.

But such an end would not be the case for Nathaniel or Joshua. Although bone-tired, hungry, tattered, and in need of a bath, both men remained sound of body and mind when Joseph E. Johnston surrendered his army on April 26. With newly inked parole papers and two days' worth of rations, they paused at a crossroads of two dirt roads. The rutted lane ran east and west—one direction toward their home in the hills, the other to Nate's new life on the seacoast.

"I take it you'll be heading east to that sassy Miss Dunn, whom I've heard so much about," Joshua said before taking a long swallow from his canteen.

Shading his eyes, Nate peered in that direction. "As fast as my legs can carry me. I truly wish I had money for train fare."

"There are no trains in this section of nowhere."

"Money to buy Amanda a nice gift, then. I hate to arrive empty handed."

"If the woman has tolerated you this long, I suppose she'll be glad to see you without presents."

"What about you? Will you head back to Balsam?"

Joshua faced west, as though his beloved blue-misted mountains could be seen on the horizon. "Nah, there's nothing for me there. The county would have claimed the land for back taxes by now. Besides, that land wasn't much good for farming, and I wasn't much of a farmer. That's one reason I left Uncle John's hog operation."

Nate felt a surge of excitement, his first since the war's inglorious conclusion. "Which way will you go, then? North? Or perhaps farther west to stake a claim in Nebraska Territory?"

Joshua turned back to him. "Reckon I might visit this Wilmington you seem so fond of. After all, unless the lady has come to her senses, I smell an end of your long-standing bachelorhood."

Nate scuffed his toe in the dust. "I don't plan to buy another store. Maybe I'll try my hand at fishing."

"You can support a family sitting on a bank with a line thrown in the river?"

"Not exactly," he said with a laugh. "I plan to buy a boat—a trawler. The sea is full of fish ripe for the taking. People in cities love the taste of seafood, same as we did back home."

"I can still taste that pickerel and trout." Joshua rubbed his belly in a circular motion. "You got money to buy a ship?"

"A boat, not a ship. And yes, long before my store burned I sold the inventory at a fair price. I've also been saving for the past five years. I can afford a small trawler, but what I need is a partner. I can't run a fishing business by myself or manage the boat alone in rough water."

"What about Miss Dunn? Doesn't she wish to become your first mate on the high seas?"

"Not hardly. I intend to fish only along the coastline and come home each night to my bride."

"Where would I live? I saved a little money, but I haven't received a pay envelope in quite a while."

"I've started building on property I own along the Cape Fear River. If Miss Dunn agrees to marry me, I will build a grander cottage than two boys from the hills ever saw."

Joshua slapped his cap against his knee. "I could never impose on newlyweds."

"You could sleep on the boat until you find a wife of your own. Most trawlers have a right-fine cabin for a man for your discerning tastes. What do you say, Josh? Will you be my partner?"

Without hesitation, Joshua threw his arms around his brother and squeezed. "I'd love to go fishing with you for the rest of my life, Nate. Maybe I can find me a sassy British lass too."

"A Carolina belle would be more likely. Now, let's whittle away some miles between us and the coast."

Two weeks later and ten pounds thinner, Nate approached the oyster shell drive of the Henthorne home cautiously.

"What's wrong?" asked Joshua. "Isn't this the house?"

"Yes, but perhaps they're still living aboard the *Lady Adelaine*." Nate dug his fists deep into his pockets.

"We'll never find out this way. Perhaps a knock on the door is in order." His brother started up the walkway.

"No, not the way we look. Let's at least wash our faces and hands around back."

"Suit yourself, but let's not stand in the street all night."

It took ten minutes for Nate to scrub off every bit of road dirt he could reach and dunk his head into a bucket to wash his hair. With wet strands dripping down his neck, he drank several dippers of wonderful-tasting water. They had yet to see a single person; the slaves from before the war were gone, perhaps on to better lives.

"We have spring water in the house for weary travelers."

The voice behind him nearly stopped Nate's heart from beating. Cobblestones shifted beneath his feet, while the stone wall seemed to wobble. Perhaps an earth tremor shook the Carolina lowlands…or maybe Amanda simply had that kind of effect on his equilibrium.

He turned to see a vision in lavender silk in the doorway—yards and yards of flowing silk, but the ridiculous hoop was nowhere in sight. "Good evening, Miss Dunn. I didn't wish to jar your delicate sensibilities with my ungentlemanly appearance."

She opened her mouth to speak but not a sound emanated. Instead, her face crumpled with emotion as she ran into his arms. "Oh, Nate, sometimes your clever wit vexes me to death!"

If not for the quick reaction of Joshua, they both might have toppled headlong into the well. "Steady on there. Let's not have your reunion become a swan song," he said, laughing as he pulled them back from danger with a firm grip.

Amanda hugged Nate harder than he thought possible for a woman. "Careful now. I will get your pretty dress wet," he whispered next to her ear.

Unbeknownst to anyone watching, she pinched his back through his shirt in reply. Then with great effort she extracted herself from the embrace. Patting her hair into place, she turned from Nate and said in her most charming accent, "You must be Joshua. Nate was supposed to save your life, not vice versa." She held the backs of her delicate fingers up to his face.

Unaware of polite conventions, Joshua grasped her fingers and pumped her hand high in the air. "Yes, ma'am, that's me. Pleased to make your acquaintance. This is your sister's place?" He gawked unabashedly.

"It is. Tomorrow you shall receive the royal tour, but tonight let's find you both something to eat." Amanda clung to the crook of Nate's elbow as they entered the kitchen. "We use this room more than the dining room these days."

Nate recognized Salome, Thomas, and Amos sitting at the table. "Good evening." He couldn't hide his surprise that they would continue to work here.

"Hullo, Mr. Nate." They chimed in unison.

"Salome, would you fix plates for our guests?" asked Amanda. "I would like to first introduce them to Mr. and Mrs. Henthorne and then bring them back to eat by the cozy fire."

"No need to look for us." Abigail glided into the room with Jackson at her heels. "We spotted Mr. Cooper from the parlor window and couldn't wait to welcome him home." Without hesitation, she brushed a kiss across Nate's cheek.

"Thank you, Mrs. Henthorne." Nate knew the color of his face matched the bowl of ripe cherries on the table.

"Well done, Cooper. I didn't think Johnston would ever give up." Jackson slapped Nate on the back.

"Word travels substantially slower without the benefit of ladies and neighbors." Nate felt inclined to give some excuse for Johnston's waiting two weeks following Lee's surrender. "May I present my brother? Joshua, this is Mrs. and Mrs. Jackson Henthorne."

This time Joshua shook only Jackson's hand before offering a small bow to his hostess. "Nate forgot to mention you two were identical," he said.

"We're not. I'm a smidgen taller," corrected Amanda.

"And I'm *infinitely* more beautiful." Abigail's jest filled the room with laughter.

Later, after they had eaten their fill of stewed chicken and dumplings, the Henthornes rose to their feet. "Allow us to show you to your quarters, Mr. Cooper," Abigail said. "I'm sure Amanda and Nathaniel would like a few minutes alone."

"Yes, ma'am." Joshua jumped up and trailed them up the steps. The servants also discreetly disappeared.

Alone with the woman he had dreamed about for months, Nate found his mouth dry as the Sahara Desert. He cleared his throat. "With the port reopening, have you given thought to returning to England? I'm sure your mother will be eager to see you. And you must be anxious to see if your changes have been implemented at Dunn Mills."

"I'm surprised you remembered my mentioning some plans. We were embarking on a heated row at the time." She refilled their cups from the teapot.

"I remember every word you said that night."

"I am planning an Atlantic crossing this summer, perhaps in July. That should give me adequate time to prepare for my departure. After all, my duties in America are finished." Amanda twirled a lock of hair around her finger.

Nate cleared his throat. "July should offer fair weather for sailing."

"And what plans have you made? Do you still plan to try your hand as a sea captain?"

"A fisherman, yes. Joshua has agreed to become my partner." He wasn't sure he liked the direction this conversation was going. Salome's delicious dinner began to churn in his gut.

"Splendid. Then our futures have been decided." Amanda's tone sounded a bit shrill.

"Uh, regarding your voyage abroad...do you intend to return someday?" He was afraid to meet her eye.

"Yes, Mr. Cooper, I do."

Nate chanced a glance at her. The queen of an invaded beehive couldn't look any angrier.

Amanda slapped her palms down on the table. "My *plan* was to sail to England on my *honeymoon*. My new husband and I would implement changes, find a suitable buyer who agrees with our vision for Dunn Mills, and then establish Mama in a flat in London—a place she has always yearned to live."

Nate ran a finger around his collar to relieve a sudden tightness in his throat. "That...that sounds like an outstanding agenda. What has vexed you now?"

"There appears to be a fly in the ointment. Thus far no one has asked me to marry him!" The thundercloud hovering over her head turned ominous.

Nate slowly pulled the silverware out of her reach. "Easy, Miss Dunn. I'm sure you were taught patience as a child." He let the words roll off his tongue, using the accent favored by coastal residents. "Can't a man relax a few minutes after a meal before getting down to business?"

She pushed up from the table, but he moved quickly. "Oh, no, you don't." He took hold of both of her wrists. "Miss Amanda Dunn, after careful consideration I have a matter to discuss that cannot wait a moment longer. Seeing that I'm awfully fond of you, and considering you tolerate me fairly well, and if I promise never to go to war again, would you agree to be my wife?" Grinning, he released her wrists. "What do you say?"

She narrowed her eyes into a glare. "That's it? That's your question?"

"It is, and I shall hold my breath until you answer."

She shrugged with consummate British indifference. "I say yes."

"You do realize I'll never be as prosperous as your papa."

"I never wanted to be an heiress, Nate. I want my children to have parents who love them and who love each other." She gave him her glorious smile. "Now let's see what Salome has for dessert."

Amanda walked the length of her suite in Abigail's house for the last time…at least as a semipermanent resident. In the future, when she and Nate came for a week over the holidays or a long weekend in the city, it wouldn't be the same. She would no longer be an Englishwoman on holiday, sent to mend fences with an estranged sibling and restore shipping lines with an antiquated society. She would also no longer be a wealthy heiress trying to find common ground with an oh-so-attractive grocer with a heart for righteous causes. Should Amanda Cooper ever lay her head on Abigail's expensive silk sheets again, it would be as an American fisherman's wife who tended her flower and vegetable gardens by day and fed her husband gourmet meals prepared by her own hands. *Or something to that effect.*

Since their simple church wedding two weeks ago, Amanda had begged Nate to take her home…*their home* along the Cape Fear River. She didn't care if it wasn't large or even finished yet. It would be theirs, built entirely by the Cooper brothers with a little help from Mr. Campbell. But Nate had refused, insisting she would see the cottage in due time. *Or when pigs take flight, whichever happens first.*

"Having second thoughts?" From the doorway, Nate interrupted her woolgathering.

"About what? Leaving Wilmington? You know I want to show you off to Mama and dazzle you with the famous Red Rose County. The sooner we board the *Lady Adelaine* and raise the sails, the sooner we can return home to North Carolina."

"No, not about leaving." He came up behind her and encircled her waist with his arms. "And it's 'fire up the boilers,' not 'raise the sails.'"

Amanda gently pinched him. "No need to get picky."

"Maybe you're worried about entrusting such a grand sum of money with my brother for a fishing boat," he murmured as he nibbled on her earlobe.

"Don't be ridiculous. It's my wedding gift to you. If Joshua squanders it foolishly, you two will be stuck fishing from a rowboat."

"Have no fear. He has been crewing for weeks on trawlers and spending his free time with Captain Russell. Besides, he's far more practical with money than I am. I might be tempted to donate the entire lot to the Confederate Widows and Orphans League."

Turning in his arms, she laid her head against his chest. "Once we sell Papa's mills, there will be plenty to fund all the charities you want. What kind of second thoughts do you mean?"

"Do you ever regret marrying me after meeting those eligible Wilmington bachelors?"

Amanda thought about Jackson's friends and burst out laughing. "Not so far, but perhaps you're still on your best behavior. Ask me again in twenty years. Besides, why would I regret marrying a man who promises me fresh oysters, soft-shelled crabs, and flounder every night of my life? Someone who doesn't expect more than simple cooking and a steady supply of tea from all over the world? A man whom I will love until the day I die. What fault could a woman find with those terms?"

Setting a finger below her chin, he raised her head and kissed her softly on the lips. "Just checking, Mrs. Cooper. I don't want to take anything for granted. Are you ready to go? We're leaving earlier than planned because we have a stop to make along the way."

"Do you mean Bermuda?" she asked as they left the room hand in hand.

"No, I mean before we reach the Atlantic."

"There is nothing between Wilmington and the sea except for Fort Fisher. Please don't take me to a place of so much bloodshed."

"No, not the fort. Just wait and see."

During the carriage ride to the waterfront and then throughout the interminable time it took to load the luggage of three Henthornes, plus hers and Nate's, Amanda tried without success to guess what the reason for the stop was. Her husband just grinned silently at her, making her even more curious. Finally, though, a long whistle blast signaled it was time to leave the coach and depart Wilmington…at least for the foreseeable future. Amanda hurried back to the open carriage where Salome and Amos sat with the last of the luggage. She hugged both in turn, along with Thomas, not caring about society's proprieties. "I shall miss you. Thank you for all your kindness," she said.

"Don't stay away too long," huffed Salome. "Now that you married Mr. Cooper, you are an American now."

"Yes, that's how I feel too."

Joining her side, Nate shook hands with the men and kissed Salome's soft cheek.

The Henthornes matched their farewell, minus the kiss. "Are

you sure you don't want to work at Oakdale for full wages?" asked Jackson. "I can only pay half wages while we're gone."

"No, thanks, sir," Thomas said. "We'll be fine watching your house until you and the mistress return." Salome and Amos nodded their enthusiastic agreement.

At the helm of the *Lady Adelaine*, Amanda spotted a familiar face. "Joshua, what on earth are you doing here? Surely you haven't decided to visit my mother in England."

"Nope. I'm just hitching a ride downriver. Captain Russell is allowing me to steer this beauty to continue my nautical education." Joshua slapped the dignified captain on the back.

"But how will you get back to town?"

"There's a horse, wagon, supplies—everything I need to keep me busy while you're gone. Stop worrying, Mandy, and enjoy your honeymoon."

Mandy. Joshua was only the second person in her life to call her that. When she turned to face Nate, her new husband was scowling at her. "Must you always stick your nose under every rock? For once I wanted you to be surprised."

As details clicked into place, Amanda blushed to her hair roots. "Our cottage! Will Joshua be finishing our home while we're on honeymoon?"

Nate nodded his head with resignation. "Along with finding a trawler for sale and then learning to maneuver it. Thanks to my demanding wife, my brother won't get a moment's rest." He guided her away from the ship's wheelhouse. "Is everyone in England this headstrong and disdainful of surprises?"

"Only half the population. The rest are men." Amanda stretched up on tiptoes to kiss his cheek.

"I hope you plan to do better than my cheek once you see the progress I have already made."

A little while later, when Amanda spotted the white frame

house, high on granite piers, with a red tile roof, wraparound porch and pebble walkway down to the river, she burst into tears. There was even a white picket fence around her future garden plot. The "doing better" came easy once they stopped by a little dock.

"It's looks delightful, Nate. Thank you. Living here will be my dream come true." She kissed him with all the passion she could muster.

"You two may stay ten minutes on land, and then I'm hauling anchor," called Captain Russell. "We've got to beat the tide or delay our trip a day."

"It won't take long to look around, Captain. The sooner we leave the sooner we can get back home," Nate said before sweeping her into his arms. Precariously, he carried her down the narrow gangway.

She clung to his neck for dear life. "I truly hope you don't drop me into those cattails. There could be snakes or toads or who knows what!"

"Have no fear, my love. I have a firm hold. If we fall into the river muck, we're going in together. I never intend to let go of you again."

Discussion Questions

1. What obstacles does Amanda face in replacing her father in the business world?

2. How could Abigail so easily adjust to her husband's slave-owning household when England had outlawed slavery long ago?

3. How does the lifestyle of western North Carolinians differ from the coastal counties in the mid-nineteenth century?

4. The death of her father places additional responsibility on Amanda's shoulders. Why does her mother suddenly become her burden?

5. Why does Jackson Henthorne take issue to the relationship between Amanda and her maid, Helene?

6. Although their attraction was immediate, why does Nathaniel conclude any romance with Amanda is hopeless after one dinner party?

7. Jackson sees the closing of other southern ports as an opportunity. Why does this also present great risk to him and his father's company?

8. What appeals to Amanda far more than the home-style cuisine during dinner at the Simses' house?

9. In what ways is the scheme proposed by Jackson's business partner dangerous? And why would Jackson take part in such a gamble?

10. What is Nathaniel hiding about his past, and how does it affect his present relationship with Amanda?

11. Why does Jackson consider Amanda a threat to his household?

12. Why would Nate participate in the clandestine rally in the woods, and what left him conflicted to his role in the war?

13. In England, a large underclass works as domestics to the gentry. How is their lot similar and how is it different when compared with slavery in America?

14. Jackson and Nathaniel each join the army during the war's eleventh hour. What caused a change of heart for each man?

15. Why would America make a better choice for the future home of Amanda and Nathaniel?

About the Author

Mary Ellis and her husband, Ken, live near the Cuyahoga Valley National Recreation Area, home to the last remaining GAR Hall in Ohio, and Hale Farm and Village, home to annual encampments and reenactments of Civil War battles. She is an active member of the local historical society and Civil War Roundtable, where she served as secretary for several years. She has enjoyed a lifelong passion for American history.

Mary loves to hear from her readers at
maryeellis@yahoo.com
or
www.maryellis.net

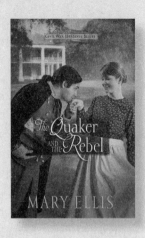

**What Happens When an Underground Railroad Conductor
Falls in Love with a Man Loyal to the Confederacy?**

Emily Harrison's life has turned upside down. At the beginning of
the Civil War, she bravely attempts to continue her parents' work
in the Underground Railroad until their Ohio farm is sold in fore-
closure. Now alone and without a home, she accepts a position as a
governess with a doctor's family in slave-holding Virginia. Though
it's dangerous, she decides to continue her rescue efforts from there.

Alexander Hunt, the doctor's handsome nephew, does not deny a
growing attraction to his uncle's newest employee. But he cannot
take time to pursue Emily, for Alexander isn't what he seems—rich,
spoiled, and indolent. He has a secret identity. He is the elusive Gray
Wraith, a fearless man who fights the war from the shadows, stealing
Union supplies and diverting them to the Southern cause.

The path before Alexander and Emily is complicated. The war brings
betrayal, entrapment, and danger. Amid their growing feelings for
each other, can they trust God with the challenges they face to provide them with a bright future?

Love, Loyalty, and Espionage…
How Does a Lady Live with All Three?

As a nurse after the devastating battle of Gettysburg, Madeline Howard saves the life of Elliott Haywood, a colonel in the Confederacy. But even though she must soon make her home in the South, her heart and political sympathies belong to General James Downing, a Union army corps commander.

Colonel Haywood has not forgotten the beautiful nurse who did so much for him, and when he unexpectedly meets her again in Richmond, he is determined to win her. While spending time with army officers and war department officials in her aunt and uncle's palatial home, Madeline overhears plans for Confederate attacks against the Union soldiers. She knows passing along this information may save the life of her beloved James, but at what cost? Can she really betray the trust of her family and friends? Is it right to allow Elliott to dream of a future with her?

Two men are in love with Madeline. Will her faith in God show her the way to a bright future, or will her choices bring devastation on those she loves?

Note from the Author

Dear Reader,

I hope you'll watch for my new romantic suspense series, Secrets of the South Mysteries, coming in summer 2015.

With sophisticated shell games, blackmail, and murder, the first book in the series, *Midnight on the Mississippi*, is a tale of searching for answers and finding self-respect and love along the way.

Best regards,

Mary Ellis

To learn more about Harvest House books and
to read sample chapters, visit our website:

www.harvesthousepublishers.com

HARVEST HOUSE PUBLISHERS
EUGENE, OREGON